JAMES MacMANUS is the managing director of *The Times Literary Supplement*. He has been a journalist most of his life working for the *Guardian*, *The Daily Telegraph* and *The Times*. His books include *Sleep in Peace Tonight*, *Black Venus* and *Ocean Devil: The Life and Legend of George Hogg*, which was made into the film *Children of the Silk Road*, starring Jonathan Rhys Meyers. He lives in London.

SLEEP
in PEACE
TONIGHT

James MacManus

DUCKWORTH OVERLOOK

This paperback edition first published in 2016 by
Duckworth Overlook

LONDON
30 Calvin Street, London E1 6NW
T: 020 7490 7300
E: info@duckworth-publishers.co.uk
www.ducknet.co.uk
For bulk and special sales, please contact
sales@duckworth-publishers.co.uk
or write to us at the address above

NEW YORK
141 Wooster Street, New York, NY 10012
www.overlookpress.com

A catalogue record for this book is available
from the British Library

ISBN 9780715650615

Printed and bound in the UK

In memory of Nicholas Strong MacManus,
who died from leukaemia in his final year at Oxford
University in 1966. He was twenty-one.

I

The seaplane came into view just as the winter sun had begun to settle into the English Channel. The plane turned into its final approach, the silver wings dipping to catch the last light of the day, before landing in a long plume of spray on the calm waters of the largest natural harbour in the British Isles. The plane taxied to the landing stage, sending a wave rippling to the farther shores of the harbour.

Brendan Bracken checked his watch. It was 3:50 P.M. The plane was late. They had been due two hours ago. The pilot had kept radio silence through the four-hour flight from Lisbon, apart from one brief coded message to say the passenger was on board and en route.

Bracken knew why they were late. With an important passenger on board the pilot had taken no chances. The four-engined aircraft had climbed to its ceiling height of fifteen thousand feet for the first leg of the journey along the Portuguese coast, and then dropped to sea level across the Bay of Biscay, before flying a dogleg into the Atlantic and then turning east into the English Channel. Portugal was neutral in name, but German agents had a free hand in Lisbon and would have noted the departure of an unscheduled British Overseas Airways flight with just one passenger on board.

The Luftwaffe had already begun to move Junkers 88 fighters to airfields along the French Atlantic coast, but in that first month of 1941 the bases were not fully operational. And in any case, an unarmed, unescorted civilian airliner flying from a neutral country to England was *supposed* to be granted safe passage by all belligerent forces.

Bracken looked at his watch again. It was 4:00 P.M. It was the word "supposed" that caused his anxiety. You could suppose nothing in the present war, except perhaps invasion and defeat. You could certainly suppose that.

He looked down from the control tower to the landing jetty and saw the pilot and crew leave the aircraft. There was no sign of the passenger. A steward clad in the airline livery– blue blazer, white trousers, and gold buttons – descended from the aircraft and waved to the shore party. He looked worried. He formed his hands into a megaphone and shouted. The word "doctor" floated over the water and up to Bracken and his driver.

"They seem to want a doctor, sir," said the driver.

Bracken looked at the man. A pool driver from 10 Downing Street. Old enough to have fought in the last war but lucky enough to be a little too old for this one.

"So I heard," he said. "Well, we don't have a doctor, do we? Come on. Let's see what the problem is."

He was huddled in a brown overcoat in a window seat at the back of the aircraft. His eyes were closed and his head rested against a pillow wedged between the seat and the porthole window. A gaunt, grey face, hollow cheeked, with wisps of hair straggling over a high brow. The steward stood in the aisle with a cup of steaming tea, but the man did not move.

"Been like this since we left Lisbon," the steward explained. "Said he wanted to sleep. I don't know whether he's dead or alive."

Bracken bent down, placed his hand on the man's shoulder, and shook him gently.

"Mr Hopkins, are you all right? You're in England. You've arrived."

The eyes opened and even in the dim interior of the aircraft cabin Bracken could see that the briefing paper from the embassy in Washington had been right:

Mr Hopkins is physically unprepossessing. Tall, at six foot two, with thinning hair. Stomach surgery for cancer in 1936 has left him with severe digestive problems and underweight for his height. He looks older than his 50 years. His distinguishing feature is the eyes. They are dark grey, the colour of slate, but with a sparkle that signals an inner vitality at odds with his general appearance. A recent profile in the *Washington Post* noted that if you watch his eyes, you will find the man.

The grey eyes looked around the cabin and then fastened on Bracken.

"England?" said the man. He shook himself, stretched, yawned, and peered out at the dusk gathering over the harbour.

It is like watching a sleepy old cat come to life, thought Bracken.

"Yes," he said. "Welcome."

"Where in England?"

"Poole, Dorset," he said. "If you're ready, we have to leave."

"Dorset?" The man seemed to remember that this was his destination." Of course. Good. Help me up, will you?"

Harry Hopkins said nothing on the drive to the station. A porter saluted him as he boarded the train, followed by Bracken and two detectives who had been waiting on the train. Once installed in a corner of the compartment he immediately fell asleep again. It was not until an hour later as they passed through the county town of Winchester that he woke up.

"Forgive me," said Hopkins. "I've been travelling for four days. Where are we?"

"Hampshire, an hour from London. Would you care for a drink, perhaps something to eat?"

The chef and waitress aboard the special train had already served Bracken and the detectives mushroom omelettes, a rare wartime treat. They were eager to prepare the fillet of beef for their distinguished American guest, a choice they had been assured he would appreciate.

"Thank you," said Hopkins, "a little whisky will do me fine."

"Scotch or bourbon, sir?"

"Scotch will be fine, thanks."

Delighted to be able to serve his guest something at last, the train steward appeared with a tray, a crystal tumbler, and a small decanter of whisky. He poured three fingers into the tumbler.

"Lots of water, please; same again," said Hopkins. He pulled back the blackout blinds and looked into the darkness. "I am sorry we were late. I was looking forward to seeing the green fields of England."

"The pilot came the long way round. It was safer," Bracken said.

"I know; he told us. Are you drinking?"

Bracken did not like whisky but nodded to the steward and accepted a glass. The two men clinked glasses.

"Here's to England," said Hopkins.

"And to the United States of America," said Bracken.

The first of the incendiaries landed close to the track as the train approached Clapham Junction station. They fell silently in clusters from the darkness before exploding in flaming fragments that briefly illuminated the back gardens and rooftops of South London.

The carriage rocked in the blasts and the train surged forward.

"Nothing to worry about," said Bracken. "We will be in Waterloo in five minutes."

The incendiaries seemed to be targeting the main line into London from the west. Hopkins peered out through the window blinds at the searchlights probing the sky with pencils of light. A curtain of fire arose along the track.

"They must have known I was coming," said Hopkins.

Bracken smiled but did not laugh. He had been thinking exactly the same thing. What better way to impress President Franklin Roosevelt's special envoy to wartime London than a raid to demonstrate the firepower and supremacy of the Luftwaffe?

The White House had hardly made a secret of the mission. President Roosevelt had announced it to the press corps only four days before.

"Mr Hopkins will go as my personal representative for a very short trip – a couple of weeks – just to maintain, I suppose that is the word for it, personal relations between me and the British government."

The journalists rose to their feet chorusing a single question: What exactly was the president's envoy going to do in London?

The president laughed. "You can't get anything exciting out of this, boys. He's just going to say, 'How do you do,' to a lot of my friends."

The press corps laughed and the president joined them.

In London nobody laughed. When the prime minister heard that Harry Hopkins was coming to London on the president's orders, he said simply, "Who?"

As his train pulled into Waterloo, Hopkins looked out at a station in semi-darkness lit only by feeble red lanterns placed along the edges of the platforms. Clouds of steam from engines waiting impatiently to leave drifted towards the arched glass roof. A few passengers were hurrying to board, but most seemed to have taken to the shelters in vaults beneath the tracks. Where wine merchants had once stored their finest vintages Londoners sheltered from the storm above. Not for them the safety of cellars deep in the countryside where the wine had been shipped on the outbreak of war.

He stepped out onto the platform and stopped in shock, as if physically assaulted by the noise. Anti-aircraft gunfire along the Thames Embankment roared into the night, throwing time-fused shells high into the darkness, where they would explode in blazing fragments. The wail of distant sirens, the shriek of departing trains, and the shrill whistles from the guards created a demented symphony that echoed around the steel-and-glass structure of the station.

The chargé d'affaires at the American embassy emerged from the gloom and introduced himself. Herschel Johnson, he said; they had to hurry. Hopkins shook hands with Bracken, shouted his thanks over the din, and allowed himself to be hurried to a waiting car.

The darkened streets were empty as the car crossed Waterloo Bridge. Some incendiaries detonated early, falling like candles from the sky while a searchlight probed the darkness, briefly holding an aircraft in its glare, while others swung their beams to trap the plane in a cradle of light. For a moment the bomber was held like an insect trapped in a web before sliding away again into the safety of the dark. Fires burnt along the river, mostly on the north bank, their glow illuminating the wedding-cake spires of Wren churches and the great dome of St Paul's. The car raced along the Strand, through Trafalgar Square, with Admiral Nelson on his column just visible in the darkness, and down Pall Mall.

"Welcome to London," said the chargé d'affaires as he was flung against the visitor by a fast turn onto St James's Street.

"Thanks," said Hopkins.

"You've arrived on a good night."

"Really?"

"Now you will be able to tell them what it is really like here."

"Them?"

"Your friends in Washington."

"I don't have many of those."

Herschel Johnson knew Hopkins was right. An unelected White House crony who was very free with the public purse – that was the standard criticism of the weary figure slumped beside him in the car. Hopkins was not popular and, however much the press may have laughed at the president's little jokes about his mission, they damned what some called "the president's back door to war diplomacy" in the editorial columns the next morning.

Johnson changed the subject.

"You know you're expected at Number 10 tonight?"

There was no reply. Hopkins was asleep.

At Claridge's Hotel a porter in a long green coat and top hat darted out from a heavily sandbagged entrance as the car drew up. He took Hopkins's bags without a word and led the way inside. Hopkins turned back to thank Herschel Johnson; the diplomat and his car had already vanished into the night.

Hopkins stepped into the hotel and lit a cigarette. The noise of the air raid was suddenly muted, muffled by sandbags and thick drapes. Two large lamps placed at either end of a black marble counter threw a soft light over a red patterned Persian carpet that extended over the floor of the large foyer. Against a wood-panelled wall stood two high-backed armchairs with tasselled cushions. Paintings on the wall featured country gentlemen from centuries past with their horses and dogs. The receptionist, a middle-aged woman in a black suit and white blouse, looked up from behind the counter and pushed a form towards him.

Hopkins felt he had somehow crossed the threshold from a world at war into the comfort and luxury of what looked like a grand English country house.

"Welcome to London, Mr Hopkins," said the receptionist. "Would you care to sign here?"

"You know my name?" he said, looking at the form.

"We were expecting you. We don't get many guests

walking in on a night like this. Your room is on the first floor, but it's quite safe. Make sure you keep the blackout blinds drawn at night. You can have shared quarters in the basement if you prefer."

"The first floor will be fine," he said. "Is the bar open?"

The receptionist looked at him with a smile.

"We don't close the bar these days. If the barman's not there, just leave a note with what you've taken and your room number. You are room seventeen, but take the stairs, please. We don't use the lift on these nights. The porter will help you."

The bar was crowded as Hopkins shouldered his way through. The voices around him were American, mostly London correspondents of major U.S. newspapers he guessed. He had been reading the back file of their reports in the brief time he had had to prepare for his trip, but he didn't feel like meeting anyone that night. He was exhausted after a journey that had begun at LaGuardia Airport in New York four days earlier. He needed a little more whisky and an early night. What he did not need was journalists buzzing around him with endless questions. He could not understand why the embassy had booked him at a hotel that had become the headquarters of the U.S. press corps.

Hopkins turned to leave. He would have that drink in his room, just one drink, and then . . . a hand on his shoulder stopped him.

"Welcome to London. Want a drink?"

Hopkins did not have to turn round to know who was talking. Like every radio listener in America, he would have known that voice anywhere. "Thanks, Ed," he said.

There he was, smiling, with a hand held out in welcome: Ed Murrow, the CBS broadcaster whose nightly radio reports famously began with his signature opening line: "This . . . is London." Murrow, who often seemed the lone voice challenging overwhelmingly isolationist opinion in America. Murrow, who had scarcely concealed his disdain for the former American ambassador in London, the pro-appeasement Joe Kennedy. Murrow, the one journalist Hopkins would stay awake all night for. Because Murrow was dangerous. He was influential. He could move opinion and, as Hopkins well knew, he needed to be watched.

The president had repeatedly told American mothers in speech after speech that he was not going to send their sons into another foreign war. The White House had good reason for such caution. Despite the war reporting from London, U.S. public opinion was, if anything, hardening against giving aid to Britain, let alone joining the war against Germany. But Murrow was on a crusade to change White House policy and he didn't care who knew it.

The two men found a table. Above the hubbub in the bar, the anti-aircraft guns in Hyde Park had started up again.

"Is it always like this?" said Hopkins.

"This is nothing," said Murrow. "Wait till the heavy bombers come over around midnight. The incendiaries light the way for them."

"How do you stand it?"

"This helps," said Murrow, raising a glass.

The two men drank until the guns fell quiet and the all-clear sounded. Murrow spoke of his passion for the British cause and poured out his contempt for a do-nothing Congress in Washington and a largely ignorant and ill-informed public across the country. Hopkins held back, saying little while Murrow attempted to probe Roosevelt's real feelings about Churchill.

"They didn't get on when they first met way back in the

last war, did they?" said Murrow. "In fact, Roosevelt detested Churchill, right?"

That was true enough, admitted Hopkins, and he pointed out that the memory of that meeting had not entirely faded from the president's mind. The idea of a global empire didn't sit very well with the president, or anyone else in Washington for that matter.

"That is hardly the issue right now, is it?" snapped Murrow.

"You don't understand, Ed," said Hopkins. "Isolationists like Henry Ford and Charles Lindbergh make it the issue. Why should American kids die so that the British can impose a dictatorship on India, most of Africa, and vast swathes of Asia? That's what they say, and people listen."

"This is not about the British Empire, for Chrissake, Harry; it's about the survival of everything we care for – freedom, democracy . . . you know, all that stuff in our Constitution."

He was angry now and Hopkins wasn't interested in a fight. He was tired and wanted to go to bed. But he also wanted to leave on the right side of the argument.

"Ed, look, it's simple: the president was not elected for a third term in order to take the country to war. He has said that over and over."

Murrow frowned and drank deeply. This was worse than he thought. Hopkins was a small-town kid who had risen to become one of the most powerful men in the White House. Hell, he actually lived in the place; Roosevelt had given him Lincoln's old study. And Hopkins had never been elected to public office in his life. No wonder people distrusted him so much.

Hopkins had a reputation as a chain-smoking, hard-drinking wreck of a man who could still stay up all night and had an eye, and more, for a pretty face. Well, there's no harm in that, thought Murrow; but the man had views on the Empire and the British class system that might have been framed in Stalin's Moscow. What the hell was he doing in London? Why had Roosevelt sent him? And more important, what would he and Churchill make of each other? It would be a disaster.

"All I can say," said Murrow wearily, "is that if you take that small-town view of the world into Number 10 tomorrow, you will have a very short meeting with Churchill."

A waiter appeared with a note from Reception. There had been a call from the prime minister's office. Mr Hopkins had been expected for a late supper. Was he intending to come? If so, a car would be sent to fetch him.

Winston Churchill was in his underground bunker beneath Downing Street when Brendan Bracken told him that the American envoy would prefer to meet in the morning.

"He's exhausted and wants an early night," said Bracken. "I don't think it is wise to press him. I am not sure he is in quite the right frame of mind for a meeting with you just now."

"And what do you mean by that?" said Churchill, who knew perfectly well what his private secretary meant.

"I mean only that it is probably as well that Mr Hopkins gets an early night. You have a lot to talk about."

"Really? I am reliably informed that he is in the bar of Claridge's as we speak, consuming whisky."

"I think you will agree, Prime Minister, that a little whisky helps a night's sleep, although in your case I believe brandy is the preferred potion."

That's what Churchill liked about the man who was variously called his personal assistant or protégé but whose official title was Parliamentary Private Secretary to the Prime

Minister. Bracken was clever, loyal, and a considerable wit. He was also a buccaneer, a man of uncertain background who had made his way from nowhere into the salons of power at Westminster. And he could talk back. That appealed to Churchill.

"What did you find out on the train?" said the prime minister.

"Very little; he slept most of the way. But you've read the briefs, haven't you? He's Roosevelt's Man Friday, disliked by everyone in Washington but adored by the president."

"A similar position to your own, then?" said the prime minister.

"Not at all," said Bracken, who knew Churchill liked to tease and had anticipated the comparison. "He's got some pretty strange views on welfare, empire, and all that. In fact, he used to call himself a socialist."

"The only thing that matters is that he has the complete trust of the president. That is why I wanted to start on him tonight," said Churchill. "God knows, we have precious little time. Ask Sawyers to come in, will you?"

Frank Sawyers was Churchill's butler, valet, and general factotum, who travelled with the prime minister everywhere. He was the weather vane by which the army chiefs, the wartime cabinet, and indeed Churchill's own family judged the prime minister's moods and especially his frequently evil temper. No one knew Sawyers's age, although he was well on in years, and no one knew where he came from, although the accent pointed to somewhere in the north. But these were unimportant details. Sawyers knew when to refill Churchill's glass, when to relight his cigar, when his favourite cat, Nelson, might suitably be placed on the prime minister's lap. Sawyers was able to suggest that a guest at the prime minister's table might not relish the third glass of vintage port that was being so generously offered quite as much as the prime minister himself.

And in those dark days when defeat beckoned and the black dog mood descended like a shroud on Churchill, it was Sawyers who could gently lift the chin and stir the heart of his master.

Bracken left the room and moments later Frank Sawyers entered. Without a word he took the prime minister's empty glass and refilled it with port.

"Sawyers," said Churchill.

"Yes, sir?"

"This is a bugger."

"Quite right, sir," said Sawyers.

In spite of the whisky and the long journey, Hopkins found sleep difficult that night. He had been shocked by the ear-splitting cacophony of guns, bombs, and sirens during the raid. News reports from London all talked of civilian deaths, the destruction of homes, the plight of the homeless, food shortages, rationing, queues, but none mentioned the deafening nightly thunder of the Blitz. He wondered how anyone got any sleep.

The next morning, as his car drove down Park Lane to 10 Downing Street, he realised that sleep was probably a dimly remembered luxury for most Londoners. Despite the cold, he wound the window down and caught the acrid smell of smoke and burning. He saw pale faces pinched with cold waiting patiently at bus stops, trying to get to work. People stamped their feet and rubbed gloved hands against the cold, craning around the queue hoping to see their bus. Others gave up the wait and trudged past still-burning buildings, heads down, hands clasping handbags or briefcases, all wondering on that freezing morning whether there would be transport home that night. They looked exhausted, hollowed out, half people.

Red double-decker buses lumbered over still-smouldering rubble strewn across the roads, weaving past piles of shattered brick and occasional geysers of water as they went from bus stop to bus stop scooping up passengers from long, orderly queues.

As they passed Hyde Park Hopkins saw the anti-aircraft crews cleaning and servicing the guns for the night ahead. Piles of expended shell cases were stacked neatly in brass pyramids under the plane trees. Elderly men and women walked dogs around the gun emplacements as if it were normal to find batteries of long-barreled 3.7-inch anti-aircraft guns in the middle of a city park.

That's the point, Hopkins realised. This *is* normal. The Blitz had been going on for four months. Twenty-eight thousand people had been killed in London alone and forty thousand homes destroyed, leaving almost half a million people displaced. And yet here on the streets on a bitter January morning people were queuing for the bus and trudging to work over the debris from the latest raid. The chargé d'affaires had been right. No one in Washington had any idea of what was happening in London.

Hopkins opened his briefcase and pulled out his letter of authorisation from President Roosevelt:

Reposing special faith and confidence in you, I am asking you to proceed at your earliest convenience to Great Britain, there to act as my personal representative. I am also asking you to convey a communication in this sense to His Majesty George VI. You will of course communicate to this government any matters which may come to your

*attention in the performance of your mission which you
may feel will serve the best interests of the United States.*
   *With all best wishes for the success of your mission I
am,*
   Sincerely yours
   Franklin D. Roosevelt

The president had announced Hopkins's mission at his
morning press conference on January 5. The letter had been
handed to him one hour later, and that evening he had left
New York on the first of five flights, making his way to the
Caribbean, Brazil, then across the South Atlantic to Gambia
in West Africa, and north to Lisbon. The safest way to travel
to Europe, it had taken four days with overnight stopovers.

His mission was to meet and get to know a man whose ego
was considerably greater than his talent, a man who seemed to
believe that a nation of 40 million people could rule 400 million around the world, a man determined to drag America
into a war. Churchill did not seem too bothered by the fact
that the United States had lost more than 100,000 men in the
Great War just twenty-three years previously.

That war was supposed to end all wars. But here they were
again, European nations slaughtering each other. Why not
just leave them to it and do a deal with the victor? Hopkins
knew how his hometown, Sioux City, Iowa, would answer
that question. Most of its residents did not even know where
Europe was. What mattered in Sioux City was the price of
petrol for the tractors and combine harvesters and the
prospects for the corn harvest. The boys liked a few beers on
Saturday nights and would try their luck with the girls in the
back row of the cinemas. That was pretty much life in Sioux
City. There was no memorial to the dead. Veterans who

hobbled and limped around the streets were reminders enough of the madness that had seized the old countries of Europe only two decades earlier. People walked past them, heads down to avoid their angry eyes, closing their ears to the occasional muttered curse that followed them down the pavement. Sioux City knew all about the Great War, and no one wanted another one.

Hopkins got out of the car in Downing Street, straightened up, ran a hand over his hair, and looked around. The entrance was sandbagged, the windows were boarded up, and the house next door, Number 11, had suffered some damage to its frontage. The United Kingdom and British Empire had been run from this small three-storey house in a London side street for two hundred years. Hopkins found it incredible.

Brendan Bracken met Hopkins at the door. "It's not exactly the White House, is it?" he said, smiling. "Come in."

Bracken led him to a small dining room in the basement where a table had been set for two. Family photographs in silver frames were arranged on side tables. Paintings on the wall depicted various well-whiskered gentlemen whom Hopkins judged to be former occupants of Number 10. It seemed a little early to eat, shortly before noon, but he told himself that nothing about his mission was going to surprise him.

"Sherry?" said Bracken, pouring him a glass without waiting for an answer.

Hopkins was sipping his sherry when a rotund, smiling red-faced gentleman with pinstripe trousers and a short black coat appeared and welcomed him to England. There was no mistaking the British prime minister. He looked exactly as he did in every photograph, perhaps slightly smaller and rounder than Hopkins had imagined, but his handshake was firm and his voice familiar from broadcasts.

They sat down to a lunch of vegetable consommé, cold beef, green salad, cheese, and coffee. A light wine and port were served as if they were essential accompaniments to lunch, which was clearly the prime minister's view. Hopkins drank, taking the edge off his hangover. He was getting the impression that alcohol was an important wartime weapon for the British.

That night in his room at Claridge's, using hotel stationery, Hopkins wrote out his first report. Roosevelt had insisted that he avoid all but essential contact with the embassy and use only U.S. naval communication channels. This involved a courier to take dispatches to radio staff operating for the naval attaché housed separately from the embassy in Grosvenor Square. The dispatches were transmitted in code to U.S. naval headquarters in Washington and then to the White House.

The president did not trust his own embassy after the disastrous tenure of ambassador Joe Kennedy. Nor, it seemed to Hopkins, did Roosevelt trust any branch of his armed services except for the navy, in which he had once held senior office. Above all, he did not trust the British.

"They will all want to know what you have to say to me," he had told Hopkins. "So write out your reports yourself and send them via courier for my eyes only. They will be on my desk within a couple of hours of you sealing the envelope. It may seem a little drastic, but trust nobody, Harry. They will watch you, listen to you, and follow you – all of them, the Brits, Americans, Free French, German agents, the lot. Say nothing, but remember: I want to know everything."

. . .

Hopkins later heard that Roosevelt had laughed out loud when he read the report of that first meeting. After a few preliminary civilities, during which Churchill pressed Hopkins to have some jelly in aspic with his beef, the envoy had remarked that some people in Washington thought the British prime minister to be critical of the president and the overwhelmingly isolationist public opinion in the States. Churchill had risen from the table, his glowering countenance matching the glowing cigar in his hand, and launched into a bitter tirade against Joe Kennedy, whom he blamed for poisoning relations between London and Washington.

"He, the American ambassador to the Court of St James, has written us off. He told anyone in America who cared to listen – and unfortunately a great many people there do listen to such rubbish – that we are finished and democracy here is dead. Do you know he twice tried to arrange secret meetings with Hitler? This was after, I repeat, *after* we were at war with Germany. He seemed to think that Hitler was a man of reason and goodwill with whom he could arrange peace negotiations. We stopped it, of course."

Having vented his ire at Kennedy, Churchill had given his guest a brief situation report, as he put it, on the current state of the war, ranging from Greece to North Africa.

Hopkins listened, captivated by the power of the oratory but wary of the propaganda that was being directed at him. When the prime minister paused to relight his cigar, he asked quietly about the possibility of invasion.

Churchill held the question up as if he had been handed a precious stone, turning it in the light to examine it from various angles. This was the question he had been waiting for. He knew that many of the American chiefs of staff had advised the president against any military assistance to Britain on the grounds that a German invasion was inevitable and that the British had little chance of preventing it.

There was no question that the Germans wanted to invade, Churchill said. The invasion barges were there, across the Channel in the French ports, carefully camouflaged and heavily defended by anti-aircraft batteries, but ready to embark. The armoured divisions the Wehrmacht had deployed to the Balkans could be redeployed to northern France in three weeks. The head of the German navy, Admiral Dönitz, was known to be nervous, but the bombastic Göring, despite the fact that his air force had lost the Battle of Britain the previous summer, was urging Hitler on.

On balance, the Germans would probably be able to cross the Channel with up to one hundred thousand men. They would incur huge losses, but they would land significant forces of infantry and light armour on the south coast. However, ten well-equipped British divisions, including heavy armour, would throw them back into the sea. The Royal Navy would complete the defeat. Naval forces would be the key, said Churchill, pacing the room, throwing out his words as if addressing the House of Commons. The air forces on both sides would fight each other to a standstill over the Channel, he said, but the British navy would be the deciding factor and would turn the sea red with Nazi blood.

He stopped pacing, lifted his glass of port from the table, and turned to Hopkins.

"Take a note of this, Harry," he growled. "We know it, and your people should know it too. An invasion would be a bloody defeat for the Germans."

Finally, after coffee and more port, the prime minister had taken Hopkins to the Cabinet Room on the ground floor and revealed the most important information of all: maps showing the routes of the Atlantic convoys from American ports to Glasgow and Liverpool and the flight paths of the German bombers trying to intercept the convoys and bomb their destination ports.

"This," the prime minister had boomed, "is where the war will be decided, not in North Africa, not along the Channel, but here on the grey seas of the Atlantic, where the lifeline of democracy is stretched to breaking point. I trust that you, your president, and the United States will help us decide the outcome of that battle."

Hopkins, exhausted and more than slightly drunk, had left Downing Street at three thirty that afternoon feeling he had personally been engaged in hand-to-hand combat with the forces of darkness now occupying much of Europe.

The prime minister had impressed upon him his admiration for the president and his love of America. Time and again he had spoken in terms of two great democracies standing side by side against the fascist tyranny engulfing Europe.

As they shook hands, Churchill had suggested that Hopkins tour the country and see other great cities now coming under attack from the air: Liverpool, Glasgow, Southampton, and Manchester. He told Hopkins he had arranged a driver, a car, and a detective, all of whom would report to the envoy at Claridge's the next morning.

Hopkins gratefully accepted the offer. In fact, he realised he would probably have agreed to anything the prime minister had suggested, just to be able to return to his hotel and stretch out for an hour on his bed. In the meantime, Churchill was going to the House of Commons to make a statement about the North African campaign.

As they left, the prime minister drew the envoy aside at the door to Number 10.

"I want you to stay here as long as possible. I do not want

you to leave until you are fully informed of our perilous situation and the material assistance we need to win this war."

Then he was gone, trailing a lingering aroma of brandy and port and raising a V sign to the cheering crowd outside. Much as Roosevelt would have been amused by details of the lunch, Hopkins knew his smile would fade when he read the last sentence of his report: "I fell asleep wondering where on earth the British prime minister found his extraordinary energy. I also reflected that he will do anything to get us into this war."

The bedside phone in Hopkins's hotel room rang at eight thirty the next morning. Half-asleep, and through the thick fog of another hangover, Hopkins picked it up.

"Good morning, Mr Hopkins. You may order breakfast in your room if you wish, but service in the dining room stops in half an hour – and there's a WAAF officer waiting for you in Reception."

"WAAF officer?"

"Women's Auxiliary Air Force, sir."

"What does she want?"

"She's your driver, I believe. Flight Officer Finch, sir."

2

Leonora Finch paused on the steps of 200 Oxford Street feeling nauseous and faint. Women with shopping bags, mothers and nannies with big four-wheeled prams, workmen shouldering ladders and shovels, and men with tightly furled umbrellas and bowler hats eddied past her with mindless urgency. A small brass plaque announced that this building, sandwiched between department stores on London's busiest shopping street, was the home of the BBC Empire Service. From here Britain broadcast to its colonies of pine and palm on which, it was said, the sun never set.

She put a hand to the wall to steady herself, looked down, and wondered whether she was going to be sick over her new brown shoes. She had slept badly and taken only a cup of tea for breakfast in her lodgings that morning. Her interview was at 10:00 A.M., in twenty minutes' time. There was still time to turn back, make a phone call, apologise, and say there had been a mistake.

And why should she not change her mind and return home to that comfortable two-bedroom house on the outskirts of

Leamington Spa, a quiet market town that seemed to exist in a different universe from the teeming anthill of London? Her mother wanted her to become a teacher and live out the war in the country. She had endlessly repeated the received wisdom of the day that the bombers would always get through and that London would be the prime target. Well, the war had begun two months ago and now, in November 1939, there were barrage balloons floating over the city, trenches had been dug in the parks, and shop windows were crisscrossed with sticky tape.

But not a bomb had fallen on the capital and such precautions were dismissed as bureaucratic nonsense in what was widely derided as a phoney war. Hitler was mocked as a pantomime villain. Christmas was coming and people were more interested in the seasonal decorations in the big stores and the bargains on offer for those who did their holiday shopping early.

Leonora took another deep breath. I am here, she told herself, because I have the language skills to get a proper job as a translator, because I can speak French fluently, because I have an ambition, ill rationalised and vague, I admit, to find work in London that would make him proud of me. And after a year of letters turning down my job applications to various government departments I finally have a reply from the mighty BBC. And that would have made him proud indeed.

She smiled, touched the shiny brass plaque with her fingertips, and remembered the cemetery in northern France. Major Leo Finch had been killed during the opening day of the Somme offensive in 1916. Like so many others, his body had never been found. Leonora had heard from survivors of that disastrous attack that her father had led his men from their trench with a service revolver in his hand and simply disappeared in an explosive burst of mud, blood, bones, and shrapnel. She had been born six months later.

When she was ten years old her mother had talked properly about the missing man in their lives for the first time. Until then Leonora had been told that her daddy was away, travelling in a foreign land. "What was he like?" she had asked as she grew up. "What did he look like?" "What did he sound like?" "What sort of things did he say?" "Who *was* he?" Her mother had found the endless questions troubling, as if they trespassed on memories she wished to keep to herself. She said that Leo had been very good-looking, tall, with tousled fair hair and deep green eyes. He was funny, she said, always laughing, full of practical jokes and madcap schemes.

The questions kept coming. Reluctantly Leonora's mother described how she and Leo had begun married life in a small two-bedroom house on the outskirts of Leamington. The house had been named Cymbeline after Shakespeare's heroine because Leo taught English at the local primary school and frequently bemoaned the fate that had given him the task of enthusing ten-year-old boys and girls with the works of the great playwright.

It was there that he and Muriel had lived for ten happy years until he was called up. He did not have to go to war, Muriel had told her daughter with bitterness. Teaching was a reserved profession, and at the age of thirty-two he could have avoided active service. As it was he took an officers' training course and became a captain in the Warwickshire Regiment. He had only been gone three months when the telegram had arrived with the opening words that brought grief to a generation of young women. Muriel had stopped, her eyes misting with tears, as she had taken the document, carefully folded and tied with ribbon, from a drawer in her desk and shown it to her daughter:

MADAM,

IT IS MY PAINFUL DUTY TO INFORM YOU THAT
A REPORT HAS THIS DAY BEEN RECEIVED FROM
THE WAR OFFICE NOTIFYING THE DEATH OF
MAJOR LEO FINCH OF 17TH WARWICKSHIRE
REGIMENT WHILE ON SERVICE IN JULY. I AM
TO EXPRESS TO YOU THE REGRETS OF THE
ARMY COUNCIL AT YOUR LOSS. THE CAUSE OF
DEATH WAS: KILLED IN ACTION.

But Muriel could do little more for her daughter than turn
the pages of a photo album and point to the smiling figure
posing on the beach, in front of a Christmas tree, on the front
lawn, outside a pub holding a pint of beer. She could not bear
the heartbreak of telling her daughter how she and Leo had
met, fallen in love, and married. She never revealed the full
story of their life together: the moment they had met as young
teachers monitoring a school dance, the risks they took lovemaking in the cornfields and woods around Leamington,
their last supper together, their last night in each other's arms,
the last kiss at the railway station. Those were her secret memories and they always would be.

Muriel Finch had deliberately avoided turning the house
into a shrine to her late husband. There was one photograph
of him in uniform with the same silly moustache every officer
wore, looking at the camera with a faint frown. She placed it
in a silver frame on the mantelpiece in the dining room. The
one she really liked showed him smiling with a stalk of wheat
between his teeth and a straw hat on his head. He was sitting
at a table outside a pub and holding a pint of beer. She had
taken the photo, and it stood framed in her bedroom on the
dresser.

Muriel had taken Leonora at the age of fifteen to France to see where her father had died. It was 1931, and by then the War Graves Commission had completed many of the cemeteries that flowered in fields of white stone over the battlegrounds of northern France.

They found the cemetery near the town of Thiepval in the Somme valley. A ceremonial arch marked the entrance commemorating the 72,194 men from Britain, Australia, and South Africa who had been killed in fighting along the ridge both in 1916 and during the German counterattacks of 1918. In one corner of the cemetery the names of 2,717 of the dead were inscribed on rows of crosses that stretched between laurel trees down the side of a valley to a small stream.

In the context of a war in which nine million Allied soldiers died, this was a small cemetery, so they quickly found him: Major Leo Montague Finch, 17th Warwickshire Regiment, 16 July 1916.

They laid their bouquet of white lilies on the cross bearing his name and Muriel read out a poem she had heard at the funeral of a friend:

"The river runs from dark to light,
So I must say farewell, my friends,
And though my ship sails from your sight,
It doesn't mean my journey ends.
It only means the river bends."

Afterwards, as they walked among the marble headstones, her mother had taken Leonora's hand and said, "I want you to love and admire your father, but I don't want you to become trapped by his memory. He would have wanted you to come here and see where he fought and died, but he would not have wanted this to become a place of pilgrimage. Bring your children here when they are grown, but until then live your own life, make your choices, and be your own person – not someone who merely carries on as a shadow of her dead father. He told me to tell you to live your life on the front line – that is what he always said."

Leonora pushed open the door and handed her letter to a uniformed commissionaire. She was told to go to room number 305 on the second floor and not to take the lift in case of power cuts.

The man who opened the door of the sparsely furnished room reminded Leonora of her driving instructor in Leamington: the same nicotine-stained teeth and fingers, the same ash-flecked cardigan. He was older, in his sixties, with thick grey hair. A pair of spectacles was attached to a loop around his neck.

He introduced himself as Richard Stobart from the personnel department of the Empire Broadcasting Service. He sat behind a desk and gestured to a wooden chair. He shuffled some papers on his desk, fished in his pocket for a cigarette, tapped it several times against its case, and put it in his mouth. Then he patted his cardigan pockets, looking for a lighter. He lit the cigarette and leant back, tipping the chair back onto two legs.

"So," he said, "you wish to join the BBC as a translator?"

"Yes, sir."

He tipped the chair forward and peered at the papers on his desk. "Why?"

The question was unexpected. He was looking at her through lidded eyes, an old grey lizard lounging back on his chair again, watchful, not friendly at all. She felt uncomfortable.

"I am fluent in French. I think that can be put to good use; after all, the BBC has a French service."

"Indeed it does. Tell me about your time at the Sorbonne."

Leonora had mentioned the four years she spent at the Sorbonne in all her job applications. The university offered a number of bursaries for the children of Allied officers who had died in the fighting, and she had been accepted to study European medieval history. For the first six months she had studied French at a language school in Montmartre. Her mother had paid the tuition fees and Leonora made just enough money waiting on tables at night to live on.

She described her four years in Paris briefly. Then he asked about her father, his regiment, the date and manner of his death. She answered the questions reluctantly. A suspicion formed that he knew the answers already. Then he turned back to her days in Paris.

"Did you have any special friends at the Sorbonne?"

"I am sorry, I don't understand."

"A boyfriend perhaps?"

"Yes, but is that relevant?"

"Miss Finch. This country is at war. We are going to fight that war in many ways. One way is to make sure we win the propaganda battle. The BBC will play an important part in that campaign."

"I understand that. But I don't understand what my boyfriend has to do with it."

He looked down at his papers again, squinted, and put on his spectacles. "Perhaps you will understand if I tell you that Philippe Masson joined the Communist Party in Paris in January this year. The Soviet Union is in alliance with Nazi Germany and since we are at war with Germany . . ."

He let the sentence trail away and smiled at her.

She looked at him in shock. How had they known about Philippe? She had not heard from him since she left Paris almost eighteen months ago. At the end of her first year she had found herself living with a medical student in a one-room fourth-floor walk-up in the working-class district of Levallois-Perret, which adjoined the wealthy suburb of Neuilly. Philippe was a country boy from Aix-en-Provence whose father ran a dental practice. He was very proud of his even white teeth and smiled a lot, which made Leonora laugh, which in turn irritated him. "The French have no sense of humour," she would taunt him, and he would reply in all seriousness by saying that the French did not have the *British* sense of humour – thank God.

Together they explored the city, learning how to ride free on the Métro, where to get free croissants after the cafés in the Latin Quarter closed in the evening, and how to make friends with the porters at Les Halles to get cheap fruit and vegetables. The political chaos of the Third Republic hardly touched their lives. France had been without a functioning government when Hitler came to power in Germany in 1933 and it was without a government five years later when the Nazis marched into Austria. That was the Third Republic. The French army fell asleep behind the Maginot Line and Paris behaved as if talk of another war was evidence of insanity, treason, or both. The events of 1938 did little to concentrate minds among the French government. Leonora graduated that summer from the Sorbonne and bade a tearful farewell to Philippe at the Gare du Nord. He was always talking about workers' rights and popular politics, but she had dismissed that as youthful posturing. Philippe a Communist? It scarcely seemed possible, but in any case, so what?

She suddenly felt angry. Why on earth should they, whoever they were, pry into her life like this? She knew she was blushing. She wanted to get up and leave. She shifted in her chair.

"I haven't heard from him since I left France. But I don't understand what this is about."

Stobart stubbed his cigarette out, got to his feet, lit another one, and began to walk around the room, circling her chair.

"Of course you don't. Let me help you. But first, two questions. You wish to do something that will assist your country at a time of great peril, and you wish to use your fluency in French and your licence to drive. Is that right?"

Leonora nodded. She had not mentioned her driving licence.

"Good. Well, I have a file here of all the letters you have written to various government departments in the last year or so. This tells us that you are determined, resourceful, and have skills well suited to the work we have in mind."

"What work would that be?"

"It would not be for the BBC."

"I thought this was the BBC."

"It is."

"So who are you?"

"Miss Finch, we can halt this conversation and you can leave this room whenever you wish."

He sat down and looked at her again, the grey lizard eyes wreathed in smoke. She half-expected a thin forked tongue to whip out at her.

"Well?" he said.

"Well, what?" she said faintly.

"Shall we proceed?"

"If you wish."

"I do so wish, Miss Finch, and I am going to assume that you do too."

For the next ten minutes she listened as the man in the grey cardigan told her the history of an organisation called the First Aid Nursing Yeomanry. It had been formed in the Great War as a women's mounted unit. The idea was that nurses on horseback could ride over the battlefields of France to care for the wounded who had fallen beyond the reach of motorised medical units. They were incredibly brave women, often working under fire. The unit, FANY for short, had won praise for its work and recently had formed another all-female unit, the Women's Transport Service, to provide secure transport for key foreign personnel working for the war effort in Britain. Hence the importance of her French.

He stopped and lit another cigarette. When he was done, Leonora stood up.

"Are you offering me a job as a driver?"

"Not exactly," said Stobart. "Let me put it this way. The Women's Transport Service will work closely with certain government departments, including the prime minister's office and the great offices of state. It will also support the work of government agencies involved in gathering information. Secret information. Driving is an important part of the job, but there are other roles. . . ." He let the sentence trail away, watching her.

"What other roles?" she asked.

"Code work, ciphers, assisting people who will be sent on missions abroad, that kind of thing."

"What sort of people?"

He leant back in his chair and blew a plume of smoke at the ceiling. "Agents, Miss Finch, British agents."

"You're nothing to do with the BBC, are you?" she said.

He ignored her response. "Let me repeat my question. Do you understand what I am saying?"

"I think so."

There was a long pause as the lizard looked at her.

"And do you have any questions?"

"Are any of the agents women?"

"It is government policy that women should not have a front-line role in this war in any of the services involved. I am sorry about that."

"So am I," she said, and stood up, brushing her skirt down. Stobart rose and shook her hand.

"But that may change," he said, and smiled.

This was the woman he wanted. All their inquiries had pointed this way.

3

Hopkins got up, took a bath, shaved, and went downstairs. He was handed a copy of the *Times* at the desk by the receptionist who had greeted him upon his arrival the previous day.

"She's over there," the receptionist said.

Standing in the foyer was a young woman in a blue-grey air force uniform, wearing a peaked cap and holding an attaché case. There was a thin white line on a broad black stripe on the lower part of the sleeve of her tunic. She was tall and had dark green eyes. She saluted him as he walked over.

"Good morning, sir."

"Good morning," said Hopkins, feeling there must be a mistake. "Are you waiting for me?"

"Yes, sir. Flight Officer Finch, your driver," she said.

"Of course," said Hopkins, vaguely recalling the prime minister's offer.

"Well, you had better come and have some breakfast."

She looked surprised. "No thank you, sir. I will wait here. We'll leave for Southampton when you are ready."

"Southampton?"

"Yes, sir. I thought it had been arranged. The prime minister's office said – "

"Yes, of course. Well, give me a few minutes."

The dining room was almost empty. He was handed a breakfast menu that listed porridge, kippers, a range of egg dishes with bacon or sausages, and prunes. The wartime rationing he had read so much about in the American press clearly had not reached Claridge's. He ordered coffee and toast with marmalade. Through the door to the foyer he could see the driver was still waiting. There was no sign of the detective Churchill had mentioned. Hopkins had no idea why they were going to Southampton and only a vague idea that it was a port city on the south coast. It had probably been heavily bombed. Good, that's what he wanted to see. Not so much the damage as the morale of the people.

The president had been specific about this: "Find out how they are taking it, Harry. Talk to the people. See if they are standing up to this bombardment." That was the word the president used: "bombardment." He was a First World War man.

Hopkins opened the *Times*. Confused by the small advertisements on the front page, he turned to page 2 and found the main news of the day. There was a plethora of wartime reports, each told in a few paragraphs and each revealing a snapshot of life in wartime Britain: "Extensive Night Raids – Quick Work by Fire Crews"; "500 Methodist Churches Bombed"; "The Duke of Kent Sees War Damage"; "Postmen's Rounds with Pickaxes"; "American Hospital for Britain."

His eye was drawn to a story close to the bottom of the page: "10,000,000 Moleskins Wanted: Exports for Foreign Exchange." The Brits were asking farmers to trap every mole they could find and sell them to the government for resale into the American market, where furriers would turn them into garments, mostly waistcoats. Hopkins had known there was an acute foreign currency shortage, but the plea for ten-million dead moles showed the level of desperation. The country was broke and was on its hands and knees hunting moles. Bartering moleskin waistcoats for guns, that was Britain in January 1941. Hopkins took out his notebook. He would make it the lead item in his next report to the president. Roosevelt loved little stories that pointed to the bigger picture.

A waiter approached his table with a large brown envelope and a smaller white one. He opened the brown one first. A cable from the White House was sealed in an inner envelope. It said simply: "Your report well received. Pursue all avenues. Good luck. Roosevelt." He ripped open the second. It was on Claridge's notepaper: "Stay in touch – Ed M."

Hopkins dozed briefly in the back of the Humber and then woke up with a start as a horn blared and the car swerved to avoid a lorry. She was driving fast through light traffic, using the gears to get maximum acceleration past a stream of military vehicles heading out of London. The air force pennant on the car's wing seemed to have a magical effect on the traffic. Hopkins fell asleep again as they cleared London. He woke as they left Guildford and climbed a hill that offered a view over green fields.

"Where are we?" said Hopkins, rubbing the sleep from his eyes.

She looked at him in the rearview mirror.

"Still in Surrey. This hill is called the Hog's Back. We take the A31 now all the way to Southampton. Should be there in about an hour."

Hopkins lit a cigarette. This was the first time he had seen the green and pleasant land he had heard so much about. It was not quite as the poets had described and the artists had painted. A carpet of frost covered the patchwork of fields and hedges that rolled away to a blur of blue hills in the distance. A little like New England, maybe.

"Sorry, sir," she said. "No smoking in the car. Service rules."

Hopkins wound down the window and threw out the cigarette.

"Does that apply to the prime minister as well?" he said sourly.

"Nothing applies to the prime minister, sir."

Hopkins smiled. That was true – except, of course, the determination to drag America into this war. That certainly applied to the prime minister.

Ten miles from Southampton, on the downs overlooking the city, the car swung into a lay-by. Flight Officer Finch jumped out to open Hopkins's door.

"Smoke break, sir," she said, offering him a cigarette from a pack of Craven "A".

Hopkins lit up and looked down at the coast. Smoke was rising from what must be the port area and also from several suburbs.

"Was there a raid last night?"

"Almost every night, sir. It's the Spitfire factory at Woolston they're after – over there." She pointed to a pillar of smoke on the west side of the city. "They flattened it back in September and they've been coming back ever since. They're very thorough, the Luftwaffe. But production has been moved into buildings all over the city and we're still making the planes."

"Looks like they hit the port as well," he said, shading his eyes against the winter sun.

"Yes. We bring down most of the coal from the north through Southampton because they have bunkering facilities, and the Germans know it. They know everything about us."

"You seem to know quite a lot too."

He looked at her properly for the first time. She had fair hair, pale skin that looked as if it had never seen the sun, and a figure that gave her blue serge uniform a pleasing shape. But it was the eyes that caught him, dark emerald-green eyes that seemed too worldly for such a young face. He guessed she was little more than in her early twenties, a little young to be an officer in the RAF, but then he'd read that they had put eighteen-year-olds into Spitfires during the Battle of Britain the previous summer.

"It's my job, sir. I am here to help you get all the information you need. When you're ready, sir."

She opened his door. He threw his cigarette away and got in the back.

She drove straight to the smoking rubble that had once been the main Spitfire factory.

"They moved out the key machinery before the raids," she said. "I'm going to show you something the Germans haven't found yet."

They toured a series of church halls, school buildings, even a semiderelict department store. Hopkins was shown a workforce of fitters, mechanics, and welders assembling the wings and fuselages of the fighter and mounting engines and the eight guns onto the frames. Under leaky roofs and in draughty halls, Spitfires were being created before his eyes. A posse of photographers trailed after them, flashbulbs popping at every stage of the tour. Reporters with long overcoats and trilbies tossed out questions. Here was the American president's envoy watching Spitfire production resume after the Luftwaffe had done their worst. They thought they had destroyed the plant. Under wartime censorship the press could not say where the plant was or give any clue as to the whereabouts of the new production lines. But the point was that Britain could take the bombing – and keep building Spitfires. "What does Mr Hopkins think about that?" "And any chance you Yanks are going to come into the war, Mr Hopkins?" Each question drowned out the last as the journalists vied for his attention.

Flight Officer Finch brushed them off with a few crisp words he could not hear.

"Have you considered that I might want to talk to the press?" he said to her.

"I am advised that the prime minister feels you should wait until you have had a chance to gather sufficient information before talking to the press. He is arranging for you to give a press conference in London later."

"Really?" said Hopkins. The woman was beginning to irritate him.

The last stop on the tour was the main garage of a requisitioned bus depot. Every inch of floor space was covered in machinery. Men in oil-smeared brown overalls swarmed around sections of fuselage suspended at head height from small cranes in a cradle of chains. Welders and riveters lined each side of the fuselage, working sheets of shiny aluminum into the shape of an aircraft that had seized the imagination of those at home and struck fear into German pilots during the Battle of Britain the previous summer. This was a Spitfire in the making, a chrysalis without wings that would soon take flight as a deadly butterfly.

Hopkins walked over to a young man in grease-stained overalls who had paused from punching rivets to light a cigarette.

"Hi," he said. "I'm over from the U.S. to see how you're doing. The name's Hopkins."

He held out his hand and the young man shook it.

"Bill Bull, sir," he said, pushing back his cap. "Welcome."

"Thanks. Can you tell me how the work is going here?"

"I can tell you I'm lucky to be alive," he said.

Bill Bull was eighteen years old, old enough to build a Spitfire and old enough to fly one in combat. He had been one of four hundred workers at the main plant when the bombers struck the previous September. They had ignored the sirens during a tea break and continued playing cards. Most of them, about one hundred men, were killed outright or died of wounds shortly after. The bombers had returned a few days later to complete the destruction and were now trying to pinpoint the new makeshift production plants scattered around the city.

"They're still after us, but they can't find us," said Bull. "Know what we say? 'Give us a roof and we will build you a Spitfire.' Amazing what you can do in a war, isn't it?"

That night Hopkins finished writing out his report in his room at Claridge's and went to the bar for his first drink of the day. He needed that drink. He had described in neutral language how the Southampton Spitfire workers had lost many of their number and their main factory in the September raids. But he had seen for himself that production was continuing thanks to a combination of ingenuity and courage that told its own story. He had ended by quoting Bill Bull in full.

In the bar he was immediately besieged by the American press corps, who had woken up to the fact that the president's envoy was in their midst.

Ed Murrow, the acknowledged leader of the press pack, took control of the situation.

"Give the guy a break," he commanded. "Harry is going to buy you all drinks and then I'm taking him somewhere quiet for dinner. If I hear anything good, I'll pass it on, OK?"

There was a muttered assent and the journalists turned back to the bar and their favourite occupation – gossiping about whichever member of their group happened not to be present. Outside the hotel, Hopkins saw the Humber waiting by the door in the darkness. It was nine o'clock. They had begun the day at half past eight that morning.

Harry leant into the rolled-down window.

"It's late. I think you should go home. We can manage," he said.

"Thank you, sir, but please get in the car," she replied. "I have my orders, I am afraid."

Hopkins looked at Murrow questioningly.

"Do as the lady says," said the broadcaster.

They drove past the boarded-up shops of Regent Street and turned into a network of small streets and alleys in Soho. The car stopped in the darkness. The blackout was impressively observed in this part of town. The only light came from the occasional flash of flame as figures moving down the street paused to light cigarettes.

Finch got out and opened the back doors. Murrow walked to the front door of a building that in most American cities would pass as a doll's house. It was three stories high, with two small windows to each story. Murrow pressed the bell three times, and within seconds a window was flung open and a sock landed on the pavement with a surprising thud. Murrow picked it up, extracted a large key, pocketed the sock, and opened the door.

"Where on earth is this?" said Hopkins, who had failed to get a drink at the hotel and badly needed one now.

Murrow went into the house and beckoned him to follow. Hopkins turned to Finch. "Are you coming in for a drink?"

"It's kind of you, sir, but – "

"You have your orders –"

"Yes, sir. Another time, perhaps."

The Black Cat Club had very few rules, but the one to which all members adhered was that no journalist should ever cross its threshold. The one exception, made on the orders of the club's owner, bartender, and occasional cook, Mrs Margot Worsley, was that Mr Ed Murrow of the Columbia Broadcasting System not only was allowed to use the club whenever it was open but also would be given the first drink free.

The club premises consisted of a single large room on the first floor and a dining room and kitchen on the second. Mrs Worsley was rumoured to live on the top floor, although no one had ever seen her ascend to or descend from those quarters, because she was always to be found in the bar when the club opened at around seven and was still there in the early hours of the morning when it closed.

The Black Cat was less a club than a permanent party hosted by Mrs Worsley, who took it upon herself to introduce everyone to everyone else regardless of whether they knew each other. She had a face that had once been beautiful and that now, beneath plentiful makeup, radiated a welcoming sexual warmth. Her lipstick was the colour of old claret and her deep brown eyes shone between long lashes coated in mascara. She wore a flowing kaftan that enveloped her from neck to ankle and a hat that looked like a turban.

There was a scatter of armchairs and tables placed around the room in no discernible order. On a wooden bar in one corner a wind-up gramophone played a slow jazz number. A coal fire burned brightly. There must have been thirty or forty people there, mostly standing and talking.

"Darlings," said Mrs Worsley, who beamed as she strode through the crowd with outstretched arms. She hugged Murrow and then turned to Hopkins. "And who is this, darling?"

"Harry Hopkins, fresh in from Washington and very important."

"I love important Americans. Do you drink gin, Mr Hopkins?"

"Sure, but whisky if you have got it."

"Any whisky, Ahmed?" she yelled to an ancient Arab behind the bar. Ahmed wore a fez with a tassel down one side and a red waistcoat over a white blouson. He looked as if he had stepped out of one of the seasonal pantomimes that were still running in West End theatres. He bent down and produced a bottle of Johnnie Walker.

"Help yourself, darlings," she said, and turned to take an elderly Frenchman by the arm to meet a woman at the far side of the room.

"But this is my wife," he protested feebly as Mrs Worsley made the introduction and sailed back across the room.

Hopkins and Murrow found a table by the window and sat down. Hopkins tried to take in his new surroundings.

"What is this place?" he said.

"Somewhere quiet to relax without a journalist in sight. That's one attraction. Dear old Mrs Worsley is the other. She is one of the grand dames of Soho. Husband was badly gassed in the last war and died a year or so after. She celebrated with a wake and the party's been going on ever since. Food is usually very good. Her potluck pies are famous. She's got a Moroccan cook who is reputed to be her lover."

"And who comes here?"

"All sorts. Dips, Free French, writers, spooks – and some classy ladies who live on their charms, if I might put it that way. But she has to like you."

"And what do they all do when there's an air raid?"

"No one moves. It's drinks on the house. If you leave during a raid, she'll never let you back in."

Murrow looked around, nodding to acknowledge several waved greetings. He could see two senior members of the Secret Intelligence Service drinking with women who were far too young to be their wives. That was the point of the place. The secrets of the Black Cat stayed with Mrs Worsley.

"Here's to you, Harry," he said, raising his glass. "You look wiped out. Tell me about Churchill."

"He's asked me to go down to his country place tomorrow."

"Chequers?"

"Yes, unless there's a full moon, when they switch to somewhere called Ditchley, apparently, in case of German bombers."

"And what did you make of him yesterday?"

Hopkins was careful with his words. The British prime minister was unlike anyone he had ever met, a politician of passionate certainty, a natural war leader and orator, still brimful of bubbling self-confidence after a career that had included some catastrophic failures. The previous summer, almost single-handedly, surrounded by appeasers and doubters, he had pulled the country through the moment of its greatest peril. But that was a battle won, nothing more.

"You've been here since the beginning, Ed, and you know

a hell of a lot more about this war than I do. So let me ask you a question. Are the Brits going to make it? A lot of folk back home think the Germans have got them beat."

Murrow took a long slug of whisky and allowed himself to think. Whatever he said was going to be on a White House desk within twenty-four hours. In his reporting he had been careful not to draw any conclusions but simply to tell his audience back home the story of England at bay, of the Blitz, and of the commanding personality and oratorical power of the prime minister.

He had described what it felt like to be on the streets at night as bombs were falling. He had slept in the Tube stations alongside thousands of frightened men, women, and children. There was little sanitation, the smell by morning was appalling, but the camaraderie and the humour during those nights were deeply moving and told a story of a people who would not be broken.

The nights in the underground shelter always ended the same way. At about six in the morning the tea came round, then people got up, shook themselves off, and headed home, if they had one left, or to work. He knew his reports of those nights sheltering with Londoners during a raid had had a big effect on his listeners. Every broadcast that mentioned the way that Londoners survived the bombing in subterranean shelters brought letters and calls from his listeners to the CBS office in New York offering help. But he never ventured an opinion as to the outcome of the war. How could he?

If you looked at the situation calmly and rationally, Britain was finished. Roosevelt was going to keep the United States out of the war. The president was running scared of the isolationist lobby led by Henry Ford and other big-business titans. The White House paid close attention to the opinion polls, which showed again and again that the American people would not stand for involvement in another European war.

Greece would fall to the Axis powers shortly and open the gates of the eastern Mediterranean to Hitler. But that was not the critical theatre of war. The war would be won or lost in the Atlantic. And the fact was that the battle was being lost. Murrow had heard appalling figures of shipping losses from sources in Liverpool but had never been able to substantiate them. Censorship and manipulation of wartime statistics for propaganda purposes made any accurate evaluation impossible. But Murrow believed his sources.

But he wasn't going to tell Hopkins any of this.

"The answer is I don't know, Harry," he said. "Right now the Nazis have all the cards. Their bombers can fly against us from French bases and their subs can operate against our Atlantic convoys from French ports. Britain is alone and I wouldn't rule out an attempted invasion this summer. But don't quote me on that; you are going to spend a lot of time with a man who is better able to answer your question than me."

Hopkins noted the use of "us" and "our." Murrow had been in London too long. He had gone native.

They left for Chequers the next morning, the Humber making slow progress through the traffic. Snow had fallen overnight, followed by a freezing fog. The white blanket over Hyde Park made the occasional statue look like a ghostly apparition in the morning mist.

Against his driver's wishes, Hopkins sat in front, listening to the rattle of the heater and watching the wiper blades swish back and forth against the shroud of fog. He was wearing the new overcoat Miss Macy had made him buy in New York the very day he left. It was camel-coloured gabardine, and just the thing for a London winter, she had said. Dear sweet Louise Macy. His fiancée. He had not even bought her a ring yet.

They cleared London on the A40 heading towards the Chiltern Hills. Hopkins had had only a coffee for breakfast and he felt hungry. He took a cigarette pack from his coat pocket and began playing with it like a deck of cards.

Leonora Finch noticed.

"Smoke break?" she said.

"Good idea," he said, and yawned. He was tired. He had only been in London two days and the trip was already killing him.

She pulled into a lay-by alongside a white wooden hut with CAFE painted in red on the side and a chimney belching out smoke. There were two lorries parked outside.

They walked into a fug of smoke, steam, and the smell of frying fat. Four men with caps pushed back from grimy faces were playing cards over mugs of tea. Behind the counter a woman with a tea towel twisted around her head and the stub of a cigarette in her mouth was shaking a large frying pan over a gas ring with one hand while pouring boiling water from a kettle into a brown teapot with the other. A hand-painted sign on the wall said NO FIGHTING. NO SPITTING. NO GAMBLING. SWEAR IF YOU MUST BUT DO NOT TAKE THE LORD'S NAME IN VAIN.

In the corner another sign would have said LAVATORY, except the first three letters had dropped off. "Breakfast?" said Leonora, anxious to provide the frail man in her care with the sustenance he so obviously needed.

"Just coffee for now," said Hopkins, lighting a cigarette. He offered her one, but she shook her head.

"They do a good baked beans on toast," she said.

"No thanks. So you know this place?"

"We drop in on the way to Chequers sometimes. The prime minister has even been here."

"What!" said Hopkins, looking around and trying to imagine President Roosevelt in such surroundings.

"Yes. We had to stop so he could spend a penny. He was most amused by the sign to the lavatory over there."

" 'Spend a penny'?"

"Well, that's what we say – translates as 'take a leak' in America, I believe. Sugar in your tea?"

Hopkins took off his new coat and laid it carefully over the back of his chair. He sat down, taking care not to put his arms on the layer of grease that covered the tabletop. The woman set mugs of tea in front of them.

Leonora produced a pack of Gauloises and lit one, blowing out a long plume of blue smoke. The distinct aroma wafted across the room, making the men at the other table look up.

Hopkins picked up the blue pack and looked at it. "How did you get these?" he said.

"The Free French brought a lot over. It's who you know in this war –"

"You must have good connections."

"This helps," she said, tapping the insignia of rank on her sleeve.

Hopkins was reminded to ask a question that had been bubbling at the back of his mind for the last two days.

"What is a flight officer in the women's air force doing driving a government car? Shouldn't you be up there somewhere?" he said, pointing to the ceiling.

Leonora smiled, red lipstick against white teeth.

"I hold an honorary rank, sir. It helps cut red tape and makes it easier to deal with petty officials and the police and so forth."

"So you are not in the RAF?"

"No, it's the women's equivalent, the WAAF, Women's Auxiliary Air Force – same thing, just a different name for us ladies."

"So who do you work for?"

"The Women's Transport Service, sir."

"And they have the right to hand out commissions in the WAAF?"

"Apparently so, sir. I don't ask questions."

And, as Hopkins understood, neither should he. He lit another cigarette. "Right. Tell me what you know about me. You must have been given a brief. That can't be confidential, can it?"

She lit another Gauloise. "You hold no formal position in the U.S. government, but you are a close adviser and confidant of the president; as such, you are an important and honoured guest of this government. My job is to make sure you get all the help you need on your fact-finding mission."

"Very nice," he said, "but it doesn't quite answer my question."

"I know about your background, sir, your upbringing in Sioux City in Iowa – such a romantic name, that."

"It's not a very romantic place."

"I know that you had what I believe in America is termed a hardscrabble upbringing."

"Correct," he said. "Any more?"

She shook her head and looked at her watch. "Sir, I think we should leave."

"Orders again?"

"My orders are to get you there in time for drinks before lunch."

Military policemen at the entrance to the drive briefly checked Leonora's documents and peered at Hopkins in the front seat. They saluted, breathing clouds into the frosty air, and waved them on. On the gravel forecourt in front of a red-brick Victorian house policemen manned a tented command post.

Brendan Bracken waited on the steps to greet them.

"Welcome," he said. "You are just in time for drinks – come and meet everyone."

The house was cold, not much above freezing, Hopkins judged as he washed his hands in a small lavatory off the hall before lunch. The radiators in the hall emitted a feeble heat, but nobody else seemed to notice or mind.

There were twelve guests gathered in a drawing room whose windows had been taped with strips of brown paper. Churchill was nowhere to be seen. Bracken introduced Hopkins to General Sir Hastings Ismay and Professor Lindemann, the prime minister's main scientific adviser.

"And may I introduce Pamela Churchill," said Bracken.

Hopkins knew all about the prime minister's daughter-in-law, the daughter of a titled landowner who had married Churchill's son, Randolph, and who was now taking advantage of her husband's posting to the Middle East to conduct a series of affairs – or at least that was what his embassy brief on those closest to the prime minister had told him.

Pamela greeted him as a long-lost friend, kissing him warmly on both cheeks. He noted raven hair, a long swan-like neck, and a brown woollen dress drawn in at the waist.

"Before you do anything let me get you a drink," she said in a low, breathy voice. "Champagne?"

"Maybe a weak whisky," he replied.

Churchill bustled into the room from his adjoining study, leaving the door open so that the lunch party could see Nelson the cat sitting comfortably on the desk amid a scatter of papers and half a dozen telephones. He shook Hopkins warmly by the hand and led the party into the dining room. Lunch that day was a command performance conducted by the premier from the top of the table as if the guests were his own orchestra. Everyone was required to perform, and not just those at the table. Occasionally Churchill would turn to one of the waitresses and ask about the price of a commodity such as milk.

"Every prime minister, every politician, must know the price of milk," he said, turning to his guests at the table having elicited the information. "Without milk you cannot have a decent cup of tea, and where would England be without her regular cuppa?"

Questions flowed from the head of the table on the great topics of the day: the German invasion intentions, the North African campaign, how England's coal-dependent economy could survive the threatened strike by the bloody-minded miners in the north, and above all the effect of bombing on morale. Could Londoners, and increasingly the population of such major cities as Liverpool, Southampton, Manchester, and Glasgow, continue to take the strain?

"What do you think, Mr Hopkins? Have you formed any views yet?"

Churchill had turned to his guest, beaming with pleasure. As usual, he had taken care with the seating arrangements. Hopkins was on his right and next to him Pamela. On Churchill's left, directly opposite the American visitor, he had placed Commander Charles Thompson. Thompson was a navy man who had served in submarines in the First World War. He was now seconded to Number 10 with a brief to monitor the Battle of the Atlantic, and as such he offered to bring the American up to date.

The question Churchill had put to him was one Hopkins

knew he was going to be asked repeatedly both in England and when he returned to Washington. In reply, he told the story of Bill Bull and the Spitfire factory at Southampton, emphasising the young man's observation that it was "amazing what you can do in a war."

Churchill was delighted with the response and immediately ordered a toast to the aircraft worker.

The lunch had been three courses: clear onion soup, to which Churchill seemed partial; thinly sliced breast of cold pheasant, with mashed potatoes and Brussels sprouts, and cheese. A different wine was served with every course, although Hopkins noticed that none of the other guests tried to match the prime minister's appetite for everything put in front of him.

Finally coffee was served with brandy. Cigars and cigarettes were lit, but none matched the Havana that Churchill produced.

"Mr Hopkins," said the familiar voice within a cloud of blue smoke. "You must be tired. May I suggest you rest? We shall have a small party in your honour this evening."

"Thank you, Prime Minister," said Hopkins, rising from his seat.

With that, the prime minister rose and left the room, trailing cigar smoke. The other guests immediately relaxed and began talking among themselves. It was as if a much-loved but imperious schoolmaster had just left the classroom, thought Hopkins.

It was dark when Hopkins woke up. For a moment he thought he had slept through the night, but his watch told him it was five o'clock. Even under the blankets he was cold. Shivering, he pulled on his overcoat and parted the curtain. It was snowing. He saw the military policemen in long greatcoats stamping back and forth and blowing into their hands. You cannot fire a weapon wearing gloves. They are going to freeze, thought Hopkins.

There was a knock at the door. Sawyers appeared with a tray of tea.

"Mr Churchill's compliments, sir," he said. "He would be grateful if you could see him when you are ready."

"Certainly. Where is he?"

"In the bathroom, sir."

"The bathroom?"

"Yes, sir. He's having his evening bath. It's down the corridor and the second door on the left. And, sir . . ."

"Yes?"

"He says that you should bring a notebook and pen."

Hopkins knocked on the bathroom door and heard a muffled command to enter. He pushed the door open and stepped into the welcome warmth of a room clouded with steam and noisy with much splashing. A bar of yellow soap escaped from the steam cloud and slithered across the tiled floor towards him.

"Bugger," a familiar voice said from within the steam. "I don't suppose you would pick that up, would you, Mr Hopkins?"

Hopkins retrieved the soap and held it out as he took a step towards the bathtub. He could dimly see a large pink figure, one hand holding a sponge, the other reaching for the soap. Hopkins half-expected to see a cigar smouldering in an ashtray beside the tub.

"Thank you. Do take a seat, and may I ask why you are wearing an overcoat?"

"I find the house a little chilly, Prime Minister," said Hopkins, sitting on a cork-topped stool.

"Well, you should work in here, then – warmest room in the house. Now, do you have your notebook?"

Churchill talked, or rather dictated, it seemed to Hopkins, for almost twenty minutes. The subject was Lend-Lease and the prime minister showed an impressive grasp of the details and complexity of the legislation that was working its way through Congress.

Listening to the voice booming around the bathroom, Hopkins almost submitted to the view that the future of Western civilisation depended on passage of a bill that would give Britain access to armaments and foodstuffs on the basis of credit. The country had exhausted its gold reserves and had nothing left with which to pay for war matériel. With the bill Roosevelt had circumvented the restrictions of the Neutrality Act by making such supplies available on condition that they were eventually returned or payment was made at a later date. But Congress in both houses showed a distinct reluctance to agree to such measures.

"Tell me, Mr Hopkins, is it going through, and if so when?"

The reply did not go down well in the bathtub. Polls showed 80 per cent of Americans were against the war and well over 50 per cent did not want to send aid of any kind to Britain. The U.S. business community had mainly concluded that Britain would soon be knocked out of the war and that Hitler was therefore the man to do business with. There was also widespread Anglophobia in the American heartland, and especially among the Irish, German, and Italian communities. But elsewhere, in the midwestern and southern states, Britain was regarded as an old lion whose time had come to face the final spear.

"Who said that?" growled the bathtub. "That stuff about the lion and the spear?"

"It was an opinion article in a New Orleans paper widely reprinted elsewhere," said Hopkins.

The figure suddenly rose from the bath, a pink, round gleaming Michelin man. Soapy water slopped over the side and cascaded across the floor.

"I've never heard such bloody rubbish. Would you be so kind as to pass me my towel?"

Hopkins wrote a letter to his fiancée that evening. It began: "Dearest Louise, nothing in this life will ever surprise me again. . . ."

Louise Macy laughed out loud when she read the letter. She reread it to make sure she had her facts straight before picking up the phone. She had a large circle of friends that reached right into the White House and she could hardly wait to pass on the news.

Twenty people appeared for the small party Churchill gave in honour of his guest that evening. A number of advisers, assistants, and their wives joined those who had already been present at lunch. They all dressed as if attending a funeral: black suits for the men and sombre-coloured dresses for the women. Having abandoned his beloved siren suit, the prime minister stood out in dark blue trousers, a maroon velvet smoking jacket, and a spotted bow tie.

To his surprise, Hopkins saw Leonora among those who were handed a glass of champagne at the door. For a moment he did not recognise her. She was wearing a plain red dress whose low neckline was set off by a single rope of pearls and high-heeled red shoes. Her hair had been tied back in a bun, revealing her long neck. As she entered, the other women in the room glanced at her, measured her in a moment, and found her wanting in tact and deference. What was the prime minister doing asking a service driver to a drinks party at Chequers? He would have the cook in next. She was very pretty, of course, and that risqué dress made much of her figure, but there was no class in the girl. In fact, she was just a little bit common and she was far too young to be in such company.

Hopkins watched her pause by the door and take the measure of the room. He walked over to her. "I thought you had gone back to London," he said.

"I could hardly do that, sir," she said. "I'm driving you back tomorrow morning, unless it snows heavily."

Hopkins walked to the window and pulled back the drapes. A long bar of light fell onto thick snow. Further flurries drifted in from the darkness above. He stepped into the alcove behind the drapes. Leonora joined him.

"Do you always come to these occasions?"

"The prime minister invited me tonight. He thought it would be nice for you to have a familiar face around."

"He was right," Hopkins said, "and it's also good to see you out of that blue serge."

She looked at him and smiled. "I bought this dress in Paris years ago. You can't find anything like this now unless you know someone on the black market."

"And do you?"

"Oh yes, we all do; that's how I get my Gauloises."

"Blackout!" someone shouted from the room, and a face thrust itself at them between the drapes.

"Are you two trying to get us bombed?" said Bracken. "Come back in and join the party. The PM has some people he wants you to meet, Mr Hopkins."

Churchill introduced his guest to Commander Thompson, opposite whom he had sat at lunch earlier. An earnest discussion followed on the need for more British destroyers to guard the Atlantic convoys. Minutes later he was talking to General Ismay, the PM's personal chief of staff, and learning about the perilous situation in Greece.

"Confidentially, I am not sure of the wisdom of reinforcing the Greeks," said General Ismay. "It weakens us in North Africa, but you know what the PM is like." He tapped his nose as if some great secret had been imparted. "By the way, did you know we have one hundred Curtiss Tomahawk planes here? We bought them from you just before the Neutrality Act came in last year. But the propellers never arrived; now if we could get those propellers . . ."

Hopkins smiled. This wasn't a party; it was more a briefing on Britain's endless list of war requirements. And what Britain needed just to survive another year of war went well beyond the provisions of the Lend-Lease legislation. The bill had not yet gone through Congress and the president wasn't even sure it would.

Hopkins saw Churchill across the room, cigar in one hand, champagne in the other, holding the attention of three of the wives. There was a gust of laughter from the group, and then Churchill turned his beaming face towards him.

"Ah, Harry, have you met my master of the black arts of science, Desmond Morton?"

As the scientific adviser whispered to him the nature of the nerve gas they would use if Hitler deployed his own biological weapons, "in strictest confidence, old boy," he said, Hopkins noticed Leonora standing with her back to the wood-panelled wall, blowing clouds of smoke into the air. She was on her own and looked bored. He was about to break off and go over when Pamela Churchill caught his eye. She was smiling at him over the shoulder of a naval officer. She gave a little flick of her head to indicate he should join her. Morton had begun a detailed description of the chemicals needed at the Porton Down research station to manufacture a new and more deadly form of nerve gas. Hopkins excused himself and joined Mrs Churchill.

"I have a feeling we're boring you," she said.

"Not at all."

"Oh, I think so. You're like that keeper at the London Zoo who feeds the seals. He steps into their enclosure with the fish and they all perform for him, and if they're good they get fed."

"Trouble is, I don't have any fish," he said.

She laughed, head back. "Oh, you Americans! You've got all the fish in the world, but you just don't want to give it to us, do you? And who can blame you? Little old England is going under – isn't that the view in Washington?"

"It's certainly not the view in the White House," he said, frowning.

"Don't look so grumpy. I'm only teasing. Now, who don't you know?"

"I don't know *you*."

"Oh yes, you do. I'm sure the embassy will have written you a brief about most people here. What did they say about me? A duke's daughter who met the prime minister's son at a cocktail party and accepted his proposal of marriage that very night?"

"Something like that. They also said that as a seventeen-year-old schoolgirl at a finishing school in Munich in 1937 you met Hitler. Is that true?"

Pamela Churchill's eyes shaded and the smile faded.

"Yes, it is, actually. Unity Mitford introduced us. He joined us for tea at our hotel."

"And?"

"Well, I daren't tell my father-in-law this, and I can hardly mention it here, but he was very charming. Eyes that bored into you while the interpreter waffled all the usual platitudes. But when he leant forward to take my hand . . . oh, his breath!"

They both laughed. Hopkins caught Leonora watching him. Pamela Churchill followed his gaze.

"Pretty, isn't she?" she said. "I can't think why she's not surrounded by the men."

"She's a driver, that's why."

"Oh, that doesn't matter anymore. There's a war on. In London everyone talks to everyone, and in the blackout they are doing a lot more than that. I think that's the dinner gong. Shall we go through?"

Dinner that night was a grander version of lunch, and as usual the prime minister was the ringmaster. Hopkins realised that Churchill loved having people around him, people to talk to, to debate with, people who shared with him the pleasures of the table and especially those of his cellar, presumably stocked at government expense. And what better way for Britain to invest in war matériel than by keeping this extraordinary figure well supplied with fine wine and brandy?

It was so very different from the White House. Eleanor Roosevelt insisted on a homely style of entertaining that bordered on the austere. The wine there was indifferent and the food no better. The president didn't seem to mind.

After dinner Hopkins excused himself, leaving the cigars and the brandy and the ever-flowing conversation and wearily climbing the great central staircase. The house was as cold as ever, but the alcohol had deadened the effect. He was beginning to think that while Britain might survive this stage of the war, he was not so sure that he would.

"Good night, sir."

He turned to see Leonora Finch at the bottom of the stairs. She was barefoot and holding her shoes and had unpinned her hair, which fell to her shoulders.

"Good night, Miss Finch. Where are you off to?"

"Bed, sir. It's late and we have to leave early."

"More orders?"

She smiled and nodded. "I am afraid so. Good night, sir." She walked to a door off the hallway and opened it.

"Flight Officer Finch."

She turned. "Yes, sir?"

"Please don't call me sir."

"Yes, Mr Hopkins. Good night, Mr Hopkins."

4

The secretary of state crossed the Oval Office, skirting papers and books strewn all over the floor, and knocked on the president's bedroom door. Hearing a muffled command from within, he opened the door and stepped inside. The drapes had been drawn and the room was flooded with the cold light of a winter's morning. Franklin Roosevelt was sitting up in bed in his pjamas, his rimless glasses perched halfway down his nose, reading documents in a cardboard folder. He waved his visitor into the room without looking up.

Cordell Hull looked around him, thinking how much the room reflected the man who slept here. Against one wall stood a dark mahogany wardrobe. A line of miniature china pigs in various colours and sizes trotted across the marble mantelpiece. Behind each pig, propped against the wall, were family snapshots. In one window alcove there was an old desk covered with white towelling, on which were scattered cuff links, a couple of silver ashtrays, a pack of Marlboros, and two cigarette holders. A wooden rocking chair faced the room in the second alcove. Two telephones had been placed on a large bedside table, along with a box of aspirin, nose drops, an ashtray and a pack of cigarettes, a leather-bound prayer book, bits of paper with scribbled notes and telephone numbers, a carafe of water, and a scatter of letters. Nailed to the bathroom door on the far side of the room was a long horse's tail, once proudly possessed by a Roosevelt family favourite, a mare called Gloucester. The bed itself was the most surprising feature. It was a narrow, white-painted iron bedstead of the kind found in school dormitories. A folded grey shawl lay across the foot.

"Good morning, Mr President," said Cordell Hull, dipping into his briefcase. "I have the overnight cables from London."

Roosevelt looked up, his face anxious and frowning. He shook the folder in his hand at his secretary of state.

"This came in this morning from Harry. You know what the Brits are asking for?"

Hull sighed and sat down in the rocking chair. He was a thin-skinned, hot-tempered man who resented any challenge to his authority. Hopkins's report from London had, as usual, bypassed American diplomatic channels and been sent through naval communications to the Department of Defense. There it had been decoded, typed up, and passed to the White House sometime in the night. The State Department never saw this traffic. It was humiliating for him and his staff, yet the president didn't notice – nor would he care if he did. Harry Hopkins, unelected, unappointed to any formal position, was the president's go-to boy. And he had gone to London, where he was once again proving to be a damned nuisance. Hull concealed his anger and rose to his feet.

"No, Mr President, but I assume you are going to tell me."

Roosevelt missed the sarcasm. "Listen to this. Harry is just passing this on, it's not his recommendation, but he thinks I should be aware of what the Brits call their basic needs to survive this year.

" 'Ten destroyers a month, beginning April 1,' " he read aloud. "*Ten!* Did you hear that? *Ten!* And they want us to recondition their oldest destroyers. . . . 'Urgent need for merchant shipping.' They can't replace what is being lost to U-boats. . . . Fifty Catalina flying boats for antisubmarine duties – fully equipped with radio, depth charges, bombs, guns, and ammunition . . . There are twenty-nine engineless Lockheed planes in England. They need fifty-eight Wright engines for them at once . . . They want to replace every one of their .50-caliber Colt machine guns with those manufactured in our own arsenals, which they say are much better."

The president threw the folder onto his bed.

"It goes on, Mr Hull, on and on: B-17 airplanes, as many as we can spare, twenty million rounds of .50-cal. ammunition, fifty million rounds for Lee-Enfield rifles. And what do they have to pay for this? Nothing!"

"Well . . . when the Lend-Lease bill goes through –"

"No, Mr Hull, not when but *if* Lend-Lease goes through. I am not sure it will. Where are we now? Middle of January. You take a look at the Senate – you think those boys are going to agree to give arms so that the Brits can hang on to their empire?"

"That's not the point, Mr President."

Roosevelt leant back against his pillows, looking exhausted. He thumped his bedside table, sending papers floating to the floor, waved at a chair by the window, and blew his nose.

"Take a seat."

Cordell Hull sat down.

"That's exactly the point. I know what has to be done, but I have to take the American people with me, and they do not want to get involved. How many times have I told American mothers that I will not send their sons to fight in another European war?"

Cordell bit his lip and decided not to confront the president with the truth. Roosevelt had said that too many times. He had made too many pledges about American neutrality. He was running scared of the isolationists, led by Charles Lindbergh. Lindbergh, the number-one Nazi fellow traveller in the United States, the man who had shaken Hitler's hand before the war and received an honour, a Nazi medal, from the German leader himself. Roosevelt had won a third term by an overwhelming majority only months earlier, yet he was worried about a loudmouth Nazi sympathiser. Goddammit, the president was there to lead. What Hull saw before him was a man prone to vacillation, a man suffering from yet another cold that was probably the beginning of flu. And that meant weeks of paralysis in the White House, with cabinet meetings being held here in this ramshackle bedroom.

The secretary of state got up. He was angry. He asked for a copy of the Hopkins file.

Roosevelt handed him the folder, lay back, and closed his eyes.

"I need Harry back here," he said wearily.

The message from the White House had been handed to Hopkins by Herschel Johnson at Euston Station in London. The night train was about to leave and the diplomat bustled through a crowd of khaki uniforms dimly visible in the smoky darkness.

"As a kid, I always used to think railway stations were so glamorous," Johnson said. "Not anymore. Take care up there; the raids are coming in every night." Then he vanished into the darkness.

The journey to Liverpool was scheduled to take five hours. Murrow had advised Hopkins to have a decent dinner before he left and the two men had dined at Claridge's on soup and game pie. Murrow was envious.

"I want to come with you, but they tie me to the studio here. I want a full report, Harry. Never mind the president; I'm the man who needs to know." He laughed and waved to a waiter for more wine. "You'd better eat well, Harry; there's no food up there, so I hear – even in the hotels."

Hopkins worried Murrow. He was a tired man with too much on his shoulders. A new American ambassador had been appointed to London, but he had not arrived yet. This figure pushing away his soup, toying with his game pie, was the de facto American ambassador. He had the president's ear. And neither man was well.

"I hear the president is sick again," Murrow ventured.

"He's got the flu. He's never in the best of health anyway."

"Don't get me wrong, Harry, but you're not looking too good either. You should take care of yourself."

Hopkins drained his glass. He was OK, just tired. It wasn't the Blitz that bothered him; it was the endless evenings with Churchill, listening to hour after hour of rolling oratory that described every twist and turn of the war, illustrated with quotes from Shakespeare, Milton, or Nelson. Occasionally, to sharpen his point, the prime minister would delve deep into the history of what he called this buccaneering isle on the rim of Europe.

The conversation only halted when messengers delivered confidential information in sealed envelopes. Churchill would rip them open and scan the contents. The news was almost always bad. He would crumple the papers into a ball and fling them into the fire. Hopkins was often at Churchill's side when bad news came, and every time the man just growled, lit another cigar, and reached for a brandy.

Good news was greeted with champagne, although there

was no cause for celebration in the month of January 1941. Not that it stopped the flow of champagne. Hopkins reported to Roosevelt that Churchill was a medical miracle, a man of almost seventy who stayed up until two or three in the morning, always with a drink at hand; never took exercise; drank and ate prodigiously; and had enough energy to exhaust men and women on his staff a generation younger. The president enjoyed such insights into life at Number 10. He was something of a medical rarity himself.

"You know your problem, Ed?" said Hopkins.

"Tell me," said Murrow wearily.

"You preach to the converted. Your radio audience is just East Coast and West Coast, and those folks are already sold on the notion that the U.S. needs, if not to step into this war right now, then at least to help the Brits with armaments. But that is not the majority. Go to my hometown of Sioux City and you'll hear a different story. Most of them don't even listen to the radio. That's the president's problem."

So now I am being lectured to by a White House know-it-all, thought Murrow, a man who sits on the president's shoulder like a parrot and repeats everything the great man says. Hopkins could be a pain.

"You know what the president's problem is?" he replied. "He's weak and he can't make up his mind. He's running scared and you don't seem to see that. You sit here and defend him, when what you should be doing is opening his eyes, telling him to stand up and give the country the leadership it expects from the White House. You have to tell him the truth."

Hopkins rose, angry. "And the truth is?"

Ed put a hand on his arm and motioned him to sit down. He leant over the table and said in a low voice, "The truth is that unless we start convoying across the Atlantic, and I mean giving those convoys naval protection, this country is finished. And it won't take long. You'll find that out in Liverpool."

A single bulb lit the first-class carriage. Hopkins sat opposite a detective from Scotland Yard finally assigned as his body-guard. He had initially refused such protection, but Number 10 had insisted. Leonora Finch had driven the Humber up to Liverpool with his overnight bag. He wanted to take the train to see how ordinary people travelled in wartime. He would put it in his next report. Roosevelt loved detail like that, which reminded him that the president had also asked for a detailed report on the wartime stamp issues in Britain.

Hopkins smiled. That was Roosevelt. In the middle of a global crisis he would be worrying about stamps. He was one of the world's great collectors and spent an hour or so every day poring over his albums with a magnifying glass. Ask the president what he wanted for lunch and he would say what he always said – "scrambled eggs." Ask him about a new issue of stamps to promote savings bonds in the United States and you wouldn't get out of the Oval Office for an hour. He said his stamps kept him sane. Churchill had his passion for the table and his champagne, wine, and brandy; Roosevelt had his stamps. That was how the two great leaders got through each day of the war.

"Cigarette, sir?"

The detective held out a pack with a bearded sailor on the front.

"Thanks," Hopkins said.

At least on the train he could smoke. A good reason to avoid the long journey by road with Flight Officer Finch. He could imagine her now pulling into a grimy transport café to snatch a quick coffee and a Gauloise among a crowd of exhausted drivers. She would talk to them, flirt a little, and then vanish into the pouring rain, leaving them to wonder what a young WAAF officer with pilot's stripes on her sleeve was doing driving a big Humber north through the night.

He opened the letter he had been handed by Johnson. It was a message from Roosevelt's secretary Missy LeHand: "The president would be grateful to know the date of your return."

Hopkins sighed. He had only been in England for three days and the old man was already fretting. He would just have to be patient.

The blinds of the compartment were drawn. In the corridors, sailors, soldiers, and civilians wedged themselves between piles of luggage. Many slept standing upright. Small children lay on top of the cases, fast asleep. Hopkins realised that getting to the lavatory was going to involve a major logistical operation.

The detective slipped a silver flask from his pocket and offered it. "It's going to be a long night, sir."

Hopkins smiled, shook his head. He had had enough to drink with Murrow. He would join the others in the compartment who were already dozing off. He drew deeply on his cigarette and expelled a long stream of smoke into the foetid air. The detective had already gone to sleep.

Sergeant Grant, formerly of the Flying Squad, had transferred to Number 10 and trained as one of the prime minister's bodyguards. A decent man with a wife and two kids somewhere in the London suburbs, he would be carrying a Colt .45 under that standard-issue raincoat. Hopkins had told Number 10 over and over again that he did not need a bodyguard. Grant would be far more useful dealing with looters in the East End of London than sitting on this train with him.

Looters were a problem never mentioned by the press, but after every big raid they always seemed to reach the ruined houses and shops before the police and firemen. Churchill had done his best to suppress newspaper stories of looting on the grounds that it was bad for morale, but everyone knew it was going on. The police often looked the other way. People were hungry and they needed food and clothes to shield them from the bitter winter.

It was raining hard when the train pulled into Liverpool's Lime Street station just after midnight. Leonora Finch was waiting for them on the platform and took them to the car. She drove slowly through the streets on the car sidelights, occasionally pausing at corners to shine a torch on street signs. Even in the darkness, Hopkins could see that the bomb damage was as bad as in London, if not worse. Whole blocks of the city had been levelled.

"God Almighty," said Sergeant Grant. "The Scousers have taken a hammering."

She dropped both men at a small hotel on the outskirts of the city. "They won't be over tonight in this cloud and rain," said Finch. "I'll pick you up in the morning, sir."

She drove off and Hopkins cursed himself for not asking where she was staying. In the hotel he was too tired to accept the offer of "one for the road" from the detective. For the first time since he had arrived in England, he slept without the sound of sirens, anti-aircraft fire, or falling bombs.

The map room of Combined Operations Western Approaches lay in a bomb-proof underground bunker near Liverpool's waterfront. Hopkins, Finch, and Sergeant Grant were led down a series of staircases into the bowels of the building. Their guide, a member of the Women's Royal Naval Service, paused before two large wooden doors and pressed a brass bell. The doors swung open and they stepped into what might well have passed for a Hollywood film set.

A massive map of the west coast of Britain, Ireland, and the Atlantic across to the U.S. seaboard covered a table in the centre of the room. Gantries of lights were slung over the table, and around it uniformed Wrens used long pointers to move markers. At the far end of the room the words "Aircraft State Readiness Board" were written on a blackboard above a map of all the airfields in the country within one hour's flight of the Atlantic. Weather maps covered the remaining walls. Women on raised walkways pinned up the latest information using a series of symbols indicating wind direction, barometric pressure, cloud, and rain.

"Welcome to the ops room," said a voice, and Hopkins turned to face a stout figure with a row of medals and service insignia on a blue naval uniform. He introduced himself as Sir Martin Dunbar-Smith, Commander-in-Chief, Western Approaches.

"It's quite a toy set, isn't it?" he said.

The British and their little jokes, thought Hopkins. No one in Sioux City had a double-barrelled name, and he doubted whether there was one to be found in any American telephone directory. Had Mr Smith added "Dunbar" because "Smith" was too common? Or did Dunbar marry a Smith who wouldn't give up her name? Or was it all some weird private joke of the British class system? Maybe Ed Murrow was right, that he was just a small-town boy from Iowa with a chip the size of an ear of corn on his shoulder. Did it matter? No, it didn't.

For the next two hours Hopkins was taken through a

series of briefings on the location, speed, and route of the convoys battering their way through the Atlantic storms at that moment. He was desperate for a cigarette, but no one seemed to be smoking. Leonora Finch remained in the background, taking notes. Sergeant Grant walked close behind Hopkins, regularly glancing at his watch, seemingly unimpressed by the flow of information. After a while he slipped away, muttering about the need to call London.

The convoy vessels were enumerated and detailed along with graphs showing the operational reach of RAF convoy-protection aircraft, mostly long-range Sunderland flying boats. As was made clear to Hopkins by Wren officers speaking in the clipped upper-class accents that made him conscious of his own midwestern twang, there was very little air cover for the convoys and not nearly enough at sea either. The loss of ten merchant vessels from a convoy of thirty was considered a success.

He was shown U-boat sightings marked on the big map with the likely course and targets plotted in red lines. Areas where U-boats were known to muster in wolf packs were given special attention. Secondary briefings covered the nature of the cargoes at sea, the number of hospital beds required for survivors of sinkings, and the attempt by the Luftwaffe to destroy Liverpool as a port and thus force convoys to move farther north to Scotland.

The Wren officer was moving seamlessly on to the location of U-boat pens on the French coast when Hopkins stood up. He felt as if he were drowning in the Atlantic like all those sailors who went down with their rust-bucket ships bringing fuel, food, and spare parts to this cold, sodden, besieged island. The room was closing in on him, or maybe it was the war. Maybe he had just realised that the British weren't going to make it. Because if what he was hearing was true, by the autumn there would not be enough food for the forty million population, let alone enough armaments to fight an invasion.

He turned to Leonora. "Let's get out of here. I need some air," he said.

They made their apologies, left, and headed down towards the docks, trailed by a protesting Sergeant Grant.

"German bombers are approaching the east coast," Grant said. "We would be better off inside somewhere; no one knows the target."

Hopkins looked to Leonora, walking briskly beside him.

"I know a good pub where they might actually have food," she said. "It's by the docks, but we should get an early warning if planes are heading this way."

The Golden Fleece stood on a corner at the bottom of a steeply sloping row of terraced houses that had been untouched by the raids. At the end of the street, cranes and warehouses marked the docks that ran for miles along the river Mersey.

A golden ram hung from a metal beam over the doorway, its two horns curled over its lowered head that looked down on those entering. Hopkins pushed open the door. It was lunchtime and the place was crowded and thick with smoke. Domino players sat around one table, while at the bar three young women giggled over glasses of gin and water. They were dressed as if for a party, with too much lipstick, knee-length skirts, and black lines drawn in crayon down the back of bare legs to create the pretence of seamed stockings. In one corner an old man on a stool was playing a fiddle. No one was listening. He had a shaggy mane of white hair and a weather-beaten face that spoke of a life at sea. He played a lament with his eyes closed, pausing only to reach for a glass of dark beer that looked as if it had been lifted straight from the Mersey.

"I bet you are hungry, sir," Leonora said.

"Harry, please."

Leonora smiled and said, "What can I get you, Mr Hopkins?"

"You won't get much here," said the detective, nodding to a small blackboard on which was chalked the single word MENU. There was a cheer from the girls at the bar as two of them began singing "Happy Birthday" to the third.

Hopkins bought the drinks – a beer for him and Sergeant Grant and a gin and orange for Leonora. The only food on offer turned out to be cheese sandwiches well laced with pickle.

They raised their glasses and toasted better times. Hopkins sipped the beer suspiciously. It tasted of hops and smelt of malt. It was flat and warm and unlike anything he had ever drunk back home.

Sergeant Grant was amused. "Not quite your style, sir, is it? We like our beer flat and tasty. You have yours all fizzed up and cold, right?"

"I don't drink beer back home," he said, putting the glass down just as a siren sounded.

The barman pulled heavy drapes across the windows and shouted, "Everyone downstairs!"

The bar emptied rapidly as people lined up to go down to the cellar. Anti-aircraft batteries began a drumbeat of fire from the riverfront.

Sergeant Grant looked at them questioningly and motioned towards the stairs to the cellar.

"I'm staying here," said Hopkins.

"I am supposed to be responsible for your safety, sir," said Grant softly. "And you, ma'am."

"You go down; we'll be all right," she said. "The Golden Fleece is a lucky name. Let's get another drink in."

Grant went to the bar, reached over for a bottle of gin and a bottle of orange cordial, and placed them both on their table with a thump. He whispered something in Hopkins's ear and then walked towards the staircase behind the bar without another word.

Leonora poured large gins for them both and they sat listening to the approaching aircraft. Only the old man with the fiddle was left in the room. His bow flew across the strings, sending the haunting notes of a familiar folk tune around the almost empty room as the noise of aircraft grew louder. The music rose to a crescendo as the windows shook with the throb and roar of their engines.

"Maybe we should go down, sir," she said.

"I would rather stay here. If this place gets hit, they'll be buried alive down there. Besides, I'm claustrophobic."

The planes passed overhead and seconds later they heard the boom of explosions from the end of the road about four hundred yards away.

The building shook and glasses fell from shelves and shattered behind the bar. A fine cloud of dust drifted down from the ceiling. It was as if the room had been in a snow globe and someone had shaken it hard. The fiddler had stopped playing and was draining his drink. Hopkins gripped his glass tighter and continued to drink. So this was what it was like to be bombed. He had only seen the aftermath of the aerial onslaught until now, but here was the Blitz in action, unfolding before his eyes and assaulting his ears.

"That's Canada Dock again," the fiddler said, and he began to play.

Leonora poured some more gin into Hopkins's glass and added the orange cordial.

"Penny for your thoughts," she said calmly.

"When I was a little boy, fireworks used to frighten me. My mother said someone let off a cracker near my cot on the Fourth of July. Anyway, I never liked them."

"And now?"

"Now I'm terrified," he said, and they both laughed.

By the time the all-clear sounded thirty minutes later, they were slightly drunk, alone in the bar with the fiddler, saying little, listening to the distant sounds of aircraft engines and the closer medley of sirens and anti-aircraft guns. The fiddler had moved on to a faster tune now, trying to drown the symphony of the Blitz outside.

"Let's go," Hopkins said, and without a word she rose and opened the door for him.

Grant appeared from the cellar, brushing dust from his hair and clothes.

"I would wait a minute, sir – there's always a straggler."

But they had already gone, hurrying down the narrow street as furtive heads peered out of doorways, towards the billowing clouds of dust and debris along the docks. Two of the great cranes they had seen earlier had fallen into each other like a pair of drunken lovers. Some buildings on the far side of the river were ablaze. Smoke poured from the deck of a ship moored midstream, and small boats fussed around it, taking off the crew.

They could see lines of Victorian warehouses along the dock front, many of whose walls and roofs had collapsed into the road. Fire engines and their crews were dragging hoses over the rubble and taking axes to jammed doors and windows. It was late afternoon on a winter's day, and the light was fading into a cold grey evening.

At the end of the street they paused as a policeman shouted at them to leave. They had just turned back into the street when they heard the plane flying low over the river. It seemed to skim the line of cranes, its swastika wing markings clearly visible, and passed overhead with the roar of a wounded animal. They quickly pressed into a doorway, holding each other. She had her arms around him, clinging to him through his camel coat, burying her face in his chest. He held her, feeling the rough serge of her uniform. She had her eyes closed and he looked up to see the blur of the aircraft as it vanished overhead.

Suddenly they fell backwards, still clinging to each other, as the door opened and a voice scolded, "What are you two dafties doing out there? Get in, the pair of you."

Scrambling to their feet in a narrow hallway, they saw a thin woman in a pinafore with curlers in her hair. She slammed the door shut behind them.

The house shook as an explosion barrelled down the narrow street, flinging debris against the shuttered houses. Dust seeped into the hallway. For a moment the woman surveyed them in shocked silence, before the sounds of falling masonry, breaking glass, and shouts and screams from outside brought her back to life.

"I am very sorry . . . ," Leonora began.

The woman shook her head and opened the door. She peered up the street.

"Pub's gone," she said flatly.

Where the Golden Fleece had stood, there was now a gaping hole. The pub had simply vanished, the destruction all the more surreal because the buildings around it remained intact, even if without windows and roof tiles. People were coming out of houses and running from both ends of the street towards the ruin, men and women with children scampering behind. Hopkins and Leonora stood on the pavement, trying to understand what they were seeing. Only minutes earlier the steaming wreckage had been the cosy bar where they had got drunk, where the fiddler had played, and where Sergeant Grant –

They began to run, joining a crowd who were clawing at the shattered bricks and masonry.

That evening they brought out the bodies under pencils of light from handheld torches. Sergeant Grant was one of the first. He looked unharmed apart from a scratch on his neck, but his moleskin waistcoat was shredded and his gold watch and chain were missing. The bodies of the three young women at the bar were shrouded in white dust and lolled like broken dolls in the arms of the ambulance crew. Expressions of terror were frozen on their faces. An ARP warden took the names of those who could be identified, but some were merely body parts, a leg, arm, or hand lying in a bloody mess among the debris. A rescuer lifted a mangled arm from the rubble and held it aloft in the beam of a torch, a ghostly vision in a theatre of the macabre. The hand was still grasping what little was left of a wooden fiddle.

Hopkins formally identified his bodyguard and walked back up the hill with Leonora. "I am so sorry," she said in a small voice.

"I hardly knew him," he said. "But he had a family and he told me his kids were safe in the country somewhere. It's just pure luck, isn't it? We were there minutes earlier. It could have been us; it could have been anyone."

"The magic hand of chance," she said, expelling a plume of smoke into the darkness.

5

"Darling!" cried Mrs Worsley, flowing across the crowded room, her arms outstretched and diaphanous gown streaming behind her. "My favourite American."

Hopkins allowed himself to be embraced and gently put his arms around her.

"You are looking a little peaky, darling. Where have you been?"

"He's been to Liverpool and he's had a tough time, so let's get him a drink," said Ed Murrow behind them.

"Ahmed, whisky," said Margot, turning towards the bar and waving. "The good stuff we got from the major yesterday."

She turned back to Hopkins. "Come and sit down, darling. I have a treat for you. A bottle of the best malt from a major who's doing something terribly secret in Scotland. Only for my absolute darling darlings. And you look as if you could eat something. How about a Welsh rarebit?"

Murrow and Hopkins sat at the same small window table with a bottle of Highland Park single malt.

"She's amazing," said Hopkins as Margot moved around

the room, pouncing on those with empty or near-empty glasses and summoning Ahmed to refill them without delay.

"Liverpool," said Murrow. "Tell me."

Hopkins briefly described the pub bombing with the same offhand understatement that he had noticed everyone used when recounting personal experiences of wartime horror. He decided this was how the Brits dealt with the daily toll of death and destruction – to dismiss such events as if they were setbacks in a sporting encounter in which one side was not playing by the rules. He then described in detail the visit to the Western Approaches HQ and had reached the point where the briefings had become a recital of endless sinkings and casualties when he saw that Murrow had lost interest. The broadcaster was moving his head from side to side, trying to see something across the room through the mass of bodies. Hopkins stood up. Pamela Churchill was at the bar, talking to a man in naval uniform. Ed Murrow got to his feet, threaded his way through the dancers, and returned with her on his arm.

"You know Mrs Churchill, I think," he said. He turned back to her. "Harry was just telling me about his trip to Liverpool and I thought you should hear it. He got himself bombed, so now he can really tell the White House about the Blitz."

"How exciting," said Pamela, sitting down beside them on an ancient leather sofa mottled with the old stains of slopped drinks. She placed a hand on Hopkins's knee and leant towards him, frowning slightly. "Are you all right?"

Hopkins nodded. The whisky was working its magic with a warmth distilled in the chilly Highlands of Scotland. "The magic hand of chance," she had said. He could see those three women in the pub with their cheap skirts, the black lines drawn down their legs, their brief day off from the drudgery of war work in the docks, their birthday gins and laughter and their sudden death. He remembered her close to him, saying, "We were lucky, very lucky, weren't we?"

"We were very lucky," he said.

"We?" said Pamela, smiling softly at him. She shifted closer to him. He could smell her perfume, a rare and exotic scent in wartime London. He thought of Leonora, clinging to him tightly in the doorway before they both fell into that house in a moment of grotesque comedy as only yards away lives were incinerated – the fiddler, the girls, his detective, all buried by a winged swastika.

"My driver, Leonora," he said.

He told them about the lone straggler and the last bomb, which had been aimed with deadly accuracy at a public house whose sign must have been visible to the pilot.

"You must tell the PM all this," said Pamela. "He'd be fascinated. He loves the idea of battle, being shot at."

"I'm more interested in those convoy figures, Harry," said Murrow. "The rate of sinkings."

Pamela sat back to let the two men talk. Hopkins noticed her hand now rested on Murrow's knee. The two were leaning into each other on the sofa with an easy familiarity.

Hopkins couldn't remember all the statistics of his briefing. Leonora had taken the notes, he explained, but the basic facts were clear: Britain was losing the Battle of the Atlantic; ships were being sunk faster than they could be replaced. Food stocks were running low at a national level and fuel shortages were severely limiting civilian transport, such as commercial lorries and buses.

Ed Murrow said, "I told you, Harry, convoying is the only way we're gonna win this war."

"I know, but you have to think about the president."

"No, Harry." He thumped the table. Pamela lit a cigarette,

seeming amused. "We have to think about what is happening here! This is our war. If the British go down, Main Street will be on the front line."

"We're not going down, are we?" said Pamela, her voice raised with mock anxiety. "Mr Hopkins, tell me you agree."

Murrow was looking over his shoulder again. "Talk of the Devil," he said, and stood up and waved.

Leonora Finch crossed the room in her air force greatcoat and peaked cap.

"Come and join us," said Murrow.

"No thank you, sir. I have a message for Mr Hopkins from Number 10."

She handed him an envelope with an official crest.

"Mr Murrow has invited you to join us," said Pamela. "Won't you sit down?"

"I really can't stay," she said with the chill tone of disapproving officialdom.

"Yes you can," said Pamela. "Here, give me your coat. I grant you express permission as the PM's daughter-in-law. Now, take off that cap and have a little whisky."

Leonora looked at Hopkins, who smiled and nodded.

"Gin if they have it, please," she said and sat down.

"You've met Mrs Pamela Churchill?" said Murrow.

"Not properly. How do you do?"

The two women shook hands formally and Pamela brushed a hand against her cheek.

"You are far too pretty and much too young to be driving around in that horrible old Humber."

"I don't know about being pretty and young, Mrs Churchill, but I like my job."

"And I have no doubt you do it very well, but perhaps in the future you will make sure our distinguished visitor doesn't get quite so close to the action."

"Actually, she saved my life," said Hopkins as he tore open the envelope. "If we had stayed in that pub we would have been killed with the rest of them."

Hopkins read the handwritten note from the prime minister: "I am sorry to hear of the danger in which you found yourself in Liverpool but very happy that you escaped unscathed. I would be most obliged if you would join me for lunch tomorrow at Number 10. WSC." He placed it back in the envelope and tucked it into his pocket.

"He's a worrier, isn't he, your prime minister?"

They all laughed and Hopkins raised his glass.

"So now I feel I can look you all in the eye," he said. "I feel like a Londoner. Thanks to my driver here, I know what the Blitz is like and I know what it is to be bombed. I feel like a true wartime Brit, so let's raise a glass to that."

They drank, ate the toasted cheese, and let the evening go in jokes, silly stories, and fruitless attempts by Margot to drag Hopkins and Murrow across the room to meet various people. Pamela Churchill left, escorted to the door by Murrow. They kissed at the doorway, an affectionate kiss on the cheek that lingered long enough to leave little doubt in the minds of those observing the scene that they were, or would soon be, lovers. Until then Mrs Worsley had ignored Leonora, who sat quietly, listening but saying little, willing the evening to end so she could go home to bed.

"Who is this, darling? I don't think we've met," said Margot, who finally recognised Leonora as one of her guests.

"She's my driver," said Hopkins. "Flight Officer Finch."

"Darling, you are so pretty. Doesn't a uniform do something wonderful for a woman?" she said, seizing Leonora by the hand. "You must meet – "

"No!" Murrow cried out. "She stays with us, Margot. She

has explicit orders from Number 10 not to let Harry here out of her sight."

"Really?" said Mrs Worsley, who did not like to be told what to do in her own club. She smiled her disapproval and wandered off.

Leonora and Hopkins pulled up to Claridge's at two in the morning. The lightless Mayfair street was deserted. They sat smoking in the car for a moment.

"You know, the last thing Grant said to me was, 'One for the road but make it quick,'" he said.

"I know. Not a good idea tonight, though, sir."

"No," he agreed. "Christ, we were lucky, weren't we?"

They both stared ahead as the smoke drifted against the windscreen, clouding the night beyond. He put his hand on hers.

"Yes," she whispered. "Very lucky."

"What did you call it?"

"The magic hand of chance."

He took his hand away, stretched back, and lit another cigarette.

"It was pure chance that the old lady opened the door for us. We never saw her again, did we? She saved our lives."

"I have her name and address, sir. A letter would be nice."

"Agreed – and I thought we had also agreed no more 'sir.'"

"Yes, Mr Hopkins."

They sat silently looking at the filaments of light that escaped the thick drapes of the hotel windows. Hopkins wound down the window and threw a glowing butt into the darkness.

"The president wants me to go back to Washington," he finally said.

"When?"

"Right now, if he has his way. I've told him it's not possible. There is a lot more to do here. Starting with tomorrow's lunch at Number 10. Is that at one o'clock?"

"Yes, sir – Mr Hopkins –and then it's Ditchley Park for dinner. There's a full moon tomorrow night."

"Are you coming?"

"I am driving you, yes."

"No, I mean to the dinner."

"I have been invited, yes."

"That's good."

"Yes," she said, and they both smiled quickly in the darkness without looking at each other.

"The PM is very pleased you could come," said Bracken, steering Hopkins from the front hall down to the basement dining room. "He wants to hear all about Liverpool. He has laid on a special lunch, cold partridge, shot on the royal estate at Sandringham."

"With more jelly?"

"Absolutely – redcurrant with game. I am sure you will like it."

Dressed in his usual siren suit, Churchill greeted Hopkins at the door and pressed a glass of champagne into his hand.

"We shall toast your survival," he said. "I was most worried about you."

"It was nothing really, Prime Minister. In fact, in a way I am glad of the experience."

"Oh?"

"Now I can tell President Roosevelt that I too have been bombed and that I know exactly what the British people are going through."

"Excellent," said Churchill. "And how is my dear friend the president?"

"Not too well; he has had a cold that has dragged on since Christmas and, as you know, he is not in the best of health anyway."

"I shall send him a bottle of the finest Madeira when you return, which will not be *too* soon, I take it?" Churchill looked anxious.

"No, Prime Minister. I'm staying as long as I have to and that will be a few weeks yet."

"Capital. Shall we go in to lunch?"

Bracken and Churchill listened in silence as Hopkins told the story of his visit to Liverpool and the bombing of the Golden Fleece.

"And may I ask what you have concluded from your visit to Liverpool, apart from the fact that the Almighty has obviously decided to take good care of you over here?" said Churchill.

"You mean, what I have reported to the president?"

Bracken and Churchill exchanged a glance.

"Yes, if that is the same thing."

Hopkins paused and wiped his mouth with a napkin.

Churchill offered him a cigarette from a tortoiseshell box. He had given up trying to force a cigar on his guest. He then filled each of their glasses with port from a crystal decanter, lit a large Havana for himself, and settled back to listen.

"What I have concluded, Prime Minister, is that you are losing the Battle of the Atlantic, as you call it, and that if the current circumstances continue the German navy will have achieved a decisive victory in that arena by the end of this year. You cannot sustain the losses of merchant shipping.

Without those ships you cannot feed your people or fuel your war machine."

"In other words, we are losing the war?" came the growl from the top of the table. A large wreath of smoke lifted to the ceiling as a plump hand raised a glass of port.

"With respect, Prime Minister, you're putting words into my mouth. But you know that if the rate of sinkings continues, that is the likely outcome."

Churchill got to his feet and began to pace the room.

"So here is my question, Mr Hopkins. What will the president do with this information? It will not be new to him. For months he has read my reports, which have spelt out the dire situation in the Atlantic. Of course, I have been careful not to draw the conclusion you have just done. I do not disagree with it necessarily, but I do not wish to be branded a defeatist. No doubt Ambassador Kennedy sent many similar reports telling of our impending defeat. But now he is hearing it from you, his own man, someone he trusts, just as I do. Neither of us trusted Ambassador Kennedy, but both of us trust you."

"What do you wish him to do, Prime Minister?"

"You know the answer to that as well as I do. We need American warships to escort our merchantmen at least halfway across the Atlantic. That would allow us to double the number of our escorts on this side of the ocean. Also we urgently – no, desperately – need more long-range aircraft to patrol the sea lanes and attack U-boats when they surface, which they must do regularly in order to communicate with the bases. That is their weakness. They must come up to receive information about our convoys and that is when, God willing and with your help, we can sink them."

His hand came down on the table with a thump that made the three glasses jump. The prime minister sat back in his chair, cigar glowing. Bracken poured him another port.

"He cannot do it, Prime Minister. Congress is fighting the Lend-Lease bill all the way and they have public opinion on their side – if the president went further now, he would lose that legislation."

"Damn public opinion! Why should that matter? He's just won a third term, hasn't he?"

Churchill had risen from his seat. Hopkins realised he had transported himself to the dispatch box at the House of Commons and was peering down at him as if he were an irritating opposition backbencher.

"Brendan, please tell our friend here that the president should pay little heed to what the people think in a great crisis like this. Should he not lead public opinion rather than be dragged along behind it?"

"I am afraid Mr Hopkins is right, Prime Minister. America is not at war and the president is beholden to the pressure of domestic politics. And let us not forget that Mr Hopkins knows the president better than anyone."

Churchill snorted, sat down, and frowned.

"So tell us, Harry, what is your best guess?" The face had set into the look of bulldog determination familiar from the wartime posters that assured the British people there would be no surrender to Nazi fascism. But Hopkins could see the anxiety in Churchill's eyes. "My best guess is your worst nightmare," he said. "The president will do nothing."

The headquarters of the Women's Transport Service occupied an old bus depot south of the river near Clapham Common. Vehicles of every kind, lorries, cars, and motorcycles, were parked in neat rows in a yard bordered by a soot-stained brick building on two sides and a garage workshop on a third. Leonora parked the Humber and entered through the front door, over which a wooden board carried a painted sign: WOMEN'S TRANSPORT SERVICE above the words FIDELIS AD MORTEM.

Colonel Stobart was waiting for her in a large well-furnished room very different from the anonymous BBC office where she first met him. He was reading through a file on a cluttered desk while a woman wearing the uniform of an army major was seated in an armchair drinking tea. The woman had short blond hair and looked to be in her early forties. A teapot, cups, and biscuits lay on the small table in front of her.

Both rose to greet Leonora as she came in. The major was much taller than she appeared when seated and had the bearing and manner of a parade ground bully.

"This is Senior Commander Ramsden from the WTS," said Stobart. "Will you have some tea?"

As Leonora fished a cigarette pack from her bag, Stobart snapped open a silver box on the desk and offered her closely packed rows of dark-papered cigarettes.

"Egyptian," he said. "I think you will like them."

She took one and Stobart lit it for her from a silver lighter. He gestured towards a comfortable armchair and they sat down. Stobart began to talk while Commander Ramsden gazed intently at the ceiling. They have rehearsed this conversation, thought Leonora.

She had made a good start in her new role, he said, and he thanked her. The Women's Transport Service did not sound like a very glamorous organisation, but its work was vital to the war effort. She had been playing a very useful role in driving an important foreign visitor. He trusted that her pilot officer's rank in the WAAF had helped cut red tape and thus assist Mr Hopkins in his mission.

Stobart paused and looked at her for confirmation.

Commander Ramsden began drumming her fingers on the arm of her chair.

Leonora nodded in agreement. As if by prior arrangement, the commander suddenly stood and continued the conversation. She described the Women's Transport Service as an independent all-female unit affiliated with the Territorial Army. She explained the title of the unit was a deliberate deception.

"As you will have heard," she said, "the WTS does a great deal more than drive dignitaries around on their official duties. Our members have driven unexploded bombs out of city centres, trucked vital blood supplies up and down the country, and also trained women in radio and code-breaking work. They are brave women doing work for which they receive little credit. We have another role for them."

She asked whether Leonora had ever heard of a new unit created to work undercover in the occupied nations of Europe.

Leonora had not.

"This is a young organisation, only formed last summer after the fall of France. But as we have quickly learnt, female agents stand a better chance of remaining undetected than men in occupied territories."

"Why are you telling me this?"

"The unit – let us call it for the sake of argument the Inter-Services Research Bureau –"

"Commander Ramsden!"

Colonel Stobart flashed her an angry glare and stubbed his cigarette out fiercely in the saucer of his teacup. Leonora realised they hadn't rehearsed the conversation after all.

"The name does not matter," said the commander smoothly. "The point is that this new force has many parents and we are one of them. You said in an earlier interview that it was your ambition to fight for your country –"

Stobart interrupted. "We thought at some point in the future you might be interested. It is something to think about. I am not suggesting that you drop your current work now – far from it. You are doing a very valuable job."

"Thank you."

"And we wish you to continue."

Ramsden spoke up again. "If I may, Colonel, I would like to clarify exactly what might be expected of Flight Officer Finch if she chose to – "

Stobart raised his hand to silence her.

"I suggest otherwise, Commander. I am sure Miss Finch knows where her duties lie at the moment. She has made her interest in, how can I put this, a more active role quite clear. That can be dealt with later."

Leonora got up. She had heard enough. She should have felt flattered that two different and differing government agencies were interested in her services. But she wasn't. The bureaucratic squabbling was depressing.

She thanked them and drove back across the river to Claridge's. Icicles were hanging from the cables on Battersea Bridge. A hundred years ago the Thames would have been solid in this weather and there would have been frost fairs on the river. Mr Hopkins had to be in Ditchley that night. The Humber was no car for frozen country roads, and they would have to leave early. That was where her duties lay, getting this exhausted middle-aged American back into Mr Churchill's company.

They arrived in Ditchley after dark under an early rising moon, which illuminated the size and splendour of the eighteenth-century mansion on the brow of a Cotswold hill.

"Why this should be safer from bombers than Chequers I have no idea," said Hopkins. "It's lit up like a wedding cake."

"The idea is that the Germans don't know the PM uses this place. It is supposed to be secret."

They both looked at the small fleet of large official cars drawn up outside the house, clearly visible, he thought, to any reconnaissance aircraft.

She read his thoughts.

"The prime minister likes company when he comes to the country. He travels with a retinue that would do justice to Cardinal Wolsey."

Hopkins was too tired, or maybe a little too ashamed, to ask who Cardinal Wolsey was.

Sawyers took him to his room and placed his bag on the bed. The room was almost as cold as the weather outside.

"I will unpack, sir, if you wish. The prime minister would be grateful if you would join him." Hopkins looked at his watch. It was six thirty. The hour at which Churchill regularly took his evening bath.

He looked at Sawyers, who nodded. "Yes, sir, he is in the bathroom."

Hopkins sighed.

"Come in," boomed the voice amid the cloud of steam. "I have a drink for you on the table over there."

Hopkins saw a glass of champagne releasing a slow stream of bubbles on a cork-topped cabinet. An open bottle of Bollinger stood in an ice bucket beside the glass. He sat down on the stool and drank, trying to imagine Roosevelt receiving visitors in his bathtub with the offer of champagne.

Two pink hands tried to wave away the curtain of steam as Churchill sat forward and examined his visitor. An empty

champagne glass stood on a chair. Churchill raised it and
Hopkins leant forward with the bottle and filled the glass.

Churchill sat back, slopping water over the rim of the tub.

"Are we looking after you properly?" he said. "Good food,
a chance to rest, that sort of thing?"

"I'm fine," said Hopkins, feeling the first glow as the
champagne worked its way into his system.

"Good. Now, I have a question of a personal and confidential nature to put to you. I know I can repose my trust in
you as a friend."

"Of course," said Hopkins, wondering whether a prime
minister who received visitors in his bath and offered them
champagne would also allow them to smoke. Probably not.

"I believe that you were in a London nightclub last night
with Mr Murrow and my daughter-in-law."

He's having me watched, thought Hopkins, and then he
realised that Pamela would have told her father-in-law about
the evening and their conversation.

"As you know, Randolph is in Egypt with the Guards and
Pamela is here in London, with not a great deal to do."

Hopkins said nothing.

"And she is a very attractive woman, I think you will
agree."

"Prime Minister, are you asking me whether your daughter-
in-law is having an affair with Ed Murrow?"

Churchill leant forward again, smiling. "That's what I like
about you, Harry. You brush aside all the pleasantries and get
to the root of the matter. I shall call you Lord Root of the
Matter from now on. Yes, that is exactly what I am asking."

"The answer is I don't know. But in the scheme of things,
does it matter?"

"Probably not, but it seems to matter to Randolph."

As Hopkins knew from his initial embassy briefing,

Randolph Churchill's own philandering in Cairo with the wives of fellow officers was well known. If Pamela Churchill had heard the gossip, she didn't seem to care. If she and Ed Murrow weren't having an affair, they would be soon. They had both been drunkenly entwined on the sofa at the club last night before they left. The farewell kiss told its own story. The prime minister would surely have heard the same thing. He seemed remarkably well informed about what went on in London after dark.

Churchill rose from the bath and pointed to the towel rail. "Pass me a towel, would you?"

Lunch and dinner for Churchill were theatrical occasions at which he could extract information, provoke debate, and draw laughter, as well as indulge in fine food and wine. But he liked to ring the changes on those he invited. "I am not a horse who likes to canter round the same course every day," he would say. At dinner that night Hopkins found a new set of guests, except for the faithful Brendan Bracken and, sitting shyly at the bottom end of the table, Leonora Finch.

The conversation began briskly over a clear hot consommé. Should a yellow metal mainly found in remote parts of Africa really underpin the world's currencies; should science not be the real purpose of study for young men and women at school and university, leaving history to be treated as mere gossip; why would the Americans never understand the British Empire?

"Surely the Americans understand the British Empire very well," said Bracken. "They were part of it, they didn't like it, and they kicked us out."

"You miss the point," said Churchill. "The secret of the British Empire is simple. But no American understands it.

The Empire was an accident. No Englishman ever sat down and said, 'We must have an empire.' They travelled the world seeking treasure, doing business, fighting wars against trading rivals, and thus acquiring vast territories along with the treasure. There is no *ideology* of empire as there is in the Nazi state, where Hitler has made a satanic religion of the belief that he can purify the Aryan race by the slaughter of millions of people and thus dominate the world."

Hopkins decided to risk a debate with his host.

"Prime Minister, there *is* an empire ideology: you believe that your rule benefits those living in your colonies and that you have, in short, a Christian, civilising mission."

Churchill pretended to ponder the argument for a few moments and then said with a throaty growl, "The first part of your questionable assertion is not a description of an ideology; it is very largely a statement of fact. As for a Christian, civilising mission, frankly, if we trail a little religion and learning in the wake of our pursuit of trade and treasure, who can argue?"

That was the problem, thought Hopkins. Many Americans would argue the hell out of that statement. Churchill did not grasp the deep and hostile feelings that empire aroused across the Atlantic – and not just among the East Coast liberal elite. In the Midwest, if they knew anything about the British it was the Boston Tea Party and the Revolutionary War that followed. Then there was the Irish question. They sure had a view about the British in Boston, and that was what was making the president's job so much more difficult.

Churchill broke away from the topic to throw out a question at Lady Cadogan, whose husband, Sir Alexander, was a Foreign Office diplomat greatly admired by the prime minister.

"This war has changed women's roles, has it not? We see

women in our factories, driving ambulances, even ferrying planes from the assembly line to front-line bases. That is admirable, is it not?"

"Of course, but there must be limits," she replied. "The soldier at the front needs to know his family is being looked after, that his children are being fed and clothed. If every woman finds a wartime job, how will that happen?"

"I see no reason why women shouldn't fly Spitfires in combat," Bracken piped in. "I should think the pilots would be delighted to have a woman on their wing."

"The navy won't have them at sea," said Churchill. "Yes, Miss Finch?"

At the far end of the table, Leonora had tentatively raised her hand.

"Well, I think women should be allowed a front-line role in this war," she said. "There is too much at stake to pretend that we can't fight just as well as men."

"If I can throw in my dime's worth, I agree," said Hopkins. "If I was a German sentry and Miss Finch came at me out of the dark with a gun in her hand and a knife between her teeth, I would be off like a shot."

They laughed. Churchill looked down the table at Leonora through his cigar smoke. "But you wouldn't argue that women have the strength of men when it comes to hand-to-hand fighting?"

"No, sir, but how much strength does it take to pull a trigger or throw a grenade?"

All the guests were now looking at the young woman and some recognised her by the same red dress she had worn at Chequers. She had slipped into the dinner late and had missed the predinner drinks in the drawing room.

"Are you in the armed services?" asked Sir Alexander Cadogan.

"I am in the Women's Transport Service, sir."

"Ah," said Cadogan, satisfied that he had an answer to the question that had been nagging him since the soup course. The woman in the red dress was someone's driver.

Churchill surprised everyone by taking just a single glass of port with the cheese and announcing his intention to have an early night. He remained at the table as his guests rose to leave.

Hopkins looked at his watch. It was eleven o'clock. He could certainly do with an early night as well. He was in his habitual state of alcoholic exhaustion. He watched Leonora walk out with the rest of the guests. He wanted to go and congratulate her on speaking up in that company. He had seen the looks of surprise among the other dinner guests when this unknown woman at the far end of the table had raised her hand. It took guts to speak up in that kind of company, and what she said was surely right. She looked back at him from the lobby and smiled as the guests walked past her and out of the door, the men muttering good night and the ladies not deigning to speak to her.

Hopkins was about to leave when a soft voice behind him said, "Would you be so kind as to join me for a nightcap?"

With a large brandy apiece, they sat in a small drawing room lit by the coals of a fire and two lamps. Hopkins had thought of politely refusing this request from a man who regarded midnight as the start rather than the end of the evening. But Churchill wanted to talk and, as Roosevelt had repeatedly told him, his prime mission in London was to listen and learn.

There was no small talk in front of the fire. Churchill lit a cigar – the sixth that evening, Hopkins reckoned – and went straight to the point. He asked for help. He didn't know how to deal with the president, how to stiffen his resolve to make the decision that had to be made if Britain was to survive. Hopkins had visited two great port cities and seen the devastation of the German onslaught. He understood surely that as the U-boats tightened their stranglehold on the Atlantic lifeline a nation starved of food and fuel would fall to Hitler.

"And then what? You think the Führer would stop there? Oh no! Nazi ambitions would not stop in Europe. Once he controlled the Atlantic, north and south, his next step would be the Americas, your soft underbelly to the south. Does no one in Washington see this? How do I persuade the president of the danger to the United States itself?"

Hopkins ground out his cigarette, the last of three packs that day, drank the remains of his brandy, and got somewhat unsteadily to his feet.

"The answer is that you should meet the president. As soon as possible. I shall advise him that that is the way forward."

The smile that lit up the cherubic face of Britain's wartime leader was one Hopkins would remember for a long time. Winston Churchill had gotten what he wanted.

6

Senior members of Roosevelt's cabinet had gathered in the Oval Office in response to a late-night summons from the president. It was a grey, bitter Saturday morning at the end of January.

Harold Ickes, Interior; Cordell Hull, State; Henry Stimson, War; and Frank Knox, Navy, sat in a semi-circle around the square oak desk fashioned from the timbers of a British frigate. Around them the usual clutter spilled onto the floor from tables and chairs – albums of stamps and photographs, ships in bottles, files, books, newspaper clippings.

From behind the door that led off the Oval Office to the president's bedroom they heard a faint metallic snap as the president buckled on his leg braces. Cabinet members knew he was being helped by an orderly as he had been to dress and bathe and that he used crutches to walk the few steps to his wheelchair. The door opened and the president wheeled himself to his desk. Once behind it, he looked like any other well-dressed man seated at a large desk, except that this desk was where the authority of the chief executive of the United States was exercised.

"Good morning, gentlemen."

The president lit a cigarette, fixed it into a holder, and placed it in his mouth at the jaunty angle that the press liked so much. This act was the signal for everyone to do likewise. Coffee was handed round by Missy LeHand, the president's secretary and the woman closest to him on the White House staff. Then Roosevelt got down to business. Winston Churchill wanted a face-to-face meeting as soon as possible. Harry Hopkins had passed on the message and urged the president to agree to the meeting.

There was a ripple of unease among the cabinet members, which extended to a deep frown from Cordell Hull. Hopkins had got in the way again, jamming up diplomatic channels with his own private initiatives.

Roosevelt knew that his cabinet resented Hopkins, as indeed did every politician in Washington. He also knew that every man in front of him that Saturday was engaged in some sort of feud with their own deputies or rival departments. He could step in at any time and replace any one of them. They knew it. So they could damn well listen to what Harry was reporting back from London and advise him on what to do.

"What do you think, gentlemen?"

They spoke in turn, a cautious view from Cordell Hull being reinforced by a more vigorous and negative reaction from Ickes. "What would America gain from such a public meeting, which would be feted by the British press and interpreted as another step on the road to war?" said Ickes. "Lindbergh and the isolationists would crucify the administration."

Knox was the most pro-British, but he came out against such a meeting. The problem was political, he said, pointing out that the following week the House of Representatives foreign affairs committee would enter executive session to hear secret testimony from Cordell Hull and General George

C. Marshall, the army chief of staff. Nineteen amendments to the Lend-Lease bill had been tabled by various representatives. There was no certainty that the legislation in any form would pass in the House or that the Senate would vote in favour when its deliberations followed.

"Any suggestion that the president is going to a meeting with Churchill would only strengthen the isolationist case and swing public opinion further behind them," said Knox.

The president listened carefully to the rest of the men in the room and made sure everyone had had their say. "Does anyone have anything else to add?" he said, wrapping up the discussion.

"Is that all Harry Hopkins had to say?" asked Cordell Hull.

"He said plenty. He almost got himself killed in Liverpool. But this meeting is the main point. Anyone got anything else?"

There was silence.

"Good," said the president. "That's decided then."

Hull said, "What's been decided?"

"I've decided that I'm going to think about it," said Roosevelt.

As they trooped out of the room, Roosevelt called Stimson back. He trusted his secretary of war above all others, except perhaps the long-serving Ickes.

"There was something else Harry reported," said Roosevelt. "He said that Churchill needs us to start escorting those convoys immediately."

"If they hear that on the Hill, we won't get Lend-Lease through."

The president held up several typed pages. "Apparently the British prime minister doesn't think much of what he hears of Lend-Lease. He says he can't fight a war with dried milk and egg powder. He wants destroyers at sea and heavy weapons for his land forces."

"In which case he should pull his army out of North Africa," said Stimson. "I don't know what they are fighting there for anyway. They're needed back in England."

"I'll send that thought over to Harry. So do you think I should meet him?"

"No question. But don't let on till after we've got the bill through. And I would advise you ask Mr Hopkins to tell the prime minister that discretion is vital."

Hyde Park presented a desolate spectacle to morning walkers in the winter of 1941. The great trees, plane, oak, beech, and ash, stood leafless in ground hardened by weeks of frost. Statues of princes, warriors, and even Peter Pan were boarded up with planks bound by rope. Vast piles of broken bricks, twisted iron, and shattered wood lined the sanded horse trails, the debris of bombed-out buildings that had been dumped in the park. The Serpentine was frozen over. The resident swans had taken flight, leaving only the ducks to forage for what little food they could find in the dank bushes along the lakeshore. A scatter of seagulls, blown inland by a strong east wind, squawked as they circled overhead. Gun emplacements on the eastern and southern perimeters of the park and their surrounding trenches provided bleak reminders of a city at war.

A few minutes before eight thirty, Harry Hopkins arrived at the arranged spot, north of the Serpentine at a point where six gravel paths met. He pulled the belt of his camel-hair coat tighter and pulled down the brim of his hat. The cold in London was different from that of Washington or New York. There you got great winters, with deep snow and freezing

weather that provided both a vista of real winter and a chance
for serious sledding. Here it was just a raw, bitter damp that
seemed to chill the marrow of one's bones. He lit a cigarette.

He soon saw Ed Murrow striding towards him from Marble Arch. The broadcaster was wearing a long grey overcoat
and grey homburg. He looked quite the English gentleman,
and Hopkins smiled at the thought. This was the kid from a
dirt-poor town rightly named Polecat Creek in North Carolina
who had grown up in a log cabin without a phone or toilet. This
was the man who had been known as a radical in his college
years, yet here he was in London walking across Hyde Park as if
he owned it, the Voice of America wearing a hat from Lock &
Co. of St James's and with a weekend shooting invitation in his
pocket from some duke.

Yes, Ed Murrow had become quite the darling of the
upper-class country set. Hopkins would enjoy ribbing him
about it, another American who had fallen into the British
class trap. If Murrow hadn't brought his beautiful wife over
with him, he would probably be chasing a duke's daughter by
now. Hopkins frowned as he remembered Churchill's question. Was Murrow having an affair with the prime minister's
daughter-in-law while her husband was gallantly fighting the
Germans in the desert? Well, hell, anything was possible in
London these days.

The two men greeted each other and stamped their feet as
they lit cigarettes.

"Thanks for coming," said Ed.

"It's a pleasure. I just love getting up at this hour and taking a stroll in these verdant pastures before breakfast."

Murrow looked at the gaunt figure smiling at him. Hopkins was reputed to have no sense of humour at all.

"I have to be in the BBC studios at ten and they keep me
there till late, so it's the best time. Sorry if – "

Hopkins said, "Don't worry, Ed, but what brings us here?" Murrow and his colleagues back at CBS had good sources in Washington. They were hearing from the State Department of alarming projections of British shipping losses in the Atlantic. The trend of the losses was clear, as were the consequences for the British war effort, but the question was this: Did Roosevelt know, and what was he going to do about it?

It was a familiar question for which Hopkins was well prepared. He had one golden rule when dealing with a journalist of Murrow's stature: if you can't tell him the truth, don't tell him a lie. And the truth was that the president was guided much more by what he knew he could not do as a politician than by what he might achieve as a statesman.

The two men duelled like a pair of fencers as they walked along the lakeshore and crossed the road into Kensington Gardens. Murrow was a good interrogator with a technique honed in a thousand interviews with devious politicians, fraudulent businessmen, and dubious celebrities. He asked questions with subtle assumptions so that any answer would confirm facts that the interviewee wished to keep to himself – an old but successful technique.

Hopkins parried, thrust back, and tried to change the subject to the grey circle of frozen water they were approaching through the trees. The round pond had been the scene of model boating for young boys since Victorian times, but now it was just a slab of ice. Churchill had been taken there as a child with his toy boats, and that had begun his fascination with the navy.

Murrow wasn't interested in Churchill's childhood. He repeated his questions about what he called the lack of leadership in Washington. Hopkins batted them away impatiently. He knew that Murrow was holding back. He had not arranged an early-morning walk in the park just to talk about the Battle of the Atlantic. He had been broadcasting the success of the U-boats for at least a week. There was something else.

The two men sat on a bench and lit more cigarettes. Hopkins coughed and doubled up as the coughing spasm took hold.

"How many do you smoke a day?" said Murrow.

"Pack or so," said Hopkins. "About the same as you, I guess."

"I couldn't work without them," said Murrow, tapping another Camel from a pack. "By the way, you hear about these new German paratrooper strike forces?"

Here it comes, thought Hopkins. This is what he really wants to talk about.

He listened as Murrow described the elite units that Hitler was creating. Britain had won the Battle of Britain the previous summer, but Hitler had learnt his lesson. There was no point in trying to beat the RAF in the air; the Spitfire was a class above the current Messerschmitt. But paratroopers landing in force to take those air bases with rapid reinforcement of airlifted armour would neutralise Britain's defensive airpower for a few critical hours while a German invasion army crossed the Channel. It would be twelve hours before the Royal Navy could arrive from its Scottish base at Scapa Flow in the Orkneys.

"Are you serious?" said Hopkins.

Murrow nodded. "The Luftwaffe has developed a heavy-lift transport plane that will take two big tanks. That's what the Joint Chiefs hear. They want the British to pull out of Egypt and reinforce at home."

Hopkins was pretty sure that if President Roosevelt had heard those fears from the Joint Chiefs he would have told him. However, Murrow was obviously not making this up.

"First I heard of it," said Hopkins, "and I'm pretty sure the prime minister is not in the loop. Besides, he's not going to pull out of North Africa – that would look terrible at home."

He wondered why Murrow had relayed information for which he clearly had very good sources in the Department of Defense back home. Perhaps he wanted to send a warning to Churchill that pressure from Washington to pull out of North Africa was only going to increase. Perhaps Murrow just wanted to share his anxiety about the direction of the war. Either way, it was too cold to continue the conversation.

They walked back to Mayfair, on the east side of the park, swinging their arms in an exaggerated fashion to work up some warmth.

"I hear the prime minister really likes you," said Murrow.

"We get on well."

"You seem to spend more time with him than some of his ministers do – bit like back in D.C., huh?"

Hopkins laughed. It wasn't a bad joke. Murrow knew how much he was resented by the president's cabinet, and it was certainly true that Churchill was giving him as much access here. The man would hardly let him alone.

"I hear he's even given you your own liaison officer now with a fancy new rank."

Hopkins concealed his surprise. Where had Murrow heard that his driver, Leonora, had been promoted in rank to a squadron officer and made his liaison officer? Brendan Bracken had suggested the promotion only a few days earlier, saying that the prime minister was aware of a certain amount of snobbery towards her within his circle and wanted to make sure she could accompany Hopkins at all occasions with a suitable status.

Bracken had enquired whether Hopkins found benefit in the attachment of such an aide, and of course he did. Leonora was an efficient problem solver who knew exactly where to go in Whitehall to get the right briefing. She also found the right medicines for his digestive problems, knew how to get the special-issue wartime stamps that he had promised the president, and had, surprisingly, established a strong rapport with the U.S. embassy.

She had, in short, become much more than his driver. Above all, when the weight of officialdom bore down on him with one querulous cable too many from the White House they could take a coffee together and talk about anything but the war.

He knew all about her upbringing, the father she never knew, the student days at the Sorbonne, just as she had heard about the simplicity and innocence of his early years in Grinnell, a small college town in Iowa. He found release and relaxation in these long conversations with a young woman he hardly knew. He told her about life as a child in a small-town Methodist household, with church five times a day on Sundays. His mother had looked at life through the eyes of a Christian missionary, while his easygoing father ran a harness store and liked a beer and bowling at the end of the day. Harry had never talked like this to anyone before, not even to his second wife, Barbara, who had left him bereft when she died of cancer.

"Yeah," said Hopkins flatly.

He threw his glowing cigarette butt onto the ice, watching as a duck waddled hopefully towards it and then turned away in disappointment. The bird looked scrawny, all bone and feather, which was why no one had bothered to kill and eat it. There were stories going around that dog was appearing on certain London menus dressed up as rabbit, and certainly horse meat was eaten quite openly in some restaurants. No wonder the swans had left.

"She's a pretty thing, isn't she?"

"If you say so, Ed."

"Oh come on, Harry; she fills that uniform very nicely."

"As does Mrs Pamela Churchill in that blue dress she wore the other night."

"When?"

"When we met at the Black Cat, remember?"

"Sure. Well, she's quite a woman, Harry."

"So I noticed."

And Murrow laughed because he knew Hopkins had come out on top in this particular joust. Murrow had got nothing of journalistic interest out of it at all.

Leonora was waiting for Hopkins at Claridge's that morning, sitting against tasselled cushions in one of the high-backed chairs in the lobby. The single stripe of a flight officer on her uniform had been replaced with the insignia of promotion, thin blue bands on two broad black stripes. Squadron Officer Finch held the equivalent rank of a squadron leader in the RAF and was now officially the liaison officer to the president's personal envoy. Brendan Bracken had explained the promotion to her, saying service conventions sometimes had to be set aside in wartime. The prime minister placed great importance on the health and well-being of Mr Hopkins, he said, and it was her job to make sure that he got the information he required when he went on what he called his meet-the-people forays, but also that he relaxed.

There was to be no more drama such as that in Liverpool. She was to stay with Mr Hopkins every waking hour of the day, and since he had refused a new bodyguard to replace Sergeant Grant she would be given firearms training and a suitable weapon. Mr Hopkins was not to know this.

The training had taken place every day at dawn the previous

week in an underground range at the Guards barracks near
Buckingham Palace. She had proved a very quick learner and
now carried a Smith & Wesson .38 in her handbag. But the
precaution puzzled her.

"Who would wish him harm?" she had asked Bracken.

"If I told you there are at least six German agents
operating clandestine radio communications to Berlin out of
London and the home counties I think you will see the point.
We cannot afford to take any chances," he said.

Leonora was dubious about her promotion but enjoyed the
weapons training that came with it. She had been given the job
of protecting a man deemed of high importance to the prime
minister. As she trained on targets, the sound of the shot and
the slight recoil of the weapon in her hand made her feel a little
less like an office girl performing meet-and-greet duties for a
visiting dignitary. And she liked carrying a gun. It was more
gratifying than the new insignia on her uniform.

As for the other instructions she had received, well, she
put them out of her mind. She appreciated the importance of
Hopkins's mission, but he seemed to spend so much time at
Number 10 or at Chequers, so what was the point in asking
her to report back on his thoughts about the war? The important point for her was that she had taken one more step
towards a real role in the war.

The lobby was suddenly full of American journalists
heading to their daily briefing at the Ministry of Information.
They marched out and onto the bus dressed almost identically
as if to conform to the cartoon caricature of what a journalist
should look like: trilby hats, cigarettes hanging from lips,
long gabardine raincoats, and heavy cameras.

She sat back and wondered if Mr Hopkins had heard of
Noël Coward. Of course he had. He must have. Coward had
become famous in Hollywood. Tonight she had tickets to his

play *Blithe Spirit* and she hoped to persuade him to come. For once there was no invitation to Number 10 for dinner, as the prime minister was hosting the Australian chiefs of staff that night. The theatres had closed the previous September when the London bombing began but quickly reopened when it became clear that people were prepared to take the risk just to get out of their homes and find some entertainment to take their minds off the daily grind of queueing for food and the nightly fear of bombs. So all the West End shows had continued to secure big audiences, and she now had tickets to the best show of them all.

The theatre evening had not been her idea. Brendan Bracken had given her the tickets and suggested that Hopkins would enjoy an evening away from the pressures of business. Bracken had chosen the Coward play less for its artistic merit than because the theatre was below ground level, although Leonora Finch knew it would not make much difference if a bomb came through the roof.

She saw Hopkins walk down the long curved staircase and into the foyer. He looked pinched with cold and rheumy eyed. This was a man in need of a good breakfast. She stood up to catch his eye. He saw her, smiled, and walked over.

"Porridge followed by kippers?" he said incredulously after she had suggested the ideal start to the day in the middle of a Blitz winter.

She nodded. "It's what Nelson had before the Battle of Trafalgar," she said. "I'll wait here."

Refreshed by what he called a meal no American would dare call breakfast, Hopkins emerged into the lobby an hour later. They drove from the hotel past Buckingham Palace to meet Fleet Street editors gathered in the *Daily Express* building. It was the first of many meetings that day. They went next to the defence ministry for a long and detailed conference with Sir John Dill, the chief of the Imperial General Staff, the umbrella group covering all three services. Later Hopkins was briefed by Charles Portal, chief of the Air Staff. Brendan Bracken sat in on all the meetings, and Hopkins realised just how much the Irishman's role for Winston Churchill mirrored his own work for the president. The eyes and ears of their masters, gundogs bringing back slain game for the huntsmen, faithful servants possessing the one attribute prized above all others by those in power – unwavering loyalty.

The question on which every meeting that day turned was one to which there seemed no clear answer: When would Hitler launch his invasion of Britain? The assumption that he would launch such an operation in the coming months was never questioned. Military opinion assumed that an attack was inevitable once weather in the English Channel improved in April or May. It was now the beginning of February. The Germans had twenty armoured divisions within two days' reach of the Channel ports. The seventeen hundred self-propelled landing craft and two hundred small seagoing ships that had been assembled the previous summer were still in harbours along the French coast. They were heavily camouflaged and bombing had not greatly reduced their number.

There was no sign that Lend-Lease would deliver the kind of military assistance that Britain needed. The bill was still stuck in Congress and the object of innumerable amendments aimed at limiting its effectiveness. Nor was there any indication that the U.S. Navy would sail to the rescue of the embattled Atlantic convoys. Britain alone stood against Hitler, as Churchill time and time again reminded his people with soaring oratory that lifted the spirits of the nation, if not the minds of those who chose to look at the situation realistically. Could the Royal Air Force and Navy repel a cross-Channel attack? The navy would have to deploy large numbers of ships from the security of its northern base at Scapa Flow to the Channel, which could take two days. Ground forces within the United Kingdom were too small and too ill equipped, and crucially they lacked sufficient armour to repel the invaders once the Germans had gained a foothold. No mention was made of the Luftwaffe's new heavy-lift transport planes, which suggested to Hopkins that Murrow had been badly misinformed – or had lied.

The briefings were for Hopkins's benefit, but he felt bemused by the volley of questions that went round and round like the raffle numbers in the steel drum at the farm fairs back in Iowa. Those summer fairs were a wonderful escape for a young kid whose father was forever busy in his harness store or on the road as a travelling salesman, while Harry's mother remained at home busy with her Bible.

The fairs were the high point of the year in the midwestern Corn Belt, breaking the boredom of life in a town where if you looked down Main Street in summer you could see the horizon twenty miles distant through a waving field of unbroken corn. No one ever took a vacation, except for a few days at Christmas. Everyone just kept on working through the summer, so the weeklong farm fair in July was the opportunity for a good time for all. The boys drank too much beer, the girls flirted and let their skirts lift in the breeze, and the fathers gathered to smoke, drink a little whisky, and think back to the days when beer, skirts, and shapely legs were the only things on their mind.

"Mr Hopkins, sir?"

He raised his head. Sir John Dill was looking straight at him. Now the questions were coming his way: polite, familiar questions he knew desperately needed answers. Lend-Lease, the Atlantic convoys, American public opinion. He lit a cigarette. There were no answers to those questions any more than there were hard facts as to Hitler's true intentions. They were all blind men in the fog of war, and that, thought Hopkins grimly, included President Roosevelt.

He didn't much like *Blithe Spirit*. It was clever, stylish, and witty but very English and very upper class, rather like its author. The theatre was full, which surprised him, and in the intermission those who shouldered their way to the small bar were rewarded with a choice of gin or whisky.

Leonora and Hopkins stood clutching their warm drinks in the crush, being pushed gently as people wriggled past them holding glasses high above their heads.

"What did you think?" she said. Maybe it was the warmth of the bar or the whisky or so many bodies pushing into her, but she looked flushed and excited and her eyes were shining.

"It's very well done," he said politely. "It will do well on Broadway."

"You hated it, didn't you?"

"Not at all," he lied.

"Yes, you did. I think we should leave. Let's walk up to that club you like."

He looked at his watch. All London theatres started early because of the threat of bombing and the difficulty of transport home. It was only 6:45 P.M. They could walk to Soho in minutes, have a drink and one of Mrs Worsley's potluck pies. Yes, good idea. He could have an early night – and a quiet night. There was low cloud and unless the weather changed there would be no raids that night.

• • •

The key in the sock fell at their feet after three pushes on the bell, and they climbed the stairs to the club room, feeling guilty at having left the most popular play in the West End before the final curtain.

The door swung open to reveal a room crowded with dancers shuffling slowly over the parquet floor. A smoky jazz number was playing on the bar-top gramophone. Through the sepia light Hopkins could see Ed Murrow and Pamela Churchill clinging to each other on the far side of the room. Margot sailed across to greet them, dressed in flowing blue silk and looking more than ever like a stately galleon in full sail.

"Darlings, how good of you to come. It's dance night and the rule is you must dance. No exceptions."

"Could we have a drink first?" asked Leonora.

"Of course, darling."

"And maybe one of your special pies," said Hopkins, who was feeling hungry after the strange combination of kippers and porridge for breakfast and a stale sandwich for lunch at the war ministry.

"Of course, anything for our distinguished American visitor. Take a seat over there and Ahmed will bring them over."

She pointed to a sofa by the window and turned and raised her voice above the music.

"Ahmed!"

A bottle of whisky was placed on the table in front of them, together with glasses, two pies on plates, cutlery, and jars of pickle and mustard.

"I wonder what the prime minister would make of this for dinner," said Hopkins, pouring whisky into both their glasses.

"I wonder what he would make of *that*," said Leonora, nodding at the dancers.

Ed Murrow and Pamela were now so closely entwined that their bodies seemed to have become one. His hand had slipped down her back, pulling her into him. Her arms were around his neck, her cheek against his cheek. The jazz riff drifted over the room in the half-light, a dark brown sound from the Deep South of the United States that stroked the dancers into a trance.

"I think he knows about that. But I wonder if Janet does."

Janet was Ed Murrow's wife, charming, beautiful, and the hostess of sought-after Sunday lunches at their Hallam Street flat in Marylebone. The lunches were well supplied with game from Murrow's weekends spent shooting on the estates of the gentry. Ed Murrow was having it every which way. He was a fixture on the upper-class social circuit, the radio voice from embattled London who entranced America, the husband of an attractive wife who preferred to spend nights at home playing bridge with her girlfriends, and here in this dark little club he was clearly the lover of the prime minister's daughter-in-law. Hopkins felt a pang of jealousy. Murrow was younger than him by more than fifteen years, a good-looking man who was going to make a fortune on the lecture circuit and with books after the war, a man who could have any woman he wanted, even if the woman he wanted just happened to be Pamela Churchill. Would that help CBS land the interview with Churchill that all the American journalists had been baying for since last summer? Maybe.

Hopkins pushed away the dishonourable thought and reminded himself to write to his fiancée, Louise. Why was he so jealous of Ed Murrow? Louise was petite, pretty, with the looks and figure of a woman half her age, and at thirty-five she was still a fixture on the social circuit. Louise Macy, who was a divorcée, had achieved a certain celebrity in Washington as the magazine fashion journalist who had escaped from Paris hours before the Germans entered the city in July the previous year. The experience had prompted her to undertake war work when she returned to America, and it was her unstinting efforts as a volunteer nurse at the Columbia Hospital in Washington that had brought her to the attention of Eleanor Roosevelt.

The president's wife was a patron of the hospital and had been impressed that a woman who had moved in the world of high fashion should now be carrying bedpans. Mrs Roosevelt invited Miss Macy to the White House and none too subtly arranged for her to meet the man she regarded as the president's social conscience and her own adopted son, Harry Hopkins.

Mrs Roosevelt valued Hopkins not just because he shared her dedication to a far-reaching and in some ways revolutionary programme of social reform but also because she thought him a good political influence on her husband.

The twice-divorced, hard-drinking Mr Hopkins may not have appealed entirely to Eleanor's more sober, straitlaced taste, but she saw in him someone who could be redeemed and Miss Macy was the woman to do it. Thus when the engagement was announced no one in Washington was surprised, although the fact that the gaunt fifty-year-old man with little left of his hair or his health should attract a smart, good-looking woman fifteen years his junior did nothing to blunt the criticism of Hopkins's role and influence in the White House.

But Louise Macy loved "my Harry," as she called him, and told friends she planned to set about having his child the moment they were married. She loved him because he was frail and she could look after him. She loved the passionate intensity he brought to his work in the White House and was impressed that her fiancé actually lived in Lincoln's old study on the second floor. Best of all, she told her friends, she loved him because he was fun. Harry at the racetrack, Harry at the theatre, Harry at Georgetown's best restaurant, Harry with half a stomach, smoking four packs a day and drinking scotch whisky if he could get it, bourbon if he couldn't – where else could you find a man like that?

But Louise was in Washington and he was here in London in the Black Cat Club with his liaison officer, Squadron Officer Finch. And he was about to have a much-needed early night. He looked at his watch. It was eight o'clock.

"Let's eat," he said, plunging the knife into the pie and opening it up.

"It may be best not to look too closely," she said.

The pie was delicious, moist, with chunks of meat that Hopkins identified as rabbit and Leonora privately thought was probably horse.

"Hey, how goes it?"

Murrow slumped down beside them.

"Damned dance night," he said. "Dear Margot won't let you have a drink unless you've had a dance. Harry, you remember Mrs Churchill?"

Harry shook hands and Ed leant over to Leonora.

"And I think we've met – you're Harry's liaison officer?"

Leonora nodded and said nothing. She had quickly learnt that in this company it was better to listen and learn. These people were great talkers and they had a lot to say. At times like these Hopkins seemed to forget she was there, which suited her well.

"Here, have some whisky," said Harry, holding out the bottle to Ed.

They drank and watched the dancers moving in a slow

circle around the small floor until they seemed to merge into a solid mass.

"I don't get this place," said Hopkins. "A bar one night, a dance hall the next."

"I told you, it's the only place people like us can relax," Murrow said. Then he ducked his head and whispered, "Wagons in a circle. Here she comes."

"Darlings," said Mrs Worsley, descending on them – less a stately galleon this time and more a giant bird that had suddenly spotted its prey. "You must dance."

She had taken Hopkins by the hand and was pulling him to his feet. Murrow sat back, smiling.

"Please, take this beautiful girl onto the floor," said Mrs Worsley. "I know you are a special guest but not special enough to break the rules – you must dance!"

Hopkins had never learnt to dance and allowed Leonora to lead him in slow twirls. She held him away from her at first, but in the throng of the dance floor they were pushed closer. She placed her hand on his shoulder and he slipped his arm around her waist.

Everyone around them was clinging to each other, legs pressed between legs, faces buried into necks, arms pulling bodies into each other. There was the smell of sweat and whisky and smoke and cheap perfume. The jazz rippled in waves over the crowd with hypnotic effect. He felt Leonora now very close to him, her body against his. Her perfume smelt of roses and the sea. He felt himself stiffen and knew she would feel him pressing into her. He couldn't help it and tried to think of Louise Macy waiting for him back in Washington in that small apartment by the hospital. When was the last time they had made love? He couldn't remember. He was hard now, but Leonora didn't break off or back away but held him tightly.

"I need some air," he said finally. "Sorry, let's take a break."

They left without saying good-bye to Mrs Worsley, collecting their coats from the lady at the top of the stairs and hurrying into the night. Leonora strode purposefully into the cold darkness and Harry followed her. In a side street off Piccadilly she opened the door of the parked Humber.

"Where to?"

"I need an early night," he said.

"So do I."

"What's the time?"

They both looked at their watches: nine thirty.

"Too early to sleep," he said. "Maybe one for the road?"

"I'll take you somewhere nice."

"Where?"

"Down on the river – not far; there's no traffic and it will be safe."

"You mean another pub?"

"Where else are we going to get one for the road?"

"We almost got killed in the last one."

"This is different; you'll like this – all Americans do."

The Prospect of Whitby stood at the end of a long cobbled street in the cluster of docks beyond Tower Bridge. The blackout drapes were so effective that the light inside made them blink as they entered; a few dockers and medical students from nearby hospitals stood at the bar. Hopkins could see why Americans were prepared to leave the well-beaten tourist trail and trek through the dark and dingy streets. The pub was pure old England: stone-flagged floors, low-beamed ceilings, and a plaque on the wall that said: FOUNDED IN 1520.

They took their beers and walked through a curtained

door to the open terrace at the back overlooking the Thames. The drifting cloud had broken to reveal strands of moonlight that laid waves of pale light on the surface of the river like silvery seaweed. The tide was high and the water lapped noisily against the steps leading up to the terrace from a landing stage. At the far end of the terrace a young couple were engaged in passionate conversation.

"Marry me and I'll give you a diamond as big as your fist," said the young man, leaning into her, waiting for a kiss.

The woman laughed. She was pretty, with good white teeth that gleamed in the darkness. "I only met you last week," she said, pushing him away. "Go and get me a drink."

The young man hurried past them to the bar.

"Are you going to say yes?" Hopkins said casually to the young woman. Leonora put her arm on his as if to steer him away from the conversation.

"Of course," the woman replied. "There's not many young men around these days. You've got to take what you can get."

"Come in here, Fiona! I've got something to show you," came a voice from the bar.

"Excuse me," said the woman, easing past them. "That'll be the diamond, I suppose." She laughed again, happy, confident, and careless of the world around her.

"Look up there," said Leonora. A line of bombers four abreast could be seen through gaps in the cloud.

"They're ours for a change, heading to the south coast, it looks like, and over to Belgium or France."

They sipped their beers in silence as the planes rumbled overhead. There was a roar of laughter and a squeal of pleasure from within the pub. The night was quiet except for the chatter from the bar and the sound of the water. The clouds

thinned further, allowing the moon to illuminate Tower
Bridge upriver and the long bend in the river downstream
where the Thames broadened as it swept past the great docks
of London.

"Was that true?" he said, suddenly remembering something she had said earlier.

"What?"

"That Nelson had porridge and kippers for breakfast on
the day of Trafalgar."

She laughed. "No, of course not. How would I know that?
I just wanted you to have a good old English breakfast because you looked so cold. And I knew that the hotel had run
out of eggs and bacon."

"Is that what a liaison officer does, check up on bacon and
egg supplies at Claridge's?"

"You're mocking me, Mr Hopkins? My brief is to look after you and make sure you have what it takes to do your job."

"I think I've done my job here," he said, flicking the glowing end of a cigarette butt into the darkness.

"I don't know about that," she said. She opened her bag
and pulled out a closely typed sheet of paper. "Glasgow, for a
dinner with the secretary of state for Scotland – that's a train
journey. Dover, to inspect the fortifications beneath the cas-
tle with the prime minister – I shall be driving you. Scapa
Flow in Scotland, to lunch aboard the HMS *Prince of Wales*
with the prime minister – that's a flight. And that's only the
next three days. This comes straight from Number 10."

"And I've got my own little list," he said, and opened his
wallet, fishing out a cable. "This is from the White House.
Let me summarize it for you: 'Come home, Harry; you've
been there too long. I am beginning to think you've gone native.' Signed 'President Franklin Delano Roosevelt.'"

"How about *this* message from Number 10?" she said,

pulling another document from her bag. " 'Do not let Mr Hopkins consider returning to Washington until he has my express permission. Winston Spencer Churchill.' So what do you think?"

"I think we'll have one more for the road," he said, and they both laughed.

The phone rang at eight the next morning. Hopkins rolled over groggily and picked up the receiver, knocking a full ashtray from the bedside table. He fumbled the receiver, put the wrong end to his ear, cursed and turned it the right way, and grunted "hello" into the earpiece.

"Good morning, Mr Hopkins. I fear we have been neglecting you."

The familiar voice sounded as if Churchill had enjoyed a glass of sherry that morning – a regular accompaniment to his kippers, Hopkins had learnt.

"Not at all, Prime Minister. I have been both busy and very well looked after."

"So I hear, so I hear," boomed the voice. "I trust you will be able to accompany me to Scotland this evening. We have an important dinner there and I think it would be wise for you to be able to report to the president on matters concerning our friends north of the border."

"Of course," said Hopkins.

"Splendid. I will see you later," came the reply. The line went dead.

Hopkins replaced the receiver. Did anyone ever say no to Churchill?

He rolled back into the bed and tried to recall the events of the previous evening. It was like trying to reassemble the scattered pieces of a jigsaw. He had drunk too much – again.

He remembered Murrow laughing as Margot Worsley dragged him onto the floor and the crush of dancers that had thrust him into an unseemly embrace with Leonora. He had been glad to get out of there shortly after. The place was claustrophobic and little better than an upper-class bordello. They had driven through darkened streets to that pub on the river. "One for the road," she had suggested, or had *he* said that? Either way, it was a bad idea, because the pieces of the jigsaw were beginning to form a picture he didn't like at all.

He pushed away the memory, but it returned, not as a doubtful recollection but as an unalterable fact. Last night he had kissed his liaison officer, Squadron Officer Finch. He had taken her in his arms on the small wooden terrace and kissed her. He had held her against the wall of the pub and he had run his hand down her skirt and pulled at the material, feeling the little bobble of her suspender clips beneath the regulation-blue RAF uniform, still kissing her, feeling her hips moving into his and –

He sat up.

They hadn't . . . not there in the moonlight against that pub wall with a raucous engagement party going on inside? No, they hadn't. He had just kissed her. A long, lingering kiss, and he could still taste her lipstick.

He sank back on the bed. He wiped his lips quickly and turned his head. . . . There was a faint trace of lipstick on the pillow. He sat up. OK, I am fifty and engaged to be married and I got a little drunk with a very attractive young woman who must be at least twenty years younger than me and we kissed. Well, so what? What's the big deal? There is a war on, not in some distant battlefield but right here in London; people are dying every night in this town and I kissed her. Yes, I kissed her; so what does that mean? Nothing at all.

She works with me, I got a little carried away and so did she, and we kissed and then –

His mind flipped back a few hours. The pieces of the puzzle were now all in place. They had left the pub and had a cigarette in the car. It was dark. Neither had said anything. Suddenly they were kissing again, her twisting towards him against the big, thin steering wheel, him turning, sliding his hand over her uniform, trying to unbutton those buttons and failing but still kissing her. The pub's front door had opened, throwing a wedge of light onto the street, and someone had walked past and shouted vulgar encouragement through the misted windows.

Then they had driven back to the hotel and he had said good night as if nothing had happened. And she had said good night as if nothing had happened – and nothing had happened, had it? Well, that wasn't exactly what Louise Macy would say, nor his God-fearing Methodist mother.

The trouble with churchgoing Methodist mothers, reflected Hopkins, reaching for his first cigarette of the day, is that they instil in you from an early age a conscience designed to keep you on the path of moral rectitude. And conscience, especially a Methodist conscience, is a needle of guilt injected well below the skin when a wrong has been committed. He felt that needle now somewhere painfully deep inside him. He should not have kissed Squadron Officer Finch. That was that. He would ask Brendan Bracken for a new liaison officer. He would explain that she was too young. He needed someone older, a man perhaps.

In the bath he soaped himself thoroughly and shaved with care. The face that looked back from the steamed-up mirror was grey with fatigue and red eyed from last night's drinking. So much for an early night. Never again did he want to hear the words "one for the road."

But then he calmly rationalised the situation over a breakfast of bacon and eggs and strong coffee. There was an excitement about London in those desperate days. You could feel it
at the Black Cat Club or down on the docks. You could see
it on the street, the swirl of a skirt, a look, a smile, a quick word,
a little joke, a glass of warm beer in a pub, two strangers suddenly finding solace in lust. Casual, anonymous sex under
cover of the blackout – that was how Londoners were facing
the bombs, and why not?

No one knew who was going to be alive the next morning.
The young woman who agreed to marry that man in the pub,
why had she done so in that carefree fashion? Because she
knew she might not have a tomorrow, so she settled for the
excitement of today, a wartime wedding, a night of long,
requited lust and the brief pleasures of a honeymoon in a
deserted seaside resort surrounded by pillboxes, barbed wire,
and anti-aircraft guns. That was why she was going to marry
him.

7

Mrs Muriel Finch took the 8:20 A.M. train from Leamington Spa to Paddington Station. She had chosen to travel on a Tuesday, thinking there might be more chance of a seat on the two-hour journey than at the start of the week. But the train had started at Birmingham and by the time it reached Leamington all the seats were taken and the corridors were packed with troops. She squeezed in and found herself wedged between two sailors, who politely made room and offered her a cigarette. She shook her head and closed her eyes.

The first thing she was going to tell her daughter when they met for coffee at Marble Arch was that the journey was extremely uncomfortable. For over a year now she had been trying to get Leonora to come home for a weekend, but again and again she had said her duties did not allow such time off.

"I'm doing war work, Mum," she would say. "I just can't get away."

Muriel suspected Leonora simply didn't want to come home and that her war work was just an excuse. She wrote regularly to her at her Pimlico lodgings and occasionally received brief notes in reply. Leonora had always been a contrary, difficult girl, maybe because she had never known her father, but now she was turning her back on her mother. It wasn't right and she would say so plainly when they met.

Life at home in Warwickshire was not unbearable; in fact, it was perfectly pleasant. Although rationing made things difficult in the kitchen, Leamington Spa was far removed from the war. With her widow's pension and her teacher's salary, she got by. What she missed was her daughter, the daughter who seemed to have vanished in wartime London, just as she had disappeared to study at that ridiculous university in Paris. Leonora had never really regarded their little house in Leamington as home. She was always heading somewhere else.

Muriel Finch had lost a husband in France; now she had lost a daughter. She remembered the exact time, to the day and almost the hour, when Leonora had broken away. It was November 1938. A few weeks earlier Neville Chamberlain, the prime minister, had returned from his meeting with Hitler proudly declaring peace in our time. But that wasn't good enough for Leonora. Oh no. She knew better. She knew a war was coming and she wanted to be in London. They had a furious argument, which had ended with a shouting match in the kitchen. They had cried and hugged and made up, but it made no difference. Leonora would not change her mind. She would not stay at home and take a teacher-training course. War or no war, she was going to London.

And so it was settled. Leonora applied for a position as a translator or interpreter with the Foreign Office and – on the off chance – the War Office, enclosing a note of her father's rank and regiment.

To Muriel's satisfaction, the replies had been swift and unpromising. Leonora was warned there was a strict process that had to be followed in order to join the Civil Service. It involved exams, interviews, and six months' further training for successful applicants. In her case, written testimonials from the Sorbonne would also be required.

This offputting response briefly gave hope to Muriel that her daughter might reconsider. Leonora did indeed relent, but only to agree to spend Christmas that year with her mother in Leamington. She would go to London in the New Year. She was adamant. And could she borrow a little money from her mother to arrange for driving lessons? That surely would help her find work when she finally got to London.

Muriel withdrew money from her Post Office savings account and watched as Leonora set off every morning in a Hillman Minx with a grey-haired driving instructor with nicotine-stained teeth and fingers and an ash-stained cardigan. Muriel had never learnt to drive, nor had she ever possessed a car. The bus and the train had been good enough for her. In any case, it was all she could afford.

Muriel had seen her daughter off on the Golden Arrow train to Paris from Victoria two years earlier. Then she saw her onto the London train from Leamington Spa to start a new life in a strange city. Muriel always seemed to be standing on a station platform waving good-bye to her daughter. Now she was on the train to London, a place that frightened her what with the bombing and reports of terrible traffic. And Leonora was not even going to be there to meet her at the station.

They met in the Cumberland Hotel by the Marble Arch roundabout at the western end of Oxford Street. Muriel had only been to London once since the outbreak of the war and was shocked by the bomb damage, the barrage balloons, and the anti-aircraft batteries in Hyde Park.

She didn't recognise her daughter at first and was quite

alarmed when an officer in a blue serge air force uniform took a seat opposite her. They exchanged a brief kiss on the cheek.

"You startled me," said Muriel. "I thought you were in the Women's Transport Service."

"I am, Mum, but they have given me an honourary commission in the women's air force – it helps with the job."

"Really, and what exactly is this job?"

Everyone asked Leonora this, or rather the few friends she had time to see always asked her. She rarely saw them because she had no time to herself. Life was work, driving that big Humber around the country and catching up on sleep in her Pimlico lodgings. She always said she was a liaison officer with the Women's Transport Service, a driver with additional duties.

"Additional duties, darling?" said her mother. "What are they?"

"I can't tell you, Mum. It's government work."

"I know – careless talk costs lives," said Muriel, "but I *am* your mother; surely you can tell me."

Leonora shook her head and sipped her tea. This place was called a coffee shop but served only tea. If careless talk cost lives, what did careless kisses cost? Was that part of her additional duties, letting a middle-aged man put his arm around her and kiss her, lean into her against the back wall of a pub?

And what had she done? Pushed him away and muttered a few demure and ladylike words of regret? No, she had kissed him back, forcefully, passionately; she had felt his hands on her legs, had pushed herself into him, felt him harden, wished he would push her skirt up farther – that's what she had done. This was an important American guest of the prime minister, a man who had the president's ear in Washington, a man who could change the tide of the war by bringing influence to bear in the White House, and she had kissed him, not once, but again in the car, when more than anything she had wanted to fold that gaunt, tobacco-stained husk of a man into her, bringing life and light to that tired body and a smile to those endless grey eyes, usually more red now with tiredness and booze. That's what she had wanted, and she could feel he wanted the same thing. This was not just one careless kiss. It was much more, or maybe not. Maybe lust and love got confused in wartime London.

"Darling, are you listening to me?"

Leonora looked at her mother and then fished in her bag for a cigarette. Her hands closed on the short-barreled .38. She felt for the safety catch. They had told her to carry it with her at all times in a shoulder holster beneath her jacket. That simply wasn't practical, so here it was among the lipstick and the cigarettes in her bag. She lit one, knowing her mother would disapprove.

"Yes, Mum, I am," she said, blowing out a stream of smoke. "It's just that I'm a little tired."

"I'm sure you are, darling, but we are all tired of this war, aren't we? I didn't get a seat on the train and had to stand all the way to Paddington."

Why didn't you remarry? wondered Leonora. You could easily have found someone, maybe a survivor of that slaughter in the trenches who needed looking after, and you could have loved him as if he was Dad. But no, you deliberately kept his memory alive, worshipped that photo beside your bed, and cut yourself off from the affection of others, including me. That's what has happened to you and me, Mum – we've lost each other because you selfishly locked yourself away in love for a dead man and expected me to join you, entombed in unspoken mourning for a name on a stone slab in northern France.

"I must go, Mum." She stood and ground her cigarette stub into the ashtray.

"Must you, darling? I thought we might have lunch."

Her mother's eyes misted with tears. Leonora leant down and hugged her.

"I'm sorry. I would have loved to, but . . ."

"I know; you have your job. Well, I want you to know I am very proud of you."

They hugged again and parted, Muriel to walk down Oxford Street and observe with shock the desolate remains of the John Lewis store, and Leonora to stride with relief into the park and across to Knightsbridge where she had parked the Humber, far enough away so her mother wouldn't see it.

The special train that took the prime minister's entourage to Glasgow stood snorting steam over the platform like a dragon. It had been painted in khaki camouflage colours over its usual apple-green livery since German fighters had recently taken to strafing trains on the move. Churchill was like a boy with a new toy as he extolled the merits of the Coronation-class steam engine and personally visited the driver and firemen to congratulate them on its performance. He asked Hopkins to join him and they negotiated the narrow corridor through the water tank and past the coal tender to the cab. There, with the countryside flashing past them and the cab rocking from side to side, Hopkins watched as the prime minister was permitted to feed the glowing furnace with a shovel of coal.

Later he insisted that Hopkins sit opposite him in the Pullman car and offered him a similar seat when the party moved into the dining car after drinks had been served at noon. Hopkins suspected that the journey had been planned to allow the prime minister to indulge in what he called a proper luncheon while travelling through the countryside at up to 100 miles an hour. There were some ten officials in the car, including Brendan Bracken, senior officers from the three branches of the armed services, and the minister for Scotland, Tom Johnston. Over the prime minister's shoulder Hopkins could see several detectives and aides to the service chiefs at a separate table. Leonora was among them. She had picked Hopkins up from Claridge's that morning and driven him to Euston Station. They had said good morning to each other and nothing further until the car pulled up at the station.

The stationmaster, wearing a bowler hat, was waiting for them on the pavement.

"About last night . . . ," Hopkins began.

She did not turn in the driver's seat but caught his eye in the rearview mirror.

"Last night a Stirling bomber suffered failure in three of its four engines when taking off from RAF Scampton and crashed into a neighbouring village, killing twenty-three people asleep in their beds," she said. She turned and smiled at him. "I think the stationmaster is waiting. I shall be joining the party when I have parked the car."

Hopkins fell asleep after lunch somewhere north of Manchester. Churchill retired to his private compartment for his usual afternoon rest. The rest of the party also dozed and tried to recover from the three-course lunch, which had consisted of smoked salmon, velouté of veal, cheese, and, naturally enough, light luncheon wines.

After just under six hours, they arrived in Glasgow at around five and went straight to the hotel, where the Lord Provost was to give dinner that night. It was Churchill's first visit to Scotland since becoming prime minister. It was important that he should rally morale north of the border as much as elsewhere, he had told Hopkins.

"Our fighting forces and most of our great Guards regiments have a disproportionate number of Scots. They are and always have been great warriors."

Hopkins noticed that whenever Churchill talked of the war or great feats of arms in British history – which was often – his voice descended to a theatrical growl.

Once again he realised that the man really was pure theatre, a cigar-smoking, brandy-swilling bulldog in a bowler hat. How would the act go down in Washington? he wondered – if he ever managed to arrange that visit. The president was being cautious about the prime minister's request, and Hopkins could see why. The isolationists had been roused to fury by the Lend-Lease bill and the Mothers of America were marching outside the White House railings every day with posters denouncing any attempt to send their boys into a foreign war.

If the president was going to meet the prime minister, it would have to be as far from Washington as possible. And then there was the issue of the British Empire. Roosevelt, like most of his party, hated the idea of it, resented its history, and privately damned its present manifestation, especially in India. Yet Churchill kept on talking about the glory of empire in Britain's hour of need and refused to be discreet about the subject, let alone apologise.

As the train drew into the station, Churchill leant over to his American guest and said, "I told you the British Empire was created by accident, Harry. Well, the Scots were the accidental heroes who assembled it. Doctors, engineers, nurses, administrators – they travelled the world. If you spend a winter up here, you will see why they are such empire builders."

• • •

As Churchill gave the after-dinner speech that night, Hopkins understood why he had been invited to join the journey north. The prime minister's dramatic rhetoric was aimed not at the assembled Scottish dignitaries but once again directly at the White House and American public opinion. He went out of his way to praise what he called "the democracy of the great American Republic." He paid graceful compliment to the president and stated that he had no wish to see American soldiers travel across the Atlantic to fight Britain's war. What he did want was the means to fight that war, and in this call he repeated an earlier famous declaration: "Give us the tools and we will finish the job."

His speech ended with a flourish and Hopkins checked his watch. It was ten o'clock. He could now politely leave and head for bed.

Then he heard his name called.

"Mr Hopkins will now give us a few words."

Churchill was smiling down at him from the top of the table.

Hopkins rose. Every eye was on him. He saw Leonora looking at him from the far end of the table, placed well below the salt, as the Brits put it. What could he say that would give hope to these people and their embattled armed forces, that would delight his genial host but give no cause for additional sleepless nights in the White House?

The words of his mother came to him: "Let the Bible be your anchor, your shield, and your inspiration." Apart from the church drudgery on Sunday, they had regular Bible readings in the evenings in their two-storey clapboard house with its dirt yard in the wrong part of Grinnell. That had all stopped when he went off to Grinnell College and embraced a godless existence of beer, basketball, and the prettiest girls in his freshman class. But his mother had been right. You don't forget what you learn from the Bible.

Speaking softly and slowly so that those present had to strain to hear, he thanked the prime minister for his gracious words and the Lord Provost for an excellent dinner.

He remarked on the courage and tenacity of the people of Glasgow and especially those working on the docks to unload the Atlantic convoys under a barrage of bombs.

And then he finally said, "I suppose you wish to know what I am going to say to President Roosevelt on my return. Well, I am going to quote you one verse from the book of Ruth, in the truth of which my own mother, of Scottish descent, was brought up: 'Whither thou goest, I will go; and where thou lodgest, I will lodge: thy people shall be my people, and thy God my God.'"

Every head strained to hear him as he dropped his voice and said, "Even to the end."

There was a moment's silence, then wild applause. Hopkins looked at the prime minister. Churchill had tears in his eyes.

Hopkins flew back alone to London at first light the next morning. He took a taxi to Claridge's, kept the cab waiting while he packed his possessions, and checked out. He was driven across town to the Savoy, where the embassy had arranged a riverfront room. He was tired of being pestered by a pack of journalists. The phone in his room at Claridge's never stopped ringing. He couldn't have a drink at the bar in peace. Every time he stepped into the lobby there she was, Leonora Finch, patiently waiting for him.

He would ask Bracken to end her assignment that morning.

There were enough titled refugees from the royal families of Europe and a host of high-ranking Free French officers in London who needed liaison officers. He didn't. His mission was nearing its end and he intended to write his final report for the president in the peace and quiet of the Savoy. He was beyond exhausted. As for avoiding the prime minister, well, he would plead pressure of work and respectfully decline the inevitable invitations to lunch, to dinner, and to Chequers for the weekend. He needed a few early nights to clear his head.

The phone rang in his room. Nobody knew he was at the Savoy except Herschel Johnson at the embassy. He picked it up.

"Hey, I hear you've been giving them Bible lessons up in Scotland. Great stuff, Harry – it's all over the wires."

"How did you know I was here, Ed?" snapped Hopkins.

"I'm a journalist, Harry, remember? Anyway, if you think you're going to hide away in this hotel, think again. The whole American press corps is moving to the Savoy tomorrow – they've been offered a big discount on the room rate and a pressroom with a dozen ticker-tape machines."

Hopkins took a second to digest this unwelcome news.

"You still there? Come and have a drink and I'll tell you the latest from Washington."

The invitation was irresistible. If anyone knew what was happening in Washington, it was Ed Murrow.

The Glasgow dinner had been a private affair and, with the exception of the prime minister's speech, all conversation was supposed to have been off the record. Indeed, the prime minister had assured Hopkins that tight censorship would be imposed on any after-dinner speeches. Churchill's own words were duly trumpeted around the world by the American press.

But Hopkins's brief speech and the lines from the book of
Ruth had apparently been given almost equal prominence.
"President's Envoy Pledges U.S. to Fight Alongside UK" was
the least of the headlines. Roosevelt would be furious.

"How the hell did you guys get those quotes?" said Hopkins, trying for a Churchillian bulldog growl but sounding
more like an angry duck.

Ed Murrow laughed so much he spilled his whisky sour
over the marble top of the bar.

"Harry, how can someone who's been around Washington for ten years be so naïve? The Brits put that out – they
suckered you. Why do you think they took you to Scotland?"

They were all lying, thought Hopkins. The Brits, the
White House, the press corps – everyone. Churchill had been
practising diplomatic deceit on a grand scale. He didn't want
the tools; he wanted the men – American soldiers, sailors,
and airmen to finish the job. As for Roosevelt, what was that
little poem by Longfellow he had sent Churchill only the
other day, handwritten and hand-carried across the Atlantic
by courier to be delivered in person to "the Former Naval
Person"?

Sail On, O Ship of State!
Sail on, O Union, strong and great!
Humanity with all its fears,
With all the hopes of future years,
Is hanging breathless on thy fate!

Needless to say, Churchill seized on this poetic offering
as evidence that the president was moving towards a more
active involvement in the war. It was no such thing, just Roosevelt playing with words, as Churchill so often did in return

and as he, Harry Hopkins, had done the previous night in Glasgow.

" 'The night cometh, when no man can work.' Saint John, chapter nine, verse four. Do you want to try the whisky sour?" said Murrow.

Hopkins wearily agreed, wondering if the old saying "if you can't beat them, join them" had any biblical provenance.

"So what's the big news from Washington, Ed?"

They were seated at the Savoy's American Bar, where Eddie Clark, famous throughout Europe for his cocktails, was shaking up a whisky sour. The wall behind the bar was covered in a map showing the long, lazy U-bend of the Thames as it flowed past the hotel on its journey through central London. On the far wall a fire burnt brightly and a door led to the outer lounge, which was where ladies were permitted to order drinks. The bar itself was for gentlemen only.

"Make it two," Murrow said to Eddie before turning back to Hopkins. "You're going to need one after what I tell you."

Hopkins sipped his drink. That was the damnedest thing about cocktails. They turned high-octane alcohol into a drink that tasted as if it were good for you.

"Inside track is that you're going to lose Lend-Lease," said Murrow. "The bill is going to fall in the debate. You know James Byrnes, the president's main man in the Senate? He doesn't think he can get it through. You may have to prepare your friend at Number 10 for some bad news."

Hopkins drank more deeply. That was the other thing about cocktails. One was never enough. If what Murrow was saying was true, he would not be the only journalist to make that deduction. In a couple of nights the bar would be swarming with journalists all braying the same questions: "What are you going to say to the Brits when Lend-Lease fails, when there are no guns, tanks, and fuel coming across the Atlantic?" "Are you going to let the Brits face the Germans with broomsticks?"

It was always personal with the press. After the backslapping and the "Have a drink, Harry," it was always, "What are *you* going to do about it, Harry?" Not "What is the president going to do," nor "Congress," just "you," Harry Hopkins. "You're so friendly with the president that you've even got yourself a bed in the White House. You know what's going on; you must make decisions in the dead of night when you're all cozied up to the president and no one's looking. So what are you going to do, Harry?"

That's what those self-seeking hypocrites thought of him, as if anyone had ever elected any of *them* to stand in judgement on politicians and other public figures.

It was time to go back to Washington. If the president was in trouble, he ought to be there. He had seen all he needed to in Britain. How many times had he said this to himself? This time he meant it. He would get Bracken to arrange a flight back. He finished his drink.

"They were very fine words last night," said a voice at his shoulder. He turned. Murrow was deep in conversation with the barman about the makings of a true whisky sour. Flight Lieutenant Finch was standing there behind him, looking a little tired, her hand on the back of his chair.

He squeezed off his barstool and helped her up onto it.

"Looks like you could do with a drink," he said.

"I wouldn't say no to a gin."

Hopkins signalled Eddie Clark, who reluctantly broke off his conversation with Murrow.

"Men only in this bar, I'm afraid," Eddie said.

"She's one of us," said Murrow.

Eddie Clark turned, poured a gin, and placed the glass in front of her.

"We missed you in Glasgow," she said. "The prime minister wanted me to drive you up to Loch Lomond and see a bit of the Highlands. You said you were Scottish on your mother's side, didn't you?"

Her green eyes caught and held him over her gin, dark green eyes searching him out. The British embassy in Washington had been very thorough in their brief, he thought, and wondered how much she had been told about him. When they weren't abusing him as a presidential crony, the press liked to call him a playboy, a man with an eye for a slow horse and a fast woman.

"Yes, distantly, back a couple of generations. I'm sorry. I should have told you – I had to get back in a hurry."

They fell into an awkward silence, glancing around the bar, which had recently been redecorated to attract the high-spending press corps from Claridge's. Framed photographs of the Hollywood stars Clark Gable, James Stewart, and Hedy Lamarr hung on the wall.

"I have to go back," he said suddenly.

"Of course. You've pretty much seen it all here, haven't you?"

Again those emerald eyes, and the smile that lit them up.

"Yes, it's been a good trip and very useful, but I have a lot to follow up on back in Washington. I will be leaving on Saturday if I can get a flight."

Saturday, she thought. Today was Wednesday.

"You might have time, then," she said, drawing a letter from her pocket. "This is from the boys of the Eagle Squadron – you've heard of them?"

Of course he had heard of them. The young Americans who had broken their own country's law to come to Britain and fly with the RAF. They had been training all the previous fall.

"Where are they stationed?"

"They've gone operational and they are flying out of a base not far from London. They wrote to the prime minister and said they hoped you would pay them a visit and take back a message to the president."

Hopkins almost laughed. That cunning old rogue had gotten him again. There he was, sitting in Number 10, planning and plotting like an old spider weaving his web of deceit, trying to enfold the president in a war most everyone back home wanted no part of; what better way than to have Harry Hopkins visit brave American boys at their British base, young men who had volunteered to fight the Nazis, and watch them fly Spitfires into the embattled sky? They would tell him their stories of why they had risked prosecution in the American courts to come to Britain and fight Hitler in the name of liberty.

There would be reporters, probably Ed Murrow and the other big names from the networks, plenty of photos and newsreel of Roosevelt's right-hand man joshing with the brave boys of the Eagle Squadron. What a story that would make for the papers back home, and how the president would be moved by American heroism at the front line.

Lindbergh and all those other creeps would rant and rave about the folly of it all – and that was the cleverest part. The more extreme the isolationists became, the more public opinion slowly would shift away from them.

"Can I see the letter?" Hopkins said.

It was just a few handwritten lines asking the prime minister if it was possible for the president's envoy to visit them at their base in Coltishall, Norfolk. There were twelve signatures. Attached was a photograph of all of them, twelve young American faces in the blue RAF uniform kneeling before a fighter – a Spitfire or a Hurricane, Hopkins could not tell which.

"Where's this?" he asked.

"That was taken at Church Fenton near York, where they have been training. They have since moved to Coltishall in Norfolk to prepare for convoy-escort duties. It's an easy drive from London."

"This a Spitfire?"

"No, a Hurricane. They will be training on the new Spitfire in the spring."

"You seem very well briefed on this."

"It's my job, sir, to make sure – "

"I know, to make sure I am fully informed and given access to all the information I may need."

He paused, looking at those faces – country boys, city boys, rich boys, poor boys, some fresh out of college, some who never got further than high school, most just twenty years old. They all wanted to fight Hitler. No one had told them they might burn to death for a minute or more, trapped in their cockpits, screaming in agony over the intercom for the radio girls to hear as their planes plummeted to earth. No one had said they might get home one day and walk down Main Street with a face that would have people crossing the road to avoid them and kids running up to point to the monster man.

"They are a great bunch. 'Kids on the ground, killers in the sky,' they call themselves."

"You've met these guys?"

"I drove Mr Bracken there in the autumn. The prime minister wanted to hear how they were getting on."

I'll bet he did, thought Hopkins. This is pure golden propaganda and he wants me to tell the president in person what an example these kids are setting. And what had she just said? Their base was an easy drive from London? Of course it was.

"Hi, you guys," said Murrow, moving between them with a fresh whisky sour in an old-style champagne glass.

He was drunk, thought Hopkins. But so what; wasn't everybody in London these days?

"Now this," Murrow said, "is what a sour should be. Here, taste it."

He seemed not to recognise Leonora as he offered her his glass.

She shook her head. "I'm on gin."

"Oh, it's the liaison officer. How is the liaising going? Is she looking after you, Harry?"

Hopkins searched his face for hidden meaning, but Murrow was too drunk for such subtlety.

"She's doing just fine," said Hopkins, wearily thinking once again that, like most everything else in wartime London, life was beyond his control.

"Here's to the Eagle Squadron," said Murrow.

Hopkins looked at Leonora questioningly.

Murrow caught the glance. "I thought we were all going to see our gallant countrymen tomorrow?" he said. "Here's to them."

8

There was still snow covering the fields and piled up in dirty grey ramparts along the roads as they drove east out of London the next morning. Leonora Finch checked her rearview mirror and saw Hopkins asleep, slumped in the corner of the backseat. He was worn-out, poor man. He had not had a proper night's sleep for three weeks; he was perpetually cold and he hardly seemed to eat. She had managed to get a plate of scrambled eggs for him that morning at the hotel and he gratefully ate the lot. Then it would be coffee and cigarettes, cigarettes and coffee, all through the day. Leonora smoked regularly, but she had never come across the three-pack-a-day habit that seemed essential to Americans.

And all poor Harry Hopkins probably wanted to do was board a plane home – back to Washington; to his warm, comfortable room in the White House; to the president he served with such loyalty; and to his petite, charming fiancée, Miss Louise Macy.

From time to time in their travels Leonora had caught that haunted look on his face, the look of a man who cannot believe what he is seeing and hearing. He had told her more than once in late conversations over a final whisky that he felt as if he had travelled to another planet. The few Americans who ventured across the Atlantic all felt the same. For the first few days they wandered around London in a state of shock, trying to find words to describe the Furies befalling the city every night and the bloody-minded courage with which Londoners lived and died under the hellish barrage.

Now he was being driven to another event, another occasion, another meeting. He had complained about it, but she knew he didn't really mind. He had to see those American flyers, knowing that Roosevelt would want a firsthand report and not some cockeyed patriotic newspaper report laced with exaggerated quotes.

Leonora had watched Hopkins change in the month he had been in London. He had arrived in a London made wary of Washington by the extraordinary behaviour of the U.S. ambassador Joe Kennedy. The ambassador had been openly critical of Churchill from the moment he became prime minister in May 1940. And Kennedy had gone to great lengths to spread around London Roosevelt's impression of Churchill after they had first met at a dinner in London in 1917. A real stinker, Roosevelt had called him, and with good reason. Within minutes of being introduced, the two men had clashed at the dinner table, Churchill as the first sea lord, pulling rank on Roosevelt, an undersecretary for the navy, as he then was. Churchill had been at his bombastic worst.

Kennedy had not got much mileage out of that, however. He loathed Churchill as a warmongering imperialist and an upper-class Englishman whose ancestors had been responsible for the great famine in Ireland in the last century. Churchill had returned the ill feeling. Number 10 had quietly let it be known that they had some interesting files on

Kennedy's shady Mafia dealings during the days of Prohibition, when the ambassador had made his fortune.

She knew all this because she had been briefed on what to say if Hopkins ever repeated or queried the poisonous gossip that had flowed from the American embassy under Kennedy. But Hopkins wasn't interested in Kennedy's intrigues and openly despised his enthusiasm for Hitler's Germany. Hopkins's wary cynicism and barbed quips about the Empire and Churchill's less-than-glorious career had vanished. He had been persuaded that America must do more to protect the Atlantic convoys. The briefings on merchant shipping losses and the lack of destroyers to escort the Atlantic convoys, together with the visit to Liverpool, had brought home to Hopkins just how close Britain was to defeat in that first month of 1941. He had told Leonora that his first mission back in Washington was to make that clear to the president and his cabinet. Churchill knew that too, which was why it had been agreed that Hopkins would return on Saturday.

She searched for cigarettes in her pockets as she drove. She was going to break regulations and have a quick smoke while her passenger slept. She would miss him. He called himself a small-town kid in a big man's world. Such self-deprecation was disarming, as Hopkins well knew, and very much part of the wry sardonic character he created for himself. Ill health dogged him, but he carried that lightly and never complained. He said the only way he had ever really relaxed was by spending a day at the races. Since horse racing was banned in Britain for the duration of the war, she had taken him to the next best thing – the dog track. The government had tried to ban that too, but there was such an outcry that the decision was reversed.

Once a week Londoners left their homes and shelters in the East End and gathered in the thousands for a few hours of dog racing at Wembley or Harringay Stadium. The races always took place in the late afternoon, as floodlighting was allowed until five o'clock, based on the curious but correct assumption that the Luftwaffe almost always bombed under the cover of darkness. The first time they went it had been a biting cold afternoon and they had drunk warm beer and eaten greasy chips and vegetable rissoles smothered in hot English mustard, which made him sneeze into his drink. They went several times afterwards and Hopkins never won a bet. She could see he didn't care. He loved the frenzied attention the crowds brought to the spectacle of half a dozen dogs chasing a mechanical hare around a dirt track.

He had taken out his notebook and written it all down: the joyous atmosphere among people able to forget for an hour the nightly bombardment, the loss of loved ones, and the daily queue for rations, the reek of unwashed bodies, the terrible food, and the rush to place bets after each race.

By the time the last dog had limped home Hopkins and Leonora were both tired. When the floodlights were turned off and the crowds streamed into the darkness, she thought he might kiss her again or at least suggest they drop into a pub for a quick drink, as if to expunge the memory of their indiscretion at the Prospect of Whitby. She wanted him to kiss her again. She wanted to feel that frail frame pressed into her, feel his arms around her. But nothing happened. He had a report to write. She drove him straight back to the Savoy. As usual, the moment he got in the car that morning he fell asleep.

RAF Coltishall lay in flat farmland a few miles north-east of the county town Norwich. The first squadron of American pilots to fly with the RAF had become operational only days earlier, in the first week of February. They had been moved from their training base near the city of York to East Anglia to fly cover for the coastal convoys that brought coal, iron, and foodstuffs from the industrial north to London.

The convoys moved slowly south within sight of shore most days of the week, shielded from surface attack by a deep minefield that stretched along the entire east coast. Just as the Germans sought victory in the Battle of the Atlantic in order to starve Britain into surrender, so they targeted the coastal convoys to cut off London and the south from vital supplies of fuel for power stations. The job of the Eagle Squadron was to stop them. Their weapon was the Hurricane, a slower plane than the Messerschmitt that came in fast and low over the wave tops of the North Sea to escape radar detection. But with its eight .303 machine guns the Hurricane packed a powerful punch, and the American pilots were not complaining.

She would have told him all this in the car as part of his briefing, but Hopkins slept all the way from London to the flatlands of Norfolk. He woke as they stopped at the gates of the air base.

The journalists had arrived earlier from London in buses organised by the Ministry of Information. There were some forty British and American reporters and cameramen gathered in a large sandbagged hangar. Arc lights had been rigged up on a makeshift platform at the far end. Hopkins could see Ed Murrow in the front row. Herschel Johnson from the embassy was beside him.

Hopkins declined the offer from the station commander of a seat on the platform. He similarly turned down a suggestion from a Ministry of Information official that he might say a few words at the end of the event. He had nothing but admiration for his countrymen who had crossed the Atlantic in order to fight Hitler, but he didn't want to contribute to the propaganda coup the Brits planned to extract from the occasion.

It was going to give the president enough problems as it was at home. He sat at the back and waited for Leonora to return with a cup of coffee.

Twelve young men in blue RAF uniforms walked onto the platform. They looked too young to be out of high school, their freshly shaven faces wearing shy grins of surprise, their ears sticking out from shorn heads, fingers twisting nervously in hands clasped in front of them.

To his amazement, Hopkins saw the press corps, both British and American, rise and applaud. He got to his feet reluctantly as Leonora passed him his coffee. He needed to see what was happening. He handed his coffee back and began applauding. He couldn't help it. Most of those kids were going to die in the skies over Europe, a long way from home but doing exactly what they wanted with their young lives. He fished in his pocket for a handkerchief and sat down.

The cameras began filming and the flashbulbs popped as the flyers introduced themselves. Tom Goodyear from Kansas City, Pete Sansom from New York State, Enrico Martinez from Tampa, Patrick McAlister from Boston, Ray Sandburg from New York City, Jamie Boland from Los Angeles, Gus Friedman from Des Moines.

The names rolled out from all over America. Hopkins craned to see the boy from Des Moines, not far from his hometown of Grinnell. He had taken the bus to the state capital many times with college friends. Those were the days before the last war, when it was easy for college kids to get a drink in a bar. That boy hadn't even been born then and his parents had only been teenagers. Had he told them what he was going to do? Had he even said good-bye to them? What on earth had they said?

The journalists jostled one another as they shouted out a barrage of questions.

"What brought you here?" "Why fight with the British?" "How do you find the Hurricane?" When will you be given Spitfires?" "What did your parents say when you told them you were going to break the law and fight with the Brits?" "What will you feel when you get your first kill and see the German plane falling in flames to the ground?"

That last question came from a British journalist. The largest of the American airmen, Tom Goodyear, who looked as if he would have trouble squeezing into the cockpit, stood up and said, "Good," then sat down.

Next came the questions Hopkins had feared. Murrow was first in.

"You have made the individual choice to join the British in the fight against Nazi fascism. Do you think your government should abandon its policy of non-intervention and join you?"

Hopkins knew the embassy had carefully tutored the flyers on the appropriate response to such questions. He didn't know whether they would stick to the script.

Goodyear stood up again and announced with the deliberation of someone who has carefully rehearsed his words, "That's not a question for us. We are here to fly and fight."

The question came back: "You have broken the laws of your own country to come and fight. How do you feel about that?"

Taking his cue from his comrade-in-arms, the youngest flyer of them all, a boy in a man's uniform, said simply, "Good."

The conference ended with ringing words of praise for the flyers from the station commander and a short speech from the Ministry of Information official about America and Britain joining hands across the ocean to fight fascism.

It was almost dark by the time the journalists clambered back on their buses, clutching thermos flasks of tea and sandwiches by way of a late lunch.

Hopkins and Herschel Johnson remained for a private briefing on the state of readiness of the Eagle Squadron. They were all good flyers and had learnt fast. In normal circumstances they would never have been considered fit for combat, but these were not normal times. By taking over the vital job of flying cover for the east-coast convoys they released regular RAF squadrons to take on German bombers and fly aggressive sweeps over northern France.

Hopkins noted the word "regular." These American boys were regarded by the RAF as irregulars, almost mercenaries perhaps, but they were happy to have them.

At the end of the briefing, Leonora handed him a white envelope with the RAF insignia on the back.

"We have to leave," she said. "The prime minister wishes you to join him for dinner with Lord Beaverbrook tonight."

Hopkins said nothing and opened the letter. It was handwritten in the careful, curling script drilled into schoolchildren from an early age in every American primary school: joined-up handwriting that looped letters into words in straight lines across the page from a young man who had now stamped the letters *RAF* on his life. Tom Goodyear, the large Kansas boy who had obviously become the spokesman for the group, had written:

Dear Mr Hopkins

 It would give great pleasure to me and all the boys in 71 Squadron if you would join us tonight for a beer in the mess we use outside the station. It is the Bull pub in the village and we would be honored by your presence around 7 p.m.

 Yours,
 Tom Goodyear

He looked at Leonora. She held the car keys in grey-gloved hands. She looked cold and tired and impatient to get back. He showed her the letter.

"I can hardly refuse," he said wearily.

Like all pubs near an air base, the Bull was having a good war. Everyone at RAF Coltishall, from senior officers to pilots and ground crew, used the pub as a means of putting distance between themselves and the violent and unpredictable world awaiting them outside. The pub had two bars, the saloon and the public bar, each partitioned from the other internally and with its own entrance. By unspoken agreement the local villagers used the latter, while anyone in uniform used the former. This arrangement caused much mocking comment about the English class system from the visiting American flyers. However the villagers noticed that the Yanks all preferred the more refined saloon bar, where the landlord, Cyril Bishop, had added to the usual pub games of darts and dominoes by installing a small baize-covered table with two decks of cards. A gramophone with a number of jazz records sat on a table by the fire. The saloon bar also had a carpet, mottled by cigarette burns and discoloured by spilt beer, but a definite improvement on the linoleum floor of the public bar.

When the Americans of the Eagle Squadron first arrived at the base, Cyril Bishop petitioned the mysterious authorities who dictated the provision of rationing cards to allow him extra supplies of whisky, bacon, and coffee. Since any American donning a blue air force uniform was regarded as a hero in the British public eye, the request was granted. Finally, Bishop had prevailed upon the local police, through judicious provision of some of his rationed eggs, to turn a blind eye to the Bull's expanded wartime opening hours.

The legal requirement that limited country pubs to opening only between eleven and two and six and ten thirty was quietly set aside. The saloon bar of the Bull was open from early in the day until well after midnight to anyone in a uniform who chose to knock on the frosted-glass panels of the door. The public bar observed official hours. This compromise, together with a regular supply of eggs, satisfied the local police.

The standing joke among American pilots in the saloon bar was the proximity of the Norfolk Broads to Coltishall. These famous inland waterways had been closed to boat traffic during the war but gave rise to many ribald comments from the newcomers. "Bring on the Norfolk broads!" and "How broad are the Norfolk broads!" were regular cries as the saloon bar door banged open. The one entertainment Cyril Bishop had not been able to provide for his American guests, as he called them, was female company. Members of the Women's Auxiliary Air Force at the base, who monitored the radar and plotted the weather, were not encouraged to join the men in their outings to the pub. The understanding, rather more subtle than the class divide delineated by the separation of the bars, was that the saloon of the Bull was for men only.

When Harry Hopkins and Leonora Finch walked in, a noisy game of darts was in progress at one end of the saloon bar and a game of poker at the other. Some twenty people, mostly Americans, were drinking, playing darts, and attempting to play dominoes. The air was thick with smoke. There was a drop in the conversational buzz as heads swung to observe the newcomers, and then Flight Sergeant Goodyear rose from the card table and raised his hands for silence.

"Boys," he said, "this is the representative of the president of the United States of America. I want y'all to make him welcome."

Harry Hopkins shook hands with every man in the room, trying to remember names and faces as they lined up to announce themselves. He accepted a drink and was given a chair by the fire, around which a crowd of eager faces immediately assembled. The darts had stopped and the cards had been laid to rest on the table.

Goodyear leant down and whispered, "Just say a few words, sir. And the lady over there, is she with you . . . ?"

Hopkins looked up. Leonora was perched on a stool at the bar with her back to him.

"She's my liaison officer."

Goodyear nodded and turned back. Hopkins heard him repeating "liaison officer" and saw the men staring at the bar.

Hopkins stood up. He had taken care to prepare an answer to the one question he knew they were going to ask him. He made it his opening line.

He was happy to tell his gallant countrymen not only that the president was proud of them but that the Justice Department would shortly announce that it would not prosecute American citizens who enlisted in the British armed forces, even though it remained an illegal act.

He went on to tell them how much the president understood their desire to fight fascism. On the other hand, he asked them to bear in mind that the president's hands were tied by Congress and that even getting the Lend-Lease bill signed into law was going to be a battle.

"What you are doing here will fire a beacon for freedom that will shine a light on the dark corners of our homeland, where they refuse to recognise the evil of Nazi fascism."

The faces around the fire stared at him blankly. There wasn't a flicker of response, not a smile of understanding or a nod of agreement. They had heard all this before, the ringing declarations from the White House about support for Britain in its darkest hour, about the courage of Churchill's lonely stand against Hitler. But such fine words were never matched by action. This was why they had broken the law to come to Britain – for action, for a chance to fight the evil of the Third Reich.

And after a drink or two these boys would admit to another good reason to wear the RAF uniform. This was the greatest excitement any American boy would ever have in his life, the chance to fly the famous Hurricane and Spitfire into combat against the Luftwaffe's finest warplanes, the Messerschmitt and Focke-Wulf. What more glorious adventure awaited any twenty-year-old from Kansas, or anywhere else in the good old United States of America? This was the chance of a lifetime, and as for the dangers, hell, you could just as soon get knocked down by a car on Madison Avenue as get shot up in the skies over Europe.

"Okay," said Hopkins, ending the awkward silence. "No more bull from me, let's all have a drink!"

At that there was a cheer and the fireside group broke up and headed for the bar. Hopkins slid onto a stool alongside Leonora. She had a half-pint of bitter waiting for him.

"Well, that was a lead balloon," he said.

"These boys just want a chance to fly and fight," she said. "They don't want to be told that, in its wisdom and mercy, the Justice Department has decided not to prosecute them when they get back home."

He laughed for the first time in a while. She was rebuking him. His pretty English liaison officer was telling him he had got it all wrong, and she was right. He had tried to imagine what President Roosevelt would have said if he had been there at the fireside. Trouble was, the president would have got the same response.

"Point taken," he said, and sipped his beer.

"Best thing is to stick around tonight, let them party, and then tell them what they really want to hear."

"Which is?" he said.

"Apart from the chance to shoot down Germans, they want a better postal service from home and some decent steaks."

"I can probably fix the steaks, but most of the post is going to the bottom of the Atlantic with all the other stuff."

Now she was giggling, not looking at him but looking into her beer.

"Share the joke," he said.

"Sorry. I don't mean to be rude, but *I* have fixed the steaks. I brought along thirty half-pound Aberdeen Angus fillets. It is your gift to the squadron, and the landlord here is going to sizzle them up tonight. I would have told you, but you were asleep all the way from London."

An hour later the steaks had been eaten, a vigorous debate had taken place between Cyril Bishop and the American guests over the difference between chips and fries, and jazz was filling the room. Hopkins watched as the landlord placed one bottle of whisky after another on the bar. If these boys could fly the way they could drink, they would be more than a match for any German pilot.

Leonora was sitting on a stool beside him at the bar. The gramophone was playing big-band music at a slow tempo. He closed his eyes.

"Mind if I ask the lady for a dance?"

Hopkins looked up. That Kansas boy again, Goodyear. He looked at Leonora.

"Fine by me, but you'd better ask the lady," he said.

"I'm game," she said, getting to her feet quickly.

Two of the Americans rolled back the carpet while a third placed a new record on the gramophone.

"Duke Ellington," he said to no one in particular, and lowered the needle onto the record.

Hopkins sipped his whisky to the sound of faster, louder music, big-band swing at a different tempo, the sound of the thirties to which he had wooed his second wife, Barbara, in their courting days in Washington.

He was a hopeless dancer and usually needed a long swig from the hip flask to get onto the floor at all. Barbara had been ten years younger, a trained nurse with soft good looks and a bouncy personality. On their second date he had taken her to a dance at the Rialto Hotel and no sooner had he put his arms around her on the dance floor than she said, "Harry Hopkins, you've been drinking without me. Take me to the bar at once." She was like that: very direct, funny, with gentle brown eyes.

She chided him about his smoking and drinking and made him buy tailored blue suits instead of the ill-fitting off-the-rack clothes he bought from Macy's in New York. "You don't need a wife," she said to him. "You need a mother." But Barbara insisted their relationship remain chaste. Hopkins was married, with three children, and although he and Ethel had separated, that made no difference to Barbara. She married him one month after he divorced, in 1931. He adored her and stayed with her to the end – through the cancer, the drugs, the delirium, and until death. They were married for just six years. He could hardly bear to think about her now.

Leonora unbuttoned her RAF jacket and kicked off her shoes. She was wearing a blue service blouse with a black tie and seamed nylon stockings. She hitched up her skirt and let Goodyear glide her around the floor, turning in slow circles that quickly became faster. Goodyear raised his arm, allow-ing her to twirl underneath, the blue serge skirt rising above her knees.

The boy from Des Moines stepped forward and tapped Goodyear on the shoulder. "May I cut in?" he said.

Goodyear looked at Hopkins, who nodded. He should have been back in London having dinner with Churchill and Beaverbrook, and here he was watching his liaison officer dance in stockinged feet, her skirt well above her knees, with young American pilots who were most likely going to get killed on their first mission.

One by one they danced with her, one always politely giv-ing way to the next. Bright faces, beaded with sweat in the smoky whisky warmth of the saloon, smiled as they whirled her around, holding her a little too close as she moved to the rhythm, leading the shy ones, helping them turn and move on the stone-flagged floor. The boys at the bar tapped out the beat on the wooden counter while people in the public bar next door craned their heads around the partition. The hands of the clock moved well past closing time, but no one noticed except Bishop, who locked the door. The record was replaced with faster music that Hopkins recognised as the latest craze in the dance halls of America, bebop, a music of jangling chords and broken harmonies that was jarringly different from the swing-band rhythm.

Hopkins relaxed in the glow of good whisky, remember-ing college dances at Grinnell, which always began with great formality and very slow waltzes, until the staff and chaper-ones moved away to gossip over tea. Then the band would lift the tempo, the girls would move closer, so you got a real feel of their tight waists, and if you were lucky someone would turn the lights down and you could slide your hands up a girl's back, pull her close, and try for a quick kiss.

These days dancing looked more like fornication; at least that's what his mother would say. He watched as Leonora teased and tantalised the young flyers, sweat staining her blue shirt with dark patches under the armpits, the seams of her stockings crooked, and her black service tie pulled loose so the knot swung against her breasts.

The kids – and that's what they were, he told himself, just kids – who weren't dancing with her were doing the jitterbug among themselves, shaking and twisting all over the floor, bumping into her accidentally on purpose and grabbing her to take over the dance.

She laughed as she changed partners, head back, the top two buttons of her shirt undone, showing her white neck and, whiter and softer still, the hint of cleft. He felt a pang of irritation, envy. He was too old for all this, too tired, too ill. Leonora was their age – well, a little older – and this was her generation, moving, gyrating, thrusting their hips at each other, smiling, laughing, and flirting outrageously. And they were loving it, especially those two boys from the Corn Belt, Tom Goodyear and Gus Friedman. They were her favourites. They cut in all the time and she let them. Hopkins shifted in his chair, planning to slip away quietly and get a taxi to the base and leave them to it. He was too old and maybe just a little jealous.

The music suddenly stopped. Bishop had lifted the needle from the record with one hand and was holding up the pub phone in the other. "It's the base for you, sir," he said, nodding to Tom Goodyear.

Breathing heavily, the Kansas boy took the phone, listened carefully for a minute, nodded, and said, "Yes." He turned to the group and pointed to the door, one finger outstretched. "Big flap on," he said. "Go, go, go."

The bar emptied fast. Goodyear rapidly shook hands with

Hopkins. Everyone blew kisses to Leonora as they bundled out the door. She flopped down exhausted beside him, breathless, her chest heaving.

"I think I have done my bit for Anglo-American relations," she said.

He handed her the remnants of her beer.

"I think you've put that unit out of action for a week," he replied.

She looked at him, grey faced and gaunt but with a smile that gave warmth to those craggy features.

"We should get going. It's past eleven," he said.

"It's too late to drive. I have arranged rooms for the night with the landlord. Number 10 is aware."

Steaks for the Eagle Squadron, rooms for the night, and the prime minister had been informed. She thought of everything.

Later, with the church bells chiming midnight, they lay in bed, two cigarettes glowing in the darkness, smoke curling to the ceiling in the dim light of the bedside lamp.

He had followed her up a narrow staircase and tripped on the top step. She had put out a hand to steady him. He had held it, regained his balance, and thanked her. She had turned and led him down a dirty carpeted corridor and opened the door to a room with a large bed squashed under a sloping roof.

"This is yours," she had said.

She had stood with her back to the door frame and one hand on the door to hold it open. He had squeezed past her, close enough to smell the sweat on her skin and the beer on her breath. His arm had touched her, curled round her waist, and suddenly they were dancing in slow, drunken circles on the frayed carpet, her mouth moving to his, and he had kissed her again and again, and without saying a word they had fallen onto the bed.

What happened to his clothes he did not know, but he had lain there naked, smoking, no longer tired. She had switched off the bedside light, and he had watched her silhouette against the pale light of the window as she slipped out of skirt, blouse, petticoat, stockings, and threw them casually over the back of the bedside chair. She had lain beside him and turned, sliding her arms around his neck, kissing him. It seemed as if they had made love all their lives, as if this were a long affair that had been going on forever. It felt like the end, not a beginning.

They lay there afterwards, panting, sweating, breathless, feeling the draught of cold air from the half-closed window. He had fumbled for cigarettes and a lighter and had snapped a flame into the darkness, lighting a cigarette and handing it to her. He could hear her heart thudding, or maybe it was his. He let his hand run over her breasts, feeling the nipples stiffen to his touch and her heart beat against her chest. Her hand took his and held it.

He wondered what she was thinking. Maybe the same as him; maybe the two thoughts met in the middle, emissaries from strangers who had become sudden lovers. She squeezed his hand, released it, and got up to close the window.

"Don't get cold," she said, and bent over to kiss him softly.

9

They left early the next morning without so much as a cup of tea, carefully stepping through the wreckage of overflowing ashtrays and dirty glasses in the saloon and quietly closing the pub's front door behind them. He took the front seat beside her as she drove fast through snow-encrusted fields. After thirty minutes she pulled into a lay-by and produced a thermos flask from beneath the front seat. She poured hot coffee into the lid that doubled as a cup and handed it to him.

"We'll have to share," she said.

He sipped at the hot liquid, coughed, handed it back, and pulled out a cigarette from a packet. They sat there for a few minutes, drinking coffee, smoking, watching the snow-laden skies move slowly overhead in darkening shades of grey.

"I'm engaged to be married," he said suddenly.

"I know."

"It'll be third time lucky. I've got four kids."

"I know. You're lucky."

He turned a questioning face to her.

"Four children is a blessing," she said.

"Their mother looks after the three boys. Diana lives in the White House with me. She's only eight years old."

"That must be fun for a child."

"It's not when Eleanor Roosevelt is bringing you up. Diana's mother died some years back. I suppose you know that too."

"Yes. I'm sorry."

"Thank you. Barbara was wonderful, a life force, but the cancer took her – at least it was quick."

She wound the window down and threw out the stub and poured out the remnants of the coffee. "We should go," she said, reaching for the keys.

"I know, but we need to talk."

She put a finger to his lips. "There's no need to talk. There's a war on. We all need a little joy in our lives."

"And that's all it is?"

"Never say no to a little joy, Mr Hopkins."

She kissed him quickly on the cheek and turned the key in the ignition.

Well after midnight, Winston Churchill turned to Sawyers, his valet-cum-butler, with glass outstretched for another brandy. He leant back in his armchair in the bunker below Downing Street, his face settled into a scowl that betrayed grief and anger. On the table beside him lay a stack of cables that had been coming in all evening.

Hopkins declined Sawyers's offer of another drink and watched while the youthful Jock Colville accepted a generous portion. Colville, the prime minister's private secretary, knew better than most that this would be a long night. The explosions on the streets above were clearly audible, but the continuing ferocity of the Blitz was not what was on the prime minister's mind.

He is like a heavyweight boxer, Hopkins thought, taking punishment in the ring, barely able to defend himself, desperate for the bell to ring to allow the corner men to staunch the bleeding and clear his head. Hopkins had seen Joe Louis batter Primo Carnera, the so-called Ambling Alp, into submission and watched the Brown Bomber destroy the German Max Schmeling. And it was a bit like that with the British, blow after blow being landed, leaving the country punch-drunk and unable to reply.

Churchill picked up the papers, adjusted his glasses, and began to list the latest disasters.

The German pocket battleship *Admiral Hipper* had left its base in Brest and sunk seven merchant ships in the Atlantic; the *Scharnhorst* and *Gneisenau* battleships had broken into the North Sea and were clearly aiming to pass into the Atlantic to link up with the *Hipper*. It was the beginning of February and eighty-eight merchant ships had been lost the previous month, totalling four hundred thousand tons of cargo, almost half sunk by U-boats.

"We can't go on like this. The losses are unbearable." Churchill spoke softly, staring vacantly at the last embers of a coal fire.

Hopkins had seen Churchill take bad news before. A few days after he first arrived he was with the prime minister at Chequers when news came through that the battleship *Southampton* had been sunk and the aircraft carrier *Illustrious* badly damaged by Stuka dive-bombers in the Mediterranean.

Back then he had swayed like a tree in a gale-force wind but had not broken. Now, for the first time, he looked defeated. The growl had gone; the voice that had lifted the British people throughout their trial by fire had fallen to a whisper.

"The Germans have their problems too," said Colville. "Intelligence tells us they have only eight U-boats on station in the Atlantic. They cannot build fast enough to replace their losses."

"Losses!" snorted Churchill. "How many U-boats have we sunk since September? Three! Just three! We don't have the ships to defend our convoys and we don't have the ships to replace those lost. Hitler knows it well. He knows the real battle is not in the desert or along the Channel. The real battle for the future of these islands is in the Atlantic. And he is winning that battle."

"Prime Minister!" Colville was on his feet, shocked.

"It's the truth, Jock, and it is as well that Mr Hopkins hears it."

Hopkins too was on his feet. He and Colville looked down on the figure slumped before them, drinking deeply from his brandy.

"Prime Minister, you know it is only a matter of time before Congress passes Lend-Lease; then we will become true allies."

Churchill stiffened and shifted forward. He wanted much more from the Americans than Lend-Lease. But he would gain nothing by allowing them to think that he had begun to give up hope.

"You know what Napoléon used to say to his generals, Harry? 'Ask of me anything but time.' We don't have time for the diplomatic niceties of congressional debates and votes. Democracy is being sunk in the Atlantic. But I will say this to you both: I cannot look the British people in the eye and promise them victory. I will pledge that I will never deliver them to defeat. We will fight on until one day you, the American nation, will join us against that barbaric fiend."

He glowered at them both, reinvigorated, reassured, his confidence restored.

There was a knock at the door. Clementine stood there in

dressing gown and slippers. "It is four in the morning, Winston. Come to bed and let these poor men get some rest too."

Churchill struggled to his feet. "I bid you good night, gentlemen. And, Harry, forgive me if I send you to bed with a few words from the Bible. You moved us all with your words from the book of Ruth in that Glasgow speech: 'Whither thou goest, I will go; and where thou lodgest, I will lodge.'"

"Thank you, Prime Minister."

"Those were fine words, but you know the verse that follows?"

Hopkins knew it well. He had deliberately omitted it from the speech.

"'Where thou diest, I will die, and there will I be buried: the Lord do so to me, and more also, if ought but death part thee and me.'"

And then he was gone, trailing cigar smoke and the perfume of old brandy.

Eleanor Roosevelt met Miss Louise Macy once a week for tea in her private sitting room at the White House. She admired the thirty-five-year-old divorcée for her work as a nurse's aide and even more because she had had the good sense to become engaged to Harry Hopkins. On one occasion Eleanor had even used her daily syndicated newspaper column, "My Day," to praise the work of Miss Macy, and all similar hospital volunteers, for putting in long hours doing the dirty work in hospitals. As a result of the volunteers' work, nurses were able to concentrate on caring for the sick, leaving the drudgery of emptying bedpans and replacing soiled bed linen to the volunteers. As Eleanor told her many readers across America, that was quite a change from Miss Macy's life as a fashion journalist for *Harper's Bazaar*.

The president's wife was a passionate activist, a woman who campaigned for social reform and raised funds for the many organisations working to improve welfare. In Harry Hopkins she had found a like mind, and as the New Deal, with its array of welfare and work programmes, unfolded, so Eleanor and Harry became close collaborators.

Now she was worried about her protégé. Hopkins seemed to have become distracted by the war; he was spending too much time closeted with the president, and she had begun to suspect that he was losing the zeal for social reform that had made her admire him so much. She was also worried about his health. Hopkins was too often at the racetrack or in fashionable Georgetown bars. And his four-pack-a-day habit was, frankly, suicidal. He needed to settle down, find someone to look after him – and, above all, someone who could give him a life away from the White House.

In Miss Macy, Eleanor Roosevelt believed she had found the answer to many of Hopkins's problems. Here was an attractive, well-connected, and socially aware woman who appeared, strangely to some, to be genuinely attached to a man both older than her by many years and in poor health. Mrs Roosevelt had introduced them at a fund-raiser and watched their romance progress with satisfaction. If she was not mistaken, Miss Macy had genuinely fallen in love. But Harry was too obsessed with the war in Europe to notice.

"When is Harry coming back?" said Louise as she sipped her tea. "I am so worried about him in London, with all the bombing."

"The president feels the same way. He has ordered him home twice now, but Harry always seems to find another good reason to stay on," said Mrs Roosevelt.

"He and Churchill have formed a close relationship, I hear," said Miss Macy.

"Rather too close," said Mrs Roosevelt. "Franklin thinks the British have got to him. He's sending over Averell Harriman to make sure he is getting the right information. As for Churchill . . ."

Her voice trailed off. She could hardly disapprove of the British prime minister's lone stance against fascism in Europe, but she suspected there might have been a peaceful and negotiated outcome if such a belligerent character had not occupied 10 Downing Street. Churchill was an imperial warrior who stood for everything that Mrs Roosevelt had fought against all her life. She knew that Harry Hopkins had shared her views, but from what little she had gleaned of his letters and cables to the president – her husband was remarkably discreet about such matters – Harry seemed to be falling for Churchill's famous charm.

She sighed. She had already lost her husband of thirty years on this issue. The president was steadily being sucked into another European war at the expense of her cherished domestic reforms. His affair with that damned woman meant that for years they had maintained the pretence of marriage for political reasons. Now it seemed she was also losing Harry Hopkins, a radical champion of New Deal reforms, a man whose career she had fostered. She had welcomed Franklin's decision to offer Hopkins a home in the White House, because it placed at the president's side a man who could keep the administration focused on the things that mattered most to America: welfare reform, antimonopoly policies, expanded social security, and public works. Now it seemed Hopkins had become the president's cat's-paw in his Machiavellian manouevring with Churchill.

The real purpose of the teatime meetings between the two women was not the political gossip beloved by Washington society but to plan Miss Macy's wedding. Eleanor Roosevelt had already offered, with the president's blessing, a wedding in the Oval Office. Naturally Louise Macy was delighted, but such a venue posed security problems. The bride-to-be reluctantly agreed that only close family would attend – a total of some forty people.

The question that preoccupied the two women at this particular meeting was the date of the ceremony. The summer of that year, 1941, was their choice, but Mrs Roosevelt found the president impossible to pin down on the subject. He was happy that his adviser, counsellor, and friend was going to marry the charming and attractive Miss Macy, but he would not be bothered by such minor details as when such an event might take place. As he pointed out to his wife with some acerbity, he was being pressured by the British prime minister and senior figures in his administration to join a war that the majority of the American people wished no part of. Steering his way through this political nightmare left little time to consider Harry Hopkins's wedding.

"So what do you think, Harry?" said Churchill, smiling, knowing that the draft of the speech he had just handed the American would be more than welcomed by the White House. Hopkins was halfway through the text in the study at Chequers when the prime minister got up and began pacing the room, speaking to the mirror over the mantel and beyond to the president in the Oval Office and to the Mothers of America, the women so passionately opposed to any intervention in the European war. His voice was clear and strong as he spoke:

"It seems now certain that the government and people of the United States intend to supply us with all that is necessary for victory. In the last war the United States sent two million men across the Atlantic. But this is not a war of vast armies firing masses of shells at each other. We do not need the gallant armies that are forming throughout the American Union. We do not need them this year, nor next year, nor any year that I can foresee."

He turned to Hopkins.

" 'No American boots on European battlefields.' That's how I finish, Harry. That's the message. You think the president will like it?"

Hopkins knew exactly what the president would think. He would view it as a beautifully crafted, and crafty, speech. It was diplomatic deception, political evasion of the highest order. It was a speech that would strain the credulity of even the most fervent Anglophiles in the White House and State Department. Because it wasn't true. Churchill's strategy was to get those American boots across the Atlantic in great numbers by whatever means he could. But he dared not say so. He wished to give the president some elbow room in his constant battle with the isolationists. He wished to reassure the powerful lobby representing the Mothers of America that their sons would not be sent to fight the Nazis. "No American boots on European battlefields" was a wonderfully reassuring message from 10 Downing Street. But it was a lie.

"I think it's fine," said Hopkins tactfully.

There was no point in arguing with Churchill. It was his last night in England. He was due to be driven to Poole the next day. From there he would take the BOAC clipper to Lisbon to start the long journey home. Leonora would pick him up after breakfast and drive straight to the harbour in Poole where the planes boarded. She had suggested the arrangement. She was staying at Chequers that night but had retired to bed straight after dinner, pleading a headache. They had had no time together since the drive back from Norfolk. What was it she had said? "Never say no to a little joy, Mr Hopkins"? And yet she didn't want to see him before he left, at least not for a final private good-bye. Her room was somewhere at the back of the building, near the servants' quarters. But he wasn't going to try to find it. She didn't want him to.

"Harry, where have you gone to?" Churchill was peering at him through a cloud of cigar smoke. "Am I boring you? You seem to be away with the fairies. I'm keeping you up again, I suppose. I'm sorry. We must both go to bed."

Hopkins smiled and got to his feet. The clock on the mantel said one thirty, an early night by the prime minister's standards.

"And we'll keep our little secret?" said Churchill.

Hopkins was embarrassed. Churchill's speech was to be broadcast by the BBC and relayed across the Atlantic by CBS the following day, and Hopkins had played a big part in rewriting the first draft. A poetic oration about two great nations united in destiny to fight the hellfire of fascism would not go down well in the Midwest or any other part of the United States. He had suggested that the thrust of the speech should be almost exactly the opposite. Characteristically, Churchill had come up with the ringing phrase about boots and battlefields that summed up the new approach.

"Of course, Prime Minister. Not even the president will know," said Hopkins. He was embarrassed because Roosevelt was sure to see the work of a hidden hand in Churchill's very public denial of the need for any American troops in the war against Hitler.

The next morning, the prime minister came to the front door to bid Hopkins farewell. Churchill was wearing his siren suit, which to an American simply looked like an outsize pair of dungarees. The belted waist, zip-up front, and breast pockets added an eccentric style to the garment that must have greatly appealed to the prime minister, if to no one else in his entourage. Leonora saluted them both, her arm rising to her peaked cap in one crisp movement and remaining there as she held the Humber door open. The salute surprised Hopkins until he remembered that Churchill was both prime minister and minister of defence. She was saluting her most senior commanding officer. Servants loaded Hopkins's luggage into the boot, including gifts from the prime minister to the president: a collection of British wartime stamps, a large truckle of Stilton cheese, and a box of pills formulated, so Hopkins was assured, to cure any ailment.

The two men shook hands. Hopkins got into the back, waving to the figure on the doorstep as the car crunched slowly over the frozen gravel. He sneezed several times, blew his nose in an old handkerchief, and within minutes had fallen asleep.

The moment the car crested the hill overlooking Poole Harbour, Leonora knew that there would be no flight to Lisbon that day. The sea was breaking in lines of white rolling waves far out into the Channel, and the landing stage was rising and falling steeply in the swell. There was no sign of the BOAC flying boat. The rough sea confirmed the weather forecast, which she had checked the previous night. She had made alternative arrangements as a precaution and now turned the car towards the neighbouring town of Bournemouth, where accommodation had been booked at the Branksome Park Hotel. From the back Hopkins sneezed again and reached for another cigarette. In the hour since they had left Chequers he had chain-smoked his way through several. Now he had caught a cold.

"We will be there in a minute," she said. "I think you need a hot bath, and if you want that cigarette, feel free – we can break the King's Regulations this once, I suppose."

He felt better in the bath. A large mug of coffee steamed on the cork-topped stool beside him, adding to the dense vapour that clouded the room. He could hardly see the door and remembered the several occasions when he had tried to write in a damp notebook while Churchill's voice boomed through the haze, dictating long memoranda about Britain's wartime needs. There was a knock on the door and before he could answer Leonora walked in, a blurred uniformed figure in the steam.

"I thought this might help," she said, and placed a half bottle of whisky beside the coffee mug. Before he could say a word she turned and left, closing the door quietly.

He was pink faced and still glowing from the bath when he met Brendan Bracken in the foyer of the hotel. The gong for lunch had just sounded and the residents were entering the dining room, where Hopkins could see white tablecloths, waitresses in pinafores, and a tureen of soup steaming on the sideboard. He suddenly felt hungry. Despite Churchill's urging, he had eaten little at breakfast at Chequers that morning.

A briefcase of documents under his arm, Bracken took Hopkins into a small office behind the reception desk. The prime minister wanted him to have the very latest briefings based on overnight cables from military commanders in the Middle East and Far East before his flight. The departure delay meant that they had arranged a tour of the local defence units after lunch. The flight was now due to take off at first light the following morning.

Hopkins reached into his pocket and pulled out a pack of Camels and a notebook.

"No need for notes," said Bracken. "These documents will travel with you. A special courier will be with you on your flight."

Bracken read from a thick sheaf of notes and began with the arrival in North Africa of a new German general named Rommel, who was regarded by the British as an exceptional tactician. There was little the RAF or navy could do to intercept the supplies of men, armour, and war matériel now being flown and shipped across the Mediterranean and with which a new desert offensive would doubtless be launched later that spring.

And so it went on. Hopkins lit another cigarette and wondered if he could break in and tell this eager, clever, pugnacious young man that none of this information was new to him. He detected the prime minister's hand in every briefing he had been given by service chiefs and those working in intelligence agencies. Britain was losing the war and desperately needed America's help. It was the message he had got throughout his stay in England and it was true enough. The country was on its knees and, for reasons neither he nor anyone in Washington could understand, Churchill had committed the bulk of his armour and his best infantry to a campaign in the North African desert.

"What is the latest intelligence on the invasion?" asked Hopkins. The shot of whisky that morning had made him feel good. Churchill usually had a schooner of dry sherry with bacon, eggs, and kidneys for breakfast and always tried to persuade Hopkins to join him. Hopkins felt queasy at the idea of sherry with his eggs. That morning he had settled for coffee and whisky. The good old boys back in Iowa would be proud of him.

Brendan paused, flipped through a few pages, and continued to read aloud: " 'It's now early February and we think in three months – when the Channel will be calmer . . .' "

He looked out the windows of the cliff-top hotel at storm clouds scudding across Poole Harbor.

"It will be a gamble for Hitler, but we are reliably informed that his generals, and especially Göring, are urging him to make the invasion his next move. Once Britain is out of the war, Germany will be the dominant force in the Western Hemisphere – and then he will be your problem. Shall we continue over lunch?"

Lunch gave Hopkins a chance to ask a question he had not dared to put to Churchill: What were the contingency plans in the event of a successful German invasion?

"The government would move to the Malvern Hills in the west and we would hold a line that would include the great industrial centres of Manchester and Birmingham – the war would go on," said Bracken.

"And Churchill?"

"Oh, he would stay in London. He would never leave. He would go down with a gun in one hand and a cigar in the other."

Leonora was seated in the lobby waiting for him as they left the dining room. She smiled and got to her feet. Hopkins broke away and walked over. "Thank you for the whisky. A little early in the day, but it certainly worked on the cold."

"I am delighted to be of help," she said, and briefly placed an arm on his to steer him towards the door and the car outside.

She drove them that afternoon on a tour of what Brendan

Bracken called the British seaside at war. The town of Bourne-mouth looked out over the Channel from a cliff-top parade of Victorian villas and hotels. Below, rows of bathing huts painted in pastel colours were strung out on a long sandy beach. Hopkins imagined the beach scene in prewar sum-mers: picnics, parasols, wet, clinging swimming costumes, sand castles, the bell tones of ice-cream vans, and everywhere a hurly-burly of children. On the cliff top, those of an age when the beach had lost its appeal would take a promenade, plan lunch or tea, dream of romantic indiscretions, and gaze endlessly at passing ships.

By the second winter of the war, Bournemouth had turned its back on such idle pleasures. Barbed wire was coiled along the beach in three lines. The huts were boarded up. On the cliff top, air-raid wardens had set up observation posts. At either end of the cliff top, the Home Guard had installed themselves in sandbagged redoubts with firing positions for machine guns. The weapons had yet to be delivered and the barrels that poked out of the gun slits were carefully painted wooden replicas. Hopkins remembered Bracken's words the previous night. The man had been drinking heavily, which was unusual for him, and his voice cracked as he said:

"We're broke, Harry. It's Lend-Lease or bust."

Leonora drove them to a nearby flight-training school and then to the local hospital, where civilians wounded during the recent bombing of the town's department store were be-ing treated. She had prepared well and knew the names of the nursing sisters and many of the men and women lying in bed with broken limbs, burns, and deep wounds from flying glass. Small children lay in cots swathed in bandages – some sightless, some limbless, all twisting, turning, and crying with pain.

"No one expected the Germans to bomb Bournemouth – it's a seaside resort," she explained. "So the store had not boarded up its windows, which is why we had so many casualties."

He could see that beneath that pale, tired face she was angry. It showed in her green eyes, which seemed to change from emerald to a dark jade as she spoke.

"And why did they?" he asked.

"Sometimes they get lost at night and drop their bombs wherever they see lights below. But this was daytime and deliberate."

"But why?"

"They have very good intelligence. They know that many Londoners, and those from other big cities, come here for a short break to escape the Blitz. It's the German way of reminding the civilian population that there is no escape in this war."

"That's terrible," he said.

"Terrible?" She spat out the word. "No, it's bestial, satanic, utterly evil, and it's what that nation stands for – all of them. There are no fiends in Hell like the Nazis, and every man and woman in Germany has the blood of these people on their hands."

She swept a hand around the ward, pointing to wounded in their white beds.

"I wish the bastards who did this eternal damnation."

She was breathing hard, jade eyes flashing as if challenging him to doubt the truth or sincerity of her words.

Hopkins and Bracken had an early dinner in the hotel that night. Leonora had declined to join them and gone directly to her room. After a brief toast to Hopkins's safe journey home, Bracken left to catch the last train to London. Hopkins saw him into a taxi at the hotel steps and watched as the Irishman clambered clumsily into the back of the vehicle with an overnight case. He first tried to shut the door while the case was only half in the vehicle and then very nearly slammed the door on his foot. The driver grumpily got out and helped his passenger assemble himself and the luggage in the backseat. Brendan Bracken was the most physically uncoordinated man Hopkins had ever met. Politically, however, he was very much in control, his master's voice, the envoy with a clear and oft-repeated message: everything he had seen that day – the beach defences and the wooden machine-gun barrels – was part of the story he was supposed to take back to the White House.

He lit a cigarette and walked across the road to the cliff top. It was a calm night with a sickle moon spilling liquid light on waves that broke close to the coils of barbed wire, defences that would no more stop the Germans than keep back the sea, thought Hopkins. His flight was due to depart at eight the next morning. He would be glad to get back to a city where the lights stayed on at night and the houses were still standing in the morning. He went back inside to the bar for a tray, two glasses, a carafe of water, and a half bottle of whisky and headed for the stairs.

She opened the door of her room and stepped back in surprise. She held a lit cigarette and was still dressed in her service uniform.

"My turn to surprise you," he said.

She smiled and said nothing but opened the door to let him in.

"One for the road again, is it?" she said.

"One for the skies maybe," he said. "My flight is early to-morrow."

"I know. I'm your liaison officer, remember? Take a seat."

She pointed to an armchair by the window and took the tray. He looked round the room. A double bed, wardrobe, washbasin, freestanding dress mirror, dressing table, and two old armchairs. An old brown hotel room that probably hadn't changed much since Victorian times.

They drank and smoked in silence for a while; then she said, "I'm sorry if I got carried away today. I just get so angry."

"I know; I understand," he said.

"I feel so powerless. I want to get out there with a gun in my hands and kill them. Stupid, I know. But what am I doing here? Driving around in a big official car."

"You've been a great help to me."

"Why? Because I slept with you?"

Now he was angry. He got to his feet and set down his whisky glass on the dressing table with a bang.

"No. Because you – all of you, everyone from that brandy-sodden prime minister of yours to those burnt babies – have made me think, made me realise what we have to do, that's why."

"I'm sorry, I'm sorry," she said. Her voice was raised. She was pale with anger. "This bloody war is driving us all crazy."

She had her arms around him, kissing him, pausing only to take the glass from his hand and put it on a table, kissing him again, breaking away to undo his tie, her smoky whisky breath on his face, her hands undoing the buttons of his shirt, fumbling at his belt buckle. There was an urgency to the way she undressed him, backing him onto the bed to unlace his shoes and pulling down his striped cotton underwear. It was as if she had suddenly run out of time and was hurrying to

beat the hands of a hidden clock that beckoned her to another assignment in a different room. Then she slipped out of
her uniform and sent the blue jacket with its stripes and the
serge skirt flying onto a corner chair. She paused in a white
slip to take the whisky and drain it in a gulp. She pulled the
slip over her head, her breasts rising as she did so, and turned
to regard herself in the mirror. He watched from the bed
where she had placed him, a voyeur to a private performance
in which he appeared to have a limited role. With her back to
him, she took her hair and pushed it up against her head, holding it there with one hand while she flipped a cigarette from
the pack with the other. She reached for a lighter, snapped it
open, put the flame to the cigarette, and for a few minutes
stood there holding her hair up, looking into the mirror, smoking. Then she turned, screwed the stub into the ashtray, and
walked slowly over to the bed.

Their lovemaking ended in sudden laughter as the bed frame
gave way with a loud crack and the mattress sagged to the
floor, burying them in a confusion of sheets and pillows.

Still laughing, they collapsed back into the armchairs. She
poured them both a drink, lit cigarettes, and pulled back the
blackout curtains to allow faint light into the room from a
cloud-hidden moon.

"Harry, tell me something," she said suddenly. "What is it
that you have to do?"

"What?"

"You said you know what you have to do."

"Oh, that. Well, that's just me. I'm nothing but a messenger boy. The president will decide what to do."

"But when you talk to him face-to-face, man-to-man,
you're going to tell him, aren't you?"

"Tell him what?"

"That this little island needs you, all of you, over here fighting with us."

"Whatever I tell him won't make much difference. He listens to lots of people, especially the pollsters."

She perched on his armchair and kissed him.

"Tell him this. Tell him we need you all here, on the front line with us."

"OK, I'll tell him."

She took the cigarette from his hand. "Promise me – on the front line with us."

"I promise."

"Swear it."

"I so swear."

10

Harry Hopkins landed in New York four days after leaving England. He had changed planes in Lisbon, flying on a Pan Am clipper south to Portuguese Guinea and then across the South Atlantic at its narrowest point to Brazil, and then via the Caribbean to LaGuardia Airport. He was both tired and ill when he arrived but found time for a brief meeting with the newly appointed ambassador to Britain.

John G. Winant, known as "Gil," was a surprise choice to many. A lean Republican with the looks of a young Abraham Lincoln, he was fifty-one and had never served his country abroad in any capacity. He had, however, executive experience as governor of New Hampshire and was an effective advocate of social reform. Thus the isolationists could hardly accuse the president of sending to wartime London a man who sympathised with Churchill's high Tory ideals and love of empire.

Winant had wanted to spend the whole day with Hopkins, but the president was waiting impatiently at the White House. The two men lunched before Hopkins took the afternoon train to the capital.

"There are only three things to remember in London," he told Winant. "Don't let Churchill refill your glass too often, he drinks more than any man I have met. Stay away from the Black Cat Club. And try to get it through the heads of those service chiefs and ministers that only Congress can declare war under our constitution – not the president. They just don't get that. They seem to think Congress will do whatever the White House commands."

"And the bombing?" asked Winant.

"That will be the least of your problems," said Hopkins. "Good luck."

Hopkins entered the Oval Office the next morning to find the president at his desk with every senior member of the cabinet seated in front of him: Harold Ickes, Frank Knox, Cordell Hull, Henry Stimson, Henry Morgenthau, and George C. Marshall. Missy LeHand, Roosevelt's long-serving personal assistant, sat in the corner. She had become close to Roosevelt in her twenty years of service and had her own room in the White House. Grace Tully, the note taker, sat next to her. Hopkins was taken aback by the sight of the president. His face was grey, drawn, and much thinner than when he had left. Hopkins knew Roosevelt had suffered from a bout of flu, but the man at the desk looked much older than his fifty-nine years.

He noticed the cabinet secretaries all held folders marked: "HH exlondon." Every report he had sent from England was in their hands. It would have been nice if the president had told him he would be handing them round to everyone. As it was, Roosevelt had just asked him to drop by the Oval Office for a meeting at ten. When they had talked on the phone the previous night, Roosevelt had sounded overjoyed to have his wandering envoy home at last.

The president looked up, held up the dossier, and smiled.

" 'Amazing what you can do in a war,' " he said. "I like that, Harry, these words from that young man you met in – where was it? Somewhere on the coast?"

Hopkins took a seat. "Southampton. Bill Bull, an aircraft fitter, worked on Spitfires."

"Great name, Harry. Sounds too British to be true; you sure you didn't make that up?"

There was general laughter.

"Well, gentlemen, let's test that young man's words," said the president. "What amazing things can we do to help Britain win this war? Indeed, should we do anything?"

The debate went on all morning. Missy LeHand repeatedly refreshed everyone's coffee; Grace Tully's pen moved rhythmically over page after page of shorthand until a completed notebook lay at her side.

Roosevelt's technique was to elicit views from his cabinet and when, as inevitably happened, two men differed, he would make both examine the reasons for their stances more deeply. Long-winded statements brought a presidential frown. Roosevelt wanted clear talking that stayed on track and didn't wander into the woods, as he put it. He had a hound dog's nose for contradiction and would lay such lack of logic at the feet of the perpetrator, asking for clarity.

Like most of those present, Hopkins appreciated the irony in this approach. Roosevelt was the master of ambiguity, a man who could make a speech that comforted friend and foe alike. He could rally support for the embattled British in a speech that would lift the hearts of those at Downing Street and then blur the meaning of the message in subsequent interviews. At moments of crisis he could often be found not at his desk but on a boat cruise in the Caribbean. It was a deliberate tactic. The president disliked being rushed into big decisions and preferred to weigh the consequences with days or weeks of careful consideration.

The cabinet was broadly in favour of as much military aid as could legally be given under Lend-Lease, if and when the bill passed. One important qualification came from the secretary of war, Stimson. America needed to improve its own arsenal and re-equip its own forces first, he said. Japan was on the move in the Far East. The United States was in no position to fight a war on two fronts, in two oceans.

The senior law officer, Robert H. Jackson, was even more cautious. He reminded the meeting that, with the America First Committee, the isolationists had formed an effective lobby to mobilise Congress and popular opinion against the Lend-Lease bill and any other form of aid to Great Britain. There were open calls from the wilder shores of the isolationist movement for impeachment of the president on the grounds that the paltry aid already given to Britain contravened the president's legal powers under the Constitution. Respected public figures such as Lindbergh had taken to platforms across the country, arguing that only Congress could approve sending military supplies to a belligerent nation in a third-party war.

The room listened quietly as Jackson concluded. "On the question of aid to Britain, the fact is we have gone as far as we can. We have stretched the executive's authority to the limit and maybe beyond, acting in certain instances without the specific approval of Congress. We have honoured the Neutrality Act in the breach."

"Meaning what exactly?" broke in George Marshall.

"Meaning we shipped millions of American rifles and

much ammunition to Britain last November without the approval of Congress. The Brits are out of money; they have no cash. We may be able to lend them goods and war matériel, but we have to have legal backing, and that means going to Congress and asking for approval."

Around noon, after more coffee and cookies were brought in, the group focused on public opinion. The president asked Ickes to report on the latest polls. They showed that the number of those opposing any aid at all to Britain was rising. Ickes noted that deep-rooted hostility to any support for Britain's war effort went far beyond the naturally hostile Irish, German, and Italian communities. The Mothers of America was the most influential of many groups seeking to mobilise opinion against the war. In fact, 80 per cent of Americans were against joining the war in Europe and 55 per cent were opposed to sending any military aid to Britain. North Carolina's tobacco senator, Robert Reynolds, had spoken for hours in the Senate decrying the millionaires of Britain, the aristocrats with large country estates and the exploiters of India, who clung stubbornly to riches that they should be devoting to the country's defence.

"I don't suppose he mentioned his own millions or what he pays his workers on those tobacco estates, did he?" said Hopkins sarcastically.

"No," said Ickes, "but he did make the very telling point that there was no point giving aid to a country that was about to be defeated by Hitler. It would be tantamount to the U.S. supplying a tyranny that we should one day have to fight."

In the pause that followed, all eyes turned to the president. He seemed to have sunk into his own thoughts while Ickes was talking and for a moment or two afterwards continued staring

down at the mahogany desk that had been a gift to a prede-
cessor from Queen Victoria. His shoulders sagged. His
cigarette had gone out in its holder. His pince-nez spectacles
had slid down his nose. Then his head came up. He pushed
his spectacles back and relit his cigarette. Then he looked
directly at Hopkins.

"Harry, is that true? Are the Brits going to go under?"

Not if we give them all the aid they want immediately,
thought Hopkins, but there was little point saying that, since
the president's hands seemed to have been tied – by the polls,
by Congress, and perhaps by his own caution.

"The Germans will try a cross-Channel invasion, but I
doubt it will happen this year. The Luftwaffe has learnt the
lesson of the Battle of Britain and next time they will wipe
out all the fighter bases with bombing and paratrooper operations. They are developing longer-range bombers that will
reach every naval base and air base in Britain. Only then will
they launch their landing craft. But Churchill knows this and
with every month that passes he is strengthening his defences."

"Then what the hell are the Brits doing fighting in North
Africa?" Stimson barked out the question as if Hopkins were
personally responsible for the Eighth Army's North African
campaign.

"That's Churchill's gamble. He thinks if he can tie down
enough German troops in the desert – and defeat them –
Hitler will not have sufficient strength to launch an invasion."

"Doesn't make sense to me," snorted Stimson.

"Well, it makes sense to Churchill," snapped Hopkins,
"and *he's* fighting the war; we aren't."

"Harry, do you think you may have drunk a little too
much of that fancy French cognac with your friend Winston?"

It was Morgenthau from Treasury, the man with the

money. And Hopkins knew that behind the sarcasm lay years of hostility to every move he had made in Washington. The president liked Hopkins, listened to him, and followed his advice – and they all hated him for it.

Hopkins got to his feet. "Gentlemen, I think we have reached a point in this interesting discussion where my departure would be my most helpful contribution. Good day, Mr President."

As Hopkins closed the door, the cabinet members shuffled awkwardly in their seats, looking everywhere but at the figure behind the mahogany desk. Roosevelt lit another cigarette, leant back in his chair, and surveyed the most senior members of his administration. They were loyal, intelligent, hardworking men, who had dedicated their lives to public service. They were also jealous guardians of their political fiefdoms who spent an inordinate amount of government time plotting against their colleagues.

He watched them in silence for a minute, turning his head so that each one felt the full force of those strong, leonine features, then leant forward and said, "Gentlemen, if you were sitting where I am as president of the United States, you would be looking at that door over there knowing that everyone who walked in wanted something out of you. You would learn what a lonely job this is, and you'd discover the need for someone like Harry Hopkins, who asks for nothing except to serve you."

The president paused and added, "And he serves this office and our nation at great personal sacrifice – I want you all to remember that."

Louise Macy met her fiancé at the grill room in the Willard Hotel. Knowing he would be tired, she had arranged an early supper, with the promise that they would return to the White House well before ten o'clock. He had been away for six weeks and the occasional letter had been short and uninformative, telling her little more about life in London during the Blitz than the newspapers.

God, he looks ill, she thought as he ambled across the restaurant to greet her. He had lost weight and his suit looked two sizes too big on his tall, bony frame. His cheeks were hollow and his face creased with deep lines. She rose from her seat at the table, her face betraying her alarm.

"You look like you've seen a ghost," he said, kissing her on the cheek. "Don't worry, kid. I'm OK."

But he wasn't OK. It was as if she were having dinner with a stranger. Hopkins began talking about Churchill, the long evenings spent drinking, the power of his oratory, the sudden moments of terror when the shrill whistle of a falling bomb seemed to mean certain death, and the crazy food the Brits were eating, like potato pie and dandelion soup. She realised that her fiancé, the man she planned to marry that coming summer, was not there at all. He was still in London. The stranger across the table was indeed a ghost; the real man was still drinking with Churchill and dodging bombs in the streets of Mayfair.

"Harry," she said, "why don't we get away, spend a little time by ourselves? You're tired and it would be just wonderful to have time together for a while."

Eyes glazed from a couple of martinis, smoke curling from another in the chain of cigarettes he had smoked since they sat down, he looked at her. He leant over and put a hand on her arm.

"I can't, darling. I'm sorry. I have to stay here. We're right on the edge."

"I thought that was Britain."

"If we turn our backs on Britain now, and that country goes down, there is no way we will get back into Europe. We need that island and if we lose it we will face Hitler alone. The man is mad and he will move into the Americas and come at us from the south. Then Japan will attack from the east across the Pacific – "

"Harry, stop it. Enough!" she said. "You're conjuring up a nightmare that's never going to happen."

"It's happening right now – over there." He yanked his arm across the table and knocked over a bowl of flowers as he pointed to the windows.

"Look, you're tired and I know you have had a really tough time. But let's talk about something real, something good."

"Like what?"

"We're going to get married, aren't we? You remember that the president said he would give us a White House wedding?"

Hopkins dropped his napkin on the floor and bent down to pick it up. "Did he?"

"Eleanor told me. She suggested it to him and he agreed. We can have the ceremony in the Oval Office. Isn't that wonderful?"

"Yes, it's wonderful, honey – and I can't wait, but right now . . ."

He had turned to the waiter for the check. He couldn't wait to get out of there, to get back to his comfortable room in Lincoln's old study in the White House, she thought. He couldn't wait to say good night to her and get back to the stream of cables from the embassies in London, Berlin, Tokyo, and Moscow.

Harry Hopkins had become a prisoner of war, she realised.

A few days later, in a Berlin cinema, the commercial attaché of the U.S. embassy, Sam E. Woods, sat down to watch a musical romance called *Wunschkonzert*. It was a Saturday afternoon, and despite the by now regular British bombing of the capital, the cinema was full. The attaché sat in the back row, close to the aisle, and placed a briefcase on the seat next to him to keep it free. Two lovers on-screen had just exchanged their first chaste kiss when the attaché lifted the briefcase to allow a man to sit beside him. The two men watched the film for a few minutes and then the American felt something placed on his lap. Without looking down, he put it in his briefcase. The man beside him left.

Back at the embassy, the attaché opened the folder and saw the words "Unternehmen Barbarossa" in heavy type on the front page of a thick document. He sat down to read, making notes as he did so. Three hours later, the document was in a diplomatic bag being carried by courier to Switzerland on the first leg of its journey to the State Department in Washington. Woods had included his own assessment of the document. His source had previously proven to be reliable, but the attaché found the contents of this document incredible. His source had been turned. This was a plant.

At intelligence headquarters in Washington, officials rapidly came to the same conclusion. The document contained details of a planned German invasion of Russia in June, just three months away. With characteristic thoroughness, the plans detailed the panzer and Luftwaffe units involved, the main invasion routes for infantry and armour, and a breakdown of the logistic requirements, including the amount of fuel and food required for the campaign. Finally there was a timetable: the invasion would be completed by the end of November, when Moscow would fall to the encircling German armies.

Cordell Hull drew up the first response to the document with his officials. There was no reason on earth why Hitler should turn on his wartime ally and commit his armies to a campaign in the east. Such a strategy made no sense at a time when the Nazi leader needed only to knock Britain out of the war to complete his mastery of western Europe. The alliance with Stalin gave Hitler access to the Russian oil fields in the Caucasus – why would he fight to get what he already had?

Despite the ideological differences between the two nations, Hitler had proved himself the master of hardheaded realpolitik. The alliance with Russia gave him a free hand in Europe and North Africa – there was no reason why he would break it now.

Military intelligence also analysed the document and concluded it was a deliberate deception. Analysts in the Department of Defense pointed out that the extraordinary detail in the supposed Barbarossa plan indicated it was a fake. The German High Command would never have allowed such compromising information to be put on paper so far ahead of an operation.

The president was informed of this German attempt at strategic deception in the daily intelligence summary, delivered by the head of a new national intelligence agency, as yet unnamed. The Germans were trying to disguise the fact that the invasion of Britain was planned for early summer. That was Hitler's real intention. The president nodded. It made sense.

Leonora Finch met Stobart in an office at the upper end of Baker Street, the third address he had used in their infrequent meetings. She had been telephoned at her Pimlico lodgings and asked to report. Unlike on previous occasions, Stobart was welcoming, almost friendly, as he ushered her to a chair and offered her a cigarette. She had thought carefully about what she was going to say but decided to find out what he wanted first.

Stobart looked the same as when they had first met a year earlier, the same ash-flecked cardigan, long grey hair, and those lidded lizard eyes. He talked briefly about the weather – it was an unusually warm spring after a bitter winter – and he enquired solicitously about her well-being, whether she had enough ration cards for food and clothes.

"Thank you for coming, Miss Finch. This is a regular review and I want to say straightaway that your work is very valuable to us," he said.

She watched the blue smoke rise slowly to the ceiling. She didn't know who "us" was, but there was no point in asking.

He told her that Harry Hopkins had personally expressed his gratitude to the prime minister for her work as a liaison officer. She may not have realised the importance the government attached to Hopkins's welfare while in London, but it was a high priority for the prime minister. She had done an excellent job.

"I was really only his driver, sir."

He smiled at her. That was the point, he said. The U.S. embassy had been pressing Hopkins to accept one of their own staff as his driver ever since he arrived. The offer had been turned down. The embassy had insisted. Mr Hopkins had again refused.

"The embassy seems to think we are trying to keep an eye on our important guest to see who he is talking to, get an idea of his views on the war."

"Are we?" she said.

He smiled again and offered her another cigarette.

"How do you get on with him?"

"He is a good man but overworked and very tired."

"Anything else?"

"I don't know what you mean."

"Let me put it this way: your relationship has become . . . shall we say, closer, has it not?"

God, they must have been watching – at the air base, that night at the hotel. Did someone creep up the stairs and press an ear to the door, or had they recorded those intimate moments at the Bournemouth hotel?

"I admire him."

"Exactly, and quite right too," said Stobart, getting up to pace the room. "He is an admirable man and a good friend of this country, wouldn't you say?"

"He has made that clear publicly in many speeches – to the Fleet Street editors, for instance," she said.

Stobart turned quickly and took two strides to his desk, turning again to face her and leaning back against it.

"Exactly. That is what he is saying in public," said Stobart. "But are those also his private thoughts? Do they inform his reports to the White House, I wonder?"

She had always known this was what they wanted, although with the ambiguity beloved of those working in the dark world of intelligence, they never made it clear. They wanted pillow talk, the casual indiscretion that might reveal a deeper truth. What was Harry Hopkins really telling his president? That's what they wanted.

"I have no idea what he is telling the president, but I don't doubt Mr Hopkins's sincerity when he says he wants America to do everything to help win this war."

"I am sure you are right, but there are certain people, senior people, very senior in fact, who would like, shall I say, reassurance on that point. Mr Hopkins in the past has expressed very strong views on the British Empire, what he calls the class system, and the need for social change. He is possessed of radical views."

"That was before the war, surely."

"Oh yes, of course, but one wonders whether he still holds such opinions . . . ?"

He looked at her, his eyebrows raised slightly.

"I wouldn't know, sir."

"Of course not, but you would tell us if you did, wouldn't you?"

She nodded and lit another cigarette. She had had enough.

"I want to ask for a transfer, sir."

He looked surprised. "Transfer – to what?"

"Commander Ramsden mentioned a unit called the Inter-Services Research Bureau. I wish to join it."

"Let us suppose such a unit exists – and I'm not saying it does – why would you wish to join it?"

"When we first met, you told me that there might be a change of policy, that women might be recruited for operational duties."

"Did I really say that?"

He appeared incredulous. What a ham actor, she thought. Their conversation had certainly been taped, so he would know exactly what he had said, and no doubt this conversation was being recorded as well.

"I want to fight in this war. I want a real job. I want to make a difference. I have fluent French. I know this unit is recruiting women to work as agents. That's what I want."

They sparred like two fencers, Stobart declining to acknowledge the existence of the Research Bureau, Leonora repeating that she wanted a front-line role in the war, not a backroom job as a driver. The conversation became circular. Stobart became impatient.

"Let me put this to you: Mr Hopkins is due to return to

London in a few months, maybe sooner. That is what the prime minister wants. Are you telling me you wish to be replaced as his liaison officer when he is here next?"

She coloured slightly and paused. "No, I would like to complete that assignment," she said quietly.

"Exactly. Shall we leave it that when you have completed that assignment, there may be some consideration given by certain authorities, of whom I am personally unaware, to the role you have mentioned?"

"Thank you, sir."

"And please remember the unit you mentioned does not officially exist."

"And this conversation has not taken place?"

He smiled in agreement. She was one of them now.

II

The spring of 1941 brought a catalogue of military disasters that fell on Winston Churchill like winter wolves on a snowbound traveller. Those were his words to Brendan Bracken as the two men examined the maps in the War Room beneath Downing Street. Yugoslavia and Greece had fallen to the Germans. Intelligence reports indicated that the British forces in Crete would be unable to repulse an expected German invasion of the island. Across the Mediterranean, Hitler's favourite commander, General Rommel, was driving his Afrika Korps towards the frontiers of Egypt, the rear base for British military operations in North Africa.

In the Far East, Japan was openly preparing to move against the British in Malaya, Burma, and Singapore. Churchill knew that Hitler saw Japan as a claw in the pincer movement to destroy the British Empire before he turned the full fury of the Wehrmacht to the home island. Meanwhile the Blitz continued to take a terrible toll on British cities. Devastating raids on Glasgow and the docks in Clydeside had left two-thirds of the population homeless. The RAF had struck back with a raid on Cologne that was carried out by almost one thousand

bombers, but the poorly trained aircrews had suffered griev-
ous losses and missed many of their targets.

Worse still, as far as Churchill was concerned, the Battle
of the Atlantic was being lost. U-boats and German naval
forces had gained the upper hand. The graph plotting the
loss of merchant ships over the previous twelve months was
climbing towards the top of the chart, leading to one grim
conclusion: by the autumn the government would be forced
to draw down its stockpile of canned and dried food to avoid
widespread starvation among the urban population.

The one small ray of light was that the Lend-Lease bill had
finally been passed by Congress and signed by the president.
But the many amendments had pared away the effectiveness
of the legislation and Churchill had received disturbing reports from the British embassy in Washington that it would
be many months before armaments would be delivered from
American factories. In the meantime, Britain could expect
little more than canned meat and egg powder from her bene-
factor.

Roosevelt had placed a wealthy American named Averell
Harriman in charge of the aid program, then retreated to his
bedroom, where he spent hours examining his stamp collection. He was a sick man suffering from a chest cold he could
not shake off. For days on end he refused to see cabinet members. Churchill had never heard of Harriman and had wanted
Hopkins to implement Lend-Lease from London to ensure
Britain got what it needed. The president demurred. Harriman would go to London to oversee the supply programme
and Hopkins would "advise and assist" the president in Washington, dealing with a military establishment that was increasingly reluctant to send any war matériel across the Atlantic.

Hopkins had pleaded with the president to reverse the decision, but to no avail. Roosevelt was adamant.

"I'm not having you drinking brandy all night with Churchill," he said. "It's bad for your health. Besides, I need you here."

Like every American who first saw 10 Downing Street, Gil Winant was amazed that what looked like a decrepit doll's house could be the centre of Britain's political, military, and imperial power.

Washington's new ambassador to the Court of St James's had been invited to meet the prime minister on the first morning of his arrival in London. He had hardly had time to sit down at his desk in the embassy before the phone rang and Brendan Bracken introduced himself. The prime minister would be happy if Winant could join them for lunch at twelve thirty. It was nine thirty.

Winant agreed. He had not even met his own staff yet. Evidently they could wait. This was a summons, not an invitation. He needed to prepare for his first meeting with the prime minister. He had been advised that Churchill's mood was swinging between desperation and defiance and that his exasperation with Roosevelt's procrastination was leading to outbursts of volcanic anger.

Bracken made the introductions, and Winant seated himself in an armchair facing the prime minister across the hearth of a blazing coal fire as champagne of a remarkable vintage was poured. They waited while the butler stoked the fire, refreshed the glasses, and brushed cigar ash from the great man's waistcoat.

"Bugger off, Sawyers," said Churchill amiably.

"Very good, sir," said the butler, promptly leaving the room.

Churchill turned towards Winant with a smile, raised his

glass in a toast to Anglo-American friendship, bade the new envoy a warm welcome, and, having lit a cigar, leant forward with a scowl.

Winant braced himself for an assault on the bedridden president, hostile Congress, and isolationist American public.

"What exactly is Spam?" asked the prime minister.

Winant could not help but laugh. To his relief, he saw that Bracken had joined in.

"Canned pork of the highest quality and very nutritious, Prime Minister. Why do you ask?"

"Because you are sending us thousands of tons and, try as I might, I cannot see how it is going to help us win the war. We cannot fire canned meat at the Germans."

The ambassador relaxed. The prime minister was enjoying his own joke. And Winant had to admit, it was a clever way to make a serious point. He could neither evade the question nor answer it. Lend-Lease had won grudging congressional approval, but what was actually going to be loaded onto British ships for the perilous journey across the Atlantic was an unanswered question. And Churchill had been right. To the mystification of the dockers in Liverpool and Glasgow, large quantities of Spam, an unknown food in Britain, had been unloaded in the first consignments.

By the time the three men sat down for lunch, a second bottle of champagne had been opened and they had been joined by the prime minister's daughter Sarah. Winant watched as Churchill unwound in the company of his third child. Sarah was young, beautiful, and unhappily married, so he had read in his briefing notes. He wondered whether his own marital difficulties had been mentioned in the brief about him that would have been prepared for Churchill.

Sarah poured wine for her father, smoothed his hair, and placed her hand on his arm. He beamed benevolently around the table, forgetting for the moment the Spam and the disasters of war in the world beyond. It was like watching a magnificent old cat being stroked and purring with pleasure in response.

"The point is, Gil, I feel I must meet the president, face-to-face. Letters and telegrams simply are not good enough," said Churchill as the port was passed around at the cheese course.

The ambassador was now "Gil": he had been accepted; Churchill liked him. No, thought Winant, he's too clever for that. He may like me, but he also needs me; he needs the president, but what he needs most of all is guns, shells, ships, and armoured vehicles – and not Spam.

Winant was well aware of Churchill's pressing need to see the president and was equally aware that there was nothing further from Roosevelt's mind. Indeed, it was hard to determine what was on his mind. After a meeting with the president before Winant left for Britain in early March, he had begun to wonder just how committed Roosevelt was to Britain's survival. The president had dismissed calls from two senior cabinet members, Stimson and Knox, to deploy U.S. warships on Atlantic convoy duties. Roosevelt seemed transfixed by the isolationist America First Committee and fearful of the public support they commanded. Lindbergh was the committee's leader and a highly effective campaigner who praised Germany's technological achievements under Hitler and openly described fascism as "the wave of the future." Blue-collar America was warming to Lindbergh's pro-appeasement views and many communist-dominated unions followed the party line after the Nazi-Soviet non-aggression pact of the previous year. Roosevelt's greatest fear was that he was losing the support of his political heartland, organised labour, which had propelled him to victory in three presidential elections.

Winant did not dare tell Churchill that even inner White House loyalists such as Hopkins were said to be losing faith in the president's ability to counter the isolationist campaign. He appeared paranoid about the wholly unrealistic threat of impeachment; he waffled in speeches about the international crisis, gave muddled answers to straightforward questions about the need to reinforce embattled democracies, and did everything to suggest to the American people that Lindbergh and the appeasers might actually be right.

"The president has forgotten his own great words: 'The only thing we have to fear is fear itself,'" Hopkins had told Winant. "You tell Mr Churchill that I am on the president's case."

Winant had tried, but Churchill had hardly listened. He was weary of hearing how Roosevelt was ill or tired or somehow beholden to isolationists.

"That's why I must meet him," Churchill growled as he and Winant went into the War Room after lunch. Churchill went straight to a large map of Europe and stabbed his finger at Poland. "Look," he said, pointing to four small red circles close to the Russian border. "These are former Polish air bases now taken over by the Luftwaffe. They have lengthened the runways in every one. The reports are absolutely reliable."

Churchill looked at Winant as if seeking an answer to the mystery of the red circles.

"Why?" said the ambassador.

"To allow heavy bombers and transport aircraft to use those runways. But that doesn't *really* answer the question. Why, Gil, why are they doing it? The Soviets are their allies to the east; to the south they control the Balkans, while to the north lie the barren wastes of Scandinavia. It makes no sense."

• • •

Harry Hopkins was slowly thawing out. He had arrived from London encased in a shell of frost and ice, exhausted, unfeeling, uncaring. He had hardly kissed her in the first few days of his return or shown any physical desire for her at all. Louise told her friends it was as if an explorer had gone to the mountains and returned as the Abominable Snowman. Now the snow was melting to reveal the man she had known and loved. Louise Macy watched as her fiancé – and she kept having to remind herself that they were engaged to be married and that she had an emerald ring to prove it – came back to life.

He began to laugh and make jokes. He insisted on doing the things that delighted her but bored him: an evening at the ballet, a visit to the Smithsonian art museum, a walk in Rock Creek Park. He slipped his arm around her waist in the park and held her close. She hated horse racing but relented and accompanied him to the Pimlico racetrack in Baltimore, where he went to great lengths to explain his system of betting and how to pick winning horses. His tactic was to scatter two-dollar bets on rank outsiders, choosing the horses on the basis of names he liked. He laughed as he lost money, claiming he would make it up on the next race. She liked to see him relax like that, crack jokes with his racing friends, drink a few beers, smoke too many cigarettes, and become again the old Harry Hopkins.

Except that he wasn't. "People change," her friends told her. "Your man is under huge pressure in the White House. He is beginning to doubt his own master and hero, the president. No wonder he is different." But that explanation did not quite assuage her doubts. The love light no longer glinted from those grey eyes. They looked darker now, more distant, the colour of ash after a coal fire.

She did not reveal her worries to Eleanor Roosevelt when they met for their weekly tea in the White House. But as usual the president's wife was very frank with her own opinions.

"He's become a warmonger," said Eleanor. "I do not like to use those words, but that's a fact. It's all he ever talks about to the president. No wonder the poor man has taken to his bed. Everyone is telling him to send guns to Churchill, to convoy ships across the Atlantic, arm the French Resistance – don't they realise we have a constitution?"

"Maybe the war over there is changing people. I – "

But Eleanor wasn't listening. She was a strong-minded woman who placed a high value on her own opinions. She had not finished with Harry Hopkins.

"I'm sorry, Louise, but I must just say this: When I first met Harry he was an idealist, a campaigner, a man driven by a desire to bring about social justice, to lift the poor from the ghettoes and give them a real life. Now I see a man who seems to have fallen for that reactionary old drunk Winston Churchill."

"But surely, Eleanor, there is a war. We are fighting fascism," replied Louise Macy with a hint of irritation.

Eleanor Roosevelt waved her hands in exasperation. "I know, I know. I am asking too much. I am a hopeless muddled old romantic and of course we have to fight Hitler, but I just think we have lost Harry."

"I know how you feel," said Louise Macy quietly, but Eleanor did not pick up on the remark. They had a second cup of tea and returned to the question of the wedding. That summer was looking difficult, given the pressure of work within the White House.

"But it has to be a summer wedding. We can dress the Oval Office with flowers and at midday the sun comes right in through the windows!" exclaimed Mrs Roosevelt.

So it was decided that Harry Hopkins was to marry Louise Macy the following year, in the summer of 1942. The women decided not to tell the prospective groom of the delay for the time being.

Hopkins usually worked from a small room close to the Oval Office. Every morning a jug of coffee, a clean ashtray, and a pack of his favourite Camels would be placed on the desk, along with overnight cables from major U.S. embassies around the world. He always read the dispatches from Britain first and paid special attention to the ambassador's personal report.

He smiled to read that Winant's first lunch with the prime minister had followed the same alcoholic path as his own. It was when the port was offered for the second time that Winant said he felt his legs beginning to lose all feeling. He had been amused by the reaction of Sawyers, who seemed to have a controlling influence on Churchill. When the prime minister had insisted that the port be passed around again, Sawyers had interrupted.

"Is it possible, sir, that this gentleman has work to do this afternoon?" he had enquired.

Winant expected an explosion at this insubordination, but Churchill had merely muttered, "Don't be so bloody impudent, Sawyers."

Sarah Churchill had laughed at the exchange. Winant saw a love of life and a delight in mischief sparkling in those blue eyes. She had rid herself of her husband, she had said, some adulterous bandleader, and was now a free woman.

Winant had taken care to exclude such personal observations from his report, but he included every other detail of his first meeting with Churchill. Hopkins read the report to the end, pausing at the point where Churchill had stabbed his fingers at the map of Poland.

He got up and walked down the corridor to the Oval Office. The president was still in his bedroom. A large globe stood on a stand by the window. He twirled it to Europe and looked at Poland. If Churchill's information was correct – and there was no reason to doubt British intelligence in this matter – then his mystification was understandable. Why was the Luftwaffe extending those runways?

The door to the bedroom opened and Roosevelt wheeled himself straight to his desk, seemingly unsurprised to find Hopkins examining the globe. The two men exchanged the normal greetings and Hopkins waited while the president lit a cigarette, shuffled papers on his desk into some order, and began reading. Hopkins took a seat on the sofa and waited.

After a few minutes, Roosevelt said without looking up, "What's on your mind, Harry?"

Hopkins told him.

The president put his papers to one side and raised his head. Hopkins spoke quickly.

"There was a paper a few days back on German plans to invade Russia, but everyone agreed it was a deception operation. I guess it is the same with those new runways, if they exist. Don't worry about it."

That night Hopkins opened the folder named "Operation Barbarossa." Circulation had been restricted to the president and officials within the State Department and Department of Defense. He had had to use the authority of the Oval Office to get the file from a reluctant William J. Donovan, the new intelligence chief about to be given the anodyne title of Coordinator of Information.

If this was a Nazi deception strategy, they had certainly put an enormous amount of work into it. Not only did the document provide minute detail of the invasion plans, but to support the hoax the Germans were lengthening runways in Poland. Was Churchill right that this didn't make sense? But then Churchill had not seen the Barbarossa document. Donovan, State, and Defense had concluded it was a deception and the president had agreed, so why distract an embattled prime minister with it? That evidently had been the argument.

It did not take long for Hopkins to persuade the president to send Churchill the Barbarossa file. It was placed in the overnight diplomatic bag to be sent to London. A new secure air route had been opened up between New York and the city of Bristol in the west of England, and it was flown by American military aircraft – a fact that had aroused hysterical comments in newspapers that were all too happy to provide a platform for the isolationists. Roosevelt had for once ignored their protests.

In the diplomatic bag Hopkins placed a letter to Winant within which was a second sealed envelope addressed to Squadron Officer Leonora Finch at the WAAF headquarters in London.

Dearest Leonora,

I hope you are surviving the bombs and the cocktails. We are very busy here, but I am saddened to be sitting on the sidelines seeing you all go through such terrible times. The bombing never seems to stop and I read that the attacks on Glasgow and the ports up there have taken a terrible toll. Life in Washington is so dull after London and I am ashamed to say I miss the excitement, the feeling of being on the front line with you all. I miss you so

much too. I have asked the president to let me return. He
is being difficult, but I am working on it.
    Take care and if you are driving Winant, look after
him – he is a good guy.
    With love,
    Harry

Leonora opened the letter in the canteen of the WAAF in
Vauxhall. She knew his writing and had almost given up
hope of hearing from him. She told herself that she didn't really mind if he wrote or not, that a brief casual wartime affair
was hardly out of the ordinary, and that he was going to get
married to Louise Macy. In any case, he was so much older
than her that the affair most certainly wasn't going anywhere,
so why worry? She told herself all those things as she ripped
open the letter and read it first quickly, skimming the words
for those that really mattered – "I miss you" . . . "With love"
– and then all over again, very slowly.

    The mug of tea cooled beside her. He missed her, or did
he just miss the thrill of being here in this bleak, blacked-out,
bombed-to-bits city? No, he missed her – and she missed
him. He wanted to be here on the front line – with her.

Leonora drove the Humber across Vauxhall Bridge, past
Victoria Station, to Grosvenor Square. Much to the irritation
of the American embassy, Winant had taken both Churchill's
and Hopkins's advice. She was to be the driver for the new
ambassador. She picked him up and drove to a small house
on Chester Street. Sarah Churchill emerged, looking pretty
in a black-and-white taffeta dress, and joined Winant in the

backseat. Leonora flicked an eye in the rearview mirror. The prime minister's daughter had invited the ambassador to join a group of friends at the theatre for a Noël Coward production. Winant had agreed and offered to give her a lift. That was all. Leonora thought it was an unusual arrangement. The newly arrived ambassador was a craggy-faced middle-aged man with, so she had heard, a formidable wife back in Washington. Sarah was only in her twenties and supposedly married to the bandleader Vic Oliver, but, well, it was London, and the Blitz, and who cared about such things?

In any event, Leonora would not be driving for much longer. She expected to transfer to her new unit after the summer. Then she would begin her training – and a new life.

After the theatre Sarah Churchill persuaded Winant to take her to the Black Cat Club. At first he declined, saying that he had been advised against going anywhere near the place. Then she said Ed Murrow was bound to be there, the most handsome American in London, and she giggled. They had been drinking and Sarah was almost snuggling up to Winant in the back of the car.

"Do you know it?" she asked Leonora.

She drove the big car through the narrow streets of Covent Garden and wondered what had become of Ed Murrow and Pamela Churchill. They would probably be in the Black Cat that night as well. Two Churchills, the American ambassador, and a famous American broadcaster – all with their husbands and wives safely elsewhere. They would invite Leonora in, but she would decline. She was going to go home to her room in Pimlico, make a cup of cocoa, and read Hopkins's letter again. Then she would write to him. But how to get the letter to Washington? In the diplomatic bag. She would ask Winant to help. He could hardly refuse.

• • •

"Can this be true?" rasped Churchill, waving the document at General Ismay; Stewart Menzies, head of intelligence; General Alan Brooke, chief of the general staff; and Brendan Bracken. Max Beaverbrook was late, but Churchill had refused to delay the meeting. Beaverbrook was always late for meetings. The newspaper magnate had been Churchill's first choice as Minister of Aircraft Production but only on the understanding that he gave up day-to-day management of his papers. Beaverbrook had agreed but somehow always found himself in Fleet Street when the presses began to roll.

The Barbarossa file had been flown to London overnight and circulated to the inner group of Churchill's most trusted wartime advisers. All had been ordered to read and analyse the content before the morning meeting at Number 10. The previous day Roosevelt had given Churchill an overview of the contents in a secure phone call but had declined to provide details. Barbarossa was, said the president, almost certainly a deception.

Having read the document, Churchill was convinced that the White House had reached the wrong conclusion. But he dared not believe what he wished so much to be true. A German invasion of Russia might well overwhelm Russia and depose Stalin. But it would last all summer and give Britain desperately needed time.

And if the Germans took longer, if the Russians held out and the campaign dragged deep into the autumn, if General Winter appeared on the battlefield and did to Hitler what he had done to Napoléon 129 years earlier . . . If . . . if . . . if . . . The prime minister's mind raced ahead, hurdling the ifs and maybes, reaching for what a small voice of doubt told him was an absurdly optimistic conclusion: that the Führer was about to make the greatest mistake of the war.

If the Barbarossa file was true.

"Well?" said Churchill.

Everyone in the room knew what the prime minister wanted to hear. But most believed it impossible that with Britain bloodied and bowed yet undefeated Hitler would turn east and attack the ally with whom he had so recently forged a non-aggression pact.

The Führer was at the apex of his conquering power. France, the Low Countries, Poland, and the Balkans had fallen to the Wehrmacht. He could now move his troops through neutral but friendly Spain, seize Gibraltar, and close the Atlantic passage to the Mediterranean. From there he could springboard into North Africa to secure Rommel's rear and expel the British from the Middle East. And of course at any time Hitler could invade Britain across the twenty miles of uncertain sea that formed the Channel.

"It's too good to be true, Prime Minister," said General Ismay, Churchill's favourite general and chief of the military staff, a man he trusted to tell him the truth and not just what he wanted to hear. "But that doesn't mean it isn't true."

"What about the runways?" snapped Churchill.

He looked at Alan Brooke, a wartime colleague, a commander he trusted despite his tendency to substitute planning for action.

"There can be no other explanation for the extended runways, and this document confirms it. I suggest the Germans are going to invade Russia with up to a hundred divisions. From the evidence I would suggest mid-June."

Churchill brooded over these words as he paced the

length of the Cabinet Room, trailing smoke from the cigar in one hand while the other was stuck purposefully into his waistcoat.

"May I add something, Prime Minister?" said Menzies.

Churchill turned, head raised, knowing that the head of intelligence had waited until others had spoken or had the chance to do so before delivering his own information.

"The wives of the head of the German and Italian diplomatic missions in Moscow have left with their children and returned home. And the German ambassador has sent his dog back to Berlin as well. Apparently he and the animal are inseparable."

Churchill beamed at Menzies, sat down, and allowed Nelson to leap onto his lap. Stroking the cat with one hand, the premier reached for the empty glass with the other, but Sawyers was too quick for him. The butler filled the glass with champagne and turned to serve the others.

Churchill raised his glass in a toast. "A man might well send his wife away from a city such as Moscow – but his dog? Never!"

The bombing of London and other major English cities intensified through the black spring of 1941. Liverpool was pounded from the air for seven successive nights in early May, and a few days later, on May 10, six hours of bombing from midnight to dawn left fourteen hundred dead in London and eleven thousand homes destroyed. It was the worst night of the war in the capital. Londoners emerged from their shelters to find fires still burning in every part of the city, major streets made impassable by rubble, and great landmarks such as the House of Commons destroyed. Churchill

told Bracken it was as if Hitler was bringing the Blitz to a
bloody climax in a final attempt to break civilian morale before unleashing his bombers on Russia.

News of the raid came too late for the morning newspapers in the United States, which carried a few brief Stop
Press paragraphs. It was only when Ed Murrow made a special
morning broadcast on CBS that the loss of life and the extent
of the damage became known to Americans.

Harry Hopkins heard the familiar voice on the radio
while he was shaving that morning. Murrow told the story
of how he and his wife, Janet, had miraculously survived the
carnage of the previous night. They had joined friends for
dinner at L'Etoile in Soho. The place had been packed and
everyone was relaxing after the first really warm and sunny
day of the year. They walked through the narrow streets of
Soho after dinner, past bomb sites where houses had once
stood, to their local pub, the Devonshire Arms. It was a
moonlit night and Janet was nervous, but they decided on a
nightcap.

The air-raid sirens had begun to sound as their drinks were
poured, but they stayed in the bar talking to friends from the
BBC until they could hear the rumble of aircraft. Janet had a
premonition of danger and wanted to go home – do anything,
in fact, but remain in that pub.

Reluctantly leaving a large whisky on the bar but promising to return, Murrow had walked his wife to their flat only a
few hundred yards away on the same street. As they opened
the front door of the apartment building, they heard a noise
like the roar and whistle of a freight train speeding towards
them. They clung to each other in the stairwell as the bomb
exploded and the building shook violently. Brushing off
the dust and debris, they ran up the stairs to the roof of the
building. Their street was on fire from end to end – and the

Devonshire Arms had vanished in a cloud of dust and rubble.

Hopkins wiped his face off with a towel without finishing
the shave. He went to his bedside phone and asked the White
House operator to put him through to the State Department.

In London that lunchtime Gil Winant was handed a brief
cable while eating a sandwich at his desk in the embassy: "Trust
you and all staff safe and unharmed after last night's attacks.
Grateful you confirm likewise your driver OK to whom
please onsend kind regards. Harry Hopkins."

Hopkins had to get back to London. It was the only place to
be. He would tell the president that he was needed there to
arrange Roosevelt's face-to-face meeting with Churchill, one
that would signal to Hitler that the New World stood side by
side with what was left of the Old.

That meeting had assumed added importance in view of
the coming German invasion of Russia. The U.S. intelligence
community, if not the White House, had swung round to
Churchill's view. Hitler was most certainly going to invade
Russia, but when? And in any case, would it change anything?
If Stalin was quickly defeated and overthrown, Britain would
undoubtedly face the full fury of a battle-hardened Wehrmacht in the autumn.

A Russian defeat seemed all too likely to Hopkins. Although Roosevelt remained sceptical about the Barbarossa
information, he agreed it should be shared with the Russians.
Stalin refused to believe it, arguing that it was a trick by the
British and Americans to drive a wedge between him and
Hitler. As May moved towards June, not a single soldier was
sent to reinforce Russian units along the border with German-
occupied Poland.

Harry Hopkins felt the sweat prickle beneath his shirt as he descended the stairs from his room to the Oval Office. It was an unusually hot day for May, but the president hated air-conditioning. He was sitting at his desk in his shirtsleeves, reading documents and tapping ash into a brass bowl. The large windows behind him were open, and through one Hopkins saw a cloud of white blooms covering an old magnolia tree, the citrus scent of its flowers drifting into the room. Andrew Jackson was said to have planted that tree when he was president 110 years earlier. Jackson had beaten the British at the Battle of New Orleans. The present occupant of the White House wasn't lifting a finger to help their old foe in its trial with tyranny.

And Hopkins knew why. In all the discussions with Roosevelt about his difficulties with a hostile Congress and a public opinion still defiantly opposed to any involvement in a European war, they never talked about what the president regarded as a clear and present danger. The taboo subject in the Oval Office framed a fear Roosevelt dared not address openly: impeachment. For three months the backroom and bar talk in both houses of Congress had been of Roosevelt's high-handed attitude towards the Constitution. Isolationist members were quietly but openly talking of gathering the required votes for impeachment.

And Roosevelt knew he was vulnerable. He had given oral authorisation for secret Anglo-American military staff talks in Washington, which had begun in January. He had been careful not to sign any documents relating to those discussions, which were attended by a senior British delegation wearing civilian clothes. The talks outlined a grand Anglo-American strategy for war against Germany and Japan in the event of hostilities.

For Churchill the talks were further evidence that Roosevelt preferred "jaw-jaw" to "war-war." But such cooperation took the president perilously close to breaching the covenant of his office, a constitution that required congressional approval before entering any "binding agreements" that would commit the country to war.

Hopkins spent the remainder of the morning with Roosevelt in the Oval Office working on a major speech, which he hoped would give heart to the British and strike fear into the Nazi regime. He passed draft after draft across the mahogany desk. The president read them carefully and then produced his pen for the inevitable amendments, passing them back with the language and tone softened into ambiguity. Hopkins would try again, only to be met with the same crablike caution.

He looked out, past the president, across the Potomac to Virginia. When Abraham Lincoln had been president, that was enemy territory. At the height of the Civil War, the Confederate troops were camped there, just across the river. Now Roosevelt feared his enemies were closer still, in Congress, waiting to impeach him and drive him from office.

12

"He's done it again," Churchill said, with more of a snarl than a growl as he thrust the embassy cable into Gil Winant's hands. "I simply cannot understand how that great man can raise our hopes to the sky at night and then the next morning turn his back on everything he promised. Does the man know what he is saying? Explain him to me, Gil; tell me I am not dealing with a madman!"

The door to the library at Chequers opened and Sawyers appeared, as ever at moments of tension, with a bottle of champagne and glasses lined up on a tray.

"Mr Harriman has arrived, sir," he said, "and Cook says lunch will be in half an hour. Shall I serve drinks?"

"Drinks? Yes, of course. But now, Sawyers, not later," snapped Churchill.

"I never said 'later,' sir," said Sawyers. "Don't be putting words in my mouth. Mr Winant, sir?"

Winant accepted a glass, marvelling at the easy familiarity and rough-and-tumble discourse between the prime minister and his butler. Churchill used Sawyers to relieve stress, much as he used champagne before lunch, wine with the meal, and port and brandy afterwards for the same purpose.

"What have you done with Harriman, man?" said Churchill.

"He's just washing his hands, sir. He doesn't rush like some people around here."

With that, Sawyers handed the prime minister a glass of champagne, placed the tray with the bottle and a remaining glass on the side table, and left.

The prime minister and his two American guests were joined at lunch by Brendan Bracken and Jock Colville.

The prime minister had intended to discuss Hitler's planned invasion of Russia with both Americans in the hope of eliciting their view as to how Roosevelt would respond to such an extraordinary change in the course of the war. But as everyone around the table was quickly made aware, Churchill's mind was consumed by Roosevelt's speech two nights earlier from the White House East Room, when the president had pledged every possible assistance to Britain and to all who, with Britain, were resisting Hitler with force of arms.

To the delight of the British government, the president had gone so far as to specifically pledge naval patrols to ensure the delivery of much-needed supplies to Britain and had promised to take necessary additional measures to deliver the goods. It was those additional measures that had caused elation in 10 Downing Street. It could only mean that American military aircraft would join their naval forces in actively fighting the U-boat menace in the North Atlantic. America was on the path to war. The Yanks were finally coming. As Churchill had said to almost every visitor to Number 10 that morning, "You can count on America to do the right thing, having exhausted every other possibility."

But it was not to be. At a press conference the morning

after his speech, Roosevelt casually retreated from his statements and airily dismissed any suggestion that the U.S. Navy would be deployed on convoy duties or that the Neutrality Act would be revised to allow U.S. forces a more active role in the Battle of the Atlantic.

The president had warned neither Harry Hopkins nor any other close adviser of his change of mind. Hopkins had immediately cabled the U.S. embassy in London, urging Winant to see Churchill at Chequers that very day. Winant should describe how wounded and weakened Roosevelt had become by the isolationists' long and savage campaign against him. He should explain to the prime minister that despite the passage of the Lend-Lease bill, Congress was still strongly opposed to any American intervention in the Battle of the Atlantic, and he should remind Churchill yet again how the executive branch was beholden to the legislative in all matters relating to war. Above all, he should make the prime minister understand that the president's tactics were dictated by domestic politics, but his strategy remained that of assisting Britain in every way to win the war against fascism – in every way except committing military forces. To ensure the message got through, Hopkins copied the cable to Brendan Bracken.

Churchill was not mollified by this information. His anger had been pouring over the table throughout lunch like volcanic lava and had not been cooled by the flow of wine. He now held up Hopkins's cable.

"Wounded and weakened! Wounded and weakened! That's us here in this island, not the bloody president of the United States of America. The bombs are not falling on Washington, are they? American ships are not being sunk in their hundreds by U-boats, are they? There are no invasion barges on the banks of the Potomac, are there? What is the man thinking?"

Winant and Harriman listened, uncomfortably aware that they agreed with the sentiments, if not the language, of the prime minister. They were privately appalled that Roosevelt had in such cavalier fashion advanced bold policies in one breath and renounced them in the next. They could do nothing but express their sympathy to the prime minister – and drink with him.

Churchill knew he had gone too far. His remarks were bound to find their way back to the White House and cause further upset. He admired both Americans at the table. They were men of high achievement and wide influence who understood and supported Britain's cause. They seemed almost embarrassed to be serving a president whose physical paralysis had become a metaphor for his lack of political will.

Neither man seemed embarrassed, however, by the way their private lives had become entangled with Churchill's family. He frowned. Gil Winant, gaunt, good-looking, a full head of dark hair that belied his fifty-two years, was sleeping with the premier's daughter Sarah. Poor, sweet, lost Sarah, trying so hard to right herself after a wounding marriage to that feckless, adulterous shit of a bandleader.

And then there was Harriman, who seemed to have replaced Ed Murrow in Pamela Churchill's bed. The premier adored Pamela and hoped she might straighten out Randolph, but his son had continued drinking, gambling, and womanising after the marriage much as before. And now he was at the Eighth Army's rear headquarters in Cairo, though safely removed from any fighting. Pamela could hardly be blamed for seeking solace elsewhere – but with Averell Harriman?

Bugger this war, Churchill thought. It is turning everything upside down. But he had no time to worry about the sexual shenanigans of his family. More important by far, he

needed to delve deep into the mind of the man who was trying to impose a new age of tyranny on the Western world.
What really lay behind the silly moustache, the cowlick of
hair over the forehead, the rigid adherence to a teetotalling,
vegetarian lifestyle, the furtive affair, if affair it was, with Eva
Braun, and the insane hatred of Jews?

Was there madness or method in the way he had awak-
ened bloodlust in the German soul? And was it madness or
an act of military genius to turn now, with Continental Europe at his feet, on his vast neighbour and ally to the east? It
was no ploy. Radio intercepts had revealed that the Wehrmacht had moved three armies close to the Russian border.
Still Stalin refused to heed the warnings. The only questions
that remained were when the blow would fall and whether
the Russians could hold out for more than a month.

"Another glass, sir?"

Sawyers was at his side, bottle in hand. Churchill looked
around the table. They had been watching him in his brief
reverie, waiting for the next outburst, but his anger had gone.
He beamed at them and nodded at Sawyers.

"Gentlemen, let us go next door and take some coffee by
the fire."

Harry Hopkins spent Saturday, June 21, at the races. Louise
Macy had gone to New York for the weekend with friends.
He was quietly relieved that she had overruled his muted
protests about her departure. Now he could enjoy himself
with a few old friends at the track and lose money over a beer
or two without seeing the faint disapproval in her eyes.

That morning he had left the president at his desk with
magnifying glass in hand going through stamp albums. The
Blitz over London had stopped several weeks earlier.

Leonora, he knew, was safe and was said to be driving a senior member of General de Gaulle's Free French staff. Winant had finally given in to the embassy and agreed to have an American driver.

The only message Hopkins had received from Leonora – at least he assumed it was from her – was an anonymous little poem, just four lines, which had been written on Claridge's stationery. The verse, like the envelope, had been handwritten in blue ink, and seeing the British stamps carrying the head of George V, Hopkins had taken it from the pile of mail in his in-box and ripped it open hurriedly.

Sleep in Peace Tonight
Remember we who fight
The fiery death that falls
From London's dazzled skies.

Hopkins smiled and folded the letter carefully, placing it in his wallet. It had to be from Leonora. He had not written to her for weeks because he dared not. He did not want to admit awkward truths to himself. In any case, what could he tell her that wouldn't contravene wartime censorship in Britain? That he felt better than he had for months? That the doctors finally seemed to have found an effective treatment for the debilitating stomach disorders that had weakened him since his surgery for stomach cancer? That the president still stubbornly refused to let him return to London? That Eleanor Roosevelt reminded him of his Oval Office wedding next summer almost every time they met?

He returned to the White House at around ten o'clock that night with twenty dollars in winnings and hopes for a nightcap to celebrate with the president. But Roosevelt had gone to bed and was not to be disturbed. Louise had left a message with the switchboard to say that she and the girls were going to a show and that he must come with her on the next New York trip. Otherwise there were no messages. The only sound was the distant hum of a vacuum cleaner. A security officer nodded to him in the corridor as he went to his room.

He turned off his bedside light at about ten thirty, by his later reckoning, and was woken by the switchboard thirty minutes later. The duty officer at the State Department reported that radio intercepts indicated that the German invasion of Russia had just begun. It was four in the morning Eastern European Time. Hitler had launched his attack just before dawn.

Hopkins was exultant. He would have done a cartwheel across the floor if he could.

The president's policy of tacit support for Britain had paid off. Hitler had turned to the east. Churchill had breathing space. And the president could now get to work on Congress and begin to mobilise public opinion for the fight that lay ahead. Should he wake him? He had the authority but decided against it. The next morning would bring the full picture. The State Department would be swamped with frantic cables from the embassies in Berlin, Moscow, and London. The Department of Defense would be scrambling to analyse the German order of battle and the strategy behind it. Radio stations and the press would be putting out wild stories and demanding briefings. Hopkins got out of bed, lit a cigarette, and paced the room. The war in Europe had come to the White House. This was the president's opportunity for decisive action.

At Chequers that Sunday morning, Churchill studied the same information with deepening gloom. The overwhelming force of the German attack, the lack of any response by forward Russian units, and the complete silence from Moscow pointed to a swift Soviet defeat. The question was no longer whether Russia could hold out until winter but whether Hitler would be in the Kremlin by late summer. In which case, Churchill had been warned by his chief of staff, the Wehrmacht could redeploy its armoured forces to the Channel embarkation ports within four weeks. They would be battle hardened and with high morale. The invasion could therefore be launched in late September before the storms of autumn made the sea crossing impossible.

The prime minister had been joined by General Ismay, General Alan Brooke, and Lord Beaverbrook, all of whom had been summoned when the news first broke. Together they looked over roller maps that Sawyers had unfurled on a long table in the library. As Beaverbrook remarked to no one in particular, they were looking at the largest invasion in the history of warfare. For once lunch had been forgotten.

Churchill jabbed an unlit cigar at the Finnish-Russian border, where the northern flank of the three-pronged invasion was under way. The objective was clearly Leningrad. The cigar moved down to Poland, the central battlefront, where the ultimate prize was Moscow. And in the south, the third prong was striking from Romania deep into the Ukraine, heading for Kiev. The invasion was only nine hours old. There were no reports of resistance anywhere.

The men stared at the maps in silence, trying to grasp the enormity of the forces that Hitler had unleashed and the incredible fact that until the very last moment Stalin had refused to believe what his intelligence agents and commanders had been telling him for weeks. The German military buildup on the border had been obvious to everyone but the man in the Kremlin. No one ever dared give Stalin news he did not wish to hear.

Alan Brooke finally broke the silence. "If it's any comfort, Prime Minister, we hear that Hitler overruled his generals, who wanted a single united drive against Moscow. He opted for the three-pronged attack to divide the Russian armies."

"Comfort?" snorted Churchill. "Look at the map, man; they'll be in Moscow in a month." He turned to Lord Beaverbrook. "Max, what do you think?"

"We've got to give them everything we can. Trouble is, how do we get it there?"

Churchill turned his back on the group and walked to the bookshelves lining the room, pulling out a large encyclopaedia and riffling through its pages.

"Sawyers!" he shouted.

The butler appeared, although no one in the room knew where he had come from, since no one had seen the door open.

"What do you make of this, man?" said the prime minister. "One hundred and twenty-nine years ago almost to the day, on June 24 Napoléon invaded Russia – what do you say to that?"

"Well, he came to a bad end, didn't he, sir. Would you like a light for the cigar?"

Hopkins took the call from Chequers over a poor line later that morning. The prime minister rarely spoke to the White House on the phone because of bad quality and the suspicion that the underwater cable across the Atlantic might somehow be susceptible to German eavesdropping.

Earlier that morning, he had sat down with Roosevelt for a breakfast of coffee and scrambled eggs, the only food the White House kitchen seemed able to produce at that time of the day. They were joined for coffee by Stimson and Marshall. The men studied cables from the embassies in London, Moscow, Berlin, and the Baltic states. The fact of the invasion was no surprise, but its scale was shocking. Over three million troops were crossing into Russia along an eighteen-hundred-mile front from Finland in the north to the Black Sea in the south. Three thousand tanks had been committed to the early stages of the assault. The armour was advancing rapidly and without opposition. In the first hours of the campaign the Luftwaffe had destroyed two thousand Soviet combat aircraft on the ground. The German High Command in Berlin was discreetly supplying this information and much more to the U.S. embassy, but it was not just Nazi propaganda. British radio intercepts confirmed the extent of the invasion.

"Harry, there are three things we must do immediately. Please convey this to the president. Together we must aid Stalin. Lend-Lease must be extended so that the Russians are given all our help to fight on until winter. Secondly, you must return to London at once in order to organise a meeting between us. The president and I need a summit to show the world that two great democracies will not be cowed by this bloodthirsty guttersnipe who has launched his mechanised armies on new fields of slaughter, pillage, and devastation."

As so often when he listened to Churchill, Hopkins felt he was hearing a speech in the making. The rich timbre of Churchill's voice was lost over the telephone line, but the words floated from the receiver in sentences that were clearly destined for a wider audience.

Hopkins agreed, conveyed the president's greetings to the prime minister, and was about to end the call when Churchill said, "And, Harry, you know what happened almost to the day a hundred and twenty-nine years ago? Tell the president this. . . ."

Roosevelt was in the Oval Office when Hopkins reported his conversation with the prime minister, including Churchill's belief that Hitler had chosen a fateful date for the invasion. Missy LeHand flitted in and out of the room, preparing for a meeting of the full cabinet at noon, the first such meeting on a Sunday she could remember.

The president listened carefully and said, "What do you think Lindbergh and that gang are going to make of this? They'll be pleased, won't they? Hitler turns on the Communists and gives the Brits a break, so there's even less reason for us to get involved. That's the way they'll measure it up, isn't it?"

For the first time in the many years he had served the president, Harry Hopkins was at a loss for an answer. Hitler had probably changed the course of the war in Europe by launching the biggest military campaign in history, and Franklin Delano Roosevelt was worried about domestic politics. Once again he had shown himself a prisoner of his own exaggerated fear of the isolationists. Once again he had shown himself to be shackled by instinctive tactical caution.

Hopkins changed the subject. "Mr President, may I direct you to the request that the prime minister has made? He has asked me to return to London."

Roosevelt noted the formal tone and the implied criticism that came with it.

"You may go to London," he said wearily. "Tell the prime minister that I am happy to meet him, but . . ." Roosevelt opened his cigarette case, placed one in the holder, and lit it. "You might also tell him that Napoléon didn't lose to the Brits at the Battle of Waterloo. He lost when the Germans turned up."

Harry Hopkins was not a man to conceal what was on his mind. It was his blunt speaking, his insistence on making the politicians and bureaucrats confront uncomfortable truths, that had made him so unpopular in Washington.

He was a populist from a hick town in the Midwest who relished his role as an outsider in a city of insiders. Franklin Roosevelt, the wealthy patrician insider, a man born for power and high office, swiftly saw how Hopkins's crusading politics neatly fit his own New Deal philosophy. Hopkins had campaigned for a revolutionary extension of welfare as a means of alleviating poverty, while Roosevelt, reinforced by his passionately liberal wife, Eleanor, had pursued the same goals through political manouevring in Washington. The president sought political achievement through serpentine ambiguity, while his adviser, confidant, and friend was never a man to dissemble. Harry Hopkins would ruefully tell friends that his Bible-reading, churchgoing mother had instilled in him values that forever denied him the chance of elected office. He could not tell a lie.

At dinner that night he told Louise that he would shortly be returning to London. He had considered saying that the president had ordered him to do so in the wake of the German strike into Russia, but she would have known it was a lie. She knew the president had resisted his frequent requests to be sent back to Britain. Eleanor Roosevelt, the president, and she were all of the same mind: Hopkins simply was not strong enough for another such mission. They had argued about this forcefully, she insisting that he was neither well enough to return nor needed at Churchill's side.

Hopkins watched her face darken as she absorbed the news. She raised her glass of white wine, drank deeply, put the glass down firmly on the table, and lit a cigarette, something she never normally did during a meal. Her face signalled her irritation, her forehead wrinkled in a slight frown and her mouth widened as if in a grimace of pain.

"He already has Averell Harriman and Gil Winant, and the embassy is bursting at the seams with Americans doing this, that, and the other. Why do *you* have to go?"

"The truth is that Churchill needs me there and the president has agreed."

Hopkins had been back in Washington for just eight weeks. She had seen little of him in that time, but at least he was out of harm's way.

"No, Harry. You mean *you* need to be there. That's the truth, isn't it? You can't stay away. You've been badgering the president for weeks about this. But why? You have so much work to do here in Washington and Harry" – she put a hand into his – "you have me here. Do I count in this? London is dangerous and – I know you hate hearing this – you're not in great health."

He stiffened. The one thing he hated was mention of his illness, the gnawing stomach pains that had been part of his life since a cancer operation four years back. They had taken out a portion of his stomach lining and told him to stop smoking and drinking and spend the rest of his life in a rest home. He had gone straight back to work, naturally, and never used his health as an excuse for taking time off. Even when he was in the Bethesda naval hospital, sometimes for several weeks, he still worked on his papers and would leave at night and dine with the president in the White House.

"The bombing has stopped. The Germans are using every plane they have on Russia. As for my health – darling, I wouldn't go if I didn't think I could do the job. Trust me."

She took his hand and looked at her fiancé: a middle-aged man riding off to war on a frail charger, a skeleton that almost rattled when it moved. Any other man would surely have stayed here, working with the president by day and looking after her at night. That was his clear duty. He knew what she was thinking and squeezed her hand gently.

"Close your eyes," she said, and raised his hand. He felt the ring slip onto his finger and looked down to see a gold signet ring inscribed with the entwined initials *HH* and *LM*.

She bent over the table and kissed him. "I understand why you have to go. But take care," she said.

13

It was a week later when Hopkins finally liberated himself from the ensnaring bureaucracy of Lend-Lease and White House last-minute briefings and boarded a plane to Gander in Newfoundland. There he was picked up by a new B-24 bomber on which he was the sole passenger as they flew across the Atlantic to Prestwick in Scotland. The new route cut days off the journey, but they had been thrown around in a storm over the Atlantic and Hopkins felt exhausted and ill when he boarded the small RAF plane for the final leg of the journey to the air base at Northolt near London.

He saw her standing by the Humber as he descended the B-24's steps. Silver needles of rain were bouncing from the tarmac. She was holding the door open and saluted without looking at him. His eyes were drawn to the officer's insignia on her uniform and the crest mounted on her peaked cap.

She turned to look at him. "Welcome back, sir," she said. "Sorry about the weather."

"Good to be here, Squadron Officer," he said. "It wouldn't be England if it wasn't raining."

Hopkins got in the car and she closed the door while an

RAF orderly loaded his luggage into the boot. She slipped into the driver's seat, turned the ignition key, and glanced in the mirror. He looked exhausted. He always looked that way. She had never seen him any other way and suspected that no one else had either.

"Where are we headed?" he asked, although he knew the answer. It was a Saturday morning and the prime minister surely would be at Chequers surrounded by ministers, advisers, aides, and family, the companionable entourage from whom he drew strength and whom he used as a sounding board for ideas, speeches, and war plans.

Only in the dark watches of the night was Churchill ever alone. Hopkins knew the prime minister abhorred solitude. He also knew the prime minister would be waiting impatiently for his arrival, for news from Washington, for insight into the president's real thinking about the new turn of the war. At least this time he had something to show the prime minister; not much, but it offered a glimmer of hope. And Churchill was not a man to look unkindly on a glimmer of good news.

"Chequers," she said.

"Are you staying there as well this weekend?"

Her eyes met his in the mirror, a flash of green below black lashes and arched eyebrows.

"Yes, sir. I have been asked to drive you to London tomorrow night. You're staying at the Savoy."

She drove as fast as ever along the tarmac ribbon of the A40, her body tilting with the curve on tight bends as if to counter the gravitational pull of the car. The summer countryside surprised him. He had supposed England at war to be an eternally bleak, grey, frozen wilderness of wrecked buildings, bomb craters, and bad food. But the rain had been a passing shower and under a hot July sun the fields not far from London were rich with crops waiting for harvest. A light wind rippled shades of gold and yellow across the tightly packed ears of wheat. The fields rolled up gently sloping valleys to wooded hills. They flashed past horse-drawn carts and an occasional tractor and through small villages with colourful pub signs. This was another country, not a country at war but one anxious for the hard work of the harvest.

Leonora had placed her cap on the front seat beside her, exposing her hair pinned into a bun. A few loose strands fell over her long, pale neck. Her knuckles were white as she held the big wheel, and when she shifted position as the car took a bend he could see she had painted her nails pillar-box red. No doubt her lipstick was the same colour. It was a convention rather than an order that members of the WAAF should not wear excessive facial makeup, lipstick, or nail varnish. But it was very much an order that they should maintain a professional distance from those for whom they worked. He looked down at his hands and felt the initialled gold ring on his finger.

Frank Sawyers met him on the steps of the great redbrick country house and led him inside. He turned to say good-bye to Leonora, but the Humber was already crunching over the gravel to the garages at the rear. He wondered if she would be included in the house party as before.

"The prime minister is in the study and will see you when you're settled in and ready," said Sawyers as he showed Hopkins to his room.

"What does that mean, Sawyers?"

"It means now, sir," he said, and Hopkins saw a slight smile crease his granite features.

Hopkins put his bags down and walked to the study. He settled for a black coffee rather than the welcoming glass of champagne and for an hour before lunch listened as the prime minister paced the small study, walking to and fro on a well-beaten path in the carpet and talking through a litany of bad news from every front of the war, including the desperate state of the nation's food stocks.

In the past, the climax of this rolling peroration of military disasters would have been the dire situation in the Atlantic, where nothing had changed and terrible losses continued. This time it was Russia and Stalin and the need to keep the Soviets in the war at least until the autumn turned roads into a quagmire of mud and the freezing winter snows could do their work.

"I do have some good news, however, Harry," said the prime minister, suddenly beaming with delight. "We reliably have learnt that not a single German unit has been equipped with winter clothing or engine oil needed to keep their armour moving."

It was Hopkins's moment to produce his own good news. He laid on the study table a torn-out page from the *National Geographic Magazine.* On it Roosevelt had traced in pencil a line that went north from the South Atlantic along longitude 26 degrees west, cut through the Azores, turned east, and curved around Iceland. The American navy would police the sector of the Atlantic west of the line, thus relieving the need for the British navy to convoy along the whole route, Hopkins said. This was the president's personal message to Churchill and one Roosevelt was sure would be warmly welcomed.

"And what does 'policing' actually mean?" said the prime minister. The smile had faded.

"It would not amount to actively engaging the enemy," said Hopkins hurriedly, trying to get the bad news out of the way. "However, it would mean U.S. naval ships actively tracking the presence of German subs or surface ships and reporting their movement to the convoy and their escorts."

Hopkins saw Churchill's face harden as he digested this piece of casuistry.

"But that is subject to further discussion," Hopkins continued hastily. "I think it fair to describe the president's policy as all aid short of war." He waited for the scowl to darken the round baby-like face, but Churchill suddenly smiled again and got to his feet.

"Well, let us have that further discussion over lunch," he said.

Churchill began the meal by proposing a welcome toast. He then asked Hopkins to give a briefing on Washington's view of the war and the president's intentions. Hopkins steered his way around the fact that had become obvious to all present, that Roosevelt intended to do nothing in a hurry. The lunchtime guests listened as yet again he tried to explain why the president had decided to make haste slowly over aid to Russia as well as just what his new policy in the Atlantic meant.

Churchill had heard it all before. He knew that the man in the White House was a cautious, cold-blooded political animal who was not yet prepared to take risks in his relationship with Britain. What Churchill wanted now was a summit of the two great leaders of the Western world, because then he, the prime minister of a nation facing the fury of Hitler's war machine, could inspire the leader of the most powerful nation on earth to join the fight for the freedom of the world.

Hopkins responded quietly, saying that he was happy to confirm that the president would meet the prime minister at Newfoundland in August aboard the pride of the U.S. Navy, the *Augusta*, while Churchill would arrive in similar fashion aboard his own flagship, the *Prince of Wales*. He watched a smile of contentment transform Churchill from a growling bulldog into a beaming cherub. Now the prime minister would have his chance to meet the man upon whom Britain's future rested face-to-face. Hopkins could almost see Churchill working on the spellbinding oratory with which he would stiffen the president's resolve to confront his political enemies and take America into the fight against fascism.

Churchill happily said good-bye to his guests at the end of the meal, but as Hopkins rose to leave the prime minister bade him stay. Sawyers cleared the table and left the two men smoking their cigarettes and cigars over the coffee and port. Churchill seemed half-asleep at the head of the table, an old cat dozing on a comfortable cushion. His eyes drooped and the cigar in his hand was left to grow a long grey tube of ash. Hopkins knew he was thinking about the *National Geographic* map and what it really meant. He decided to pre-empt the inevitable questions that would fall to him.

"I wonder if you could help me with a detail of military history, Prime Minister?"

The eyes opened. The grey ash fell onto the polished mahogany table as the cigar was lifted to his mouth. "Winston, please, Harry. Of course I can help you."

"May I ask whether Germans were present at the Battle of Waterloo?" he said.

Churchill sat up, looking puzzled, seeking the true meaning of the question. "Why on earth do you ask that, Harry?"

"Someone in Washington suggested that the Germans rescued Wellington when he was about to lose to Napoléon at Waterloo."

Churchill leant forward, smiling, and reached for the salt and pepper cellars.

"Someone in Washington? Perhaps we can give Mr Someone-in-Washington a lesson in history – Sawyers!"

The butler materialised as usual without the sound or sign of a door opening. "Mustard, please, Sawyers."

"Mustard, sir?"

"Don't repeat what I have just said – mustard, man, mustard!"

Sawyers disappeared and reappeared in seconds with a pot of mustard, which he placed on the table with a flourish.

"Goes well with port, does it, sir?"

For a moment Hopkins thought the butler had gone too far. Churchill glowered at him, then seized the salt and pepper and placed them some distance apart on the table.

"This is Napoléon on the hilltop overlooking the valley. The time is three in the afternoon."

The pepper pot moved across the table.

"And here is Wellington on the far ridge."

The salt cellar moved into position.

"And this" – he moved the port bottle in its silver coaster – "is the farm where British and French troops are engaged in fierce hand-to-hand combat. The battle turned on that fighting. And here" – he placed the mustard pot some distance away – "is Blücher, with his Prussian forces."

Churchill sat back, surveying the deployment of forces on the table.

"You can inform Mr Somebody-in-Washington that when Blücher finally arrived, the balance had already tipped against Napoléon. Victory was not certain but it was moving Wellington's way. The arrival of the Prussians made it certain."

A cloud of cigar smoke descended slowly on the battlefield. Hopkins knew Churchill was looking down on those heroic redcoats with their muskets, swords, and staves, troops beloved of their commander, Wellington, on his chestnut mount. Then, as now, the fate of Europe had been in the balance. There, around a ruined stone farmhouse, history had been made by a small group of men, their faces bloodied and blackened by smoke, their muskets out of ammunition, jabbing and stabbing with swords, clubbing with gun butts, punching and gouging with bare hands.

Hopkins looked at the bottle of port on its coaster, the two squat glasses glowing red with the last of the fine wine, the carefully placed condiments, and he too saw Napoléon flee the battlefield in his coach, heading into captivity and exile.

"It was a very close call, Harry. It could so easily have gone the other way. Damned close."

With that, Churchill rose, smiled at Hopkins, and left. There were tears in his eyes.

The rain arrived in the night, pattering against the windowpane riding on a wind that blew the drapes into ghostly shapes in the half-light of dawn. It was still raining when they left for London after breakfast the next morning. He had excused himself from another lunch, saying, quite truthfully, that he had an urgent meeting at the American embassy with Gil Winant. Churchill saw him off from the steps, cigar in hand, smiling, waving, with new battles ahead and Waterloo once again a London railway station.

Hopkins wanted to stop for coffee, or more likely tea, at the café where he and Leonora had paused briefly on their first journey to Chequers. He remembered the way every head had turned as she entered the place and how the diners continued to stare as they both sat down. That was the first time they had talked at any length. But now it was closed, so she drove on through the rain until they reached the out-skirts of London.

"We've got time for a coffee at the Cumberland, if you'd like?" She gave him a quick smile before looking back at the road; red lipstick had smudged onto her white teeth.

He nodded. "Good idea."

He wanted to talk to her. They had hardly exchanged a word in the hours she had been driving him since he got off the plane. It was as if there had been a pledge of silence be-tween them, as if their past was a secret in which they alone were complicit. What was it she had made him say? "I so swear." She had asked him to promise to work to bring America into the front line with Britain. And he had promised. He had crossed his heart in front of her, naked in that hotel room with the collapsed bed, and sworn to die. But once back in Washington all he had done was try to forget her.

At his desk in the White House it had been easy to erase memories of a little wartime fling on the far side of the Atlan-tic, easy to dismiss it as nothing more than a narcotic to deaden fear when the bombs were falling. It was said that everyone fell in love in London during the bombing; it was only natu-ral. It wasn't love, of course; it was just frightened people clinging to each other in blacked-out hotel rooms, on creak-ing beds, while the shrapnel rattled on the roof and the win-dows blew in. They called it love because it sounded better, because love somehow justified their betrayal, and they were both traitors, weren't they? Perhaps a few lonely, frightened souls had truly fallen for each other in those long nights. But not him; he was no different from the rest. All he had wanted was the pleasure of a warm, womanly body after the sirens had sounded and the whisky glow had begun to fade into fear.

And now he was back and she was in the front seat with wisps of dark hair falling over that long white neck and a smile smudged with cheap lipstick. She agreed to have coffee with him near Marble Arch, a short walk from Grosvenor Square and his appointment with the ambassador. He could have so easily and politely thanked her for the drive and offered some meaningless pleasantry about seeing her again sometime.

But he couldn't. He could not let her go. It was as simple, and as complicated, as that. They found seats in a crowded coffee shop where the tables were so tightly packed that every conversation was shared with people on either side.

Afterwards he walked from Marble Arch along Oxford Street for a while before turning towards Grosvenor Square. London had changed in the few months he had been away. The bombing had stopped, and unless it was his imagination, everyone seemed less war weary and exhausted. There were more people on the streets, and although they weren't smiling, they had lost that bewildered, fearful look that had been so prevalent in the winter. The damage was still evident, but some of the shops had pulled aside the makeshift shutters to display their goods, mostly women's clothes that appeared old-fashioned and dowdy compared with what was worn on the streets of Washington and New York. He realised he had forgotten to bring her a present and peered hopefully in the windows for a silk scarf.

The biggest change on his short walk was in Grosvenor Square. It had become a little America in the middle of London. Every accent on the pavement was American, from the clipped nasal New England twang to the slow Texan drawl. The clothes were smart: dark blue suits with big lapels and trouser turnups and button-down cotton shirts straight from American department stores.

On the doors of almost every one of the elegant eighteenth-century houses lining the square strange nameplates had been placed to conceal rather than announce the activities within. NORTH AMERICAN COORDINATED FOOD RELIEF PRO-GRAM; JOINT AMERICAN HOSPITALS TRUST AID PROGRAM; U.S. SCIENTIFIC RESEARCH FACILITY; OVERSEAS OBSERVER GROUPS ONE, TWO AND THREE. And everywhere American men and women with the stance, shape, and haircuts of military personnel were trying to look like civilians.

The embassy on the west flank of the square clearly had been unable to accommodate the new arrivals and had expanded to take over the whole area. Hopkins crossed the green gardens in the middle of the square wondering whether the isolationists realised what was happening in London.

He was late and Gil Winant took him straight into the main conference room for what was described as a "three-sixty situation report." There were fourteen faces sitting around the table and Hopkins instantly knew this was a meeting with a hidden agenda. He had been to many such sessions in Washington where the VIP guest had failed to spot the trapdoor in the middle of the room. Gil Winant introduced him and went round the table asking everyone to identify themselves. There were military attachés, air attachés, naval attachés, political attachés, and a man and a woman who loosely identified themselves with Bill Donovan's new intelligence service. They were all American. There was not a Brit in the room.

The typewritten agenda was handed round by a secretary who left the room. Hopkins scanned it and found the trigger to the trapdoor in Item 8: "The high risk of UK's continuing campaign in North Africa in light of invasion threat." He congratulated himself. You had to be a veteran of political warfare in Washington to see just what that meant.

The meeting droned through reports on Britain's food

shortages, the prospects for the summer harvest, the techni-
cal inadequacy of the standard anti-aircraft gun, and industrial unrest due to wildcat strikes that were holding up
production of war supplies in the north-east. The information was no more than a useful update on reports that he and
the president had already discussed at length. Every report
was a piece in a jigsaw that would, when complete, answer
the question that kept Roosevelt and his cabinet awake at
night: Could Britain resist an invasion if Hitler gained a
quick victory over Russia?

Leonora had told him that the Free French general she had
been driving was certain of a Russian collapse and a full-
frontal cross-Channel attack by early autumn. She had not
seemed worried and made him laugh with the account of the
Frenchman's attempts to seduce her. Champagne, scent, and
foie gras had all been used in the preliminary skirmishes, and
after every advance had been repulsed the assault had been
made under cover of large quantities of wine and a late-night
drive back from a special forces airfield in Hampshire.

"What happened?" Hopkins said, perhaps a little too urgently.

"He made me stop the car and climbed into the front seat.
I got him by the balls and squeezed hard," she said, laughing.
"It works every time."

They had talked for half an hour over cooling coffee that
tasted like stewed acorns. He told her how pleased he was to
be back in London, where he could do a real job and share
the excitement of working to the point of exhaustion with the
chiefs of staff, military intelligence, Lord Beaverbrook, and,
above all, the prime minister himself. It made the petty politics of Washington seem impossibly boring and small-minded.

They had chain-smoked nervously while the words flowed back and forth, getting tangled as one spoke over the other. They weren't listening properly; they were both eager to talk, she wanting to know whether there had been any movement on America's neutrality, he seeking news of life in London and how she had lost her job driving Winant. She said an American had been appointed as the ambassador's driver for security reasons.

"Security reasons?" he asked.

She smiled. "You Americans don't trust us; didn't you know that?"

He didn't tell her that he had suddenly realised in Washington how much he'd missed her, how the long hours in the White House, the late-night dinners with Louise, the weekend afternoons at the track, were like so many doors he was trying to close on the life he had led in London. He had tried to forget her and he felt ashamed. When they left, she said, "Aren't you going to ask me?"

"What?"

"What I did with all that champagne and foie gras?"

"Well?"

"I still have them in my digs."

He had laughed at that as he walked away, leaving her on a corner of Oxford Street, and he was still smiling at the thought of a champagne feast in a poky little room in Pimlico when he reached the embassy.

"We're on the B-17 item. Harry, are you all right?"

He looked up. All eyes were on him. The briefing was being given by an air attaché from the embassy.

"Sure," Hopkins said, and reached for the coffee, proper

ground coffee from Brazil, flown in with the rest of the supplies so essential to American life in wartime London.

The attaché explained that the previous December, when the Justice Department had manipulated the logic of the Neutrality Act and authorised the president to send Britain rifles and ammunition, the U.S. air force chiefs had smuggled six B-17 bombers into the consignment on the basis that they needed to be tested in wartime conditions to make them fully effective in the event of America entering the hostilities. Roosevelt had managed to keep the shipment from the eyes and ears of the press on the grounds of national security until the arms had arrived, but he had done so to a chorus of complaints from his own staff, advisers, and cabinet, all of whom had told him he was committing political suicide. Once the information had been released to the press, Roosevelt had ridden out the storm of criticism in the papers with a White House press conference in which he displayed his usual mix of folksy charm and political ambiguity.

The RAF had immediately trained on the B-17s, the so-called Flying Fortresses, and flown the bombers in combat. They were found to be slow and vulnerable to ground fire. The RAF had then made changes to the armour and armaments of the planes to increase their firepower but had asked the U.S. air force to pay for and ship in the extra weapons and armour plating required.

"So the question is, would any such agreement lie within the executive power of the president, given the legal requirement of the Neutrality Act?" said the air attaché, staring at Hopkins.

"It would. Do it," said Hopkins, looking at Winant and rolling his eyes to the ceiling.

There was a stir around the table as the meeting turned to

the next item, the Eighth Army campaign in North Africa. Everyone had a dog in this fight, thought Hopkins.

Winant put the issue simply: The deployment of the British Eighth Army in North Africa seriously weakened Britain's ability to defend itself against invasion. Churchill had already resisted very strong suggestions by the U.S. Joint Chiefs of Staff that he adopt a purely defensive posture to safeguard the Suez Canal and return some of the infantry and armoured divisions from North Africa to Britain. The reason for urging this course of action on the prime minister again was the latest intelligence from Germany. Hitler had kept back sixty thousand paratroopers from the Russian campaign. The Luftwaffe had also developed and was now flying a new Messerschmitt transport plane capable of lifting two of the heaviest German battle tanks at a time over a range of two hundred miles. Those two facts added up to a new German strategy for the invasion of Britain: airborne landings to seize key airfields along the south coast and the rapid introduction of heavy armour into such bridgeheads.

Hopkins listened as the attachés, the intelligence people, and the military experts debated the issue for over an hour. Ed Murrow had been right about that new heavy-lift plane. He was probably better informed than most people in the room. But no one around the table seemed to know what to do with the information. This was what happened when you placed fourteen people in a room and put a sign on the door saying "MEETING IN PROGRESS." Everyone had to have their say, nobody listened to anyone, and everyone had to repeat what they had already said.

Hopkins gave up on the meeting and thought back to coffee at the Cumberland Hotel. She had orders, she said, to drive him to the south coast the next day. The RAF was to conduct a large-scale daylight bombing raid cross the Channel. She must have very high security clearance to be given such information, he had said. Her orders had come from Number 10, she replied. That explained it. Churchill wanted him to see the RAF in control of the skies over the Channel. The prime minister wanted President Roosevelt's envoy to see Spitfires flying cover against the Me 109s while the bombers pounded away. Churchill probably knew all about the latest attempt by the Joint Chiefs to get him to divert forces from North Africa. The old man was well ahead of his young yet-to-be allies in this game.

Hopkins hauled himself to his feet. It was his turn. He was the president's man and they wanted to know whether the White House would agree to further pressure Churchill to strengthen the home defences.

"The sixty thousand paratrooper reserves and the Messerschmitt transport plane – has that intelligence been shared with the British?"

All heads around the table nodded.

"In which case, leave them to it. I have said this before: they are fighting this war and we are not."

He sat down and watched the disappointment ripple throughout the room. He knew that whatever he said would go straight back to the president and that was surely the reply he himself would have given. Roosevelt was not so much walking a tightrope as using it to strangle the British. Hopkins's mother had once told him how much her faith had been tested by her brother's death in the First World War. He felt Roosevelt was testing his faith, and that of many other close advisers, in this war.

They joined an observation post on the cliffs above Dover just after 11:00 A.M. He had slept on the way down and, looking at his watch, he could see the drive had taken just over two hours. They entered a small sandbagged hut whose walls were covered in maps of the Strait of Dover and the French coast between Calais and Boulogne. Mud had seeped through the straw matting on the floor and the air was thick with tobacco smoke. The room was in semi-darkness, lit only by two oil lamps swinging from a beam overhead. There were three men in the room wearing black military uniforms of a type Hopkins had never seen before. On one side, steps led to a narrow platform from which a long glassless slit window looked out over the sea and the enemy coast in the distance.

They were handed tea in chipped enamelled mugs while one of the observers explained their position on the maps. They did not mention the raid or ask what they were doing there. Hopkins and Leonora were given binoculars and told to focus on the cliff tops running west of Calais. There was a haze over the cliffs, but within minutes the Spitfires became clearly visible as flashing silver dots diving like birds of prey onto unseen targets on the ground and rising again to wheel and turn into another dive. The harsh drumbeat of anti-aircraft fire rolled across the water.

Hopkins watched the action, catching an occasional close-up of a Spitfire with the familiar RAF roundels on its deep wings.

"What are they attacking?" he said to no one in particular.

"The fighters are trying to take out the anti-aircraft batteries before the bombers arrive. The targets are a railway marshalling yard, possible embarkation points for the self-propelled invasion launches, shipping in the harbour, and anything that looks German, I suppose," said Leonora.

She stood next to him, hunched forward, gripping the

binoculars. Once again, he thought, she had been briefed about this outing in great detail.

Hopkins stepped down into the darkened room and lit a cigarette. An observation officer made notes while another man talked quietly into a telephone in the corner of the room.

"Come and look at this," she said. She was excited and swung round, beckoning to him.

He saw her face half-turned, eager, anxious, as she shifted from foot to foot in excitement. It was the same face he had seen in the moonlight on the little terrace behind that pub on the Thames, and on the dance floor of the Black Cat Club, and resting on the shoulder of the American pilot at the pub near the Eagles' air base. He remembered the way she had laughed when the bed collapsed that night and how she had stood naked against the light of the window in the hotel in Bournemouth. But each image and memory quickly faded as if part of a slide show that moved on too quickly. He could not locate her place in space and time. It was as if she were a creature of his imagination, a mythical being in a dreamworld beyond reach of reason. It was as if she were always somewhere else.

Yet there she was, across the muddy matting, silhouetted against the glaring sunlight visible through a slit window, turning and beckoning to him. Her flat black shoes were covered in mud, and flecks marked her seamed nylons.

He felt the air pressure change in the room as the sound of heavy explosions reached across the water.

"Come on," she said again, and put out a hand to help him back up the steps.

He saw the bombers coming in from the west, looking like black dragonflies skimming low along the cliff top before climbing to deliver their payloads. Clouds of smoke rose through the haze, and the noise of explosions and anti-aircraft fire thudded more loudly across the sea.

"It's our biggest daylight raid yet on the French coast," she said, putting down the binoculars and moving closer to him on the platform. "Mr Hopkins, you are looking at a little history here."

Hopkins grunted and stared into his binoculars.

She turned back to stare across at France, leaning out of the slit window, knuckles whitening on the glasses.

"Come on, boys, give the bastards hell!" she yelled, slamming a fist into the wooden frame of the slit window.

Heads turned when the tall figure walked into the Black Cat Club that evening. He had the kind of face you knew you had seen somewhere before but couldn't quite place. His well-pressed grey business suit stood out in a room full of uniforms. He looked around, evidently searching for someone, then stepped sideways from the door, resting his back against the wall, and waited. The room was crowded and people quickly turned from the familiar stranger by the door to their drinks. They knew that shortly Margot would sail across the room, through the smoke and jazz riffs, to determine the identity of the stranger and whether he was welcome or not.

"Welcome, darling. Are you meeting someone here?" Margot was almost shouting over the music.

The stranger shifted away from the wall and straightened up, thinking it best to offer his hand to this exotic lady with the peacock-feathered hat.

"Actually, I am supposed to meet Mr Hopkins here. He said eight, but I am a little early."

"Come in, darling, come in – have you got the key, darling?"

The man handed her the key, which had almost knocked him out on the pavement below, and allowed himself to be led to the bar.

"Whisky?"

"Thank you."

"Ahmed, the usual!" bellowed Margot at the bar. The fez-zed head dropped below the counter and popped up, a bottle in hand.

"Harry will be here soon, but I must introduce you. It's against house rules to be on your own here. Fiona darling – come here, sweetheart."

Mrs Worsley had detached a middle-aged lady in the uniform of the Wrens from a group of officers and pulled her over.

"Fiona, this is a friend of Harry Hopkins and he's American, and what did you say your name was . . . ?"

"James Stewart; people call me Jimmy."

"Jimmy, this is Fiona and she is something terribly important in the Wrens, but no one knows what she does. . . ."

Mrs Worsley paused and looked at the smiling face above her. Jimmy Stewart, he had said. *The* Jimmy Stewart? The hubbub was quieting as heads turned again to inspect the stranger who had suddenly become *very* familiar to every woman in the room.

They were looking at the garlanded Hollywood actor who had starred in *Mr Smith Goes to Washington* two years ago. James Stewart, whom the papers said was due an Academy Award for *The Philadelphia Story*, which had opened in British cinemas that spring following critical and popular success in America. James Stewart, a film star at the height of his fame, here in London in the Black Cat Club, wearing a smart grey suit and smiling the slow, easy smile that had captivated audiences since his early days at the MGM studio.

James Stewart picked up his glass of whisky and half-raised it to the room, acknowledging the attention. It was a rule of the club that very important people who were brought as guests or who came of their own accord, having been given the code, should be treated the same as everyone else. The only celebrity at the Black Cat Club was Margot Worsley, and she was not inclined to surrender her status to a visiting American film star.

"Come over here, darling, and tell us what you are doing. We all loved *The Philadelphia Story*." Margot took his hand and began to lead him into the middle of the room.

The door opened at that moment, and Harry Hopkins walked in with Leonora Finch. He had never met Stewart but had learnt from the embassy that the film star had travelled to London in defiance of his studio. Why no one knew. Hopkins had suggested a meeting and Stewart had swiftly agreed. Hopkins was almost as infamous in Washington as Stewart was famous in Hollywood.

He had insisted Leonora accompany him. She protested. She loved the club for what it had once been: a bohemian hangout for jazz-loving artists, writers, poets, and gossip-hungry journalists. She hated what it had become: a den of drunken, lecherous men in uniform who were forever talking a great war without any intention of fighting it. He had reminded her that as his liaison officer she was duty bound to join him for the occasional after-work cocktail.

Hopkins spotted Stewart and waved across the room. "Follow me," he said to Leonora. This time he was going to surprise her. This time he would show her something different, exciting, something even more memorable than Spitfires flying cover over bombers attacking German positions in France. He was going to introduce her to a Hollywood movie star.

They ended the night in a little Italian restaurant on a Soho back street. James Stewart told the story of how he had defied his forceful studio boss, Louis B. Mayer, to join the military; how he had been turned down on health grounds; how he had appealed the decision; and how he had finally been drafted. He had reported for induction on March 22 that year at Fort MacArthur in California. He said he was an accomplished civilian pilot and his aim was to turn his back on stardom for the duration of the war and serve with the RAF.

He spoke with such quiet conviction that neither Hopkins nor Leonora dared break the flow of conversation. He paused often to say that he was talking too much, but they insisted he go on. Leonora could hardly believe that here in the blacked-out city a man with a Beverly Hills mansion, an MGM contract, and glamorous actresses queueing to date him was telling them he had crossed the Atlantic to this dark and dangerous city to fly and to fight.

There was a silence when he had finished. It was almost midnight and they were the last in the restaurant. The grey-haired owner, who had already secured the film star's signature on a menu, made no move to eject them. Instead, he placed a bottle of Chianti on the table and shook James Stewart warmly by the hand.

"So, Jimmy," said Hopkins, "what are you doing here right now – I mean, you're in the army, aren't you?"

"Army Air Corps," corrected Stewart. "I took some leave because I wanted to understand what was going on here. I wanted to see if the Brits were really going to fight, because I sure as hell wasn't coming over here to stick my neck out if you were about to run up the white flag."

"Have you seen any white flags?" Leonora asked.

Stewart leant over the table, took the bottle, and poured them each a large glass. He raised it to them: "Hell, no. I have only been here a couple of days, but I have walked the streets of this city night and day. And I raise a toast to the bravest people I have ever met. You're in this to the bitter end – and so am I."

They drank and Hopkins said quietly, "There's a real fight on at home, Mr Stewart."

"Jimmy, please."

"Jimmy. The isolationists have got the president penned in. He needs help."

"So you think I should be back there speaking up for him?"

"There are plenty of pilots here and not a lot of Hollywood stars to take on Lindbergh and that gang back home."

"Spoken like a good White House man," said Stewart. "But forgive me for not agreeing. Plenty of good people *are* standing up against Lindbergh. Clark is one; he's really campaigning hard on this. He's talking up the need for us to get stuck in, and like me he plans to show folk back home that he means business."

"Clark?" Leonora said.

"Sure, Gable. He's coming over to fly as well. The studio is as mad as snakes. But there's nothing they can do; his contract doesn't say anything about not fighting in foreign wars between films."

He laughed a good, rich, deep laugh that went right back to hometown days in Indiana, Pennsylvania.

"But you see my point, surely?" said Hopkins.

"No, I want to be here, on the front line; that's the only way to fight this war."

"You're right," she said. "You're so right." Her voice was raised. She was slightly drunk, her face flushed.

Stewart looked at her, surprised by her vehemence. "Can I ask what you got those stripes for?" he said.

She shook her head and raised her glass. "I have done nothing for them yet," she said, slurring her words. "Here's to the front line."

James Stewart vanished from London as mysteriously as he had arrived. The press corps only learnt that the famous film star had been in their midst when he was back training at Moffett Field near San Francisco. Newly commissioned as a second lieutenant, he was interviewed on network radio and asked as usual why he had abandoned a luxurious lifestyle in Hollywood for the rigours of life as an air force pilot.

"I sneaked across to London recently," he had said. "Didn't tell anyone; I just went. I met good folks there and saw what was happening with the bombing and all. That told me I had been right all along. This is a war we all have to fight."

"Did you know James Stewart was coming over here?" Murrow fired the question across the breakfast table at the Savoy. He was irritated. Of course his friend Harry Hopkins had known. He knew everything. The White House had probably arranged the visit. It had been Roosevelt's way of rewarding a famous face and name who was speaking out against the isolationists.

Hopkins looked up from his plate of scrambled eggs. "Sit down, Ed. I've got a story for you."

Murrow pulled up a chair and beckoned a waitress for a coffee. "Well, did you?"

"No, as a matter of fact I didn't. He told nobody."

"But you met him?"

"Sure, but he wanted it kept quiet and that was the way I played it. Now, do you want to hear about this story or not? It's just for you."

There are few things a good journalist won't do to beat colleagues to a story. Murrow scribbled furiously on the back of a breakfast menu as Hopkins briefly outlined plans for the meeting between Churchill and Roosevelt, taking care not to give dates, locations, or any other details.

"You can't use it yet," warned Hopkins.

Murrow threw down his pen.

"For Chrissakes, Harry, you can't tell me stuff like this and expect me to keep it quiet!"

"I promise that you will be the first to break the story. We haven't got all the details yet, so be patient."

"OK, but tell me what they are meeting for. What's the agenda?"

"They need to get to know each other, Ed. Churchill wants to know what's really in the president's heart and mind, and the president likewise. These are two big egos, Ed, and it has to be handled carefully, but it is also a message to Hitler."

"Any press going on the trip?"

"No, but I'll keep you informed. Don't worry."

Murrow sipped his coffee, watching Hopkins forking egg into his mouth. The president's envoy was about to hurry off to another meeting at the embassy, then on to Number 10, and after that to the Ministry of Defence. This frail figure would lunch with some bigwigs, hurtle through more meetings – and Leonora would always be at his side, taking notes, sitting in on the most sensitive meetings and excluded only when Hopkins went one-to-one with the prime minister. In the evening they would drink and maybe eat at the restaurant Hopkins liked so much. They never charged him there. Hopkins was an American hero in London, well known for his crumpled suit, broad-brimmed hat, and endless cigarettes – and that smile quick to spread on his grey, gaunt face. He couldn't buy a drink or pay for a meal.

The man was in love. Everyone in the press corps knew it and so did the diplomats at the embassy. The FBI had agents in London and they had certainly reported back the same story. The president's envoy had fallen for a British girl twenty-six years his junior, a young woman whom the prime minister had assigned to him as his driver and then liaison officer.

Now that woman, Squadron Officer Leonora Finch, had become his full-time companion – and, Murrow reckoned, his lover. The two were inseparable, doing the official rounds by day and appearing at every party on the embassy circuit at night. London was at war, but the Blitz had stopped and the summer season was in swing. There was not much by way of food and fine drink, but that didn't matter; the gin was cheap and black-market whisky plentiful.

Everyone wanted an excuse for a party that July, and Hopkins was at the top of every invitation list. Harriman was on a mission for Churchill in the Middle East and Winant had buried himself under paper at the embassy, when he wasn't to be found at Sarah Churchill's small flat. Harry Hopkins was the favored American guest for London's wartime hostesses, when they could extract him from endless meetings with Churchill, Beaverbrook, or the service chiefs. And Leonora was always with him.

Murrow knew it all. It was a good story but not one he could use. That was not what worried him. Leonora Finch with her green eyes, she was what worried him. "Are you taking your liaison officer with you?" asked Murrow.

"Where?"

"To Newfoundland for this meeting."

"Sure. I can't do without her; she makes everything happen."

Murrow bit his lip and lit another cigarette. "Harry, let me tell you something."

"I don't have time, Ed." He got up and dropped his napkin on the table.

"Flight Officer Finch got promoted to squadron officer, right?"

"Right, so?"

"Well, it was not gazetted in the WAAF daily orders. All

promotions to officer ranks are published in internal announcements and circulated to the RAF top brass. They have to be – it's military regulations."

"How do you know?"

"I checked, Harry. I'm a journalist, remember? You can check it out too."

"So what are you saying?"

"I am saying maybe she's not in the WAAF."

Hopkins paused, swilled the dregs of the coffee around. "Spit it out, Ed. I hate riddles," he said.

"You two are real close. Maybe you should ask her who she really works for?"

Murrow got to his feet. He picked up his hat, leant across the table, and patted Hopkins on the shoulder. "Don't make me wait too long on that story, will you? I'll kill you if anyone else gets it first."

In the first week of the German invasion, Stalin retreated to his dacha outside Moscow, refusing to believe the disastrous news that was pouring in from the three fronts. He took no calls from his commanders, refused to see anyone from the Kremlin, and admitted only his secret police chief, Lavrenty Pavlovich Beria, to his presence. It was rumoured in Moscow that the Soviet leader had suffered a nervous breakdown. Government was paralysed and the leaderless Red Army was being annihilated at every contact with the invading forces.

It was Beria, the man who had masterminded the slaughter of the Soviet officer class in the thirties, who finally persuaded Stalin to return to the Kremlin and take command of his crumbling military in early July. The news remained grim. The Germans had captured Smolensk and bombed Moscow.

Their advance on the capital was slowed only by physical exhaustion and supply problems. The watching British and
Americans took some comfort from the fact that the Russian
leader was at last trying to rally his people with a call for a
scorched-earth policy to slow the invasion.

Churchill and his generals looked at the map of eastern
Europe spread as usual across the long table in the Chequers
library. As usual, he was using his cigar as a pointer. When
Hopkins entered the library, Churchill turned to him and indicated the small flag markers on the map. He had been invited
that weekend to complete the planning for the Anglo-American
Atlantic summit.

"We don't have long, Harry. They'll be in Moscow by the
autumn."

"If I may, Prime Minister." It was Ismay, his favourite general.

Churchill turned and nodded.

"We may be overlooking something. You remember that
Hitler's High Command had argued for a single overwhelming
thrust on Moscow and that he overruled them and insisted
on the three-pronged attack we see here."

"Go on," said Churchill.

"The Wehrmacht was right. An overwhelming thrust
through the centre would certainly have put Hitler in the
Kremlin by October at the latest. But with three armies moving on a eighteen-hundred-mile front, Hitler has a problem.
That's three armies to feed, fuel, and resupply with ammunition. It's a logistical nightmare. Much of the German supply
transport is horse drawn and slow. If the autumn rains are
heavy, as usual, General Mud will be a powerful ally."

Churchill said, "What do you think, Dill?"

The general shifted, looking down at the map. Churchill
always tested one general's opinion against the next.

"It's a fair point, but the Germans have momentum and high morale, and I don't see their advance slowing significantly before autumn."

Churchill prowled around the long table, examining the coloured flags from every angle: red for the Soviet armies; blue for the northern invasion front; green, Hitler's favourite colour, for the centre; and yellow for the south. He scowled. The minutes passed as he paced the room restlessly. The map yielded no answers. No one said anything, sensing that the prime minister's thoughts were forming into thunderclouds. He looked up, saw Hopkins, and smiled. Churchill seemed to have forgotten the presence of his favourite American.

"Come and cheer me up, Harry," he said, guiding Hopkins through the double doors to the study across the hall.

Churchill turned with relief to plans for his summit with President Roosevelt. The prime minister was excited. This meeting was to be a hinge of history on which the door to a new world would swing open, a world free from the tyranny of fascism and the racial hellfire that burnt in Hitler's mind. He and the president would forge an alliance that would send their two great nations into battle to liberate Europe.

Hopkins listened patiently, knowing as well as ever that the rhetoric flowing across the study was shaping into another speech. He also knew that Churchill's expectations of the summit were grossly optimistic. Roosevelt had no intention of sending a single American into battle to liberate Europe.

"I think, Prime Minister, that the president sees in this meeting an opportunity for you two to get to know each other better and understand how you can work together more closely."

Churchill must have caught the note of caution and paused. Hopkins knew Roosevelt better than anyone in the administration and probably better than anyone in America. And he was right. Churchill did not really know the enigmatic figure who presided over the world's richest and most powerful nation from a wheelchair. The prime minister needed to learn everything about the president. What hours did he keep? Was he a night person or an early-morning riser? What books were his favourites? What gift would be most appreciated in the White House? What could Mrs Churchill send Mrs Roosevelt by way of a present? What was his favourite food? What did he drink?

"I think it fair to say that the cuisine of the White House does not quite match the standard of Number 10 and Chequers, Prime Minister," said Hopkins. "Mrs Nesbitt is famous for her spinach and scrambled eggs, but that's about all he eats."

"Spinach and scrambled eggs? Mrs Nesbitt?"

"The White House cook. She has been there forever. It's her favourite recipe."

"Perhaps I should take the president a gift of a new cook?"

They enjoyed the joke but decided in the end that signed copies of Churchill's early books would be a more diplomatic present. As the cigar and cigarette smoke drifted towards the ceiling, they pondered whether a good malt whisky might also be welcome.

"The president usually takes a cocktail in the evening. He rarely drinks anything else," said Hopkins.

He slid his cuff up slightly and glanced discreetly at his watch. It was almost lunchtime. There would soon be drinks in the drawing room; then other guests would join them for lunch. Sawyers would bring in bottles of fine wine. The prime minister would leave his glazed house party at around three o'clock and retire for his afternoon nap.

Hopkins wanted to get back to London in reasonable

shape for dinner at the L'Etoile restaurant in Soho. He had booked a special table in an alcove at the back, well away from the window. He did not relish Churchill's reaction when he insisted on having water at the table. Nor did he look forward to Churchill inviting him to describe to his guests the grand alliance that would be forged at the Atlantic summit. The meeting would change nothing in Washington. If anything, the crumbling Russian front had only convinced the isolationists of the need to stay out of the war.

Churchill thought cocktails were an abomination, a waste of good whisky, gin, and brandy. He decided to take the president a bottle of single-malt whisky in any case. "Do you think he'll appreciate that?" he said.

"Put it this way," said Hopkins. "He'll probably give it to me and I'll certainly appreciate it."

Churchill laughed. "We are going to make history, Harry," he said, standing up. "Let us join the others for a drink before luncheon."

He saw her enter the restaurant and look around. She ignored the small and officious maître d' with a clipboard who hopped from foot to foot in front of her, trying to catch her eye. Seeing Hopkins, she smiled, gave a little wave, and walked slowly through the restaurant, squeezing sideways past close-packed chairs. Diners turned and watched her progress to the alcove table at the back.

She was wearing a modest dark green dress with a white rose pinned to the lapel. Her hair was swept back, revealing a single rope of pearls around her neck. Her green eyes were lit by the colour of her dress. The women in the restaurant watched as she kissed him on the cheek and sat down by his side. They were a little too close and the kiss had been a little too firm for a meeting between father and daughter, the women decided; this was a lecherous middle-aged man who had made money on the black market and his young popsy.

They drank cocktails, toasting the friendship of their two countries, the health of the prime minister and the president, and finally the downfall of Hitler and his henchmen.

She giggled, feeling a little drunk.

"We haven't even ordered yet."

He slipped his hand onto her leg, pushed down against the skirt, and closed his hands on her thigh.

"I give you lust," he said, raising his third gin sling.

"And I give you my new job," she said, smiling.

He put his glass down.

"New job?"

"Yes. I am being transferred to a new branch of the service."

"You mean I am losing my liaison officer?" He took his hand off her leg.

She had needed the cocktails to tell him. She nodded.

"Don't ask me, please; it is secret. But I will be here in London and I will work with you until the end of your mission here."

Hopkins signalled the waiter. He needed time to think. He tried to remember exactly what Ed Murrow had told him. The waiter handed them long, elaborate menus printed on thick cardboard.

"Tell me about this branch of the service."

"I can't; I told you, it's classified."

"No, I mean tell me about the service you are transferring from."

"You know that, the WAAF."

"Leonora, they have no records of you."

"Are you ready to order?" said the waiter.

She sighed, glanced briefly at the menu, and ordered an omelette. Hopkins asked for grilled chicken.

"I know: it's complicated. I am officially a member of the First Aid Nursing Yeomanry, FANY for short. It is a high, grand name created in the First World War for some very brave women who rescued the wounded from battlefields. Now they train women like me as drivers, wireless operators, parachute packers, code breakers, all sorts, and we are transferred to various units."

"I don't understand," he said. "You were assigned as my driver and turned up in an air force uniform with one stripe on your sleeve. Then you got promoted, got two nice new stripes, and now you are transferring to a unit you cannot name from a unit that apparently doesn't recognise you."

She leant over, kissed him on the cheek, and put her hand on his. "Does it matter? It's wartime and a lot of silly secret stuff goes on. We're on the same side, aren't we?"

"Are we?" he said.

"Come here," she said, and took his face between her hands, pushing him back against the leather banquette and kissing him until his lips ached.

The women in the restaurant nodded to themselves. They had been right and, worse still, the couple were making an exhibition of themselves in a very smart restaurant. It was the war, of course. Young women thought they could get away with anything these days, and with all these foreigners and refugees wandering around at night in the blackout it was no wonder. The government should have closed the cinemas and dance halls, that's what they should have done, and then you wouldn't have flibbertigibbets like that tart over there with her hands all over that old man behaving in that way. It was scandalous. It was amazing the maître d' had let her in in the first place.

When Hopkins woke the next morning she had gone, leaving only a note that carried a row of crosses below the words "Leonora – always."

14

The report of Stalin's war demands was long and detailed, right down to the calibre of the anti-aircraft guns, which were his highest priority. Roosevelt went through the report carefully and noted that Harry Hopkins had not only revealed the strengths and weakness of the Russian military, but he had also done so by penetrating the dark heart of its monstrous leader, Joseph Stalin.

Hopkins had only been in Moscow for three days and yet his report had more information about the battlefront status and more insight into the thinking of that tyrant than the U.S. embassy had given Roosevelt in three years.

It was a classic Hopkins operation. He had been sent at short notice on a long and arduous flight from Scapa Flow in Scotland to the port of Archangel in northern Russia. From there he had flown to Moscow for two long meetings with Stalin. Hopkins had asked for minimal ceremony and had opened the first meeting with a single question to the Russian leader: What do you need in order to stay in the war with Germany?

Eight hours of blunt talking followed, spread over two meetings in the Kremlin. Some of Stalin's demands were politely dismissed. He wanted production lines of Soviet tanks established in American factories. Hopkins pointed out that this was practically and politically impossible. Stalin was well aware of this, Hopkins realised, but provoked the refusal in order to strengthen his request for the war matériel he really needed: a range of light anti-aircraft guns, 20mm cannon to upgrade the armament on his fighters, aluminium to manufacture planes, .50-calibre machine guns; the list went on and on. Hopkins enjoyed the bluff and counterbluff in the negotiations, which took place with just an interpreter present. No officials were on hand to take notes. Agreement was signalled by a handshake at the end of each meeting.

Roosevelt had been reluctant to let him go. The president felt Hopkins was not strong enough for such a mission and in any case should remain in London to work on the Atlantic Conference. Churchill had insisted. Hopkins was the president's man and Stalin would welcome such a high-ranking visitor. Keeping Stalin in the war was now Britain's strategic priority. Roosevelt disliked being gainsaid by the British prime minister but in the run-up to their summit decided not to argue the point.

Roosevelt put the list to one side. He had no intention of provoking the isolationist lobby by trying to meet Stalin's extravagant war needs. But he was interested in the man himself, the leader with whom one day he might have to sit down and negotiate a postwar settlement in Europe.

"Listen to this," he said to Missy LeHand. "Here's Harry on Stalin." The president adjusted his glasses and picked up a typewritten document.

" 'No man could forget the picture of the Russian dictator as he stood watching me leave – an austere, rugged figure in boots that shone like mirrors, stout baggy trousers, and snug-fitting blouse. He wore no ornament, military or civilian. He's built close to the ground, about five foot six and one hundred and ninety pounds. His hands are huge and as hard as his mind. His voice is harsh but ever under control. He never wastes a syllable. If he wants to soften an abrupt answer or a sudden question, he does it with that quick managed smile that can be cold but friendly, austere but warm. He curries no favor with you. He seems to have no doubts. He assures you that Russia will stand against the onslaught of the German army. He takes it for granted that you have no doubts either.' "

Roosevelt had plenty of doubts: about the outcome of the war in Russia, about the prospect that Germany would turn back to Britain again in September, about the poisonous rhetoric of the antiwar movement that was swaying opinion in Congress. Meeting in the Oval Office with his cabinet, he had even heard doubts whether they could get the Selective Service bill through Congress. The measure would extend the current twelve months' military service for young men. Without passage of the bill, America would not have a coher-ent army. Congress did not seem to care. The war seemed more remote than ever for most Americans, with the Japa-nese bogged down in China and the Germans driving deeper into Russia.

At least Harry Hopkins was back in London and the At-lantic Conference would finally give Roosevelt the chance to meet and measure the man who had kept Hitler at bay for almost two years. Roosevelt had read many briefings about Churchill as a wartime leader and as a man: his appetite for fine food and the best wines; his childish love of excitement, of action, of making things happen around him; his high emotion, which often made him cry openly and unashamedly; his intellectual ability to outthink his cabinet colleagues and his generals; his rash, impetuous decision making that had so often led to military disasters. But the president still did not know the inner man.

Roosevelt had cabled Hopkins, asking his opinion:

TELL ME IN A SENTENCE WHAT THAT MAN IS
LIKE, WHAT DRIVES HIM FORWARD, WHAT HE
REALLY BELIEVES IN. I STILL HAVE NOT GOT TO
THE HEART OF THE PERSON WITH WHOM I AM
TO SIT DOWN AND SPEND TWO DAYS IN CON-
FERENCE NEXT MONTH.

Hopkins had sent a brief cable back:

ALL YOU NEED TO KNOW ABOUT CHURCHILL
IS THAT HE HAS MOVED THE GROUSE-
SHOOTING SEASON FORWARD BY TWO DAYS SO
THAT HE CAN TAKE TWENTY-FOUR BIRDS
SUITABLY CHILLED ACROSS THE ATLANTIC TO
PRESENT TO YOU AS GIFT. HE CAN BESTOW NO
HIGHER HONOR ON YOU. HE IS A TRADITION-
ALIST WHO WILL BREAK TRADITION, A LEADER
WHO WILL CROSS THE PERILOUS WATERS OF
THE ATLANTIC TO MEET YOU, A MAN WHO
WILL AGREE WITH EVERY SENTIMENT YOU
EXPRESS ABOUT THE BRITISH EMPIRE BE-
CAUSE HE IS DRIVEN BY A SINGLE UNALTER-
ABLE TRUTH WHICH GUIDES HIM AS THE
EVENING STAR GUIDED THE THREE WISE MEN
TO JERUSALEM. THAT TRUTH IS THAT THE

BRITISH CANNOT BEAT HITLER WITHOUT
AMERICAN ENTRY INTO THE WAR.

The president had laughed when he read it and said to
Missy LeHand, "Ask Mrs Nesbitt if she knows how to cook a
grouse."

Missy LeHand looked puzzled. "Of course."

"And if she doesn't know, please ask her to get a good
recipe."

Throughout July, Hopkins attended the weekly meetings of
the British cabinet as the prime minister's special guest. Ob-
jections raised privately by a senior civil servant, Alexander
Cadogan, about this unorthodox arrangement were dismissed
by Churchill. He wanted the man he now regarded as a friend
at his side while planning the Atlantic Summit.

Roosevelt had initially suggested that the conference should
be an intimate, informal meeting between the two leaders with
minimal staff on either side. He also insisted that the meeting
be kept secret until the last moment.

Churchill robustly argued with Hopkins for a different
approach. The conference should be announced in advance
to the world as symbolising the union of two great democracies in the fight against fascism. He would travel with all his
military advisers aboard the battleship *Prince of Wales* to the
rendezvous in Placentia Bay in Newfoundland. There they
would discuss the great issues of the war: Japanese aggression
in the Far East, aid to Russia, the North African campaign,
and Lend-Lease. There they would shake hands, sending a
message to Hitler that Britain was no longer alone.

Arguments about the shape and purpose of the conference flew back and forth between Downing Street and the

White House that month. Hopkins found himself the arbitrator as two men with masterful personalities clashed in long secret cables to each other and short telephone conversations. British and American diplomats in each capital were manouevred like chessmen by their masters as each leader strove to shape the conference to his own ends.

Finally the matter was settled with creative ambiguity that suited both Atlantic partners. Roosevelt would travel to Newfoundland from Washington in secrecy under cover of a relaxing fishing trip. He would not inform his military advisers of the true nature of the trip until two days before the meeting. The aim would be a joint declaration of an Atlantic Charter announcing great principles of peace and war. For his part, Churchill would agree to keep the meeting secret, which in any case was essential given the presence of U-boats in the North Atlantic.

Hopkins stressed to the prime minister that the closing declaration at the end of the conference could not mention increased military cooperation between the two sides or suggest that America was moving closer to a combat role in the conflict. Churchill merely beamed benignly at such advice and said nothing.

Hopkins's life in those weeks was defined by a triangle of the Savoy Hotel, 10 Downing Street, and Chequers. He moved between these three points with an increasing burden of information about the Russian front, movements of the twenty German divisions still deployed in northern France, and fierce accusations from the isolationist lobby in Washington that Britain was selling Lend-Lease supplies to raise foreign exchange. Leonora no longer drove him on his frequent journeys to the prime minister's country house, but she remained at his side in London, arranging meetings, preparing briefs, ferreting out research from secrecy-obsessed government departments.

He had been given an office in the war ministry a few yards across Whitehall from Number 10. It was the usual featureless Civil Service office, with a desk, chair, bookcases, and paint-flaking radiators. The best thing about it was the view over the Thames through the plane trees at the back. Leonora brought a kettle and coffee percolator and, through the good offices of Frank Sawyers, obtained real ground coffee.

He had placed her name on the list of those travelling with the prime minister's party across the Atlantic. She had demurred, saying it would not be possible.

"I could talk to the prime minister about this," he said quietly.

"Please don't, Harry."

"This old bag of bones needs you. You hold me together."

He got up to put his arms around her, but she backed away.

"Don't be silly."

"I'm not. I'm trying to get two big beasts to drink from the same watering hole without locking horns. It's tough and the Atlantic relationship depends on it."

"Oh, I see," she said, smiling. "Now I am essential to Anglo-American relations, am I?"

"No, you're essential to me."

"Listen, Harry. James Stewart told us that he was training to come over and join the RAF and fly bombers against the Germans. He is a Hollywood star who is prepared to sacrifice everything for that ideal. That's his personal choice. My choice is the same. I want a real place in this war."

"I know, on the front line."

"Well, as close as damned possible. So don't try to stop me."

"And you won't tell me how you are going to do this?"

"On a need-to-know basis, Harry, even you don't need to know. Trust me."

She was just twenty-four years old and she was telling him what to do, or rather what she was going to do, against his wishes and judgement and no doubt against the orders he could undoubtedly bring to bear. There was no changing her mind. The green eyes were flashing red now.

Then she kissed him.

More than any other American journalist in wartime London, Ed Murrow wrapped himself in the British cause and the British way of life. Just as his nightly radio broadcasts had made him a celebrity in the United States, so he became a famous figure in London. Tall, lean, with dark good looks, he slipped easily into the camouflage of an Englishman about town. A corner of a white linen handkerchief pushed up from the breast pocket of his well-tailored Savile Row suits, and his shoes were from Lobb's of St James's. But above all his easy conversational manner made him a favourite, whether in his local pub or in society drawing rooms.

He enjoyed a pint of beer in an East End pub as much as a vodka martini at the bar of the Savoy. He told his audience in America of the fervent admiration he felt for the sheer bloody-minded guts of the ordinary working-class Londoner. He enthralled his listeners in America by allowing them to share startling imagery of London at war. Walking home in the rain early one morning after a raid that destroyed much of the city of London, he said during a broadcast, "The windows in the West End were red with reflected fire and the raindrops were like blood on the panes. This was a night when even the rain caught fire."

Murrow's fame and his passionate advocacy of the British

cause won him invitations to weekend house parties. Although many of the grand country houses had been taken over by the armed services, there were still plenty of shooting parties on the smaller estates close to London throughout the autumn and winter. Murrow took shooting lessons and quickly accepted invitations to blaze away with borrowed shotguns at pheasant and partridge.

His hosts were happy to have the most famous American in London and Murrow was equally happy to mix with the titled and landed English gentry. He guiltily admitted to himself that despite strong egalitarian political views, shaped by an impoverished upbringing, he enjoyed the company of dukes, knights, baronets, and their impossibly grand wives.

He told his wife that it was useful to get out of London occasionally and breathe air that was not acrid with smoke and the smell of burning. Janet dutifully accompanied him at first, but it soon became clear that her husband was the main attraction at such gatherings and her presence was a social obligation rather than a pleasure for her hosts.

So Janet Murrow remained in London most weekends, preferring her war work – gathering castaway clothes for refugees with Clementine Churchill and occasionally working for the mobile canteens that dispensed free food and hot drinks after a big raid. She teased her husband about the new wardrobe he had acquired for his country parties: hacking jackets, brogues, flat peaked caps for the shoot, and tasselled loafers, blue blazers, and expensive shirts from Jermyn Street for the evenings. "Dear God, look at you! Dressed like that, they wouldn't recognise you in Polecat Creek," she would say, and they would both laugh. She turned a blind eye to his fling with Pamela Churchill, telling herself that she had already really lost her husband to the Blitz. He sometimes wondered whether her indulgence of his own infidelity was because she had found solace with her own lover, but he immediately dismissed the thought. Janet was just too good, too upright, for adultery.

Even while in London Murrow was rarely at home. He spent his waking hours walking the streets, interviewing survivors of the latest bombing, and beaming their stories across the Atlantic. When the major bombing raids halted in the early summer that year, his relentless energy took him on tours of the country, visiting factories, schools, and hospitals, always seeking out human stories to illustrate Britain's perilous battle for survival. He would come home to their flat in Marylebone, his chiselled good looks diminished by the pallor of exhaustion, dump his dirty laundry, sleep a few hours, and then head to the BBC studio a few blocks away.

In their brief snatched conversations over coffee or at a local restaurant, when Janet could lure him away from his schedule, he would talk of nothing else but London and Londoners. "If this city falls to the Nazis, it will be Manhattan next," he would say, a view she had heard many times before.

There was another reason Murrow enjoyed his country weekends. The shooting parties brought together senior figures in the intelligence and military worlds. Murrow began hearing classified information about clandestine operations and secret units. Such talk took place well after the port had circulated and always in coded conversations. Nevertheless, as an American ally, a damned decent chap, and a reasonable shot, Murrow was taken into confidences that would never have been vouchsafed to any other member of the foreign press corps. Murrow enjoyed the gossip and the social life that went with it, but he was aware of the irony of his social celebrity in Britain: here was a kid from across the tracks in a dirt-poor town in North Carolina enjoying the clubby, class-dominated lifestyle of the English gentry that many Americans treated with contempt until they could embrace it.

Murrow was anxious to keep track of Hopkins. He wanted to break the story of the Atlantic summit in one of his broadcasts, and he was fearful that the news would leak to the British press first. He had asked his news desk at CBS in Washington to monitor White House announcements for any sign that President Roosevelt was changing his daily routine to travel to any unscheduled meeting.

Towards the end of July it was announced that the president would take a short fishing vacation on the New England coast in the second week of August. Roosevelt was known to love fishing trips and frequently found relaxation on board the presidential yacht, *Potomac*. The president's vacation that summer differed only in that he usually went south to Florida to fish. Ed Murrow was not informed of the brief White House announcement.

Throughout the war the Savoy and Claridge's duelled for the custom of the free-spending American press corps. In the summer of 1941 the German invasion of Russia brought a fresh wave of reporters, cameramen, and their assistants to London. They were joined by the growing U.S. diplomatic and intelligence presence in the capital. Now the bars, restaurants, and bedrooms of both grand hotels were packed with Americans. Harry Hopkins found his favourite bar at the Savoy had been transformed from a haven for a quiet drink into a nightly riot of unruly, questioning newsmen. The bar at Claridge's had gone the same way. It was impossible to hold a conversation amid the throng of thirsty journalists and embassy staffers.

He briefly considered moving his headquarters to the

Dorchester hotel on Park Lane, which had mostly been taken over by the wealthy and their families. Many had closed their London houses and moved in full-time for the duration of the war, bringing their servants with them. The attraction of the hotel was its underground levels, which provided bomb-proof shelter during raids. Hopkins soon gave up on the Dorchester. The residents gossiped in the bars and restaurants about nothing else but money, the shortage of servants, and the best place to garage their Rolls-Royces during air raids. He could not stand the place.

He and Ed Murrow fell back on the reliable Black Cat Club. It lacked the comfort and cocktails of the other bars, but Margot stuck firmly to her rule that no journalists were allowed except for Ed Murrow. He and Hopkins met there every week, and in late July, as they reluctantly pondered another of Margot's potluck pies, she drew them aside and whispered, "We have a few sausages tonight, darlings – frankfurters, would you believe? All the way from the USA."

"There you go, Harry – Lend-Lease is working," said Murrow, who laughed.

"Which makes it your round," replied Hopkins. He was not amused, since Lend-Lease was becoming a political millstone for the president.

The two men sat in their usual corner, ordered whiskies, and began the traditional jousting between those who held official information in the name of national security and those who desired it in the name of the public interest.

"So?" said Murrow, knowing he did not have to ask the question.

"I'm going to level with you, Ed," said Hopkins. "It's going to happen soon, but I can't tell you when or where. The president has demanded total secrecy. He hasn't even told his cabinet. Only Hull and Ickes know."

"This is the biggest story of the war, Harry. You can't sit on it."

"I can, Ed, and I am."

"All right, but tell me this – you're going?"

"Sure. I am travelling with Churchill."

"And you're taking your liaison officer?"

"I would, but she can't come. Why?"

"I just wondered."

"No, you didn't; you're trying to tell me something."

"Harry, you're fifty years old. This kid is twentysome-thing."

"She's not a kid. She's twenty-four. So what?"

So you're in love, you mad old fool, thought Murrow, in love with a young woman who was placed alongside you for exactly that purpose, to make you fall in love. And maybe you are right not to tell me any of your White House secrets, but what the hell have you been telling her?

Murrow tapped out a cigarette and tried not to think how many he had gone through that day. Three packs maybe, and it was still early evening. He passed one to Hopkins and both men snapped lighters and inhaled.

Murrow let the conversation die. When you are fishing for information, sometimes it is best to sit back and say nothing. Hopkins was miles away, lost with the fading cigarette smoke.

"It doesn't matter. She's ending her assignment with me and joining some unit," he said.

"Which one?"

"I don't know. Some secret outfit where she can do real war work, so she says, maybe even overseas somewhere."

Murrow admired Harry Hopkins. They were alike in many ways, men who had fought their way up from poor back-grounds to achieve powerful positions in public life. In any other situation he would even call Hopkins a friend. But this was different. A huge story was about to break and he, Ed Murrow, was going to be the first with the news. And he had just been given the lucky break that every journalist needs on a big story.

"I think I know which unit that is," he said.

Hopkins looked up, suddenly alert. "Go on."

Murrow leant back and blew a smoke ring to the ceiling. Take your time when you have a fish on the line.

"Deal, Harry? I tell, you tell?"

Hopkins paused, chased a smoke ring to the ceiling, and nodded. "OK."

"It's called the Special Operations Executive. Very secret, formed late last year and now launching sabotage and terror ops against the Germans and collaborators in Europe." There was a pause and then Murrow said casually, "They are recruiting women, Harry; it is the first time the ladies will have a front-line role in this war. Churchill has personally approved it."

Now he had Hopkins. The man looked shocked and drained his whisky, holding up the glass for a refill without shifting his gaze from Murrow. "Front line – that's what she always said she wanted."

"I know, I have heard her; that's why I am pretty sure that it's the SOE."

"How do you know this?"

"It's quiet talk in certain very well-informed circles, Harry, trust me. I mix with the right people. I listen and learn."

"What will women do in the SOE?"

"Same as the men. They'll be radio operators, couriers, and all the rest of it."

"The rest of it?"

"Cutting communication lines, blowing bridges, railroads, killing Germans – that sort of stuff."

Murrow watched the frown deepen on the haggard face.

"Deal, Harry?" he said softly.

Hopkins sighed and reached for his glass. It was empty again. He held it aloft and Ahmed hurried over to refill it.

"All right. Placentia Bay in Newfoundland, week after next," he said. "Just the two leaders and their staff – no journalists and no prepublicity. There will be a joint declaration afterwards, but there is no agreement on what."

"Are you sure? We haven't heard a squeak."

"You have, but you weren't listening. The White House announced the president is leaving next week for a routine fishing trip up in New England."

"Jeepers. You'll be there?"

"I told you."

"And you'll look after me?"

"I'm there to look after two very different, very difficult, very determined men, but, sure, I'll give you a call when I'm back in D.C."

Murrow cut short the evening, telling Hopkins quite truthfully that he needed sleep much more than whisky. He then went straight to his studio at the BBC and called his news desk in Washington.

"Did you get an announcement about a presidential fishing trip?"

There was a pause, a rustle of paper.

"Yeah, he's taking a week's vacation off the New England coast. The annual fishing trip."

"Why didn't you tell me?"

"Didn't think it was important – Why? Is it?"

"Never mind," said Murrow.

15

Leonora Finch received her orders to report to her new unit at a short meeting with Colonel Stobart in the same bleak office on Baker Street where she had last met him. Unlike at their previous meetings, he seemed disinterested, almost bored by their conversation. The folds of his eyelids drooped even farther, reminding her again of the lizards she had seen in the zoo. He thanked her for her work in the WTS and said that she would be contacted by Major Ramsden for the details of her training. All her current duties were to end with immediate effect and she would need to return her uniform to WTS headquarters in due course. She would be given a week's leave and would then receive a full briefing about the Inter-Services Research Bureau and undergo a final assessment as to whether she was a suitable candidate.

He looked up. "That is what you want, isn't it?"

"Yes, sir."

"Good," he said, and returned to his document.

She was not to mention the name of the organisation to anyone and, if asked about her war work, she was to say that she still had a job in a clerical capacity for the Women's Transport Service. He reminded her that she was no longer to wear her uniform or use the rank that went with it.

"Are there any questions?" he said, looking at his watch.

"Can I be clear? My job as liaison officer with Mr Hopkins is to end?"

"Yes."

"Why? It seemed so important the last time we talked."

The lizard eyes closed to slits.

"Certain senior people, very senior people, have no further interest in information from that source – and let's be fair, it wasn't as if you told us anything anyway, was it?"

"I think I did a very good job, but perhaps not one your department would recognise."

He smiled. She was angry. He admired that. She would have made an excellent agent in his own organisation, but now Ramsden had her. He didn't like the sound of the Inter-Services Research Bureau, which was in any case a ridiculous cover for the unit's real name, the Special Operations Executive, referred to by all in the know as SOE: all gung-ho madcap characters running around Europe with sticks of dynamite up their bottoms, trying to set Europe ablaze, in Churchill's words.

The prime minister loved this sort of derring-do and was as happy with the idea of the SOE as a schoolboy with a new train set. But it was madness, really. The Germans were already picking up SOE agents in Europe, torturing them, and breaking into local Resistance groups with the information obtained. This woman was going to be thrown into the thick of that mess. Ah well, such is war, he said to himself, and turned his thoughts to lunch at the Travellers Club.

"I would offer you lunch," he said, getting up to show her out, "but it's a sandwich at the desk today, I'm afraid."

She said she understood. If you live in a world of lies, it quickly becomes difficult to know what is true, she thought. But she didn't say that. She said good-bye and left.

Once out on the street, she gave a quick hop and a skip of pure joy.

They met at a little-used pub off Fleet Street and sat at a wooden trestle table on a warm evening at the end of July. She got there first and he was surprised to see she was not in her air force uniform. She was wearing a pleated blue skirt and sleeveless white blouse and sat with a half-pint of beer and a pencil poised over a newspaper crossword.

"Hi, stranger," he said, and flipped his hat onto the table.

"Hardly a stranger," she said, laughing as she remembered the surprising energy of this frail figure the last time they were in bed together.

He smiled and joined her. She was right. She was not a stranger. But he had not seen her for well over a week. He had missed her. They drank warm beer and smoked, and she told him what he already knew, that she was transferring to a new unit, and also what he did not know, that the transfer was with immediate effect. She was no longer a civilian.

"But there's a big conference coming up. I need you there."

"I'm sorry, Harry. I've told you I can't do it."

"Why not? You're my liaison officer."

She put a hand on his arm. "Not anymore. I have been transferred."

"I know. And I know where you are going. You're joining some madcap unit called the SOE."

She was surprised and took a quick look round the bar.

"You shouldn't mention that name. And you know I can't talk about it."

He leant forward and took her by the arm. "Look, I know this is what you want to do, get on the front line and all that stuff, but at least grant me this. Finish your mission with me. Come to this conference."

"Where is it?"

"I can't say. Overseas. The week after next. We will travel by ship in the prime minister's party."

She laughed. "Neither of us can say where we are going, can we? War makes us keep our secrets, I suppose. Come on, let's walk."

They walked the warm pavements through dusky streets, not knowing where they were going but following their footsteps. They looked into the cavernous nave of St Paul's, whose majestic interior had been stripped bare of tapestry and ornament. Above them Sir Christopher Wren's great dome rose over a sea of surrounding ruins. They walked past block after block that had been reduced to rubble until they came to the Monument, a tower of stone that marked the Great Fire of London 275 years earlier and had so far survived the present destruction.

"Dickens walked here," she said as they turned into Lower Thames Street and headed east, both now knowing their destination.

"He complained that every time he came along here, a beautiful small building had been pulled down to be replaced by something taller and more ugly."

"Good job he didn't go to Manhattan, then."

"But he did, and he loved it."

Somewhere beside the warehouses lining the dank streets beyond the Tower of London he took her hand, and she held it, swinging her arm in unison with his, until they came, as they knew they would, to that riverside pub.

It was late and the last of the light was settling on the

Thames as they entered and pushed through a group of medical students wearing their white hospital coats. A few tomato sandwiches curling at the edge in a smeared glass case were the only sign of food. Hungry from the walk, they bought two and a beer for her and whisky for him and went to the back terrace.

"It's Newfoundland off the Canadian coast," he said. "We're going on a battleship. You would have your own cabin. You would work with me, see history in the making. It would only take a week."

"I can't do it, Harry. I'm sorry." She wasn't looking at him, staring instead at the muddy flow of the river bearing driftwood, debris, and unseen bodies to the sea. She had been told that many victims of the Blitz were simply blown into the Thames by bomb blasts and never seen again.

"I may never see you again," he said.

"You will; of course you will. Why wouldn't you?"

"Because – "

She put a finger to his lips. "Don't say anything."

She drew the finger down his chin and kissed him.

"Tell me you love me," he said.

"I have never met a man like you in my life. You astonish me. You never stop, do you? It's as if you are carrying the weight of this war on your shoulders."

"And?"

"And I love you."

"Leonora. Look at me." He turned her towards him and cupped her face in his hands. "Marry me. Now. Here in London."

She stepped back and laughed a nervous, shocked laugh. "Don't be silly."

"I'm not. I'm serious. We will live in Washington together in the White House."

"But you're engaged to be married," she said.

"Not for long," he replied.

She shook her head and turned to the river.

"What, am I too old?"

She shook her head again and reached for a handkerchief from her handbag.

"Too old to fall in love?" he asked.

Leonora shook her head.

"Too old to make love to you?"

She turned and smiled. "You know very well that's not true."

"So?" he said.

"You're American and I want to live here in England," she said.

"I'll make a fine Londoner after the war," he said. "I want to see this city rise from the ashes."

"You don't know who I really am," she said.

"I know you were never a WAAF officer," he replied. "And I think the Brits have been using you. If I had been Churchill, I would have done the same thing. But I also know that what you feel for me is real."

Leonora coloured and turned away. "You don't understand. We have all lost too much. I can't leave now. We have to finish this thing, this war, this bloody, bloody business."

"Finish it with me. Side by side. We're in this together, aren't we?"

He put his arms around her, holding her close, and felt her soften in his embrace.

"I wish we were, Harry, I really do. But we're not," she said, breaking away. "We must go."

They walked wordlessly back to the main road and boarded a crowded bus heading west into the city. They climbed the stairs to the top deck and sat in the front where the windows had been wound down to ventilate the sweaty, smoky atmosphere. They didn't speak or look at each other. She held his hand until the bus reached the Temple Tube station on the Embankment. She rose and gave him a quick kiss on the cheek.

"This is where I get off. Good-bye, Harry."

He turned and watched her walk through the crowded top deck and vanish into the stairwell. As the bus moved away, he saw her climbing the steps to the Tube. She turned and blew him a kiss.

Franklin Roosevelt delighted in fooling the White House press corps. He had in the past allowed stories to be leaked about the huge size of the fish he had caught off the Florida coast and then jokingly publicly chided the journalists concerned when they printed such tales. On this occasion he went to great lengths to sustain the hoax that he was going on a summer fishing trip when he left Washington by train on August 3 for New London, Connecticut, where the presidential yacht, *Potomac,* awaited him. Details were given to selected correspondents of the type of rods and bait the president favoured and why he expected to find larger marlin and tuna in northern waters than off the Florida coast.

His only companions were old fishing friends who knew nothing of the historic nature of their slow, weeklong voyage up the New England coast. They noticed nothing unusual about the president except that he spent more time in his cabin working, he said, on his papers than he did fishing.

He had told none of his senior military advisers about the true nature of his holiday. Only an inner circle of his cabinet were made aware of the forthcoming summit. There were good reasons for such secrecy. He did not wish his first wartime meeting with Winston Churchill to be overshadowed by the inevitable uproar from the isolationist lobby. Newspapers across the country duly reported brief White House communiqués that the president was enjoying a well-earned rest aboard the *Potomac* and managing to catch fish.

It was only when the *Potomac* reached Nantucket Sound off Cape Cod and the battleship *Augusta* appeared with the accompanying cruiser *Tuscaloosa* that the real nature of the vacation became apparent. The president bade farewell to his surprised fishing friends and transferred to the *Augusta,* which immediately sailed for Newfoundland.

Except for his doctor and a naval aide, the president was unaccompanied. By then Winston Churchill and his party of thirty-five military, political, and scientific advisers were at sea on the *Prince of Wales.* The two leaders were sailing to the summit aboard their biggest battleships with very different views as to the purpose of their meeting.

Churchill shrugged off warnings of the presence of U-boats and treated the Atlantic crossing as a much-needed vacation. Harry Hopkins had remained in his cabin feeling seasick on the first night. The next day the prime minister commanded his presence in the stateroom and began a series of backgammon games that would continue until their arrival in Canadian waters.

Hopkins lost at backgammon just as he failed to persuade the prime minister that the real purpose of the summit was for the two leaders to get to know each other. Churchill thought otherwise. He was indeed curious to meet and understand the enigmatic character who had won an unprecedented third term in the White House, but the prime minister was also looking for a momentous agreement that would place the

United States at Britain's side. He wanted a mailed American fist raised to Japan in the Far East and a sword drawn to confront Hitler in Europe.

Hopkins reflected glumly that the clichéd stereotype of any meeting between a British and American statesman was about to be reversed. The blunt, plain-speaking English politician was going to be trumped by an American Machiavelli.

It was only when Churchill returned to England and retreated to Chequers to weigh the outcome of their meeting that he realised that all Hopkins's subtle attempts to lower his expectations about the meeting had been well motivated. President Roosevelt was not the comrade-in-arms Churchill had hoped for.

The ceremonial side of their meeting had been uplifting, almost spiritual. The president had greeted the prime minister standing on the *Augusta,* supported by his son Elliott and with his back to a deck rail. It was the first time anyone could remember the disabled president standing to meet a foreign dignitary. "The Star-Spangled Banner" had been played and a marine colour guard had presented arms. Churchill had invited the president to attend a Sunday church service held under the big guns of the *Prince of Wales.* The prime minister had personally chosen the hymns and prayers that were said and sung by British and American sailors under blue and sunny skies.

Lunches and dinners had flowed between the two sides. Hopkins was ever present at the president's side and attentive to his every need. Churchill noted this with interest and a pang of regret. Hopkins seemed a different person from the man with whom he had spent so many hours at Number 10 and Chequers, plotting the course of the war. Hopkins's loyalties now were very clear.

Roosevelt too noticed that his aide and confidant seemed to have changed, but in a different way. The president had worked closely with Hopkins for more than five years – in fact, hardly a day had passed in that time when they had not met, lunched, shared a cocktail, or just sat and talked in the Oval Office. Harry was White House family, Roosevelt used to say, but there seemed to be something wrong with Hopkins on this great state occasion.

When he and Churchill held their first meeting alone and without even secretaries to take notes, the president raised the subject.

"Harry seems a little off-colour," he remarked.

"He's tired. That Moscow trip took it out of him."

"We should never have sent him," said Roosevelt.

Both men knew that the emissary and counsellor from whom they expected so much was breaking under the burdens they placed upon him. Both also knew that Hopkins had accepted that price, allowing them to do likewise.

The eight-point Atlantic Charter issued at the end of the three-day summit was a declaration of principles that both sides agreed would govern the postwar world: liberty, justice, prosperity, and security for all.

Isolationists insisted loudly that there was a secret agenda to the summit and that confidential arrangements had been made to bring America closer to war. They brushed aside White House denials as blatant deceit.

In Britain people hoped that there were such secret arrangements, because they were more worried about renewed bombing and rationing than democratic ideals. Churchill tried to persuade his cabinet that he had at least achieved a good working relationship with the president and that the two men now knew each other better. He was in a stronger position, he suggested, to steer the United States into the war.

His ministers were sceptical and they were right. It wasn't true. After the conference the president had resumed his fishing trip off the Maine coast and airily dismissed suggestions that America was any closer to war. Instead, he pointed to the success of the meeting as being the affirmation of principles that would underpin world peace.

"Waffle waffle waffle!" snarled Churchill. He was alone in his study the day after his return. The V signs he had given the crowds, the triumphant statements to the press, and the glow of optimism that had carried him back across the Atlantic had become bitter memories.

It was the hour before lunch and the first glass of champagne had been poured. His guests had been delayed by a fallen oak tree across the main road a few miles from Chequers. Sawyers appeared.

"Did you call, sir?"

"Waffle, man, waffle – we can't fight a war with waffle."

Sawyers knew well the mood of his master; the black dog of depression was growling at the door to the study.

"Well, sir," the butler said, taking the proffered glass and refilling it, "I am sure you are right. But at least the Germans are sticking it to the Russkies and not bothering us."

Churchill contemplated Sawyers and not for the first time wondered whether the man was really a mental defective or just acting the part.

"Don't be a fool, man. They're on the move again. They'll have Kiev in a week and then it will be Moscow. And then where will we be?"

"I expect we will all still be here, sir. By the way, that nice Mr Hopkins left his hat behind."

Churchill wasn't listening. "Waffle," he said. "All we got was waffle."

He paused. What had Sawyers said – something about Harry Hopkins's hat? Yes, Hopkins; the man was an enigma like his master. Just whose side was Hopkins on? He had seemed so supportive, so attentive to British needs. He understood that the war could only be won with U.S. boots on the ground here in Europe. And yet he trotted around the Atlantic Conference at Roosevelt's side and said not a word when the president produced all this flannel about principles in the postwar world.

Had it not occurred to either of them that there would not be a postwar world unless the White House became an ally in the war against fascist tyranny?

Harry Hopkins was well aware of the disenchantment in London. The summit had evaded history rather than made it. It had produced nothing but fine words, empty promises, and two dozen chilled grouse that were even now sitting in the refrigerator in the White House kitchen. Mrs Nesbitt had not taken kindly to the gift and Hopkins suspected that the birds would be quietly disposed of with the pretext that they had "gone bad," if the president ever asked.

Hopkins knew too that he was unlikely to be sent back to London. The president liked to exercise total control over those who worked most closely with him. Roosevelt had publicly praised Hopkins's missions to London and Moscow in the month of July but once he was back had urged him to take a rest and spend time with Louise Macy.

Behind the benign advice, the easy smile, and the camaraderie lay a wary, calculating mind that weighed the nuance of every move and utterance of his inner political circle. He needed Hopkins to regain his strength and remain at his side in Washington as the isolationists prepared a new campaign against him in the autumn. Roosevelt's every political antenna was now tuned to domestic political battles to come. Hopkins knew he would be seeing the world through White House windows from now on.

Saddest of all, Hopkins admitted to himself that he was not looking forward to his welcome-home dinner with Louise. Eleanor Roosevelt had offered the couple a private dining room in the White House. He was tired and would otherwise have accepted, but the mere thought of Mrs Nesbitt's cooking made him book a fashionable restaurant in Georgetown.

He knew he would drink too much, hear the latest details of their wedding plans, and fend off questions about his work in London. Hopkins could not dissemble. His face always betrayed irritation or boredom. And he was bored with talk of a wedding that was still a year distant. He also didn't want to repeat all the old Churchill stories he had told Louise after his first visit. Above all, he felt acutely uncomfortable when Louise raised, as he knew she would, the question of what he did in his spare time in London. The Blitz had ended for the time being, the theatres and cinemas were open again, and the restaurants had begun to expand their menus, or so the American newspapers had reported.

"So what did you do with yourself in the evenings, darling?" she asked.

She looked very attractive, leaning forward, her dark eyes

gazing into his, one hand on his arm and a leg pressed against his under the table.

The champagne sat in an ice bucket beside them; the first course had been ordered and the waiters at the Chantelle were keeping their distance. He was lucky. Here he was, a shambolic old wreck with a life-shortening history of stomach surgery and intestinal problems, sitting beside a fiancée fifteen years his junior, who looked as if she had stepped out of the fashion magazines for which she once had reported.

He leant forward and took her hand.

"He's a monster. He consumes your time day and night and even when you are not with him he's on the phone or sending couriers round with documents."

"Phooey," she said. "The man's running a war. I'll bet you spent your nights drinking with Ed Murrow and that gang, didn't you?"

Hopkins admitted that, yes, he had spent too much time with the journalists, but that was part of the job, trying to understand their side of the story and flagging up reports that were going to cause problems for the president. It had been fine when the Blitz was on, because the correspondents had a daily story to write. Now they were running round digging up embarrassing news about Lend-Lease goods being sold to Latin America and the sudden increase in venereal disease in London.

"And all those women? London is full of lonely women, they say."

She had buttered a corner of bread and bit it off, looking at him.

He shook his head.

"London is full of people without enough food, without homes, with their kids scattered around the country and worrying when the Germans are going to start bombing again," he said wearily.

She took his hand.

"Don't get irritated, darling. I'm trying to understand."

"I'm sorry."

It was clear that London had been too much for him this time, she decided. He spent his nights with Churchill and his days running around government offices. Then that trip to Russia must almost have killed him. The president had a lot to answer for. She would talk to Eleanor and ask that Harry never be sent overseas again.

Leonora reported to a former hotel near Baker Street that had been requisitioned for wartime use. The note delivered to her Pimlico flat had merely given her the date, time, and place of the interview, which was to assess "the furtherance of her service career."

Colonel Stobart was nowhere to be seen; instead she was shown into a room stripped of all furniture except for two chairs and a desk. There were blackout blinds on the windows and a single dim bulb in a dusty lampshade.

She waited there for fifteen minutes and was thinking of leaving when the door opened and Commander Ramsden walked in with an armful of cardboard files. Leonora stood up, but the major motioned her to sit down. There was no smile, no greeting, and no reference to the fact that they had met before.

Ramsden put the files on the desk with a thump, sat down, and frowned at Leonora, as if trying to remember who she was and what she was doing there. The commander opened a file, scanned it, and then looked up again. She smiled.

"Welcome," she said. "I am sorry to have kept you. Now, let's get down to it."

She said that Leonora was to be assessed for induction into a new unit that carried out sabotage operations in Europe. In her case, she was being considered for the section that sent agents into France. She had expressed a wish to join such a unit and, given the high security clearance she had already been granted because of the nature of her work with the Women's Transport Service, she was regarded as a strong candidate.

"Is this the Special Operations Executive?" asked Leonora.

Commander Ramsden snapped the file shut. "I don't know who told you that, but they shouldn't have. Yes, it is, but I suggest you forget that name." Then she slipped into French, questioning Leonora's motives for volunteering for such dangerous work. Most young women would have been happy to do their war work in vital jobs such as manning radio communications and code work. Why was she different? Did she realise the dangers? Had she thought about how she would react to torture if captured? Did she realise what the Gestapo did to women under interrogation?

Leonora replied in French. After fifty minutes the questioning stopped. Commander Ramsden rose from the desk, walked across the room, and opened the door.

"You will hear from us," she said.

Leonora would only realise later that the strangest aspect of the interview had been that her interrogator had neither offered her a cigarette nor smoked one herself.

In the next fortnight, two further interviews in the same room followed in quick succession, each lasting one hour without the offer of cigarettes, tea, or even a glass of water.

In the last interview Ramsden for the first time confirmed the name of the unit Leonora would be joining: F Section of the Special Operations Executive. She had been accepted for training. She could change her mind now, but once training had begun she would have to be fully committed. Once again Ramsden spelt out the risks. The chances of survival after being deployed into France were no more than fifty-fifty. A clean death was not the likely end for those who did not survive. Capture meant torture and execution, or transportation to a concentration camp, which amounted to the same thing.

"What happens if I do change my mind once training has begun?" Leonora asked.

"It has never happened. We may change our minds about you during training, but you will not have the privilege."

Finally Leonora was reminded of what had been said at their first interview. The work she was to undertake was secret. No one, not even close family members, could be told what she was doing. The cover story if she needed one would be continuing work for the Women's Transport Service.

"Do you understand this?" said Ramsden. "I want you to think very carefully, not later but now, before we go ahead."

She nodded. "I understand," she said.

There was a moment's silence. Ramsden produced a cigarette case for the first time and offered her one. They sat smoking, saying nothing for a few minutes. Then Ramsden stood up, shook her hand, opened the door, and handed her an envelope.

"Good-bye and good luck," she said.

On the street outside, Leonora breathed deeply, trying to slow her thudding heart. She felt the heat from the pavement on her legs. She noticed the number of horse-drawn carts among the traffic. Petrol rationing had brought the return of a slower and more civilised kind of transport in London. The horses looked ill nourished and tired. She walked briskly towards Hyde Park Corner. In the tearoom of the Cumberland Hotel she placed the envelope on a table. Her hands were shaking. She gripped the salt cellar and looked around for a waitress. She had sat here only weeks earlier with her mother arguing about her war work, as if driving an official Humber had anything to do with the war. Now that work was about to become very real. What was she going to say to her mother? She opened the envelope.

> Wanborough Manor near Guildford in Surrey at 10 A.M. Monday 14
> August. A car will meet the 8.45 A.M. train from Waterloo to Guildford.
> Bring a suitcase and prepare for a stay of three weeks.

The note was unsigned and written on unheaded paper.

Like most young women, Leonora Finch thought little of her health and never considered her physical fitness. She had enjoyed lacrosse at school but otherwise had played no sports. In Paris she and Philippe had walked everywhere, and in London it was the same. Buses were irregular and often full and taxis were exorbitantly expensive. She had bought a bicycle and had kept it chained to the railings outside her Pimlico lodgings, but it had vanished one night in the Blitz. London's criminal fraternity had learnt to take full advantage of the blackout early on in the war.

So in her free time she joined the throngs of Londoners who walked the streets of the city and enjoyed the parks and private squares that had been opened to all after removal of their iron railings. She felt and looked healthy, even if she did not believe the many newspaper reports that claimed war-time rationing was actually beneficial because it reduced consumption of sugar and fat.

After a week at Wanborough Manor she understood what an overweight, prematurely middle-aged wreck of a human body she had been dragging around for so many years.

At least that was the description given to her and the other nine members of the group in the discreet house in the Surrey hills by a tall, commanding figure in battle dress. The man looked to be well into his sixties and announced himself as Major Roger de Wesselow. After breakfast of coffee and croissants on the first day, he gathered them in what had once been the ballroom. He was their commandant, he said in fluent French. That was to be the lingua franca during the course. They were forbidden to speak English.

The next day they would be woken at around 6:00 A.M. and taken for a three-mile run and would progress to eight miles by the end of the course. He would join them. The rest of the days would be taken up with further cross-country runs, swimming in a local lake, and courses such as map reading. They were only to use first names to each other and should not discuss or speculate on the nature of their work or where it might eventually lead. Each one had been chosen for her aptitude and skills, but not everyone would progress to the next course. They would be given free time in the evenings and would be allowed to visit the pub in the local village, where they would describe themselves as medical students and doctors from St Thomas's Hospital in London who had been evacuated to the manor to escape the bombing. They were not to make contact with anyone in the village and above all should not discuss the nature of their training.

"Is that clear?" said de Wesselow.

Looking around, Leonora saw that some of her group understood perfectly what they were to do and why they were there, while others, especially a plump young woman with ringlets of red hair, seemed confused.

"I'm Claudette," she said to Leonora after their induction talk. "I answered a government advertisement for a bilingual secretary and found myself here. Do you know what's going on?"

After three weeks of cross-country runs and lake swimming, Claudette and every other member of the group knew exactly what they were doing in the Surrey hills. Theoretical map reading had been followed by night-time route marches. Two people would be dropped off at around midnight in open country twenty miles from the manor with only a compass and a map for guidance. Those who failed to return by first light were made to repeat the exercise later that day.

Then the communications training began. The first day was spent learning how to assemble and break down simple short-wave radio sets. The next few days the group was taught clandestine techniques in the use of radio, which began and ended with a golden rule: no transmission was to last more than five minutes. The Germans, like the British, scanned traffic on every wireless frequency night and day. Since all private broadcasts were banned, any such traffic was deemed to be hostile. Operating from the Gestapo headquarters on the Avenue Foch in Paris, the Gestapo and their French collaborators were adept at pinpointing the location of radio operators foolish enough to remain on the air for more than a few minutes.

On the final day of the four weeks they had spent at Wanborough the ten volunteers assembled in the hall. They had packed and a bus waited outside to take them to the station. De Wesselow thanked them for their hard work and handed each an envelope with the warning that they should not open it until they reached London.

Leonora and Claudette found themselves in the same carriage and on arriving at Waterloo at midday decided on a cup of tea and a sandwich in the station buffet. They sat in a corner and opened their envelopes.

Leonora read: "Report to Colonel Parker 64 Baker Street at 1600 hours this afternoon."

When Claudette saw her smile, she nervously put her own envelope back in her handbag. "Congratulations," she said. "I knew you were going to pass."

"I'm sure you have too," said Leonora. "Go on; open yours."

Claudette giggled and shivered. "I can't; I'm all goose bumpy. There's gin at the bar; let's have a drink first."

Claudette told her that her father had been a French officer who had been killed escaping by sea from Dunkirk. He had survived a long fighting retreat from the Belgian frontier with his unit, which had been virtually wiped out by the time it reached the coast. He had embarked safely on one of the hundreds of small boats that had crossed the Channel and had been only a few miles from the English coast when the boat was attacked and sunk by a German fighter. The plane had returned for a second run to machine-gun survivors in the water. That's when her father had been killed – trying to swim to safety.

Claudette told the story in a matter-of-fact way, sipping her gin and staring down at the table. She seemed to be talking to herself, Leonora thought. The survivors had been picked up, and one of them had told Claudette's mother what had happened, she said. Her father's body had never been recovered.

Her mother had met Claudette's father while on a student exchange visit to Lyon soon after the end of the First World War. He was a young lecturer and she wanted to be a teacher. They had married in Lyon, which was where Claudette had been born. The family had moved to London when her father had got a job at the French Institute in Kensington. He had returned to fight for his country when war broke out in 1939. Her father had been a wonderful man, warm, passionate about the great French poets of the nineteenth century – de Vigny, Lamartine, Musset, Rimbaud – and a great cook. He had bright red hair like hers. That was her story.

Claudette laughed. "I shouldn't be saying any of this to you, should I?"

"Open your letter," said Leonora.

Claudette slid a long fingernail along the flap of the envelope and drew out the same unheaded notepaper. She smiled and gave Leonora a long hug.

Claudette had received the same instruction, but the time was an hour later. "I don't know what we have let ourselves in for," she said, "but let's have another gin, if they've got one."

16

Churchill had called the first months of that year, 1941, his black spring. Harry Hopkins reflected that with summer over, they were now heading into an even darker season of the year. The trees were in their autumn beauty as he drove with Roosevelt to the president's family home, Springwood, in the town of Hyde Park in upstate New York. They both needed a few days' peace to recover from weeks of wearying political combat in Washington. Sunlight played on the glow of yellow, orange, and amber leaves around them. Black would have better suited the president's state of mind, thought Hopkins.

Both men were exhausted. For the first time in his career Roosevelt was bereft of political ideas. There were no more rabbits in the hat, he told his friend. If anything, he was the rabbit now, staring helplessly at the oncoming headlights. He needed time to think, to recover the confidence and optimism that had been the hallmark of his radio broadcasts and presidential addresses to the American people throughout the years of the New Deal in the thirties. It seemed that the people were no longer listening.

It was October. In Russia the Germans were driving towards Moscow across a 375-mile front. In Japan a supposedly moderate government had fallen, to be replaced by an avowed advocate of war, General Tōjō. In America every opinion poll showed that the public mood had hardened further against involvement in the European war.

In Britain Churchill was still awaiting a victory of British arms after the disasters of Norway, Dunkirk, and Crete. In every battle the Germans had outfought and outthought the British, with troops who were better armed, better trained, and better motivated. Hopkins knew this was Churchill's secret fear, the gnawing thought that the British soldier was no match for the German. In the lonely midnight hours with only his closest advisers around him the prime minister had confessed that the men who had fought over the centuries in Europe from Agincourt to the Somme were no longer to be found in the British army. The slaughter of the First World War had caused such public revulsion that the army had been left to languish afterwards. Money and men had gone into the air force and the navy.

He had poured out his fears, speaking to Hopkins over the transatlantic phone as he spoke to none of his senior military men.

"I can talk to you, Harry," Churchill said, "because how can I face my generals and tell them that their men don't have the stomach for a fight, that they prefer retreat to battle?"

Hopkins knew too that Churchill, ever alert to public opinion, had become alarmed by open criticism in Britain of America's continuing neutrality. In mid-October the U.S. destroyer *Kearny* had been hit by a torpedo 350 miles south of Iceland, with the loss of eleven members of the crew. The ship limped safely to port, but there was not a ripple of protest or concern among the American public. Days later, again near Iceland, a U-boat torpedoed another U.S. destroyer, the *Reuben James,* this time sinking the ship, with the loss of 115 members of the crew. Again the American public did not react. They seemed more interested in the annual Army–Notre Dame football game.

The isolationist lobby used these losses to taunt Roosevelt, challenging him to go before Congress and ask for a definitive vote on whether America should go to war. Roosevelt ducked the challenge, knowing he'd face a humiliating defeat. He responded with words, because they were his only weapon. In the annual Navy Day speech at the end of the month in Washington he said, "The shooting has started. And history has recorded who fired the first shot. In the long run, however, all that will matter is who fired the last shot."

The press dutifully reported the speech but gave plenty of space to the mockery that Charles Lindbergh and other isolationists heaped on the president's words. Hopkins guessed that German, Italian, and Japanese diplomats in Washington had sent back equally derisory reports to their governments.

This was a president, after all, who had defied his cabinet and decided against asking Congress for another small amendment to the Neutrality Act to allow American vessels to be armed in war zones. He knew that in the Senate and House the elected representatives of the American people would fight him all the way. He knew too that they would have the great majority of their constituents with them. And he knew that in all probability he would lose the vote.

The cabinet assailed the president for his decision. Stimson and Morgenthau vigorously argued that only by standing up to the isolationist lobby could the president hope to swing public opinion to his side. Americans respected a fighter; it was in their history to support an underdog against the bully, they told him, and "you, Mr President, are being bullied, unfairly attacked by a political pressure group that is bewitching the great American people with the fantasy that we can stay out of this war." Take them head-on, Roosevelt was urged; appeal directly to the American people.

But he dared not. The man who had told his people they had nothing to fear but fear itself was fearful of confronting his political enemies.

And then there was Churchill. The long, almost daily cables from Downing Street were supplemented by phone calls made from the secure booth in the basement bunker. The prime minister had placed two clocks in the booth, one set on London time and one on Washington time.

"He always seems to be on our time," remarked Roosevelt as he directed Hopkins to take yet another call from Downing Street. This time the president had been called by Churchill at his Hyde Park birthplace, the sanctuary Roosevelt had returned to throughout his life. Tea had been poured in the elegant drawing room when the White House put the call through.

Hopkins answered. The voice on the end of the phone was subdued. The growl had gone. Churchill was almost pleading to be understood.

"Harry, I do not know what we will do if England is fighting alone when 1942 comes," he said.

And then he delivered more bad news. In the previous two days British shipping losses in the North Atlantic had been fifty thousand tons. The sinkings had all been well east of the 26th Meridian, which Roosevelt had deemed the eastern limit of U.S. naval presence in the Atlantic. U-boat commanders knew exactly where America had drawn the line. British naval intelligence reported that there were thirty U-boats strung out across the route that British convoys had to take to reach and return from American ports.

"Tell me, Harry, do you have any hope of good news for us in the near future?"

By which Churchill meant: Was there any remote prospect that America would enter the war anytime soon? It was a question to which Churchill already knew the answer. But he never gave up hope. Hopkins looked across the room to where the president sat at his desk, cigarette holder in hand, reading a file of high-priority cables sent over from State that morning. He knew that Roosevelt was half-listening to his end of the conversation.

"I am sorry to say, no, I don't, Prime Minister," he said.

They bade each other farewell with the usual good wishes. Hopkins replaced the receiver, took a chair in front of the desk, lit a cigarette, and waited. He watched the president working his way through the cables, scribbling notes in the margins of some, which he placed to one side. The man was very tired. The lines that creased his cheeks from nose to mouth were deeper. Behind the rimless glasses his eyes lacked lustre.

The president sighed and held up a closely typed document.

"He wants to ship forty thousand more troops to the Middle East and he requests the loan of our passenger vessels to do it. Doesn't his embassy here tell him what's happening on the Hill?"

"I'll talk to him," said Hopkins.

Roosevelt pointed his cigarette holder at the phone. "You just have."

"No, I mean let me go back to London. Sit down and have a real talk. I will try to get him to see that North Africa should be a sideshow."

"No, Harry. You're staying here. You're not strong enough, and anyway, I need you."

"I could iron out a lot of problems over there."

"I am sure you could. But you're due for your checkup next week and that comes first."

"He's getting desperate, you know."

"He will have to wait, just as we will."

Eleanor Roosevelt rarely travelled to Hyde Park with her husband, preferring to remain in Washington to work on her daily newspaper column and oversee the numerous committees on her favourite cause, civil rights, especially those of the Afro-American minority.

Her marriage to the president was an arrangement that suited both sides. Years earlier she had moved out of the marital bedroom, following an affair he had conducted with lack of due discretion, but she had agreed to maintain the relationship for the sake of his political career. She had nursed him through his attack of polio and subsequent paralysis and stayed at his side throughout the years of his presidency.

Some in the White House called her the president's conscience, and it was true that Eleanor Roosevelt scorned the inevitable political compromises and wheeler-dealing as Roosevelt forced through the New Deal reforms in the thirties. He in turn chided her for an unbending approach to politics, to which she snapped more than once, "I value principles more than politics, Franklin."

She lived in a suite of rooms in the south-west corner of the White House, a large sitting room, a small bedroom, and a bathroom. Her office was on the first floor, but it was to her own quarters that she invited Hopkins upon his return from

Hyde Park. He was going into the hospital the next day and she wanted to wish him a speedy recovery over tea and cakes.

Hopkins knew he was being summoned rather than invited. He also knew that he would hear yet again Eleanor Roosevelt's firm views on America's slide to war. He would hear her expound calmly and methodically the view that fascism must be fought and conquered but not at the expense of 400 million Indians who remained in British colonial servitude. And although she would not say so openly, she would let him know how disappointed she was in someone she had once thought of as a fellow crusader for social justice.

"You're looking tired, Harry; what are they going to do to you this time?"

"Just a checkup, the usual stuff."

"I hope it does you good; you need a rest."

"I'll be fine."

"You've been off-colour since you got back from London."

"It was a tough trip, Moscow and all."

"I worry about you, Harry; we all do."

"Don't worry; the doctors will fix me up."

Eleanor Roosevelt was not to be deterred. She was smart. She knew something was wrong with the man she had watched over for years.

"That's not what I mean. You've changed."

"We all change, Mrs Roosevelt."

"Did anything happen in London?"

"A lot happened in London."

"No, that's not what I meant. You seem so distracted now, as if you left half your head over there."

"Maybe I have, Mrs Roosevelt. I am dealing with two prima donnas."

"You went to London to help the British and came back

wanting to send our boys over there to fight for their empire. That's not the Harry Hopkins I know."

"It's not quite like that, Mrs Roosevelt."

She smiled thinly and put down her cup. The tea was over. They talked briefly about family matters, the weather, and then she stood up and offered him her hand.

"I wish you a quick recovery, Harry. The president needs you," she said.

Harry Hopkins walked quickly along the corridor to his rooms in the south-east corner. It was four thirty, which made it nine thirty in London. He crossed his large bedroom with its huge four-poster and went into the smaller bedroom next door that served as a study. He picked up the phone and asked the operator for Ed Murrow's home number in London. He had to talk to Murrow. He had been back from Britain for three weeks. In that time he had received not a line, not a word. He had written to Leonora every week: long, funny letters about life in Washington, about his daughter, Diana, about his latest disasters at the racetrack, and about how he missed her. And not a single word in return. He remembered that she was supposed to be training for some secret unit, but surely they would forward letters to her? He would give Murrow the address in Pimlico and ask him to go round. Murrow would understand. He'd know what was going on. Murrow was as much a friend as any journalist could be to anyone.

"Hunter Two-Five-Four-Seven." It was Janet Murrow, her voice faint and crackly. She told him Ed was "out, *as usual*," and laid heavy emphasis on the last two words.

"You'll probably see him before I do," she said. "He's going over to New York in a couple of weeks for a speaking tour."

Hopkins was in the State Department listening to a briefing on Stalin's strange disappearance from the Kremlin when the call came to report to the Oval Office immediately. He hurried up Pennsylvania Avenue, reflecting that he had never been asked to report to the president before. It had always been: "Come by, Harry." "Drop in for a cocktail, Harry." "Give me a moment, will you, Harry."

He was breathless when he entered the Oval Office. The president waved him to a chair and held up a piece of paper.

"Things are going to change around here, Harry. I am sick and tired of this."

"Mr President?"

Roosevelt leant over the desk and handed Hopkins the paper.

It was the printed menu for that day, Tuesday, 14 October 1941. Breakfast was spinach omelette and coffee; lunch was spinach tart, fried potatoes, and grilled corn; and dinner was vegetable soup followed by scrambled eggs and apple strudel.

"It's got to stop. The doctors say this type of food is doing me no good. I am going to ask Eleanor to let Mrs Nesbitt go."

Hopkins stood up, patting his pockets for cigarettes. He lit one, his hands shaking slightly. Stalin had not been seen in Moscow for over a week. German armies were now only fifty miles from the capital. In Britain rations of meat, butter, and bread had been cut again, leaving people on subsistence level. The Japanese were moving large-scale forces down Burma towards Singapore, and their battle fleets had reportedly put to sea in strength. And the president of the United States was worried about his diet.

"Mr President?"

"I want you to tell Mrs Roosevelt. She'll take it from you."

Hopkins nodded and turned, feeling sick. He would call Stimson, Knox, and Hull, get a meeting of the inner cabinet, and agree on a direct and, if necessary, brutal approach to the president.

He had his hand on the doorknob when Roosevelt said, "By the way, Harry, I am going to let Churchill have those ships."

Hopkins turned back. The president was smiling, leaning back, his cigarette drifting smoke to the ceiling.

"And I am going to ask Congress to amend the Neutrality Act. It will be a fight, but we should get it through. We have got to put guns on our merchant ships. You know U-boats won't waste a torpedo on our ships – they just surface and sink them with those deck-mounted guns?"

"I do know that, Mr President," murmured Hopkins.

"Good. Well, you'd better get working."

"Yes, Mr President. May I ask a question?"

The president had returned to his papers and spoke without looking up.

"Sure."

"What changed your mind?"

Roosevelt looked up, not smiling now.

"I didn't change my mind, Harry. I made up my mind. There is a difference."

The hills that rolled down to the coast at Arisaig in the western Highlands offered some of the most bleakly beautiful vistas in Scotland. The cold blue waters of the Sound of Arisaig and nearby Loch Ailort washed up against giant boulders of grey, weathered rock and granite cliffs that rose to a mantle of bracken and pine. In good weather the green hills of the islands of Eigg and Rum and the mountains of Skye broke the horizon, but there was rarely good weather in Arisaig. Rain-laden clouds were almost as much a feature of the landscape as the broad-winged kites that floated over the forested hills.

The new arrivals at Arisaig were taken by bus from Mallaig railway station some miles distant and dropped at a large country house well away from the main road. Here they assembled in the draughty hall under the gaze of magnificently antlered stags' heads and learnt for the first time the real nature of the organisation they had joined.

Leonora looked out of the mullioned windows at the rain and the shrouded hills beyond. She was sitting with twelve others on hard wooden chairs as a colonel in battle dress addressed them. Yet another moustachioed middle-aged man trying to find a role in this war to redeem the fact that he had survived the last one. He could be my father, thought Leonora. The age would be about right. But no, Dad would have been different; he wouldn't have been stupid enough to get back into uniform. He would have been a doctor, a teacher. He would have stayed out of harm's way.

His name was unimportant, said the colonel. But their names were important because they must now forget them. Each would be given a new identity with a field name. They were not to contact family or friends until the end of their training. In the event that anyone dropped out of training, they would be required to spend several months in a cooler house somewhere in Scotland before returning to ordinary life.

The SOE had been set up a year earlier to create sabotage and terror against German occupying forces in Europe. They were the people selected to carry out those missions. They had been brought to this remote region because it was far from prying eyes and completely secure. The whole area had been declared a zone prohibited to the public. In their month at Arisaig, they would be taken through a syllabus that included small-arms training, use of explosives for demolition, silent killing techniques, basic infantry tactical training, and practice in the destruction of railroad tracks and rolling stock.

The evenings would be spent building up the relatively simple knowledge they had already acquired in the use of Morse code and clandestine radio. Those who passed this stage of their training – and not everyone would – would continue on to parachute training at an airfield in the south of England.

"Is that absolutely clear?"

The voice was patient, kind, and expected no more than a dutiful nod of heads.

The heads duly nodded and then one hand was raised. It was Claudette.

"What is a cooler house?"

"It is a place to which those who leave the course will be taken for a few weeks in order to reorient themselves to their former civilian lives and to prevent any leakage of classified information. Anything else?"

There was silence for a few moments and then a hand went up, Claudette again.

"If we are changing our identities, how are you going to pay us?"

Everyone laughed except the colonel in battle dress. He looked at the redheaded woman sitting in the front row. Attractive, with a good, plump figure and red curls, she had a better chance than most of talking her way through a roadblock. And she was gutsy, good leadership material. But she was too confident. That could be dangerous in the field. He would get her name later.

"Your accounts will be credited every month and your

pay will be waiting for you upon your return. That will be all for now."

"*If* we return," muttered Claudette, standing up and catching Leonora's eye.

That evening they were given a welcome drinks party in the main drawing room. There was no wine, just whisky or gin with water or tonic as mixers and bottled beer. Two elderly women circulated, making sure their glasses were kept topped up. The colonel was there with two younger men in civilian clothes who introduced themselves using surnames only: Sykes and Fairburn were to be the group's instructors.

"You know what they're doing, don't you? Trying to see how much we can drink before we fall over," said Claudette.

Leonora nodded and looked over their colleagues, all young men from very different backgrounds, from what little she had learnt on the train. There were two members of de Gaulle's Free French army, a teacher, a barman, and the rest had all volunteered from regular units.

She was to learn during the course that they had two things in common, like her and Claudette. They spoke fluent French and wanted a real fighting role in the war. If they completed their training and joined F Section of the SOE, in a few weeks they would be in France working with a small circle of Resistance fighters.

And that was the point, wasn't it? They would be fighting, killing Germans, Vichy traitors, blowing up ammo dumps and troop trains, gathering information for bombing raids, helping release prisoners from jails in every large city. That was what she wanted, wasn't it?

She looked at Claudette talking to one of the instructors, a handsome older man. Alcohol was obviously not the only trap on this course. Leonora had heard that voluptuous blondes would appear ostensibly to test the French of the men. Seduction would follow and those who fell for the bait would be quietly sent to the cooler house. It looked like a similar test would be applied to the women. From her animated conversation, Claudette seemed well able to handle the challenge.

Claudette had had no idea what she had volunteered for when she first arrived at Wanborough Manor; now she was as eager as the rest to complete training and join the Resistance in Europe. Why? Why were they all doing it? Did Claudette want to avenge the death of her father murdered in cold blood in the waters of the Channel? And had that really happened? The story seemed curious, a little too obvious to Leonora. Or were they both trying to prove that women could, after all, play a real fighting role in a war created by men for men? Did that make sense? Did anything make sense? Not really.

For her there was something else, something she needed to discover in herself. They risked torture and unimaginable horrors if captured. And they had been warned over and over again that the chances of capture and interrogation were very real. So why risk it? Like Claudette, was she trying to avenge the death of her father? If he had been alive, he would have been horrified at the risks she was taking. And what would Harry Hopkins think? She knew the answer to that. She had tried to push him out of her mind, that tall, gangling American with his big hat and a Camel permanently stuck in his mouth.

He made her laugh, which was probably why she was half in love with him. He thought he was in love with her, but he wasn't. He was just lonely, looking for love or lust, call it what you will, while he grappled with the big man in Number 10.

Had he really wanted to marry her? If she had said yes, what would he have done? Probably obtained a special licence, married her in a registrar's office, and taken her back to America. That's where she could have been now – in the White House under the unforgiving gaze of Eleanor Roosevelt.

"I say, are you coming through?"

It was Sykes. The others were trooping through to the dining room. She finished her whisky and placed the glass on a table beneath another set of antlers. How many stags had been slaughtered to decorate the walls? She wondered what they did with the hides.

At the end of the first week in Scotland, the F Section intake had learnt how to strip, reassemble, load, fire, and maintain a range of British, American, and German pistols, rifles, and submachine guns. They concentrated on a new British weapon, the Sten gun. With only four components – barrel, body, butt, and magazine – it was easy to break down and hide. It fired single shots or short bursts with 9mm ammunition that was interchangeable with the standard German weapon of the same type, the Schmeisser MP 38.

"If you run out of ammo in a firefight, grab a Schmeisser off the nearest dead German and use the magazine."

It was Fairburn talking, a burly ex-police inspector who had learnt every method of killing from years working on the Shanghai waterfront.

The Sten was designed for close-range fighting. With a high fire rate and a twenty-eight-round magazine a single burst would empty the weapon.

"So fire only two shots at a time – double tap, we call it. The beauty of the Sten is that you can drop it in muddy water or bleed all over it and it will keep working. Have you got that?"

They'd got it. They learnt to turn and fire snap shots from

the hip at moving targets. They shot at targets while lying down, sitting, and even through their legs. They shot at fast-moving flickering lights at night in the open and again in the damp darkness of a cellar below the house. Fairburn made them lie on camp beds in a darkened room and would remotely snap on a light to see how fast they could roll off the bed, reach for a Sten concealed beneath it, and fire at a target on the door.

"I want you to love this gun, because it's going to save your life," he said. "And if you are badly wounded and the Gestapo are closing in, it has the great advantage of a short barrel. That makes it easy to turn it on yourself, but make sure you have saved that last bullet. It's either that or having your fingernails torn out one by one."

"He's all heart, isn't he?" said Claudette. "I sometimes think they want us to give up on the whole thing."

"Well, do you?"

Claudette shook her head. "It's funny, isn't it, but if someone asked me why I was really, truly doing this, I wouldn't say it was because I want to fight the Germans or because of what happened to Dad, but because it's exciting. I like that. I suppose I get bored easily."

Sykes and Fairburn were with them every hour of the day, from the unchanging breakfast of porridge and brown sugar until drinks after dinner.

Sykes was the silent killing expert. He showed them the short, sharp-bladed commando knives that would be standard-issue in the field. A quick slash to the throat was the fastest and most silent way to kill, he said. The victim would be dead before he hit the ground, but it was messy. The

attacker would almost certainly be covered in blood. They
practised on dummies strung from the ceiling of the cellar.
The blades of the knives were smeared with red paint and
they had to stand with their backs to the dummy, turn, and
slash at exactly the point below the chin where the carotid
artery lay. An inch to either side of it and they would fail to
kill outright.

They were advised, where possible, to use karate killing
techniques, which were almost as fast and just as deadly. The
beauty of these techniques was that they required no great
strength. Two hard thumb thrusts into vulnerable tissue on
either side of the neck would drop the victim unconscious
to the ground, where he could be throttled in seconds. The
problem was getting close enough to carry out the attack.

"The best way is to deceive your victim. He's your lover,
he's in your arms or in your bed, he wants you, he reaches out
for you, then you step in close and do the work."

"What happens if we're trying to kill a woman?"

Sykes looked at the class and saw the redhead at the back.
That half-French woman Claudette again, always asking
bloody stupid questions, except, as he acknowledged to
himself, it wasn't a stupid question. The Gestapo used women
on their snap roadblocks, rightly thinking they could more
easily spot disguised female Resistance fighters. And women
torturers were said to be more effective in extracting
information than men.

"Use your knife," he finally said.

The final days of the course were spent tramping the hills with
packs and Sten guns to map reference points where further
directions were concealed. They walked through rain clouds

and mist, pausing only for a tea break from thermos flasks. The
final destination was always a point along a three-mile line of
railway track that branched off the main London line.

Sykes and Fairburn would arrive on an old engine and
teach them how to plant their explosives and where to lie in
ambush. The charges detonated with a satisfactory bang and
threw a cloud of earth into the air but left track and train intact. They were made to carry out these attacks for hour after
hour. The initial detonation was always followed by small-
arms fire on targets nailed to wagons behind the engine. Towards late afternoon, Sykes and Fairburn would leave on the
engine, while they were left to hike back to the manor house
in the enveloping darkness.

Most of the F Section trainees became quieter and more reserved as their training drew to an end. The next step was a
short parachute course and then they would be sent into
France to join their Resistance circuit. The prospect concentrated minds. The nightly lectures on the Axis order of battle
or how to write condensed reports for radio transmission always gave way to evening drinks in the drawing room. There
the group sank into silent gloom as they drank their whiskies,
read newspapers, and smoked.

Only Claudette seemed unaffected by the contemplation
of the dangers ahead. She told Leonora that pretending to
blow up trains and firing magazine after magazine at rusty old
wagons was the best fun of their time at Arisaig. She seemed
to regard the course as a glorious school outing with guns and
explosives. Leonora knew it was just an act, Claudette's way of
coping with the knowledge of what was to come, but others in
the group disliked her flamboyance and shunned her.

Claudette helped Leonora realise what she was doing on the

rain-sodden Scottish hills, cold, wet, hungry, and sometimes frightened. Claudette, with her red ringlets and personality, could have done anything in this war. She could have attracted a wealthy husband in London, used her money to leave for America, or simply worked as a desk intelligence officer, with her knowledge of France and French. Instead she had chosen the darkest and most dangerous path of all, and Leonora found faith and comfort in joining her friend on that journey.

On their final night at the manor, the colonel whose name was unimportant gave them a short talk before dinner.

"From an early age we deceive ourselves, just as we deceive those closest to us. None of us are quite what we appear, even to those who think they know us best. We all have our secrets and we all tell lies to conceal those secrets. If you doubt what I am saying, just pause and think back over your lives for a few moments."

Claudette looked sideways at Leonora and put her hand over her mouth to suppress a giggle.

The colonel sat on a chair and took a small notebook from the side-flap pocket of his trousers. He began to flick through the pages. Minutes passed. People shifted in chairs, breaking the silence. The colonel got up.

"The power to deceive is going to be important in your fieldwork," he said. "When you go to a restaurant or a café or walk down a city street, you will be wearing the mask of an innocent civilian. You will use that mask to deceive the police when they stop you – and they will. But just as you deceive the enemy, so they will try to deceive you. They work hard to penetrate our circuits in France and our operations here – and they sometimes succeed. So trust no one except those closest to you in the chain of command. Good luck."

It was late November when they left and their final morning brought a surprise. Only eight of the twelve who had begun the course assembled to take the bus to the station. The other four had left in the night, having failed in some way to satisfy Sykes and Fairburn. They would now spend weeks comfortably incommunicado in a remote area of Scotland.

"They may be the lucky ones," said Claudette as they took a last look at the green-grey hills of Arisaig, where they had learnt to kill, to deceive, and to face the fact that capture meant certain torture and shipment to a concentration camp.

17

The festive tree on the White House lawn shined brightly against the gloom of the winter's day. It was three o'clock and just over two weeks until Christmas. Franklin Roosevelt was having a late lunch at his desk in the Oval Office. Hopkins had joined him, sitting at the other side of the desk eating Mrs Nesbitt's spinach and scrambled eggs.

At the same moment, Winston Churchill was dining at Chequers with Gil Winant and Averell Harriman. Sawyers had cleared the table and placed the port decanter before the prime minister, leaving the men free to discuss the growing crisis in the Far East.

In the darkness over Ringway airfield outside Manchester, Leonora Finch was falling through the freezing air, having jumped from an aircraft at a thousand feet. As instructed, she waited for five seconds, then pulled the rip cord. She felt as if someone had jerked her upwards like a giant puppet. In the light of a quarter moon she could see the white canopy of Claudette's parachute below. They had jumped together on the last night of their training.

The hands of Leonora's watch glowed. The time was just after 9:00 P.M. Swinging in the night air above a darkened city, she suddenly felt freed of all doubts about the journey she had embarked upon.

Back in Washington a telephone call from Knox, the secretary of the navy, interrupted the president's lunch. Hopkins took the call, listened briefly, and put the phone down.

"Knox has just received a message from the commander in Honolulu saying there is a big air raid on at the moment. It's not a false alarm and there are casualties."

Roosevelt was silent for a moment pondering the news. "It's the Japanese," he said slowly.

"I doubt that," said Hopkins. "Why would they want to attack us?"

Churchill rose from the table, switched on the radio on the sideboard, and returned to his seat at the table. He had missed the start of the news but caught reports about fighting on the Russian front and in Libya. The last item concerned an unconfirmed report of a Japanese attack on American ships in Hawaii in the Pacific. The broadcast moved into the next programme.

The prime minister sat upright in his chair, gazing at the radio, straining to make sense of what he had just heard.

"Did you hear that?" he said to Harriman.

"Something about a Jap attack on our ships," said Harriman. "Must be a mistake. Probably a false report."

Sawyers entered the room. "Excuse me, Prime Minister, I couldn't help overhearing what you said. It's true. The Japs have attacked the Americans. We've just heard it on the radio."

Churchill left his cigar burning in an ashtray on the table and walked across the hall to his office, where two secretaries were on duty. He put a call through to the White House. Minutes later Roosevelt was on the phone.

"They've attacked our base at Pearl Harbor," the president said, speaking slowly to give emphasis to every word. "The losses have been heavy. We're all in the same boat now."

Leonora landed well, rolling forward as she had been told and then lying breathless for a moment, looking up at a scatter of stars in the clear sky.

The next time she landed she would be in France. Men would emerge from the darkness and hustle her away to a safe house. There she would assemble the radio, send a brief message to confirm her safe arrival, and quickly talk through her instructions with the local Resistance. They would know her by her field name, Yvonne. Her circuit was called Monkeypuzzle, operating in the heart of the Loire Valley, home to the Forty-Seventh Panzer Division. She was to be the courier between the radio operator and agents in the field. Their task was sabotage and intelligence.

She gathered the folds of her chute and walked to a hangar. For a few more days she would remain Leonora Finch, and right now Leonora Finch needed to shed her flying gear and sit down with Claudette in the mess bar and drink a lot of gin.

Claudette was standing with the group of instructors, hopping from foot to foot and bursting with excitement.

"Have you heard?" she said. "The Japs have attacked the Americans. The Yanks are in the war!"

In the tumble of events that followed the devastating attack on Pearl Harbor, the last thing President Roosevelt needed was a visit from the British prime minister and his entourage. The American political and military establishment had been turned upside down; public opinion, long indifferent to a distant war, had swung to shocked outrage and demand for revenge.

Leading isolationist politicians and businessmen suddenly fell silent. America was at war with Japan and Germany. Hitler had pre-empted any doubt in Washington about a two-front war by declaring war on the United States four days after Pearl Harbor. The president faced a formidable array of diplomatic and political problems, but he gave Hopkins the most challenging task: that of coordinating businesses large and small to fire up the sluggish American economy and place it on a war footing.

Hopkins's job was to tell business leaders that America needed tanks and guns now, not fridges and automobiles. Roosevelt knew this role played to Hopkins's strengths, his ability to cut across political lines and mobilise business leaders and unions behind a common cause. That is why he had once made him secretary of commerce, a post he held until illness forced his resignation. Now the president wanted Hopkins to shake off the depression that had descended upon him since the summer and get back to work.

Despite none-too-subtle messages from Washington that the president would prefer a visit in January, Churchill had insisted and Roosevelt reluctantly agreed. The wartime alliance between Britain and America would be sealed in Washington during the Christmas holidays. Churchill would stay in the White House in a room opposite Harry Hopkins's on the second floor.

"That's so you can keep him happy," said the president. "But don't let him keep you up all night drinking. This is not Downing Street."

The president tried briefly to keep to his normal evening routine after Churchill and his party of service chiefs, aides, and secretaries descended on the White House three days before Christmas. On the first night Roosevelt mixed gin and vermouth cocktails as usual at six thirty and Churchill accepted the alcoholic abomination with good grace.

Dinner followed at seven, with Hopkins joining the two leaders. Mrs Nesbitt produced a thick broccoli and spinach soup for the first course, through which Churchill briefly stirred his spoon before leaving it untouched. Hopkins remembered too late that the prime minister liked only clear broth.

After dinner Roosevelt would usually relax with a film or his stamp collection. On the first night the three men joined their military staffs in the Oval Office. Hopkins placed a large brandy in the prime minister's hand, while the president surprised everyone by asking for a glass of red wine. The conversation went on until eleven o'clock, when Roosevelt ended the meeting. Churchill wheeled him to the lift.

"This is probably an early night for you," said Roosevelt. "But I expect you need some rest."

Three hours later Hopkins and Churchill were still talking in the map room that had been set up next to the prime minister's quarters. Maps of every theatre of war – the Atlantic, the Russian front, North Africa, the Malay Peninsula – and a detailed map of the city-state of Singapore had been hastily fixed to the walls.

Below them side tables were piled with festively wrapped Christmas gifts for the Roosevelt family, the White House staff, and the British visitors.

Outside, the lights of the Christmas tree danced in a sharp north-east wind, throwing a paint box of colours against the windowpanes.

By then even Churchill was tired. The brandy bottle was half-empty and mounds of cigar ash filled several ashtrays in the room. He rose to leave.

"One question if I may, Prime Minister," said Hopkins.

"Of course," said Churchill, gazing at the red flags marking suspected U-boat positions in the Atlantic and blue flags showing convoys.

"It is of a personal nature."

Churchill sat down and waited.

"You were kind enough to provide me with a liaison officer in London."

"Indeed, I remember," said Churchill.

"I have tried to thank her for the excellent work, but my letters to both the organisation for which she worked and her home address in London have gone unanswered."

"Harry, in London people go missing all the time. I am sorry you have lost touch with, er, umm . . ."

"Squadron Officer Leonora Finch."

"Yes, quite. A woman of great spirit, I believe."

"I would like to know what happened to her, if possible."

Churchill rose from his chair, walked to the sideboard, and poured another brandy. He returned to his seat.

"I hardly have to tell you, Harry, that in this time of war on our little island, people are called on to do extraordinarily difficult and dangerous things. We all of us play our parts in various ways. The milkman on his rounds has to dig people out of the rubble of their homes. The postman has to help put out fires. Women play just as big a part as the men. I am sure Miss Finch is doing her bit, but where and how I do not know. Now forgive me, the president will be upset if we stay up too late."

In the twenty-four days that the British delegation spent at the White House that Christmas, the president and prime minister lunched and dined together every day but one.

In Berchtesgaden, where he spent Christmas, Hitler had laughed off the Allied coalition that was forming across the Atlantic. He told a gathering of admirers, mostly old colleagues from the early Nazi Party days, that American troops were soft, overfed, and undertrained and would have no stomach for a fight, especially against his mechanised forces.

He was supremely confident and talked quite openly of his strategy for global victory. The Germans would break through in the Middle East while the Japanese stormed into India. The two Axis powers would then join forces, pool resources, and turn on Russia to finish Stalin. After that, it would be the turn of Britain and then the Americas.

This was exactly the prospect that so disturbed Churchill, Roosevelt, and their commanders. Following the carnage at Pearl Harbor, the sinking of the great British battleships *Repulse* and *Prince of Wales* had left the Pacific a Japanese lake. Roosevelt began to wonder whether in their triumphalism Japan might even attack the West Coast of the United States.

Despite the unaccustomed late nights and drinking more than he was used to, the president was exhilarated by Churchill's company. The prime minister's secretaries, aides, officials, and service commanders hurried through the corridors of the White House with urgent cables, red boxes, and messages from London and the outer reaches of the Empire, especially Australia, all day and deep into the night.

Mrs Nesbitt and her kitchen staff agreed that they had never seen such thin, pasty-faced, malnourished people in their lives. The kitchen rose to the challenge with a succession of meaty stews, grilled meats, and thickly crusted fruit pies with lashings of ice cream. These were served to the British staff and their American counterparts in a communal dining room in the basement.

The drinks with which the two men began their evenings were now champagne for Churchill and the usual cocktail for Roosevelt. Neither man liked breakfast meetings; in fact, both insisted on having the first meal of the day in bed. So the evening was the first time they could quietly talk alone, compare notes, and dig over the day's work. Although always invited to such sessions, Hopkins preferred his desk and absorbed himself in the task of mobilising a wartime economy. Even the prospect of high-voltage gossip that flowed between two men with long political lives behind them could not entice Hopkins from his work.

It was on the last day of Churchill's visit that the president again voiced his concerns about Harry Hopkins.

"Harry does a great job for me, you know," Roosevelt told the prime minister.

"I know. A remarkable man. He has our admiration and trust completely."

"But he's been very distracted since he came back. He's not his usual self. Eleanor and I are both worried about him. What did you do to him over there?" Roosevelt made the last remark with a half laugh.

Churchill puffed on his cigar and said, "London during the Blitz was a dark and dangerous place. People vanished in front of friends and loved ones. It was natural to reach out for a little comfort and company in that situation. Many people found passing friendships amid the wreckage."

Roosevelt pondered these words.

"Will you talk to him, Winston?" he said. "See if there is anything you can do. I may be missing something here. Eleanor tells me Harry hardly sees Louise Macy these days. And she will be his salvation."

Churchill gave a noncommittal grunt. Two of the mightiest British battleships had been sunk, the Japanese were at the gates of Singapore, and he was being asked to consider the private feelings of a presidential aide. Admittedly, Hopkins was a vital figure in the coalition that was taking shape and someone Churchill both liked and admired. But he had always regarded the private lives of his inner circle and his own family as of secondary interest to the job at hand, a job on which the future of Western civilisation depended, as he saw it.

His own daughter, he reflected, had abandoned her husband for the American ambassador, and dear Pamela was in the arms of either Ed Murrow or Averell Harriman – or both. The prime minister's intelligence people brought him reports of these infidelities and many more, but he ignored them.

Hopkins was, however, a little different. It was not so easy to dismiss his problem as just another wartime fling. The workload imposed by the new dimension of the war and the demands of the festive season left little time for the task that the president had proposed. In any case, Churchill disliked the idea of prying into the personal life of a man he admired and trusted.

"I will of course, Mr President," he said.

On the eve of his departure Churchill suggested to Hopkins that they leave the maelstrom of the White House and dine quietly at the British embassy, where, apart from any other consideration, Mrs Nesbitt was not in charge of the kitchen.

"I have lost sight of you these past few days. I feel the need to refresh myself with your knowledge, insight, and opinions before I leave."

Hopkins enjoyed the compliments because he knew the prime minister meant them.

The two men talked for over an hour at the table, with the British ambassador, Lord Halifax, hosting the dinner. Churchill's address to a joint session of Congress on Boxing Day had been a triumph. His relationship with Roosevelt had been deepened. The meetings between the British and American service chiefs had gone well, although competition for scarce military resources meant that mutual suspicion remained high.

Above all, Churchill had achieved his supreme objective: the American war strategy was to be Germany first. Roosevelt had agreed to prosecute the war in Europe before turning against the enemy in the Pacific. It had been a hard-fought battle, with many in the administration arguing for exactly the opposite course of action. But the president had accepted the prime minister's eloquently argued wishes.

As the coffee was poured, Halifax withdrew, pleading urgent business. Hopkins and Churchill lit up and the prime minister raised his glass. "To you, Harry, a true friend to Britain in its hour of need."

Hopkins smiled and waited. Churchill would not have left Roosevelt's side without good reason. Nor would the ambassador have slipped away at such an opportune moment.

"Harry, I was told as a schoolboy that if you grasp a nettle swiftly and hard enough, it will not sting you," Churchill said.

"I have heard that but never tried it, Prime Minister."

"Winston, please. Anyway, you mentioned the other day your concerns about your liaison officer in London."

"Leonora Finch, yes."

"Well, I have made inquiries. What I have to say goes against her wishes. But I think it for the best to tell you that she has joined a secret unit that will conduct guerrilla operations in occupied Europe. She has completed her training and has been deployed into France. I can tell you no more except that she is an exceptionally brave woman and this was her choice."

"That unit is the Special Operations Executive?" said Hopkins.

Churchill looked surprised. "Yes, but the name is held closely."

Hopkins sank back into his chair, his knuckles whitening around his glass. "How did this happen?"

"She volunteered, Harry."

"Did she volunteer to spy on me?"

Churchill caught anger in the white face staring at him across the table. He rose, walked to the sideboard, placed the bottle of port on the table in front of Hopkins, and began to pace the room.

"Those were her orders. Wartime orders, Harry. We didn't know anything about you. You surely understand that."

"What did she tell you about me?"

"Nothing that we didn't quickly find out from you, yourself: that you were a close and loyal ally in our darkest hour, that you gave us hope when we had none, and that you brought that to-the-root-of-the-matter mind of yours to bear on some of our intractable problems. That's what we found out from you."

There was a long pause. Hopkins took the bottle, poured a glass, and stared at it, swilling the dark red liquor against the crystal.

"Is there anything you can do?"

Churchill shook his head.

"I can only tell you to forget her. You have a wonderful life ahead of you with Miss Macy, a remarkable woman. This is a cruel war and our only task is to win it. Nothing else matters."

In spite of her parachute training, it was by Lysander aircraft that Leonora was finally sent into occupied France, arriving in the central Loire department some thirty miles from the city of Tours on a night of bright moonlight. After three days waiting at a special forces airstrip in Hampshire, she had flown with a radio operator, both hunched up behind the pilot in the small single-engine plane. They carried with them packages of stores that included plastic explosives, ammunition, and several spare Sten guns.

The final briefing had repeated everything she had learnt about her mission in the previous weeks. She was to be known only by her field name, Yvonne. She would be given the field names of those immediately below and above her in the command chain. Apart from that, she would identify others in the Monkeypuzzle circuit only by passwords. Her job was to convey instructions from a radio operator to agents throughout the Loire region, but especially on the Atlantic coast. The radio operator would be moving to different safe houses regularly to avoid what the SOE had belatedly begun to realise was a highly effective Gestapo system of scanning and pinpointing broadcasts to London.

Monkeypuzzle was one of several circuits operating in occupied France. The region south of a line roughly through the centre of France was controlled by the Vichy collaborationist regime and lay outside the scope of SOE's activities for the time being.

The strategic aim of the Monkeypuzzle agents was to organise and equip paramilitary groups that would harass German army units by blowing up road and rail communications in the event of a large-scale raid by British seaborne forces. The tactical mission was to map the whereabouts of the various units making up the panzer division in the Loire area, locate sites for weapons dumps, and reconnoitre possible landing beaches along the coast.

Above all, SOE wanted to impress rival organisations such as the Secret Intelligence Service with the quality of their information from occupied Europe. Civilian morale, the behaviour of off-duty German forces, black-market operations, the cafés, restaurants, and brothels used by German officers and their French collaborators – all this was grist to the intelligence mills grinding out secret briefings in London.

"And it is your job to keep your radio operator busy. That means that you will be on the move throughout the Loire region. The first snap checkpoint you come to will be the most dangerous because you will be nervous. First rule is: do not make eye contact with those checking your papers. Look around you, look bored, pick your nose, cough, sneeze, whatever, but don't look at them directly or look at the ground. They have been trained to regard such behaviour as suspicious."

He was a young man said to have been flown out of the Monkeypuzzle circuit from an airstrip near Tours only weeks earlier. SOE always tried to give their agents a final briefing from those who had recently returned from the field.

It was the same young man who had rudely woken her a few nights earlier at four in the morning. He had shaken her, ripped the blankets from her bed, and torn off her nightdress, all the while shouting questions in English. In the final weeks of the course they had been ordered to speak only French. She passed the test, cursing him fluently with a string of Gallic expletives.

The flight to France was an anticlimax. They flew low, below radar, deep into the Loire region and landed by flare light at a rough airstrip. People had appeared from the darkness and unloaded the plane, and within minutes the field was in darkness and the aircraft aloft again. She spent the first night alone in a hayloft with only cows for company in the barn below. The radio operator had been given sanctuary elsewhere. Rough hands had helped her up the ladder to the loft with her small suitcase and a pack containing her Sten gun and ammunition. Bread, cheese, and a pitcher of wine followed her up the ladder. No one spoke a word. She was in France with the Resistance. She was where she had wanted to be for years.

It was the week before Christmas. By the light of her torch she hacked off some cheese and a chunk of bread with the commando knife. She ate and drank the wine straight from the pitcher. The cows stirred in their stalls below, sensing the presence of a stranger. She lay back against the prickly hay and thought of Harry Hopkins preparing for Christmas in the White House. There would be a decorated tree, presents, crackers, pudding, and festive turkey. Maybe he and Churchill would join the president and sing carols.

She knew the prime minister had hastened to Washington after Pearl Harbor. The BBC had been trumpeting the news for days and especially in broadcasts to Europe. She wondered if he would think of her and maybe raise a silent toast. Or had he fallen back into the arms of Louise and forgotten all about her. Did it matter? She had done her duty and deceived him. But he had known, hadn't he? And he had forgiven her. And he had written all those letters to which she was forbidden to respond: long, gossipy letters laced with love. Poor man, she had not been able to tell him – nor her mother. No one had known she was to be flown by night into Nazi occupied France as an agent of the Special Operations Executive. Her life had become a secret known only to a few strangers in the duplicitous world of intelligence.

She thought of Muriel worrying at home in Leamington Spa. The last letter Leonora had sent had been a month earlier. All she could say was that she was going to be out of touch for a while on war work. She had received an agonised letter in return demanding at least a farewell meeting. She chose not to reply. It would only make matters worse.

And what had happened to Claudette, her funny friend with whom she had shared so much in their training? Claudette had disappeared during those final days at the Hampshire air base without a good-bye. But that was the way of the SOE. No one ever knew anyone else's name, what they were doing, where they had been, or where they were going.

As Fairburn, their instructor at Arisaig, had said, two people can keep a secret as long as one is dead.

18

Hopkins checked back into Washington's naval hospital in the first week of the New Year. He was emaciated and suffering the same roiling stomach pains that had signalled his cancer seven years earlier.

For the first time he decided to ask his doctors to judge the length of life left to him. Usually on regular visits to what he joked had become his second home he took the optimistic view that the blood transfusions, X-rays, and special drip-fed high-nutrition liquids were no more than regular services – like those required to keep Mr Ford's automobiles on the road.

Hopkins knew he had deceived himself. Now he wanted the truth. It could hardly be worse than the news that followed him to the hospital from the White House. The president had refused to send him any daily bulletins or confidential reports, telling him to concentrate on getting better. But no one knew the back channels of the executive mansion better than him. Hopkins was probably better informed in his hospital bed than at his desk, with more time to read and reflect on the reports that arrived twice a day in plain brown envelopes.

The grand coalition between America, Britain, and Russia that had been assembled with such hard work and festive cheer over Christmas had done nothing to challenge Hitler's mockery or his mastery of Europe.

Far from turning the tide of the war, it had been a harbinger of disaster. The Japanese had followed up the devastating victory at Pearl Harbor with island-hopping conquest after conquest in the Pacific. They were at the gates of Singapore and within striking distance of Australia. Never had an empire collapsed as swiftly, in only a few months, as that of the British in the Far East. More British ships were sunk in the Pacific, finally bringing home to the Admiralty in London the fact that battleships without air cover were simply target practice for land- or carrier-based aircraft.

And in North Africa Rommel was on the move, pushing the British back yet again.

Churchill had returned from his American visit to face harsh criticism over his war leadership. To the prime minister's fury, there was much sniping in both Parliament and the press at the length of his stay in the comfort of Washington. Hopkins read the reports from London with incredulity. How could the British turn on a man who had sustained the country's morale and steered them to survival against Hitler for the last two years? The answer was that this was the third winter at war for the British and they were plainly fed up. Churchill was to face a vote of no confidence in the House of Commons.

The American people were also restless. They wanted quick revenge for the disgrace of Pearl Harbor. What they got was a number of humiliating U-boat attacks on American shipping. Some merchant ships were torpedoed within sight of the U.S. East Coast. German radio gloatingly reported that a number of U-boat commanders had claimed to see the lights of Broadway as they surfaced to attack ships leaving New York.

In Washington the politics of war erupted in a vicious power struggle within the White House. The Joint Chiefs of Staff had not given up and were still urging the president to make the campaign against Japan his priority. But the president stuck to Churchill's demand for a Germany-first policy.

Hopkins pushed the papers aside. If this went on, the isolationists would be back on the airwaves again saying, "We told you so."

As for America's preparedness for war, Hopkins knew that the country had neither the men nor the armaments to enter any conflict. For years it had been said that the American military had all the time and no money, and now it had all the money and no time.

And that was Hopkins's real worry: time. How much time did *he* have?

The doctor stood by his bed, peering at him over a sheaf of notes.

"If . . ." The doctor paused, trying to add emphasis to the words that would follow. "If you look after yourself, get plenty of rest, eat well, and cut down on your smoking, I could reasonably say you have several good years ahead of you."

"Several?"

"It's difficult to pin down a number."

"Try."

"Say three to four years. I am sorry."

He was not yet fifty-two. That would make him fifty-five at most. Hell and damnation, why now when there was so much to be done? And there was Louise – how could he allow her to marry a man with a death sentence? She knew, of course. He had been frank with her about his illnesses and she had said she didn't care. She was remarkable, beautiful, and really seemed to like him. But . . .

There was always that "but."

He would have to go back to London – one last time. The president would let him if he worked on him. Churchill was going to need every friend that spring in 1942. The previous year had been bad enough, but 1942 was going to be worse. And Hopkins was pretty sure he could get Roosevelt to agree.

Arguments about how to turn the war against Hitler were already dividing the three allies. Marshall wanted a sledge-hammer attack across the Channel to draw German divisions from the Russian front. Churchill was nervous and wanted an invasion of North Africa in Tunisia to take Rommel in the rear. Stalin wanted a second front now – not tomorrow, not the day after, but now!

Hopkins knew what the Brits would call it: a bloody shambles, or as the boys back in Sioux City would say, a real bastard boondoggle. And he couldn't sort it out from a hospital bed. But he could do one decent thing now. He would tell Louise of the doctor's verdict and break his engagement. She was an honourable woman. She would argue and refuse. He would insist. There would be a row, but he would prevail with simple logic: What point was there in marrying a man who would be dead in a few years? Better by far that she should find herself a new life with one of her many admirers in Washington.

Winston Churchill never gave interviews to individual journalists, on the basis that while by so doing he might please one of the gentlemen of the press, as they liked to be called, he would certainly alienate the rest. In any case, there was also too little time, and he preferred speeches as a means of talking to the British people and the world beyond.

In the late spring of 1942, however, he made an exception for Ed Murrow. For months Hopkins had been urging the prime minister to give America's most famous broadcaster an interview. Murrow had petitioned Number 10 relentlessly, but then so had every other member of the growing U.S. press corps in London.

But Murrow was different. His was a voice that found an attentive audience in Washington and rippled out to listeners in the cornfields of Kansas, down to the muddy delta of the Mississippi, and across to the California coast. It had been pretty hard to get the folk in San Francisco or San Diego to pay much attention to news of the war in Europe, but after a Japanese submarine had surfaced in plain sight offshore and fired a few shells into an empty ranch in February they began to do so. And it was to Ed Murrow's Sunday-night programme that they tuned their radio sets to find out what in hell was happening in that weird world overseas.

The war was going badly for both Atlantic allies. Roosevelt had foolishly given a hostage to fortune by promising Stalin a second front in Europe. The president then had to backtrack, explaining that it just wasn't possible that year. The Kremlin rumbled with accusations of capitalist treachery.

Stalin had lost his key ally in the struggle against the invading German armies. Winter had given way to spring. The snows melted and quagmires of mud dried out, firming the ground for tanks and armoured vehicles. Hitler sent his troops back into battle on the eastern front. All the Russians could do was retreat behind vast numbers of their dead.

The Battle of the Atlantic was once again at a tipping point. And worst of all for Churchill, the Joint Chiefs of Staff in Washington seemed to be getting the upper hand in the battle to persuade the president to change his mind and strike first at Japan.

Brendan Bracken sat in the study at Number 10 looking nervous. He watched as Ed Murrow set up his microphone on the prime minister's desk. It was just after six in the evening, a time the broadcaster had requested, knowing that Churchill would prepare himself for the interview with a glass of champagne. Churchill had in fact had several glasses and was now pacing the room reading from a sheaf of notes.

Bracken had advised against the interview. He was not worried about what Churchill was likely to say. What message do you have for the people of America? That would be the first bland question. The prime minister would rise to his feet behind the desk, grasp his lapel, and talk until Murrow gently cut in with a follow-up question. Churchill's message would be a simple one of the need for a united fight against fascism but dressed in a majestic cloak of words that would make the drowsy farm boy in Kansas sit up, rub his eyes, and listen. It was what would follow the interview that worried Bracken. He hated being the messenger of bad news. And what he had to tell Murrow was very bad news.

After the interview, Murrow was hoping for a long and bibulous discussion with the prime minister, but Churchill made his apologies, saying he had to make a speech at a dinner at the Savoy hosted by Lord Beaverbrook.

"Stay and have some dinner with Brendan; he knows everything," the prime minister had said.

It was more a command than an invitation. Murrow agreed. He liked Bracken. They were outsiders, self-made men who had risen from obscure origins to commanding heights in their professions, exactly the kind of men that Churchill liked. Unlike most Brits in the wartime government, Bracken did not use diplomatic language as a cloak to conceal errors or mask his true intentions. He was Irish and he said what he thought.

Sawyers appeared and led them to the dining room, which had been laid for two.

"There's a special on tonight," he said, "Cook's fish pie."

"Bring on the pie," said Bracken, and poured them a glass from the decanter.

"Did you know Hitler is a teetotalling, vegetarian non-smoker?" he asked.

"Yes, vaguely; I don't know why you don't try to assassinate him. There must be a chance down at Berchtesgaden."

"Ah," said Bracken. "Don't think we haven't thought about it. But the PM ordered the plans to be scrapped. He wants to leave Hitler in place. He thinks he's mad and making big mistakes."

"Such as?" said Murrow.

"If he had followed his generals' plans and opted for an overwhelming thrust against Stalin on one front, they would be in Moscow by now. We want him to go on making those mistakes."

Sawyers brought in the pie and served it onto two plates.

"There's more news from Russia tonight, gentlemen, and it's not good," he said, and left.

"Does he listen to everything we say?" asked Murrow.

"Probably. But he can deal with Winston's appalling moods, which is more than most people around here, me included."

Sawyers reappeared, swept away the plates, and placed cheese on the table.

"They've taken Kiev again," he said, and left again.

The two men smiled. Sawyers always seemed to know more about the war than they did. They pushed their cheese plates to one side and lit cigarettes.

"How's Harry?" said Bracken.

"The hospital treatment back in January did him good. He's much better apparently."

"But no longer engaged, I hear?"

"No, you're wrong there. He tried to break it off, but she wouldn't have it. That's one tough babe."

He turned and said, "Ed, do you remember that woman who was Harry's liaison officer?"

"Yes, I do. Harry was mad about her."

Bracken raised his eyebrows.

"It was no secret, Brendan; everyone knew."

"I see. Well, she undertook secret war work after Harry left."

"I know. Harry told me she wanted an active role in the war."

"And she was sent into France."

Murrow had an intimation of what was coming. He said nothing.

"Well," Bracken said, looking at the ceiling, hoping to find the right words. "She was working with the Resistance in France. She was betrayed, captured, and interrogated. She is almost certainly dead. We just think someone should let Harry know."

"Jesus, what happened?"

"A complicated story, but a member of her own circuit either was turned by the Germans or was an agent all along. A woman Finch knew and had trained with, apparently. Anyway, Finch was arrested in a safe house in Tours. There was a firefight. Some of the German Sicherheitsdienst got killed. The local police worked on her and then the Gestapo took over."

"And she's dead?"

"We're told the Gestapo held her for weeks. She was barely

alive when they finished with her. She was put on a train with the others on her circuit and sent to Ravensbrück."

"Where?"

"A concentration camp for women. We're told she died shortly after arrival. No one gets out of that place alive."

"Are you sure of all this?"

"A member of her group evaded capture and got back via Spain. We've confirmed his account through other sources. It's not a pretty story."

"And you want me to tell Harry this?"

"We think someone should."

"We?"

Bracken said nothing but poured each a port.

"The PM regards Hopkins as a good friend as well as an ally. He wants the best for him."

So this is where they had taken her. This is where they said her life would have ended even if she had reached the camp alive, which was very doubtful.

Hopkins traced a road north from Berlin, his finger moving along the map to the town of Fürstenberg on the river Havel. A pretty place close to a region of lakes and forests, according to the gazetteer in the Library of Congress. The town had fine churches, some well-preserved medieval buildings, and several locks along the river. But this was not what had attracted Heinrich Himmler to the area in 1938. The Nazi leader was looking for somewhere out of the way, a small village far from prying eyes but within a day's drive of Berlin. He wanted somewhere close to a town with a good working crematorium. Fürstenberg had such a crematorium.

Three miles away in marshland lay a small village called

Ravensbrück. It was there in May 1939 that eight hundred women prisoners arrived, shackled, their heads shaven, to become the first prisoners in the only Nazi concentration camp for women.

Hopkins's finger rested on the small black dot that marked the place on the map. He held it there, trying to judge the distance to the coast. Twenty or thirty miles maybe. Even if anyone got over the high wall and through the electrified barbed wire, there was nowhere to go.

He lit a cigarette, sat back at his desk, and picked up the State Department's brief. It was April 1942, and in the three years since the camp opened the number of inmates had risen to an estimated twelve thousand.

Prisoners included every kind of woman marked for torture and death by the Nazis: Jews, Gypsies, lesbians, communists, Jehovah's Witnesses, prostitutes, and criminals deemed to be antisocial, such as black marketeers. They had coloured triangles sewn onto their uniforms to denote categories. Yellow for Jews, purple for Jehovah's Witnesses, green for criminals, pink for lesbians, and black for political prisoners. It was very efficient, very German, very Heinrich Himmler.

Hopkins had had to struggle to get State to do the research and write the report. They were too busy, they said, and Nazi concentration camps were hardly a matter for the diplomatic service. He had persevered and pointed them to the Swiss Red Cross. They would know. They had an office in the city and sources – German officials with a conscience who whispered about atrocities or pushed scrawled letters under the door.

He had tried the Brits too and begged Brendan Bracken to find out what he could. But it was Murrow who came back with the reply.

"Look, Harry, you've got to get a grip. There's a war on. Bad things are happening all over the world and you are going to get married in a couple of months. She's gone, Harry, gone. The Brits are sure of it. You have got to let go. We all need you, here in London and there in Washington, working at full steam, not losing yourself in this nightmare."

Hopkins knew Murrow was right. The Swiss had reported that there were no coloured triangles for French Resistance fighters or the British who fought with them. They were tortured, starved, or worked to death within weeks of arrival at that little village called Ravensbrück.

He wished he had brought a hip flask with him. He was shaking like an aspen leaf and a quick snort now might stop the trembling. Nothing he had experienced in London during the Blitz had made him quite so nervous. It was five minutes to noon on 30 July 1942, and Harry Hopkins was standing in the Oval Office facing Reverend Russell Clinchy. Hopkins knew Clinchy well. The pastor had presided at his wedding eleven years earlier when Barbara Duncan became Barbara Hopkins and thus the lodestar and love of his life. Beside him President Roosevelt, wearing a white linen suit with matching shoes and a red carnation, sat resplendent in his wheelchair. Roosevelt handed up a silver flask. Hopkins took a quick swig and smiled. He steadied himself. His hair was neatly combed and his blue suit well pressed. He looked around the room.

There were roses in small vases on the mahogany desk. The mantel was covered in white chrysanthemums and gladioli placed on either side of the French antique clock. Over the door to the bedroom old Grandma Roosevelt beamed down from a gilded frame. There were three rows of chairs occupied by family and a few White House staff. Eleanor Roosevelt sat at the front beside Hopkins's four children: three boys, David, Robert, and Stephen, and Diana, his daughter. The daughter Barbara had given him.

This is my wedding day, thought Hopkins. The first wedding here in the White House since Alice Lee Roosevelt, eldest daughter of President Theodore Roosevelt, had married Congressman Nicholas Longworth in 1906 – and I'm plain terrified. He fished for the ring in his waistcoat pocket and smiled weakly at his children and other relatives.

Thirty-three guests rose from their seats as a marine band in the long hall outside struck up. Miss Louise Macy, wearing a dark blue dress and carrying a spray of purple flowers, entered the room on the arm of her father. She walked slowly through the room smiling at several guests she knew and joined Hopkins. She took his arm and squeezed it. Ten minutes later they were married. The band played a popular song, "I Married an Angel," from the Broadway show of the same name, and Hopkins stood swaying as his hand was shaken and people slapped him on the back.

"Are you all right?" Louise said anxiously. Her husband was pale and looked like he needed to sit down.

"I'm fine," he said. "But pinch me. I can't believe we just got married in the Oval Office."

The wedding breakfast ended in toasts and speeches. Roosevelt read out a telegram from Winston Churchill.

" 'For a man who spends far too much time with his doctors I am delighted to see that Harry Hopkins has decided that the administration of matrimony is a better treatment than any blood transfusion.' "

Then Roosevelt raised his glass and said, "I wish I could

tell you that Harry and Louise were going on a fine honeymoon and returning to a new house in Georgetown. I urged him to do both. But they are not. They have asked to make their home here in the White House and Harry wants to get back to work tomorrow. When I said I didn't think Louise would appreciate this arrangement he wrote me a note, and here it is."

The president adjusted his spectacles and read:

" 'We wish to keep faith with the young men and women who will be our future and with our friends, allies, and loved ones who have died for that future.

" 'We believe we should all use every waking minute of every day in the fight for our freedoms. The war will be won both on battlefields around the world and here in this house. Louise and I would like to work for that victory with you under this roof.' "

Roosevelt looked up. "And I agreed."

19

The day Franklin Roosevelt died, on 12 April 1945, the war in Europe had been all but won. The president spent his final days at his winter quarters in Warm Springs, Georgia, with the woman he had loved for most of his life, Lucy Mercer. Eleanor Roosevelt had remained in Washington. His last phone call to the White House was to make sure he would be sent a new stamp commemorating a United Nations conference he was shortly due to address in New York.

That same day in Berlin, the philharmonic orchestra gave its final concert of the war attended by leading Nazis. As they left, members of the Hitler Youth held out baskets filled with cyanide pills wrapped to look like candy. Hitler did not attend. He remained in his bunker as the Russian forces closed in on the city.

One by one the Nazi concentration camps fell to the Allies as they fought their way into Germany in the early months of 1945. The Russians had liberated Auschwitz on January 27 and the full horror of Hitler's Holocaust began to become clear to an incredulous world. Buchenwald was taken by the Americans on April 11. The atrocities therein were filmed and released as newsreel to be shown in cinemas throughout North America, Europe, and the United Kingdom. British forces took Belsen on April 15, having cleared a path through thirteen thousand corpses that surrounded the camp.

That left Dachau and Ravensbrück. Hopkins had followed the final stage of the war in Europe with the same intense and jubilant interest shared by all those in the White House. But he did not share the general morbid fascination with where and how Hitler would meet his fate.

Instead his mind was focused elsewhere. Leonora was dead, he told himself, a memory buried under the rubble of war. But he wanted at least to know how and when her life had ended. Dachau in Bavaria was in the path of the American advance. But Ravensbrück in the north would fall to the Russians. They had been slow to provide details of what they had found at Auschwitz. What would they find at Ravensbrück and what would they share with the world?

Partly through pride and partly because he felt her fate was a painfully private matter, Hopkins did not seek any more information about Leonora Finch from his well-placed friends in London. He could just imagine them sighing over the phone and repeating the same old platitudes: "What's the point, Harry?" "Why obsess over a woman who is dead and gone?" "You had an affair with her – so what? Who didn't have a fling if they could during those Blitz nights?"

In any case, he doubted British intelligence knew more than the scant press reports about the liberated camps coming out of Germany. Berlin was the prize and the big story was Adolf Hitler's last stand.

If anywhere, the answer to Ravensbrück lay in Moscow. And it was Averell Harriman, now the American ambassador to Russia, to whom Hopkins turned. He had never been close to Averell, disliking his inherited wealth and the patrician ease with which he had charmed Roosevelt and Churchill and seduced the prime minister's daughter-in-law. But Hopkins and Harriman had put Lend-Lease in place together and had given the British the wherewithal to survive and fight on during the desperate days of 1941. He knew Harriman admired him. And he knew that if anyone could help him, it was Averell Harriman. Within forty-eight hours he received a reply. The confidential cable from the Moscow embassy was decoded and forwarded to the White House by the State Department:

Dear Harry,

I am afraid I cannot throw much light on the fate of the woman about whom you enquire. The situation in Ravensbrück remains confused some days after liberation, but a few facts are clear.

The SS guards forced two thousand inmates – all women, of course – on to what they described as a death march when the Russian forward troops were a few miles from the camp. They took them into the surrounding forests.

In the days before leaving, the guards shot a number of high-profile prisoners, including a Frenchwoman named Anna Rizzo, who had organized an escape network for Allied airmen in France. They also burnt a large number of files in the camp incinerator that had been specially built on a large scale to take over the work of a similar facility in the neighboring town of Fürstenberg.

A gas chamber had also been built close to the camp.

*There were 3,500 prisoners alive when the Russians took
the camp and all have been identified by the Red Cross,
although many have died since. There are no British na-
tionals among the survivors, nor are there thought to
have been any among those forced into the death march.
The Soviets overtook that column, killed the guards, and
freed the survivors. But many had already died. They
were mostly Poles and German Jews.*

*The Russians confirm what is largely known by the
Red Cross, namely that British prisoners, and especially
those in the SOE, were killed within days of arrival at
Ravensbrück.*

*I do not wish to extinguish all hope, but nor do I wish
to raise it. We may never know what happened to Miss
Finch. In the chaos of the final days at Ravensbrück, it is
faintly possible that she may have escaped, but if so, I am
sure we will hear from her very soon. Otherwise, I am
afraid you will have to accept she shared the terrible fate of
so many others in that bestial camp.*

With my warm regards,
Averell

As Harriman well knew, this was not the whole truth.
There were unsubstantiated reports that two British prisoners
had survived the death march and were in Russian hands.
The Russians denied it, but the reports persisted. There was
no point passing these rumours on to Hopkins. It would
drive him mad.

• • •

When Harry Hopkins had seen Roosevelt for the last time
that April, both were tired and ill and knew that each
other had not long to live. Both also knew that the imminent

victory over Germany was shadowed by the spectre of a cold war with Russia.

Despite the new conflict in Europe that was rising from the ashes of the old, the two men talked of the political battles they had fought in the days of the New Deal in the thirties and drank cocktails, much as they had done every weekday punctually at six o'clock for most of Roosevelt's presidency.

Bereft of the man who had been his friend, mentor, and leader for over ten years, Hopkins was further shocked by Churchill's loss of office in the British general election in July. The two men he had served and with whom he had helped shape the course of the war had gone.

Leonora and London in the dangerous days of 1941 were now memories he would retrieve, cherish, smile over, and put away with a painful heart. He remembered her as she once was in the dark nights of the Blitz and on summer evenings at that pub by the Thames. He could not bear to think of how she had met her death. He consoled himself with his wife, Louise, and his memories as his long-borne illness entered its final stages in the autumn of 1945.

Epilogue

Harry Hopkins died on 29 January 1946, in New York's Memorial Hospital. The funeral took place four days later at St Bartholomew's Episcopal Church in the city. The service was attended by several hundred people, including representatives of all the Allied governments. Mrs Louise Macy Hopkins led the mourners, with Hopkins's three surviving children. His third son, Stephen, had been killed in the Pacific campaign in 1944. Winston Churchill was unable to attend the service, but the British ambassador and several senior figures who had worked with Hopkins in London occupied front-row seats. A gracious tribute from Churchill was read out by the ambassador: " 'His was a soul that flamed out of a frail and failing body. He was a crumbling lighthouse from which there shone the beams that led great fleets to harbour.' "

At the end of the service, before anyone had moved from their seats, a woman dressed in black and wearing a veil rose from her seat at the back and limped up the aisle with the help of a cane. She carried a wreath and laid it on the coffin. The woman lifted her veil and turned to the Hopkins family.

She wore a patch over one eye. Her pale face was marked with a long, livid scar running from her temple to her chin. Her good eye was the colour of jade. She looked at Louise Hopkins, smiled, dropped the veil back over her face, and walked away.

The attached note read simply: "Leonora – always."

Historical Note

Between 1939 and 1945 an estimated 130,000 women passed through Ravensbrück concentration camp. The majority either were executed or died of maltreatment. Four women members of the Special Operations Executive were among those who died in the camp. They were Denise Bloch, Cecily Lefort, Lillian Rolfe, and Violette Szabo. The four had been operating separately in France for the SOE when they were captured. Two of the four, Cecily Lefort and Lillian Rolfe, had been recruited in London from the Women's Auxiliary Air Force. All four were executed between the end of January and early February 1945 in a frenzy of killing at Ravensbrück as the Allies closed in on the camp. Three women members of the SOE did, however, survive their ordeal in the cam

Acknowledgments

This book is a work of fiction in which I have tried to convey accurately the crucial role played by Harry Hopkins in the unfolding relationship between Winston Churchill and Franklin Roosevelt during those momentous early years of the Second World War. A novelist's imagination and the historical record are not natural bedfellows, but where possible I have used published accounts in my description of Hopkins's many meetings with Churchill and his ministers, his communications with the White House, and his relationship with Franklin Roosevelt and his cabinet.

I wish to gratefully acknowledge the key texts which relate to the events described in this book between the years 1941–46 and which have been central to my research. *The White House Papers of Harry L. Hopkins, Volumes 1 and 2,* by Robert E. Sherwood (Harper, 1947) were my starting point. *Roosevelt and Hopkins* (Harper, 1948), also by Sherwood, was an important resource. *Harry Hopkins* by George McJimsey (Harvard, 1987) and *Wartime Missions of Harry L. Hopkins* by Matthew B. Wills (AuthorHouse, 2004) helped my understanding of the man and his mission.

The literature about Roosevelt and Churchill in World War II is vast. I list here only those books that have a direct bearing on the story of Hopkins at that time. The third volume of Winston Churchill's history of the Second World War gives a warm and illuminating account of the impact tha-Hopkins made when he arrived in London in 1941 and how the American emissary became "the most faithful and perfect channel of communication between the President and me."

John Colville's *The Churchillians* (Weidenfeld & Nicolson, 1981) includes a brief but telling passage about how the two very different characters of Churchill and Hopkins forged a bond that was to lead to a lasting friendship.

Every major biography of Churchill makes room for Harry Hopkins in the dangerous years of 1941–42, and almost all promote the strategic importance of their relationship. In the same way all biographies of Franklin Roosevelt recount the president's dependence on Hopkins as a counsellor and friend in the White House. Frances Perkins's *The Roosevelt I Knew* (Harper, 1946) gives a telling insight into Hopkins's influence over New Deal policies in the 1930s. She also provides a fascinating glimpse into the president's personal world with a beautifully observed description of Roosevelt's bedroom at the White House.

Finally I hope the reader warms to the character of wartime London, especially during the Blitz months from September 1940 to May 1941, in this book. The living and the dead, the lovers and the looters, the fire crews and those manning the anti-aircraft batteries, nurses, barmen, and clerks, they all had their roles to play in life, as they have in this book. I have drawn on contemporary newspaper accounts, especially from *The Times* of London, to ensure their stories are truthfully told.

There are many people without whose guidance and

advice this book would never have been written, let alone published.

First and foremost, I owe Thomas Dunne a debt of gratitude I hope one day to repay. Tom may not thank me for calling him the grand old man of New York (and thus American) publishing, but the tenacity and vision with which he conducts his business, which reflects the way he treats his authors, richly earns him that sobriquet. Thanks so much, Tom.

I have been lucky in Peter Joseph, my editor at Thomas Dunne Books, an imprint within St. Martin's Press. The relationship between a writer and editor is not always easy, especially when the Atlantic Ocean separates them. Peter has been the driving force in getting this story from first draft to the bookshops. I owe warm thanks also to his colleague Melanie Fried, who tracked down bad grammar, lazy style, and plain wrong facts on far too many pages. She didn't let me get away with a thing.

To Barbara Wild, who copyedited the final version with forensic diligence, I owe a huge debt of gratitude.

Tim Waller in Cambridge, England, worked on the first edit of the text and made all important changes, not least in adapting language and grammar for an American readership.

Kate Trevelyan Kee, who has worked in publishing most of her life, read an early version of this book and made important suggestions.

Mrs. Deborah Keegan, my executive assistant in London, kept my life on track while I researched and wrote this book.

The story of Harry Hopkins has been with me since I was taught American History at St. Andrews University by a visiting lecturer from Texas. He was a well-rounded figure with a love of cigars whose ash would fall to the floor and drift around our feet as we talked. Sadly, I cannot recall his name and nor can the university identify him from their records. I salute my forgotten tutor as a great teacher.

In London I am, and will remain, indebted to my agent, Sophie Hicks, who knows just how much an occasional large glass of red wine in the Groucho Club means to a struggling author. It is to Ed Victor, Sophie's boss, that I, like so many other authors, also remain truly grateful. Also by James Mac-Manus

Also by James MacManus

Midnight in Berlin

Berlin, 1939. In the British embassy, military attaché
Colonel Macrae, is preparing to defy his ambassador and
his government and assassinate Hitler. The military parade
to mark the Fuhrer's 50th birthday will be his opportunity.
In an elegant suburb of Berlin, Sara Sternschein plays her
nightly role as the lead attraction in the Gestapo's infamous
brothel, the Salon Kitty. The young Jewish woman has no
choice; her twin brother is being held in a concentration
camp.

And in the Gestapo Headquarters, Obergruppenfuhrer
Joaqim Bonner waits and watches, a spider at the centre of
a web of intrigue. Sara Sternschein is Bonner's secret weap-
on.Gathering intelligence for his mission Macrae is drawn to
Salon Kitty and its mysterious hostess. In a city of lies, spies
and secrets does Sara hold the key to thwarting Hitler –
or is Macrae being manipulated?

Based on extensive research, *Midnight in Berlin* takes the
reader into the dark heart of Berlin on the eve of the Second
World War.

Out now in hardback and ebook